A PURER TASTE

THE WRITING AND READING OF FICTION IN ENGLISH IN NINETEENTH-CENTURY CANADA

The fiction of early English Canada was the product of a distinct cultural milieu – colonial, conservative, and occasionally philistine, yet alert to the need for national self-definition and to the role that popular fiction could play in shaping the new nation's political and social attitudes. Carole Gerson discusses the respective roles of writers, readers, cultural leaders, and commentators in the days when romance was English Canada's preferred genre and Sir Walter Scott the presiding spirit.

Among the topics she examines are reading preferences and opportunities; the reception of fiction in nineteenth-century English Canada; the problem of legitimizing Canada as a location for fiction; the debate between the few advocates of moderate realism (represented by the journalism of Sara Jeannette Duncan in the mid-1880s) and the many advocates of romance (represented by Goldwin Smith's 1870 address 'The Lamps of Fiction'); the importance of historical fiction to the development of political and literary nationalism; the appeal of French-Canadian history and local colour to English-Canadian writers; and the beginnings of regional and social realism around the turn of the century.

Gerson draws on a broad range of periodicals, unpublished archival materials, and little-known fiction as well as the few currently well-known works from this era to produce an illuminating portrait of a central aspect of Canadian cultural history.

CAROLE GERSON teaches in the Department of English at Simon Fraser University, and is the editor of *Vancouver Short Stories*.

A PURER TASTE

THE WRITING AND READING OF FICTION IN ENGLISH IN NINETEENTH-CENTURY CANADA

CAROLE GERSON

UNIVERSITY OF TORONTO PRESS

Toronto Buffalo London

© University of Toronto Press 1989
Toronto Buffalo London
Printed in Canada

ISBN 0-8020-5820-5 (cloth)
isbn 0-8020-6733-6 (paper)

Printed on acid-free paper

Canadian Cataloguing in Publication Data

Gerson, Carole
A purer taste : the writing and reading of
fiction in English in nineteenth-century Canada

Bibliography: p.
Includes index.
ISBN 0-8020-5820-5 (bound)
ISBN 0-8020-6733-6 (pbk.)

1. Canadian fiction (English) – 19th century –
History and criticism.* I. Title.

PS8195.G47 1989   c813'.4'09   c89-093143-7
PR9192.4.G47 1989

Cover illustration: Franklin Brownell, *Lamplight*, 1892, oil on canvas,
38.6 × 30.6 cm; National Gallery of Canada, Ottawa, gift of the
Royal Canadian Academy of Arts, 1893; reproduced courtesy of
Eric Franklin Stremer

This book has been published with the help of a
grant from the Canadian Federation for the Humanities,
using funds provided by the Social Sciences and
Humanities Research Council of Canada.

For Martin

and for Ruth and Mickey

In the minds of children, imagination exerts a weird and fascinating influence, and while we think the faculty a good one, when properly controlled and regulated by the understanding, – on the other hand, we regret that, in the present system of family discipline and education, it is allowed, like bad weeds, to hinder the growth of rich and fragrant flowers. The morbid excitement for novel reading, and the numbers of sensational works published at the present day – in which crime and its evils are so darkly portrayed, is but one of the many evidences of the truth of our remark. We hope to see soon the dawn of a purer and more correct taste, when writers of fiction will inculcate wiser lessons of life, and stimulate a taste for all that is pure, noble and refined. (George Stewart, jr, 'Novels and Novel Readers,' *Stewart's Literary Quarterly Magazine* 1 [1867] 34)

Contents

Preface and Acknowledgments

[A] literature is *not* an accumulation of books ... Literature is a relationship between writers and readers.[1]

If we are to compose valid criticism of work produced in earlier stylistic periods, we must do so in terms of conventions established at a time contemporary with the works themselves. If we fail to do so, we shall miss the integrity of the works we study, not to mention their significance, frequently profound, for their original audiences.[2]

To understand the relationship between the readers and writers of fiction in English Canada during the nineteenth century we must first attempt to reconstruct their prevailing frame of mind. Out of the amorphous mass of books, periodicals, letters, and personal papers which constitute the detritus of our cultural history it is possible to discern the conventions and expectations that shaped the writing of fiction and responses to that writing, as expressed by the English-language population scattered across the vast area that eventually became Canada. The geographical terrain embraced by this study is immense, yet consistency overrides regional variation. Each English-speaking community undertaking the process of cultural individuation drew on the common heritage from Britain, grappled with the torrent of publications from the United States, and strove towards the creation of a national literature that distinctively and appropriately referred to Canada. As we shall see, the constancy of the difficulties besetting the writing of serious fiction in nineteenth-century Canada was temporal as well as spatial. Throughout the period under consideration, authors of both literature and criticism continued to encounter the same set of recurring problems, subject to minor modifications. The order of these chapters is therefore loosely chronological, beginning with the issues faced by the first literary pioneers and concluding with the situation of Canadian fiction just before the modern era. However, human events seldom conform neatly to the time frames imposed by their chroniclers. For the sake of convenience this book's subtitle refers to the nineteenth century, yet its subject more precisely begins in the 1820s and continues until at least 1904, the year of the publication of *The Imperialist*. The title, *A Purer Taste*, derives from a statement issued the year of Confederation by a man who was to play a significant role in shaping his country's cultural ethos.

Running as warp threads through this study are several basic questions that reflect the attitudes of the community in which and for whom most Canadian authors wrote: whether the reading and writing of fiction were acceptable activities, especially in a society preoccupied with the task of nationmaking; whether Canada could supply the elements required by the genre of the novel; and whether writers and readers could agree upon definitions of romance and realism and an appropriate balance of the two. The discussion of these problems focuses upon an eclectic group of novels, chosen because they or their authors at some time achieved a degree of public recognition, or because they were (however briefly) the subjects of contemporary response in the form of reviews or commentary. At the same time, less attention than might be expected has been paid to some of the better-known novels from the turn of the century because much more has been written about the texts of Gilbert Parker and 'Ralph Connor' than about the cultural environment in which they were produced and received. To understand that environment it is necessary to 'open up the canon,' in Leslie Fiedler's phrase – to acknowledge that '"literature" is effectively what we teach in departments of English,'[3] and to recognize that particularly in the field of early Canadian fiction, the current limited canon more accurately reflects the choice of a few professors and publishers than the actual cultural situation of the last century.

Many of the opinions and responses discussed in this book have been culled from early Canadian literary periodicals whose selection has also been rather eclectic, governed by the vicissitudes of preservation and availability. Major significance has been granted to the periodicals of central Canada, whose importance has been generally acknowledged by modern literary critics, especially *The Literary Garland* (Montreal 1838–51), *The Canadian Monthly and National Review* (Toronto 1872–8), and *The Week* (Toronto 1883–96).[4] However, the temptation to concentrate on the most convenient sources has been tempered with copious references to other periodicals spanning the temporal and geographical field of this book. Newspapers, on the other hand, have in the main been excluded with the exception of obviously relevant literary contents such as the columns written by Sara Jeannette Duncan for the *The Globe* (Toronto) and *The Daily Star* (Montreal), and *The Globe*'s now celebrated 'At the Mermaid Inn' column of 1892–3, which featured the opinions of Archibald Lampman, Wilfred Campbell, and Duncan Campbell Scott.

This approach is supported by Paul Rutherford's content analyses of leading Montreal and Toronto dailies from 1849, 1871, and 1896. On average these newspapers devoted less than 2 per cent of their space to 'culture and entertainment.' Their meagre literary showing was restricted primarily to serial novels, 'almost all ... foreign imports from Britain, America or France' chosen to hook a broad, continuing readership.[5] The obvious inference that most major newspapers regarded fiction as a utilitarian component of marketing, leaving to the cultural periodicals with circulations that were substantially smaller (but probably more dedicated) the concern with developing a local and national literature, was drawn by Sara Jeannette Duncan in 1886.

'Why do you print no book reviews?' I asked the editor of a leading journal recently.

'People don't care about them, and it interferes with advertising,' was his truly Philistinish response.[6]

It must be immediately recognized that this book recounts the literary history of a cultural élite. Dedicated, articulate, and usually privileged by education or economic status, the men and women whose views fill the following pages took it upon themselves to shape the writing and reading habits of their compatriots. Their opinions and tastes recorded in the literary publications deemed worthy of preservation thus predominate; the unexpressed views of the mass of Canadian readers must be inferred from their leaders' comments and frequent diatribes against dime novels, 'yellow-covered literature,' and illustrated papers, most of which were American and hence doubly reprehensible to the conservative, nationalistic Canadian mind.

Illumination on the problem of shaping a national literature is cast by John Garvin, who in 1922–3 attempted to bring out a twenty-five volume series of 'Master-Works of Canadian Authors.' His initial choice of poets – Charles Mair, Charles Heavysege, Charles Sangster, Isabella Crawford,

Charles G.D. Roberts, Archibald Lampman, Bliss Carman, Duncan Campbell Scott, W.W. Campbell, and Pauline Johnson – demonstrates remarkable consistency with the canon currently preserved in pedagogical collections of Canadian literature, as does his selection of Thomas Chandler Haliburton, Joseph Howe, Susanna Moodie, and Anna Jameson. When he came to fiction, however, Garvin gave serious consideration to many writers and titles which today would hardly be recognized by those who compile and teach from the familiar anthologies. William Kirby's *The Golden Dog* and Gilbert Parker's *The Seats of the Mighty* were obvious selections; less so was the latter's *Pierre and His People*. In addition to *Wacousta*, John Richardson was to be represented by *The Canadian Brothers*; James De Mille's *The Dodge Club Abroad* and *Helena's Household* were given the same weight as *A Strange Manuscript Found in a Copper Cylinder*. Other proposed titles included Norman Duncan's *Dr Luke of the Labrador*, *The Span O'Life* by William McLennan and Jean McIlwraith, W.D. Lighthall's *The False Chevalier*, McIlwraith's *The Curious Career of Roderick Random*, Agnes Laut's *Lords of the North*, the stories of E.W. Thomson, and when Garvin thought he could not obtain copyright clearance for Roberts' poems, the latter's *A Sister to Evangeline* and *The Canadians of Old* (his translation of Aubert de Gaspé's *Les anciens canadiens*).[7]

Even a casual critical glance will note the impress of a taste for costume romance at the expense of social realism, as well as the virtual absence of women writers. It is now difficult to sketch the outline of Canadian fiction before the First World War without thinking of Frances Brooke, Thomas McCulloch, Catharine Parr Traill, Rosanna Leprohon, Sara Jeannette Duncan, Charles W. Gordon, L.M. Montgomery, and D.C. Scott, now that their work has been made available in modern reprints, or to ignore the genre of the animal story. The point to be emphasized here is that the canon of early Canadian fiction has never been as constant as that of early Canadian poetry. The current perspective on early Canadian literature has been shaped by the editors of recent anthologies and reprint series; Garvin, closer to the era and more in touch with its standards, was expressing a literary outlook outmoded by the modernist generation that followed.

Garvin's preference for writers who chose to conserve the formulas of historical romance provides an appropriate introduction to the problem of the relation between popular taste and literary performance. In the larger world the tradition of the novel has always included considerable debate regarding the nature of the genre; from Cervantes and Sterne to the post-modernists, novelists have written as much against the prevailing forms of fiction as within them, stretching both the structure and content of fictional narrative into ever more flexible modes. In Canada, however, the practice until recently has been to write almost exclusively from within the received patterns, refraining in both form and content from challenging prevailing cultural norms. In the past, very few Canadian authors of fiction possessed sufficient tenacity, vision, or private income to pursue literary endeavours that did not promise imminent recognition or recompense. Popular success, not high art, was the goal of most of the writers considered here. James De Mille's comical subversions of ephemeral romantic fiction are amusing but scarcely revolutionary; Susanna Moodie and Sara Jeannette Duncan were radical only in Canada when they advocated fiction dealing with some of the less pleasant realities of common life. Yet despite its significance to Canadian cultural history, early popular culture has been omitted from the standard academic view of Canadian literature. South of the border, Robert E. Spiller's *Literary History of the United States* (1948) has been counterbalanced by studies such as James Hart's *The Popular Book: A History of America's Literary Taste* (1950) and Herbert Smith's *The Popular American Novel, 1865–1920* (1980);[8] the British picture has been filled in with classic studies by Q.D. Leavis and Amy Cruse, followed by Margaret Dalziel and Richard Altick.[9]

A Purer Taste does not alter the received notion that Canadian literary history is the history of a conservative colonial culture; rather, it illuminates that history by presenting it on its own terms – establishing, in the words of a modern critic, 'the context that would make [Canadian literature] significant to imaginations formed on European cultures.'[10] The fictional writings of this colony acquire new importance when viewed as documents in literary and cultural history, for which an understanding of their intended audience is crucial. Key elements in the horizon of expectations[11] of the culture in which they were written, they reflect the aspirations, preconceptions and limitations of an emerging nation struggling towards self-definition and both seeking and creating its identity through its literature.

For their encouragement at various times over the years that this book was in preparation I am grateful to M.W. Steinberg, Donald Stephens, Fred Cogswell, the late Susan Wood, the late Roy Daniells, Carl F. Klinck, Laurie Ricou, Diana Brydon, John Lennox, Clara Thomas, Peter Buitenhuis, Mary Lu MacDonald, Ann Munton, and above all, W.H. New, and Kathy Mezei. The research could not have been accomplished without the generosity of Anne Yandle, Head of Special Collections at the

University of British Columbia Library, and the determination of that university's Inter-Library Loans staff. I would also like to thank the many librarians and archivists across the country who have lent assistance, in particular Anne Goddard at the National Archives of Canada and Leon Warmski at the Archives of Ontario. The Canada Council awarded the Doctoral Fellowship under which this project was initiated many years ago, and the Social Sciences and Humanities Research Council the grant which allowed its completion. Without the encouragement of Gerald Hallowell at the University of Toronto Press this book would still be languishing in manuscript. Cheryl Siegel, librarian at the Vancouver Art Gallery, generously combed through the history of Canadian painting in search of a suitable cover illustration – and discovered that readers were not a major subject in early Canadian art. Jean Wilson provided meticulous editing, and Melanie Houlden, Carol McIver, and Marjorie Lang assisted with several phases of the research. I alone am responsible for errors or omissions.

Letters from the William Kirby Collection are quoted with permission from the Archives of Ontario; the letter from Thomas McLean to Louisa Murray, owned by Louisa King, is quoted with the permission of the York University Archives; the letter from Daniel Wilson to J.W. Dawson is quoted with the permission of the McGill University Archives; the letter from William Kirby to George Stewart is quoted by permission of the Houghton Library at Harvard University; manuscript materials in the National Archives of Canada are cited by permission. It has not been possible to trace the descendants of E.W. Thomson and G.M. Fairchild, whose letters are held by Queen's University Archives. Quotations are cited in their original form, with a few minimal silent corrections in spelling and punctuation. Every reasonable precaution has been taken to trace the owners of copyright material and to secure permission and make due acknowledgment; any error or omission will be gladly rectified in future editions.

Above all, for their love and patience I must thank my husband and computer consultant, Martin Gerson, who has known this undertaking almost as long as he has known me; and my children, Daniel and Rebekah, born into this project as the wards in Jarndyce are born into a suit in Chancery, but more fortunate in seeing it come to a definitive conclusion.

A PURER TASTE

THE WRITING AND READING OF FICTION IN ENGLISH IN NINETEENTH-CENTURY CANADA

1 Readers and Writers

A scant four months after Confederation, Thomas D'Arcy McGee addressed the Montreal Literary Club on 'The Mental Outfit of the New Dominion' and posed the rhetorical question, 'Who reads a Canadian book?' His answer was not heartening: 'very few, for Canadian books are exceedingly scarce.' He then proceeded to soften the blow by listing several resident writers and entering a plea 'on behalf of those who venture upon authorship among us, because I believe the existence of a recognized literary class will by and by be felt a state and social necessity.'[1] A modern response to McGee can begin by subdividing his question into several parts: 'Who was reading?', 'Who was reading books?', and 'Who was reading Canadian?' Answering the first entails a brief overview of literacy in nineteenth-century Canada.

From 1861, Canadian census takers measured literacy regularly, if not always consistently. Earlier comments indicate that during the second half of the eighteenth century illiteracy among English Canadians, while not as high as among the French, was a topic of considerable concern.[2] The public education movement that swept western Europe and North America in the early nineteenth century seems to have been especially effective in the settled English-speaking areas of British North America, according to one interpreter of the 1861 census.[3] Paul Rutherford treats the same statistics rather more cautiously. He estimates that '[a]round 1850, about one-quarter to one-third of the adults in the mainland colonies could not read,' and from his analysis of subsequent census figures concludes that 'By the end of the century the level of illiteracy (again the inability to read) among adult Canadians must have hovered around nine or ten per cent ... the dominion now ranked slightly behind France as well as England and Wales.' Omitting Quebec improves the picture by several points. In both 1871 and 1901 literacy rates for each of the major Canadian cities were consistently higher, by three to eleven percentage points, than for the towns and countryside comprising the remainder of the provincial territory.[4]

Despite the difficulty of computing precise literacy rates, it is evident that the systems of public and private education that evolved in nineteenth-century English-speaking Canada succeeded in the basic task of creating a functionally literate population. The degree to which that literacy was applied to 'literature' was not measured by census takers and must be inferred indirectly, from the encouragement of reading provided by booksellers, libraries and Mechanics' Institutes, and literary societies.

In his speech, McGee lamented, 'Of public libraries I grieve to say that we have not, so far as I know, a single one in the whole Dominion.' He was aware of 'a Society Library in Quebec' (presumably that of the Literary and Historical Society of Quebec) and of college, law, and parliamentary libraries, but he believed that in 1867 there was 'no public library in any of our chief towns.'[5] It may be that McGee defined 'public library' to exclude subscription and public school libraries or those maintained by Mechanics' Institutes, parishes, Sunday schools, or local booksellers. In any case, his negation of public libraries implies that whatever facilities were in existence had made little impact − at least on a resident of Montreal. During the following decade James Douglas, jr, President of the Literary and Historical Society of Quebec, likewise deplored the state of the country's libraries, yet by the time of his 1875 report[6] they had become quite numerous (in Ontario if not Quebec) although meagrely stocked.

Ontario's first public subscription library had been founded in 1800 in Niagara-on-the-Lake (then known as Newark) and in the early 1820s a free, public Quaker library was established in Aurora.[7] From the 1830s to the late 1850s, many Mechanics' Institutes functioned essentially as public libraries; in 1858 '143 Mechanics' Institutes and Library Associations in Upper and Lower Canada had received government aid.'[8] Upper Canada was well served by Egerton Ryerson's plan for County Common School Libraries, of which there were 1535 by 1870.[9] According to the National Council of Women's summary of Canadian libraries published in 1900, at the turn of the century there were 535 (non-school) libraries in the Dominion of which 418 were in Ontario, 50 in Quebec, 44 in the Maritime provinces, and 19 in the West.[10] Although Quebec did not have a free lending library until 1885 when the Fraser Institute was founded in Montreal, the reading public of the lower province was not entirely without access to books. In addition to the libraries of colleges and religious institutions there were 'bibliothèques paroissiales,' intended to 'promote suitable reading for the faithful ... By 1860 about half the parishes of the province had some kind of library, with an average of 200 to 300 titles in each.'[11]

Closer to home (for McGee) was the Mercantile Library Association of Montreal, which in 1843 had absorbed the holdings of the Montreal Library/Bibliothèque de Montréal.[12] In 1859–60 *The Family Herald* (Montreal) followed this library's activities, in particular the decision to issue ladies' tickets which for an annual fee of two dollars would permit their holders to attend lectures and borrow books. The *Herald* anticipated that the presence of women, with their presumed interest in 'the current literature of the day,' would offer 'a tolerably strong guarantee that books, and not newspapers as heretofore, will become the leading feature of the Association.'[13] Such refinement in public reading taste, replacing newspapers and current local politics with books and more tasteful literature, was seen as a desirable stage in the development of a national literary consciousness by several mid-century commentators. The 1838 contributor to *The Pearl* (Halifax) who lamented that instead of engaging in 'literary pursuits,' 'Every novice in composition ... imagines the stormy sea of politics to be the proper element over which his genius may expand' was echoed by Susanna Moodie in her preface to *Mark Hurdlestone, the Gold Worshipper* (1853), where she deplored the disinterest in polite literature manifested by native Canadians, who much preferred 'a good political article from their newspapers' to 'romantic tales and poetry.'[15]

That the word 'literary' connoted distinction is evidenced by the frequency of its appearance in the names of Canadian clubs and social associations throughout the nineteenth century. In the 1830s and 1840s there existed 'an astonishing number' of literary societies in the Canadas – eight in Quebec, seven in each of Montreal and Toronto, and eight more in smaller communities – of which two-thirds were English and few survived more than a couple of years.[16] Their numbers increased as the century progressed; an 1890 account of the same phenomenon in England theorized that 'Literary societies appear to be the natural successors of "mechanics' institutions," which some forty and fifty years ago did good work in the way of mental improvement.'[17] This description certainly applies to the Ottawa Literary and Scientific Society, which was formed by the 1870 merging of the local Mechanics' Institute with the Natural History Society of Ottawa. And like many such organizations it was less literary in practice than in name. In its published programs from

1898 to 1901 and even more so in its published papers from 1897 to 1907, the Society demonstrated greater interest in science than in literature. A similar paucity of literary activity was noted by the historian of the prestigious Literary and Historical Society of Quebec: 'En fait, il eut été plus juste de baptiser la LHSQ: "Société historique et scientifique de Québec".'[18] In 1838 Halifax had a Literary and Scientific Association largely concerned with 'the art of Public Speaking';[19] similarly on the west coast the all-male Burrard Literary Club of Vancouver (1894–1904) was essentially a debating society interested in current political topics, its 'literary' aspect protruding only in occasional programs on heavyweights like Shakespeare and Carlyle, and, once, a paper on 'Canadian Poets and Authors.'[20]

The tendency of men's literary societies to sidestep literature in favour of current events, science, and history was echoed in the interest the latter held for many women's literary societies if the Women's Literary Club of St Catharines may serve as an example. Founded in 1892 to balance the local Men's History and Science Club, the Women's Literary Club selected as its first undertakings the writing of a 'Life of Laura Secord,' the placing of markers at local historic spots, and the initiation of a series of pilgrimages to historic sites. In the record of the highlights of the Club's first eighty years compiled in 1972, activities relating to social services and local history overshadow literary events, which were represented by a visit with William Kirby in 1896, a lecture by Laura Goodman Salverson in 1913, and a poetry reading by Bliss Carman.[21] However sparse, this organization's literary activities exceeded those of the now famous Toronto Women's Literary Club, founded in 1876, which exploited the presumed gentility of the term 'literary' to dissemble its members' feminist and suffragist projects.

Certainly some literary organizations did engage in the activities implied by their titles, such as the Calgary Women's Literary Club (founded in 1906), which studied Shakespeare and Browning and helped establish the Calgary Public Library in 1912.[22] Among women the popularity of 'literary and reading societies and clubs' at the turn of the century is indicated by *Women in Canada*'s list of thirty-five, mostly in the major cities of Quebec and Ontario, followed by the names of another fourteen towns where such organizations were known to exist. The most westerly of these is Port Arthur; adding prairie and British Columbia groups would significantly increase the total.[23] However, as revealed in the surviving records, the existence of an association calling itself 'literary' does not necessarily imply significant literary activity or a group of committed readers. Further pursuit of McGee's query requires consideration of the reading material available to Canadians from their local booksellers and publishers.

By the end of the nineteenth century most adult Canadians could read, many valued the notion of literary activity, and the majority had access to some kind of organized collection of library materials. How many of these works were Canadian? Allan Smith's research on the books reviewed by the major central Canadian literary periodicals between 1852 and 1887 reveals that the volumes most frequently noticed in the press were published in the United States but written in Britain – a continuation of the pattern of the previous two decades, when the majority of the books imported into the Canadas were American editions of British texts.[24] Before Confederation, fewer than a quarter of the titles reviewed by *The Anglo-American Magazine*, *The British-American Magazine*, and *The Saturday Reader* issued from Canadian presses and about two-thirds came from the United States. After 1867 the nationalistic *Canadian Monthly and National Review*, *Belford's Monthly Magazine*, and *Rose-Belford's Canadian Monthly* lent increased support to local publishers, giving frequent notice to books that were published in Canada or were Canadian editions of American publications (thereby boosting the publisher of the latter two, the Belford brothers, who specialized in bringing out cheap editions of unprotected American and British books).[25] However, this policy was not continued by *The Week*, nearly half of whose reviews during the period surveyed were of books emanating directly from American presses.

The Week paid a similar proportion of its attention to American authors: of identified writers, 48 per cent of those reviewed were American, 28.5 per cent British, and 16.5 per cent Canadian. In *The Canadian Monthly*, *Belford's*, and *Rose-Belford's Canadian Monthly*, the proportion of Canadian authors reviewed was somewhat higher: about 22.5 per cent, compared with 23 per cent for American and 44.5 per cent for British writers. *The New Dominion Monthly* (Montreal), despite its name, demonstrated the least interest in new dominion writers: Canadian authors received only 6.5 per cent of its reviews, in contrast to 37 per cent for British writers and 40 per cent for Americans.[26] If there is any correlation between the reviewing of books and and their subsequent audience it would appear that the products of Canadian writers and publishers did not, as a group, have a major impact upon Canadian readers. At the same time, however, it must be remembered that the usual practice was for a book to be reviewed only when an editor received a free review copy. Hence these figures may speak more accurately about the lassitude or poverty of the

Canadian publishing industry than about the reading opportunities of their public.

Best-seller lists did not begin to be compiled in Canada until the very end of the nineteenth century, at which time they confirm the reading orientation suggested by the earlier figures from book reviews. Mary Vipond's analysis of data from the 1899–1918 period concludes that 'Canadians read more American fiction than anything else in the first two decades of the twentieth century. Of the approximately two hundred novels on the best-seller lists, about 44 per cent were by American authors, 36 per cent by British and 21 per cent by Canadian.'[27]

The schema initiated by McGee's question would be incomplete without some examination of who was writing Canadian books. Census figures from 1861 to 1911 show that 80 per cent of Canadians who were not French declared themselves of British descent, roughly one-quarter coming from Scotland. The proportion of those originally from Ireland and England shifted over the half century, the Irish segment decreasing from 50 per cent to 27 per cent with the English portion increasing reciprocally. Among literary writers, however, English and Scottish Protestants of the professional or 'middle middle class' predominated, their fathers being primarily teachers or professors, clergymen, lawyers, civil servants, or doctors. Contrary to the current notion that women were well represented among early Canadian writers, according to the few existing studies of the sociology of authorship in Canada they accounted for only 13.5 per cent of Canadian authors born before 1899 (deemed worthy of inclusion in later reference books), whereas of British writers from the same period 19 per cent were female.[28] In the 1830–50 period, women accounted for about 22 per cent of the English-language creative writers in the Canadas, the majority being 'educated, urban and middle class' males, just under half of whom 'were either lawyers or clergymen.'[29] The socially ascendant orientation of this literary fraternity is suggested by the fact that nineteenth-century Canada, unlike its sister dominion of Australia, developed no local popular press to supply the lowest stratum of readers with indigenous pulp fiction. Though the country's cultural leaders were consequently able to take pride in the relative cleanliness of their national literature, one modern critic has wondered about the long-term effects of this lack of 'ordinary material written and published for common Canadians.'[30]

Throughout the nineteenth century the reception of literature in Canada was steered by nationalists who, in chorus with the Reverend Hartley Dewart, advanced the familiar notion that 'A national literature is an essential element in the formation of national character.'[31] They formed a vocal community of editors, commentators, publishers, and promoters which expressed itself primarily in the periodicals it founded (and in many cases promptly buried) and among which it shifted about with considerable ease. Mobility of editors and writers has always been a significant feature of Canadian literary history, beginning in Montreal with David Chisholme, founding editor of *The Canadian Magazine and Literary Repository* (1823–5), who then left that magazine to start a rival and equally short-lived publication, *The Canadian Review and Literary and Historical Journal* (1824–6). Chisholme also edited *The Montreal Gazette* and later *The Montreal Herald*;[32] this combination of newspaper and literary work was characteristic of many male editors and authors like John Sparrow Thompson of Halifax. Thompson edited *The Halifax Monthly Magazine* from 1830 to 1833, *The Pearl* (1837–40) during the last year of its brief existence, and Joseph Howe's more enduring newspaper, *The Novascotian*, in 1838 and again from 1840 to 1842.[33]

Before women began to establish a noticeable presence in the major newspapers in the 1880s, their primary arena was the literary periodicals, where at mid-century a few proved their mettle as editors.[34] Less physically mobile than their male colleagues, many nonetheless developed a broad web of literary connections. Most prominent in the pre-Confederation era were the Strickland sisters, Susanna Moodie and Catharine Parr Traill, who spread their genteel literary taste across the Canadas by contributing not only to *The Literary Garland* (1838–51), but also to many of the more ephemeral literary magazines, including *The Canadian Literary Magazine* (York 1833), the Moodies' *Victoria Magazine* (Belleville 1847–8), *The Anglo-American Magazine* (Toronto 1852–5), *The Maple Leaf* (Montreal 1852–4), *The Family Herald* (Montreal 1859–60), and *The British American Magazine* (Toronto 1863–4).

After Confederation the pattern of interrelationships within the dominant literary élite of central Canada became even more evident. Civil servant and constitutional legal expert John George Bourinot, the author of *Our Intellectual Strength and Weakness* (1893), founded the Halifax *Herald* and contributed stories and articles relating to Canadian culture and history to *Stewart's Literary Quarterly* (St John), *The New Dominion Monthly* (Montreal), and the Toronto periodicals *The Canadian Monthly and National Review* and *The Week*. Another Maritimer and prominent critic, George Stewart, jr, founded *Stewart's Literary Quarterly* in St John in 1867, went to Toronto in 1878 to edit *Rose-Belford's Canadian Monthly*, and a year later moved to Quebec, where he edited *The Morning Chronicle* from

1879 to 1896 and *The Quebec Mercury* from 1898 to 1903. Scotsman Graeme Mercer Adam married the daughter of John Gibson, editor of *The Literary Garland*, and was closely associated with many major Toronto publishing ventures and periodicals before he emigrated to New York in 1892. Missouri-born John Talon-Lesperance began his journalistic career in St John and was then variously connected with a number of Montreal newspapers and periodicals, including *The Gazette, The Star, The Canadian Illustrated News*, and *The Dominion Illustrated*. Presiding over the entire scene was the leonine figure of Goldwin Smith. Internationally prominent before he arrived in Canada in 1871, Smith quickly established his local significance with his involvement in the founding of *The Canadian Monthly and National Review* in 1872, *The Telegram* in 1874, *The Bystander* in 1880, and *The Week* in 1883.

These men clustered around the literary periodicals which they edited and to which they contributed, and around the literary section of the Royal Society of Canada, founded in 1882. Lack of faith in Canada's literary practitioners initially jeopardized the inception of the Society's English-language literary division when Daniel Wilson tried to persuade J.W. Dawson to abandon it entirely, arguing, 'It is certain, looking to the material out of which such a section has to be formed, that it will either do nothing, – or a great deal worse.'[35] Although the 'English Literature, History and Allied Subjects' section went ahead with Daniel Wilson as president, one of its founding members soon admitted that 'the weakest point' of the Royal Society of Canada 'rests in the literary sections.'[36]

At the Society's first annual meeting Bourinot, Stewart, Smith and Talon-Lesperance rubbed shoulders with James M. LeMoine, author of six volumes of *Maple Leaves* (1863–1906) and many other works on Quebec history and folklore; his close friend, William Kirby, whose novel *The Golden Dog* he had inspired; their acquaintance and fellow man of letters, Benjamin Sulte; John Reade, literary editor of the Montreal *Gazette*; nationalist and imperialist George Taylor Denison; and poets Charles Sangster, Evan McColl, and Louis Fréchette. In later years these charter members were joined by William Withrow, editor of *The Methodist Magazine*; bibliographer and cataloguer Henry Morgan; literary commentators J.W. Longley, W.D. LeSueur, and Andrew MacPhail; poets Charles Mair, Wilfred Campbell, Archibald Lampman, Charles G.D. Roberts, Duncan Campbell Scott, and William Henry Drummond; fiction writers E.W. Thomson and Charles W. Gordon ('Ralph Connor'); and staunch literary nationalist W.D. Lighthall, editor of *Songs of the Great Dominion* (1889). A similar group portrait of the cultural power-mongers of Victorian Canada can be found in the guest list of the 1897 banquet of *The Canadian Magazine*, which included prominent politicians, bankers, university presidents, newspaper editors, authors, and poets – all male of course – a virtual who's who of the country's literary tastemakers.[37]

The exclusion of women from the Royal Society (in 1947 Gabrielle Roy was the first admitted to the literary section) did not likewise inhibit their contribution to their country's literary milieu. After 1867 the most prominent women writers included Agnes Maule Machar ('Fidelis'), a substantial contributor of fiction and literary journalism to many periodicals, including *The Canadian Monthly and National Review* and *The Week*; Ethelwyn Wetherald, poet and active journalist in *The Globe* and *The Week*; Susan Frances Harrison ('Seranus'), author of fiction and poetry and contributor to *The Week*; and Sara Jeannette Duncan, whose relatively radical literary opinions and exuberant style enlivened the pages of *The Week*, the Toronto *Globe*, and the Montreal *Star*.

These literary men and women, together with less easily identified editors of and contributors to nineteenth-century Canada's cultural periodicals, participated in the debates that characterized discussion of Canada's literary development throughout the last century and on into the next – debates that produced the colourful rhetoric and dramatic declamations that pepper subsequent sections of this book. On one side ranged the optimists,[38] many of them editors and publishers, who convinced themselves if not the country at large that Canada's obvious potential for material prosperity would inspire a cultural golden age. On the other sat the realists, including many writers, who felt that the country's general readership took little interest in its authors.

The two positions scarcely altered over the decades. Optimism frequently possessed recent immigrants who were unable to conceive of a social order which lacked a powerful literary tradition and therefore asserted that with only a few years of encouragement the New World would produce a respectable literary showing of its own. Typical was John Sparrow Thompson, an Irish Methodist who arrived in Nova Scotia in 1827. As founding editor of *The Halifax Monthly Magazine* in 1830 he informed his readers that 'we are confident, that with the rapidly advancing general prosperity of the Province, its literature will not remain stationary, and we hope to gain largely from the spirit of enquiry which is now at work, and from the literary efforts which will be the fruit of that spirit.'[39]

Yet for the rest of the century the theme of disappointment with the country's current literary performance coupled with faith in its imminent improvement echoed a familiar refrain.[40] In the optimistic 1880s William Kirby echoed his compatriots in his anticipation of a new era for Canadian writers. Telling George Stewart of his 'regret that a few men I know could not live by literature purely in Canada – as they might in any other Country speaking our language,' he added cheerfully, 'I doubt that day is a good way off yet for us. We ask in the Dominions about where the U States were fifty years ago – as to literary encouragement, but as times change so much faster now, one may expect that in a score of years there will be a genuine pride spring[ing] up among our people for their own writers – as now patronize our manufacturers.'[41] And in 1897 *The Canadian Magazine* announced, once again, that 'We are nearer ... than ever before' to having a commendable national literature.[42]

The optimists expressed great confidence in the power of literature as 'a missionary of civilization and refinement'[43] despite the reluctance, or economic inability, of Canadians to subscribe to the journals established for this purpose. Indeed, their high mortality rate (few survived more than three years) lends support instead to Reverend Dewart's blunt denunciation that:

There is probably no country in the world, making equal pretensions to intelligence and progress, where the claims of native literature are so little felt, and where every effort in poetry has been met with so much coldness and indifference, as in Canada. And what is more to be deprecated than neglect of our most meritorious authors, is the almost universal absence of interest and faith in all indigenous literary productions, and the undisturbed satisfaction with a state of things that, rightly viewed, should be regarded as a national reproach. The common method of accounting for this by the fact that almost the whole community is engaged in the pursuit of the necessaries and comforts of life, and that comparatively few possess wealth and leisure, to enable them to give much time or thought to the study of poetry and kindred subjects, is by no means satisfactory.[44]

Both sides of the issue were experienced in full by the tempestuous John Richardson. In 1841, after publishing *Wacousta* (1833) and *The Canadian Brothers* (1840), he adopted the rhetoric of the optimists in his petition for a government pension for his efforts 'to introduce into [Canada] that spirit of refinement, through the instrumentality of literature, which is the first indication of moral superiority in a people, and the surest guarantee of order and well regulated submission to authority.'[45] Denied the rewards he thought owed to him, Richardson then switched his tune and lambasted both the Canadian public and their administrators for not caring 'a straw whether the author was a Canadian or a Turk,'[46] who might as well have published 'in Kamschatka.'[47]

After Confederation, cultural nationalists continued to lament the Dominion's apparent failure to encourage its own writers. In 1875 James Douglas, jr reluctantly admitted that 'our intellectual acquirements have not kept pace with the growth in material wealth of our country.'[48] To provide encouragement some critics requested special consideration for Canadian writers. In its call for 'Justice to Canadian Authors' *The Canadian Illustrated News* declared: 'While platitude should never be encouraged because it is of native growth, mediocrity might be treated with indulgence, and where there is real excellence, it should be proclaimed precisely because it is Canadian.'[49] This position irritated Sara Jeannette Duncan. Cautioning against indiscriminate literary nationalism while trying to infuse her country with a sense of culture, she finally threw up her hands in despair at Canadians' 'blinding lethargy' in literary matters, denouncing her compatriots as 'the imported essence of British Philistinism, warranted to keep in any climate.'[50] The turn of the century saw little improvement: Robert Barr's vehement 1899 accusation that Canada 'would rather spend [its money] on whiskey than on books' directly echoed John Richardson's complaint of sixty years earlier that Canadians 'would far more rejoice in a great distiller of whiskey than a writer of books ...'[51]

During the post-Confederation era, responsibility for English Canada's disappointing literary achievement was attributed to three major obstacles: copyright laws, which failed to protect books not published in Britain or the United States; the perceived limitations of Canadian subjects and markets; and the country's inferior political status, which was not conducive to literary inspiration. The copyright problem, which has received full treatment in George L. Parker's comprehensive study, *The Beginnings of the Book Trade in Canada* (1985), will here be summarized very briefly.

The Imperial Copyright Act of 1842 was designed to protect works published in London or Edinburgh and to prevent the colonies from reprinting copyright works or importing unauthorized reprints (ie, cheap American editions). It was amended by the Foreign Reprints Act of 1847, in force until 1894, which 'permitted the importation and sale of pirated British copyright works'[52] at a duty of 12½ per cent. After Confederation, Canadian publishers campaigned for the reprint rights enjoyed by American publishers, whose advantageous position allowed them to be the primary suppliers of the Canadian market. The loudest voices belonged to 'the most cunning publisher of the day,' John Lovell, whose creative approach to legal problems transformed his Montreal printing establishment into a wealthy international enterprise,[53] and to Graeme Mercer Adam, who argued in the 1870s that 'the anomalous state of our copyright law represses all native publishing enterprise, and retards the development of an industry which would have much to do with the educational and intellectual advancement of the country, were the trade relieved from the disabilities that now trammel it.'[54] The 1875 Canadian Copyright Act improved the situation more for Canadian publishers competing with American pirates than for Canadian writers. Much local literary publication was financed by the author or by subscription and often poorly edited and produced. The economic insecurity of Canadian publishers left them unwilling to take risks on local literature or to seek international markets for Canadian works. Illustrative of the extremities of the situation are the well-known misadventures of *The Golden Dog* (1877) whereby William Kirby lost his royalties, control of his copyright, and any further inclination to write Canadian fiction.[55]

Hence to secure meaningful copyright registration, aggressive marketing, and adequate remuneration, many Canadians chose to publish in Britain or the United States and, especially towards the end of the century, to remove themselves bodily as well. As Sara Jeannette Duncan commented in 1887, 'The market for Canadian literary work of all sorts is self-evidently New York.'[56] And as the career of mass market Toronto publisher John Ross Robertson suggests, New York supplied the bread and butter of cheap Canadian publishing. In the 1870s and 1880s, when Robertson successfully exploited the saleability of pirated popular American fiction, the sole Canadian on his list was May Agnes Fleming, a New Brunswicker whose move to New York in 1875 and steady stream of novels bearing scant evidence of their author's origins presaged the course that would be taken by many later Canadian writers.[57] It is ironic but scarcely surprising that at the turn of the century many of Canada's most successful fiction writers were expatriates, including Gilbert Parker, Charles G.D. Roberts, Bliss Carman, E.W. Thomson, Grant Allen, Lily Dougall, Robert Barr, and Sara Jeannette Duncan. The latter's necessary 'abandonment of Canada' in her first novel, *A Social Departure* (1890), was seen by Graeme Mercer Adam as symptomatic of the Canadian writer's disadvantaged position in the larger literary world:

To patriotic Canadians, who are at the same time ardent book lovers, it will be a matter of regret that a Canadian writer has thus, in her own interest, to ignore the native book market and even to assume the piquante guise of an American girl, to enable her to win the ear of an adequate and appreciative public. This is but another evidence, however, of the disabilities common to the status of a dependency and of the national effacement that is forced upon a clever and aspiring writer, who is only a Colonist.[58]

To Goldwin Smith, laissez-faire liberal and ardent advocate of a 'free union' between Canada and the United States 'like that into which Scotland entered with England,'[59] the prominence of so many literary expatriates patently proved that 'A writer of mark appearing in Ontario, still more one appearing in any of the minor Provinces, would seek the larger market of England, that of the United States, or both.' In Smith's continentalist eyes, the problem was compounded by Canada's physical geography and cultural apathy:

A writer in Ontario has hardly any field outside his own Province. Quebec, saving the British quarter of Montreal and the British remnant in Quebec city, affords him none. There is very little chance of his reaching beyond Quebec to the Maritime Provinces. On the other side neither Manitoba nor the Territories have as yet much of a reading public, and British Columbia is in another world. Ontario is his sole constituency, and Ontario is a farming Province with little over two millions of people; while among the wealthy class reading is not very much the fashion nor are libraries very often seen.[60]

Smith had already couched a socio-political explanation of the problem in his rhetorical question 'What dependency ever had a literature?'[61] As the century neared its close his view was repeated in Sara Jeannette Duncan's declaration that 'in our character as colonists we find the root of all our sins of omission in letters,'[62] in J.G. Bourinot's admission that 'Literary stimulus seems to be more or less wanting in a colony,'[63] and in Graeme Mercer Adam's regretful conclusion that 'The history of colonies, it has been said, is seldom written and never read. The same, it is to be feared, is true of their literature.'[64]

During the nineteenth century the topic of Canada's literary development grew so obsessive that one young observer finally quipped, 'We shall soon be able to compile a bibliography of what has been written about Canadian literature, more voluminous than the literature itself.'[65] Cultural commentators usually identified the obstacles to Canada's literary development as the country's pioneer and colonial condition, the difficulties imposed by copyright laws, and cultural apathy due in part to a necessary preoccupation with material progress.[66] While these impediments affected all forms of artistic endeavour, the stories and literary commentary found in nineteenth-century cultural periodicals reveal two additional problems besetting Canada's establishment of a national voice in fiction. Widespread doubt about the acceptability of fiction as a literary mode and an undercurrent of diffidence regarding the validity of Canada as a location for fiction produced a set of internal cultural attitudes which viewed the novel as an inferior genre, considered popularity a writer's primary goal, and discouraged serious innovation. Local applause was reserved for writers who shared their community's preference for the unthreatening entertainment of popular romance, and often set that romance safely beyond the borders of their own prosaic terrain.

2 The Reception of the Novel

'Man can no more do without works of fiction than he can do without clothing,' audaciously proclaimed Australian writer Frederick Sinnett in 1856.[1] In Canada's subarctic climate the subject of attire required more serious consideration; nonetheless, during the nineteenth century, in Canada as in the rest of the English-speaking world, fiction captivated the general reading public. As early as 1806 a visitor contemptuously remarked that 'novels and romances are most in request among the Canadian ladies, as they indeed are among the ladies of Europe.'[2] At the time of Confederation, Thomas D'Arcy McGee cited the claim of a Montreal bookseller that fiction accounted for 44 per cent of the volume of his sales. In 1870 novels comprised two-thirds of the circulation of the library of the Montreal Mechanics' Institute, and in 1880 over three-quarters of the circulation of the library of the Toronto Mechanics' Institute.[3] While the public's reading taste was frequently disparaged, few English-Canadian commentators took a position as extreme as that of some of their French-Canadian counterparts, whose maxim 'Les peuples honnêtes n'ont pas de romans' was echoed even by a novelist who claimed that 'Le roman, surtout le roman moderne, et plus particulièrement encore le roman français me paraît être une arme forgée par Satan lui-même pour la déstruction du genre humain.'[4]

During the nineteenth century the English-Canadian response to prose fiction reflected many of the disputes familiar to English and American observers of the novel's struggle for approval. As a relative newcomer it lacked the sanction of classical precedent. As a species of fictional creativity it disturbed the utilitarian, evangelical bias of the middle class who generally distrusted imaginative self-indulgence. The dramatic expansion of the reading public over the course of the century further accentuated the apparent power of the novel to alter and possibly corrupt a large segment of the population.

Nina Baym has argued that contrary to the current prevailing interpretation of United States literary history, the novel was well received in antebellum America. Her *Novels, Readers, and Reviewers*[5] suggests that hostility to Hawthorne and Melville was not indicative of hostility to fiction in general, but of popular distaste for the writers now placed at the cornerstones of the American literary tradition. While Canadians appear to have read novels as avidly as their American cousins, their taste met with less approval from their cultural arbiters. On the whole they echoed their British predecessors, transferring to a Canadian context the issues documented by John Tinnon Taylor in his study of *Early Opposition to the English Novel*.[6]

Canadian literary opinion reveals a spectrum of attitudes (all tinted conservative) ranging from absolute abhorrence of the novel, to restrained attraction to it, to qualified justification of prose fiction as a didactic instrument or a harmless way to 'while away an idle hour, or fill up the blanks of a wet day.'[7] After Confederation, overtly nationalistic fiction gained increasing acceptance due to the political need to create for Canada an identity distinguishable from that of the United States. Canadian commentators acknowledged the astonishing ability of prose fiction to seize the imagination, arouse the emotions, and consciously or subconsciously persuade the reader. They dreaded the abuse of this power by unscrupulous writers and dolefully warned of the detrimental effects of excessive novel-reading upon the morals and industry of an infant nation. On one level the reception of the novel resembled the attitude towards alcohol: many indulged, but the practice was officially condoned for medicinal purposes only. Within this broadly conservative framework there appeared many variations of opinion as reviewers and editors presented different definitions of moral and entertainment values and occasionally expressed quite divergent views on specific books or authors. A detailed examination of the reception of the novel in Victorian Canada shows how seriously the subject was regarded in an emerging nation which recognized the importance of literature in shaping its national character.

While the arguments for and against prose fiction shifted somewhat over the century, central Canada and the Maritimes consistently retained an educated and influential élite who excluded the novel from the highest realms of literature. One of the earliest expressions of this position appeared in 1824, when *The Canadian Review and Literary and Historical*

Journal defined literature as 'the study and knowledge of the languages of Poetry, of History, and of Philosophy.'[8] At mid-century Mary Jane Katzmann admitted science and philosophy to the fold: 'Like the fruit and lighter matters at dinner, a romance is occasionally acceptable; but as solids are necessary to man's strength, in as great a degree does his intellectual system require good literary food – a course of study calculated to interest and strengthen the mind, such as is afforded by science, history, or philosophy, but never by the contents of a baseless novel.'[9] Four decades later Charles Mair echoed Matthew Arnold's maxim that 'The crown of literature is poetry'[10] when he opened a discussion of Canadian literature with the stipulation 'By the term Literature you mean, of course, poetry.'[11] And in the introduction to his *Headwaters of Canadian Literature* (1924), published a full century after the quotation cited at the beginning of this paragraph, Archibald MacMechan followed suit by defining literature as 'poetry in all its branches.'[12]

This disdain for fiction coloured the reception of Canadian imaginative writing from its beginning. Reviews of the two major Montreal literary productions of 1824, Julia Catherine Beckwith Hart's *St Ursula's Convent; or, The Nun of Canada* and George Longmore's *The Charivari*, disclose a clear predisposition to favour the poem over the novel. David Chisholme candidly admitted that he bothered with Hart's book only because it was 'the first native novel that ever appeared in Canada.'

Chisholme's comments are worth quoting at length because they explicitly establish the tenor of the environment into which the first Canadian novel was launched. While Chisholme acknowledged fiction to be 'the most alluring of all species of composition,' he refused to grant it any lasting value:

We must, in the first place premise, that we have not yet arrived at a satisfactory conviction of the utility of novel writing, especially of those light, amatory, and romantic tales which, under this title are daily issuing from the press ... and that until that is the case, we cannot help thinking, that the genius and talents of young writers of both sexes, might be applied to much greater advantage to themselves and others in commencing their labours, by pursuing some more serious and important course in literature than *fiction* ...

Chisholme conceded that fiction could be acceptable and even useful if it were 'made subservient to the highest sentiments of morality and virtue.' But he wondered what attraction the genre could possibly hold when all that was truly valuable was to be found in abundance in the real world:

In the actual occurrences of life there is a natural beauty, as well as a moral principle which the invention of the highest genius can never equal; and in reflecting upon them, a feeling and generous mind, is often struck with awe and veneration at the happy or unfortunate results to which they lead in human affairs. As the recollection of these are as useful and important for the preservation of social and patriotic feelings, as the worshipping of their household gods by the ancients, we could wish that all young persons aspiring to the enviable rank of authorship, instead of distracting their minds for the purpose of drawing an unnatural and insipid picture of humanity by means of a tale of fancy in the form of a novel, would apply themselves with assiduity to collect the scattered fragments of what may have happened in real life, and by combining them with those scenes of rural beauty of which nature has, almost, in every country, been so profuse, present them to our view in the unassuming garb of facts, which must inevitably lead to some moral deduction.[13]

Consequently Chisholme advised the young author to turn to history and he concluded his review by offering to send her a copy of the 'History of the British American Colonies' (a book which it has not been possible to trace).

Not all Chisholme's contemporaries shared his views. At least one pre-Victorian journal was willing to recognize the legitimacy of imaginative prose fiction so long as it contained 'beauty and philosophy, and historical information, and natural truth.' In 1830 (presumably with Walter Scott in mind) John Sparrow Thompson, editor of the *Halifax Monthly Magazine*, distinguished between the gothic romance of the past and the more realistic novel of the present. He condemned the former for being 'filled with exaggerated pictures, and froathy sentiments, and producing in the minds of their readers, a worthless dream-like enjoyment,' but praised the latter's 'truth to nature,' noting that 'Some of the brightest names in the literary annals of the world, have been identified with these comparatively light works.'[14]

The topic of reading material for children inevitably led to questions regarding the value of fiction. While Canadian commentators concurred in defining education as the fostering of morality and reason and advocated a factual, rational approach to the real world, they differed significantly regarding the role of the imagination in the intellectual development of the child. Overtly didactic tales like those by Susanna Moodie and Catharine Parr Traill were generally the most acceptable form of children's literature because they contained a clear moral structure. However, in 1827 Truro schoolmaster James Irving advocated unusual leeway in children's reading. While he assumed that the ultimate goal of literary education was 'imagination brought under subjection to reason and rendered submissive to its direction,' he also acknowledged children's general preference for fairy-tales over 'historical facts and logical inductions.' Hence he argued that

The recital of such tales, or their perusal, undoubtedly is to the young mind what light food is to the young body: – it imperceptibly prepares it to receive, and induces it to relish, what is stronger and more nutritious ...

That such tales recited or read, engender in the young mind a dislike to truth and wholesome nutriment, is essentially erroneous: – they foster the imagination, and feed it with itself, till the gradual development of reason impel it to seek for more solid matter.

Enjoying an eighteenth-century trust in the natural power of reason and assuming that well educated children will normally discard the fictional world as they mature, Irving even allowed young people unexpurgated editions of the ancient and modern classics. But only the classics: 'in leaving youth the liberty of choice I would not be understood as recommending an indiscriminate Library – a "Candide" by the side of a "Rasselas," a "Purcelle" by the side of "The Exiles of Siberia," or a "Don Juan" by "The White Doe." Works evidently pernicious and immoral, however recommended by genius, are in no wise defensible, – can in no wise conduce to any salutary end.'[15]

The liberal-mindedness of Irving's approach to imaginative literature was soon to be stifled by the encroaching gentility of the Victorian era represented by Robert W. Lay, editor of *The Maple Leaf* (1852–3), a Montreal magazine initially intended for children. Although his periodical did publish fiction, including didactic tales and a serialization of *Uncle Tom's Cabin*, Lay continually ranted against literature dealing with 'the unreal.' When he began to serialize Catharine Parr Traill's 'The Governor's Daughter,'[16] which is less a novel than a series of nature lessons presented in a fictional framework, Lay felt compelled to justify himself in italics:

it is not intended to introduce thrilling descriptions of imaginary adventures, or a history of wonderful characters living in an ideal world, far above the stern realities of life; but we wish and intend to develop the Natural History of this country, in a faithful and pleasing manner ... 'Truth is stranger than fiction,' is a proverb in common use; and really there is so much of the true and substantial, so much information of the most enticing

character, so many things existing to write about, that we deem it *worse than folly* to
enter much upon the unreal.[17]

This view was shared by Catharine Parr Traill herself, who had
suffered from extreme boredom during her voyage to Canada in a ship
whose library was 'unfortunately ... chiefly made up with old novels and
musty romances.'[18] Evidence of her preference for pragmatic literature
appears in her practice of treating juvenile fiction as a vehicle for
communicating practical and moral information, her tendency to document the factual sources of her stories,[19] and her warning that children
allowed a steady diet of fiction suffer because 'superstition, credulity and
a love of falsehood are by degrees established in the infant mind.'[20] Traill
found a supporter in Henry Youle Hind, prominent scientist and editor
of the Canadian Institute's *Canadian Journal*, who declared that 'the habit
of reading for amusement alone' destroys the moral and intellectual
capacities of the child's mind.[21]

Distrust of the imagination and the consequent subordination of the
reading and writing of fiction to other literary activities persisted into the
last decades of the nineteenth century. That the novel was valuable only
insofar as it participated in more elevated disciplines such as politics and
philosophy was implied by Goldwin Smith's 1880 remark that in his
journal, *The Bystander*, books would be judged 'not as literary works but as
events and landmarks in the history of opinion.'[22] In 1878 a critic of
George Eliot hailed the advent of the psychological novel because it finally
raised fiction to the level of 'science, philosophy and theology.'[23] In this
climate it is scarcely surprising that John George Bourinot, author of a
series of important assessments of Canada's cultural standing, considered
the novel markedly inferior to the more factual discipline of history.

In *Our Intellectual Strength and Weakness* (1893) Bourinot appears at first
to encourage prose fiction when he opines, 'I do not for one deprecate the
influence of good fiction on the minds of a reading community like ours.'
Yet he proceeds to discuss the novel in qualifying and pejorative language
which instead reveals a distinct bias against imaginative prose. The genre
is described as 'a necessity of the times in which we live' especially suited to
'women distracted with household cares.' Bourinot hopes that Canadian
writers will not 'bring the Canadian fiction of the future to that low level to
which the school of realism in France, and in a minor degree in England
and the United States, would degrade the novel and story of every-day
life.' The irony of his perspective fully surfaces when he praises in
historical writing the features of narration and characterization which
drew their strength from the powerful influence of the novel:

To my mind it goes without saying that a history written with that fidelity to original authorities, that picturesqueness of narration, that philosophic insight into the motives and plans of statesmen, that study and comprehension of the character and life of a people, which should constitute the features of a great work of this class, – that such a history has assuredly a much deeper and more useful purpose in the culture and education of the world than any work of fiction can possibly have even when animated by lofty genius.[24]

Such doubts regarding the value of prose fiction despite its vast appeal to the reading public discomforted many literary periodicals. Journals whose emphasis was primarily informative or political, such as *The Canadian Monthly and National Review* (1872–8), easily justified the inclusion of some fiction as part of their nationalistic mandate or as lighter diversion from their more serious articles. But periodicals that published significant quantities of prose fiction, like *The Literary Garland* (1838–51), felt called upon to vindicate their presence, their contents, and where applicable, their profits. In the case of the *Garland* self-justification was accomplished in annual editorial declarations that the spread of polite literature assisted the refinement of morals and manners in a frontier society, and by publishing articles and book reviews in which the boundaries of acceptable prose fiction were carefully delineated. Disregarded were the ultimate implications of items like the 1850 piece on 'Novels and Novel Readers' whose conclusion that 'There is far more real poetry in science than in fiction'[25] questioned the very nature of the periodical in which it received publication.

In the same volume, the Reverend Henry Giles intoned:

Constant indulgence in fiction weakens both mind and motive, it incapacitates the one for thought, and the other for action. It surrounds the life of its victim with an atmosphere of unreality, and it puts within it a fountain of uneasy desire ... Useful and sober studies are not simply neglected, they are loathed ... We get so habituated to the landscapes of romances that in these only we luxuriate, and we turn from the actual to rejoice in a fanciful creation.[26]

To counteract the potentially debilitating effects of fiction the *Garland* editorially reminded novelists of

the obligation under which an Author rests to his readers, that in furnishing them with amusement for an idle hour, he should not only avoid presenting to them language, which it might be beneficial to forget, and ideas or characters which it would be pernicious to emulate; but that, on the contrary, he should endeavour to entwine the fictitious and real portions of his subject in such a manner, that many, who have only commenced its perusal for the purpose of acquiring some useful information, or banishing a tedious hour, may have a pleasing recollection of its most striking passages.[27]

The practice of reducing fiction to amusement for an idle hour permissible only after the completion of 'graver studies'[28] effectively recognized the potential subversiveness of the imaginative world. In nineteenth-century Canadian literary commentary it was usually taken for granted that while there was a distinct and obvious separation between the 'real' world of everyday experience and the 'unreal' world of literary adventure, the unreal possessed extraordinary influence over the real. To be judged acceptable, fiction at best had to promise to improve the real world and at worst promise to do no harm.[29] Intolerable were all novels whose effects could be pernicious for one of two reasons: because through their plots they engaged the reader in sympathy with characters or activities which would be reprehensible in real life, or because their style could arouse sentiments and ideas which would incapacitate the reader to function usefully in the real world. The problem of the connection between literature, imagination, and ordinary life extends back at least to Plato, and a conflict between literary representation and external reality has accompanied the novel ever since Don Quixote set out to enact the ideals and events of literary romance. But the subject that Cervantes approached with humour Canadians of the Victorian era usually regarded with solemn concern. Novel readers were pictured as simple-minded innocents, easily misguided and corrupted by the wrong sort of literature. Hence almost every discussion of the novel included admonitions against books designed 'to gratify some particular passion or fancy.'[30] Reading merely for pleasure encouraged egotism; as The Canadian Literary Magazine cautioned in an 1833 piece appropriately titled 'The Effects of Literary Cultivation on Morals,' 'In the bosom of him who neglects every other pursuit in his love of books, the streams of humanity, benevolence, and charity are dried up; the feelings of affection and sympathy in the joys and sorrows of his fellow mortals are banished from his heart; and, in short, every virtue included under piety to God, and love to man, is totally neglected and contemned.'[31]

During the Confederation era, as technological and marketing advances appeared to forecast that the usual flood of cheap American-produced fiction would swell to a tidal wave, a countervailing deluge of dire predictions issued from the Canadian press. In 1867, at the tender age of nineteen, George Stewart, jr, rising scion of the Presbyterian middle class, founded his own periodical to save the youth of New Brunswick from the corruptive effects of popular fiction:

The reading of 'Dime Novels,' and other books of that ilk, has wrought incalculable injury to many a bright and promising lad. Tales of buccaneers, murderers, and highwaymen; of 'fast young men,' and 'gay and festive gamblers,' deaden the moral sensibilities – familiarise the mind with crime and lead it on to moral ruin. It is true that there are no highwaymen now with mask and pistol, demanding 'your money or your life!' nor blood-thirsty pirates, compelling unfortunate victims to 'walk the plank!' – but if your youth cannot find work of this kind to do there is something else for them: they can learn to drink and smoke and swear and swagger in the truest dime novel style, and become the heroes and haunters of bar and billiard rooms. That numbers have been ruined in the way indicated is beyond question, but how many, eternity only will reveal! It behoves everyone to use his influence to free his country from the vice breeding literature with which it is now flooded.[32]

Revealing for its implied vision of Canadian society is the response to the prevalence of pulp literature that appeared in the Montreal *Family Herald*'s editorial answer to the query 'if it would be proper to lend a young lady "Tom Jones".' The reply was that 'the mind of every well educated young lady presents a stronger barrier to the seductive influences of such a work as "Tom Jones" than does the mind of any young man whatever.' Although the editor had little praise for Fielding's morality, he preferred it to the 'vulgar immorality circulated weekly in the American Pictorial Press, and hugged to the bosoms of thousands of the families of Canada' and concluded, 'We would have far more hope of the integrity of our youth, and the virtue of our young women by their reading Fielding from Joseph Andrews to Amelia, and Smollett from Roderick Random to Humphrey Clinker, than by one twelvemonth's perusal of these American Pictorial seductive sheets which are scattered broad cast over Canada.'[33] Implicit in the foregoing is a constellation of notions about sex, class, literature, and nationality which not only upholds (and subliminally links) myths of female and Canadian moral superiority, but in its acceptance of rather risqué eighteenth-century novels also reveals 'the vestigial class motivation' underlying much bourgeois anxiety about popular literature.[34]

In Canada, anxiety was aroused as well by serious current British novels reflecting their own society's mood of self-criticism, as when artist Daniel

Fowler found his values roundly challenged by Wilkie Collins' *The New Magdalen*. Writing in *The Canadian Monthly* he gave Collins 'full credit' for enlisting 'all the sympathies of the reader and spectator for an unfortunate woman,' but found in the narrative the dubious moral that 'it must be better to be sinful and unfortunate than unfortunate and sinless; it must be better to sin and confess than not to sin at all; and she who passes her life in alternately sinning and confessing, must accumulate, if she live long, a vast amount of virtue.'[35] Interestingly, not only does Fowler refrain from commenting on Collins' use of Canada as the country where one of the characters is educated to be an unforgiving snob, but his affinity with the views of this person suggests that Collins intuited the Canadian national viewpoint with surprising accuracy. Reading novels as prescriptions for social behaviour proved a constant habit in Canada; J.G. Bourinot's 1895 descent to this level when he advised that Du Maurier's *Trilby* was 'not a model for the maidens of Canada'[36] echoed the mid-century fear of *The Literary Garland* that fashionable sentimental novels would be mistaken for true pictures of life.[37]

The practice of including within novels characters whose vision has been distorted by their reading habits was a feature of the European reaction against the novel that was quickly absorbed into the self-reflexive conventions of the genre it criticized. Frequent in nineteenth-century Canadian fiction are individuals like Austen's Catherine Morland, Scott's Edward Waverley, and Flaubert's Emma Bovary, whose education has consisted of reading for gratification and whose judgment is consequently impaired. The comic side of this convention was developed by the Reverend R.G. MacGeorge in the character of Miss Laura Matilda Applegarth, a backwoods Canadian female Quixote and

a devoted member of the sisterhood of novel readers, and as such profoundly tinctured with the essential oil of romance. For every thing in the shape of the common place or prosaic she entertained a generous contempt, and would rather have tramped bare-footed through the world, with a knight errant of the orthodox olden school, than have submitted to the degradation of wedding an unpoetical agriculturalist, whose only crusades have been against the weeds which invaded his acres, or the foxes which depopulated his hen roosts![38]

Rosanna Leprohon expanded upon the tragic implications of such misguidance in two of her serialized novels, 'The Stepmother' (1847) and 'Ida Beresford; or, The Child of Fashion' (1848), as well as in her best-known work, *Antoinette De Mirecourt; or Secret Marrying and Secret*

Sorrowing (1864). When innocent Antoinette is placed under the tutelage of her cousin, Mrs D'Aulnay, whose moral sense has been corrupted by 'novels, love-tales of the most reprehensible folly,'[39] the younger woman becomes entangled in intrigues that nearly destroy her. Susanna Moodie found the convention appropriate to the didactic tone of 'Jane Redgrave' (1848) and *Matrimonial Speculations* (1854) and Agnes Maule Machar used it in two novels serialized in *The Canadian Monthly*, 'For King and Country' (1874) and 'Lost and Won' (1875).

In the eyes of most nineteenth-century Canadian critics the most reprehensible crime an author could commit was to depict vice and depravity. Novels which appeared to advocate immorality were universally condemned because they would 'inflame unsteady and romantic young men with a brigandish *furore*.'[40] *The Literary Garland*'s unidentified J.P. spoke for the Canadian cultural community at large when he lamented that 'in some of the pages of Sue, Dumas and Ainsworth, and in most of those of Reynolds, Soulie, and De Balsac ... crime is represented in a *couleur de rose*, the criminal is decked in a species of heroism, and the hideous features in his character are partially, if not wholly, hid, by the dramatic manner in which they are portrayed.'[41]

Such writing was usually denounced as 'sensational,' under which label was lumped all that Canadians found offensive in the way of criminality, deviant behaviour, revolution, irreligion, and sexual realism. In the 1820s and 1830s the word was often attached to gothic fiction, in Upper Canada when *The Canadian Literary Magazine* deplored the 'spectre-mongering' of Monk Lewis and in Nova Scotia when Senex complained in *The Acadian Magazine* of 'German Tales' of 'some supernatural mountain monster' and 'contracts with the devil.'[42] Later in the century the term was reserved for fiction regarded as socially and politically subversive, as when *The Anglo-American Magazine* denounced G.W.M. Reynolds, claiming that his 'unvarying task' was to 'minister to the coarsest and most depraved sensual appetites – to inflame the poor against their richer brethren – to demonstrate that aristocracy and guilt are synonymous terms – and to sneer at every thing in the shape of revealed religion.'[43]

Tirades against sensational fiction increased in volume and vituperation as the century progressed. In 1869 a contributor to *Stewart's* remarked that 'It is not a very easy matter, in this age of sensations, to horrify or even astonish the reading public; for, thanks to Miss Braddon, and her doubtfully successful imitators, our modern heroes are almost all murderers, adulterers, or devils incarnate, our heroines Cleopatras, Helens of Troy and Beatrices de Cenci, or possibly Hecates, Scyllas and

Astartes.'[44] According to *The Saturday Reader* the 'mission' of sensation
novels was to 'supply morbid food to depraved appetites.'[45] The literary
policy of *The Canadian Monthly and National Review* was to 'throw down the
gauntlet to the sensation school of novelists.'[46] *Belford's* feared that 'the
taste of the ordinary novel-reader has become ... vitiated with the
sensational plots of the day,'[47] and Sara Jeannette Duncan, the most
liberal Canadian critic of the 1880s, added her voice to the chorus by
deploring the 'cheap Coney Island realism' of the American sensational
press.[48]

It was easy enough to attack overtly sensational fiction; more problematic were realistic novels with a corrective purpose. The likelihood of
confusion between authorial intention and readers' responses troubled
The Literary Garland:

> There is something so poisonous in the very atmosphere of vice, especially that of
> a sensual character, that we can hardly breathe in it without contamination. The
> delineation of it in all its odious and disgusting particulars, although accompanied
> with a detail of the ruinous consequences to which it inevitably leads, has a natural
> tendency to produce an effect the very opposite to that which the generality of the
> novels writers of the old school, and not a few of the present day, seem to have
> anticipated.[49]

However, the *Garland* maintained sufficient flexibility to publish several
articles expressing the opposing view. Miss Foster's 1848 defence of *Jane
Eyre* argued against condemning a work as immoral for the improbity of
its 'hero' without examining the larger moral structure, and Susanna
Moodie championed 'our great modern novelists' who described social
evil to campaign for reform.[50]

In the 1880s Emile Zola provided a convenient focus for Canadian
discussions of the boundaries and abuses of fiction. His works bewildered
some of his detractors since, as Goldwin Smith admitted, 'They do not
seem to be exactly obscene or even immoral; at least there is nothing in
them calculated to inflame the passions.'[51] In *The Week* Zola attracted a
colourful array of pejorative adjectives: repulsive, slimy, foul and
prurient, debased, and degraded. That periodical's 1891 review of *Money*
termed it a 'dull and disgusting book' like 'a photograph of a cage full of
lecherous and greedy monkeys' and described Zola's realism as

> dulness with superadditions of the odour of onions, whiffs from the sewer, smells
> of decayed vegetables, marks of beer glasses on the tables, greasy table napkins,

inane conversation, stupid ribaldry. No undegraded person with a nose, ears and eyes voluntarily lives in such an environment, or voluntarily reads one of Zola's books. They are the worst garbage of modern literature, wholly inartistic, essentially false as descriptions of life, and to be avoided not because of their immorality (for who can call putridity immoral?) but because they are emetic in an excessively nauseating way.[52]

This reviewer's claim that he cannot find Zola 'immoral' is decisively undercut by the violence of his language, which indicates the extent to which Zola's picture of the real world posed a clear threat to all that Victorian Canada valued in life and literature and to its sense of the proper interaction between the two.

Graeme Mercer Adam, who was sympathetic with (and possibly the author of) the above condemnation of Zola, identified another source of literary corruption as the 'new woman.' The increasing prominence of women as authors, consumers, and subjects of fiction added a sexual dimension to the subversiveness of popular novels and particularly aroused the ire of several influential males. Back in 1867 Thomas D'Arcy McGee, 'though no enemy to a good novel,' raised 'a warning voice against the promiscuous and exclusive reading of sensational and sensual books, many of them written by women, who are the disgrace of their sex, and read with avidity by those who want the opportunity equally to disgrace it.'[53] Four decades later Adam opened an 1895 survey of 'Recent Fiction in Britain' by castigating 'the degeneracy of the novel in the hands of the new woman' and going so far as to predict that 'The outpourings of this class of fiction, if the defiling stream is to continue, would reconcile us to a censorship of the press, which should be despotic as well as stern.'[54]

The criticism of Duncan Campbell Scott and Sara Jeannette Duncan (the latter will receive fuller attention in Chapter 4) contains a more measured assessment of the permissible range of the late nineteenth-century novel. Duncan tended to restrict her attention to Howells and James, admiring their innovations in style and subject but cautioning that the depiction of mundane experience required the leavening of art:

A cabbage is a very essential vegetable to certain salads, but we do not prostrate ourselves adoringly before the cabbage bed in everyday life, and it is a little puzzling to know why we should be required to do so in art galleries and book stores, however perfect the representations there of cabbages, vegetable or human. If we do it is certainly the art we admire, not the nature. And so we take the liberty of thinking that literature should at its best be true not only to the objects upon and about which it constructs itself, but faithful also to all the delicate attractions and repulsions which enter so intimately into the highest art, and which, curious as it seems, are quite as distinctive of Mr Howells' work as what has been called, with an approach to accuracy, his 'photographic process.'[55]

D.C. Scott replied to Zola's vilifiers in one of the most broad-minded critical statements published in pre-modern Canada, arguing that

It is childish to restrict to that which is within the scope of polite conversation in society the powers of a genius bent on searching life. The great problem of existence is worked out far beyond the parlours, and the laws of life are wider than the decalogue by which society steers its empty ship ... he is at bottom a vicious man and a barbarian who would allow his daughter[s] to read the newspapers and to refuse them the great moral novels which deal with the severer aspects of life.[56]

Few of Scott's contemporaries shared his values. Nineteenth-century Canadian commentators seldom deemed fiction a valid or valuable form of entertainment unless they found the fictive world to be unequivocally upholding the ideals and principles by which they believed society to be motivated in the real world. 'Moral utility,' the 'supreme esthetic principle' of nineteenth century culture in the United States,[57] held equal sway in Canada. With a few notable exceptions the prevailing view was that the purpose of literature was to instruct: morally by presenting examples of proper conduct and pedagogically by providing useful information. Hence the emotional power wielded by the novel was expected to work solely for what the critic defined as good, and protection of the reading public from fiction lacking meliorative value devolved upon authority figures, including book reviewers. Most commentators would have agreed with the description of the responsibility of the literary reviewer that appeared in *The Literary Garland* in 1840: 'There will always ... be scope for the legitimate exercise of the lash, as long as ignorance and vanity shall find vent through the press; books of doubtful moral tendency, or those designed to pander to the vicious appetites of the many, will always offer a fair mark to the reviewer, whose pen is dipped in gall. In such cases severity is a virtue, and he that can scourge the guilty into a proper respect for honour and decency, is a public benefactor.'[58]

The moral responsibilities of the novelist were generally taken for granted, but there was less accord regarding his subject-matter. Early in the century, when simple entertainment was suspect, fiction was required to demonstrate its utility. As the two Montreal reviews of *St Ursula's*

Convent indicate, this was to be accomplished either by providing useful information or by supporting 'the highest sentiments of morality and virtue.'[59] Praiseworthy novels were expected to contain an extractable moral; for example, in 1832 *The Halifax Monthly Magazine* applauded James Fenimore Cooper's *The Bravo* as 'an admirably constructed illustration of the evils of bad government.'[60] The *Literary Garland* habitually construed novels as elaborated fables as when it described *The Scarlet Letter* as 'a thrilling portraiture of the inner man, shewing the resistless force of uncurbed passion, and the might and certainty of the retribution, which follows its indulgence. So strikingly is the great moral developed in the story, that all who read must involuntarily ask themselves if they are living a life of hypocrisy, or if the great and divine law of Truth is the guide and safeguard of their hearts.'[61]

Particularly well received were novels with an unimpeachable purpose such as temperance or the abolition of slavery. The instantaneous international success of *Uncle Tom's Cabin* inspired editors of several faltering Canadian periodicals to serialize Stowe's whole novel to boost their circulation[62] and others to treat their readers to extracted scenes.[63] A sense of moral superiority seems to underpin Canada's eager embrace of anti-slavery fiction; less welcome were novels examining complex social problems whose ramifications touched more directly upon Canadian life.

At mid-century Susanna Moodie took the most radical position to be found in Canadian criticism at that time when she praised 'our great modern novelists,' Dickens and Sue, for venturing into the realm of 'the murderer, the thief, the prostitute,' to depict 'heart-rending pictures of human suffering and degradation.' The value of the work of 'these humane men [who] bid you step with them into the dirty hovels of the outcasts of society, and see what crime really is, and all the miseries which ignorance and poverty, and a want of self-respect never fail to bring about' lay in the social reforms they advocated:

If these reprobated works of fiction can startle the rich into a painful consciousness of the wants and agonies of the poor, and make them, in despite of all the conventional laws of society, acknowledge their kindred humanity, who shall say that these books have been written in vain? For my own part I look upon these men as heaven inspired teachers, who have been commissioned by the great Father of souls, to proclaim to the world the wrongs and sufferings of millions of his creatures, to plead their cause with unflinching integrity, and with almost superhuman eloquence demand for them the justice which society has so long denied. These men are the benefactors of their species, to whom the whole human race owe a vast debt of gratitude.[64]

While Moodie shared Dickens' middle-class reluctance to envision social reform being implemented through action more traumatic than a change of heart on the part of the rich, few mid-Victorian Canadian commentators went as far as she and none went further in allowing the novel to wander into the nether regions of human experience. Because the great European novelists of the latter half of the nineteenth century were engaged in expanding the literary and social frontiers of fiction, Canadian critics frequently found themselves in a problematic position. Their original tendency to distrust literature that was purely entertaining and to require a concrete moral connection between the fictive and the real was increasingly disconcerted by their apprehension that this requisite didacticism was being directed towards radical ends. Hence they were left with several unsatisfactory options. They could continue to insist that literature be instructive and simply rail against those novelists who educated readers about features of contemporary life they would prefer not to acknowledge. They could concede the literary greatness of the best writers while bewailing their immorality. Or they could cease to expect that fictional literature relate directly to everyday life and instead call for a return to the good old days of Sir Walter Scott.

Examples of the first two positions abound in *The Literary Garland*. The *Garland*'s predilection for literature 'alike elegant in style and diction' with a 'high tone of religious and moral feeling' initially spelled trouble for Charles Dickens. A commentator on *Oliver Twist* felt uneasy about the kinds of characters who receive the author's attention, yet as a reader couldn't help responding to Dickens' narrative power: 'It is true that a good deal of the character [the book] delineates, is not such as to impart much benefit, except by teaching to shun those whose portraits are exhibited; but for interest, mirth, or pathos, no pen surpasses that of Boz, and no production of that pen surpasses "Oliver Twist".'[65] In *The Chimes* not even the author's literary gifts could redeem him from the charge of fomenting class discord, but with *Dombey and Son* Dickens was judged to have redeemed himself.[66] Disraeli, a writer of 'high genius,' was likewise chided for breaching the acceptable limits of fiction by expressing his Chartist sympathies in *Sybil*. So threatening were his politics that the *Garland* warned, 'it is our firm conviction that were the tone assumed by the author to be generally adopted, we should ere long witness the decline of Great Britain from the eminent position she now holds among the nations of the earth.'[67]

Attempting to assess fiction directed towards a European public, many Canadian commentators found themselves caught between their predetermined standards of what a novel should be and their actual aesthetic response to great literature that transgressed those standards. The quandary created by a critic's simultaneous approval of a writer's artistry and disapproval of her morality could produce direct self-contradiction, as in an 1849 article on George Sand. After acknowledging that 'as a mere writer she decidedly stands alone, unparalleled, and far above every other of the present day' the anonymous commentator added: 'No writer, however, since the days of Rousseau and his "Heloise," has done so much harm as George Sand, or has tended more to demoralize society at large ... Totally without either principle or religion, her whole object seems to be to cast a stigma upon every feeling we are taught to value – upon every institution we hold sacred.'[68]

At times the conflicts within a critic's response manifest themselves more subtly and, as in the passage from Bourinot discussed earlier, are to be discerned from his language rather than from his overt opinion. Subtext nearly subverts text in an 1878 discussion of *Manon Lescaut* which says of the heroine that 'The author paints in the warmest colours her matchless beauty and grace and charming gaiety, so that while we read we almost forget to condemn the infatuation which she inspires.'[69] With the little word 'almost' this critic interrupts his own engagement with the fiction as he attempts to assert social propriety over the pleasure of the text. Later articles occasionally present a critic in the process of working out divergent responses and attempting to reconcile a novel's obvious achievement with its less acceptable elements. *The Week* found artistry to justify content in *The Mayor of Casterbridge*, which earned Hardy praise for having given 'the inalienable charm of truth' to material 'of the coarsest fibre,'[70] and also in *Anna Karenina*. Reading the latter as an account of 'the inevitable consequences of a transgression of virtue,' the reviewer was able to conclude that 'This is a masterpiece of fiction, and though dealing with a delicate subject, a profoundly moral book.'[71]

But some topics, however masterful their presentation, were simply untenable. To late nineteenth-century Canada's most important cultural journal Tolstoy's 'Kreutzer Sonata' was so 'brutally frank' that 'we fail to find anything in the book to justify its existence'[72] and George Moore's *Celibates* was 'intensely disagreeable': 'It consists of three stories, the second of which [containing an unacknowledged attempted rape and subsequent suicide] should never have been written. All three deal with unpleasant subjects and persons, and though we fully recognize their ability and also we regret to say their truthfulness as possible sketches of real life, we confess to have obtained little from their perusal.'[73]

The tension generated by the conflicting requirements that fiction justify itself by propounding a socially relevant message but that this message not subvert the prevailing conservative social vision received different resolutions in different periodicals. When Canadian commentators of the second half of the nineteenth century requested that novels avoid unpleasant social problems they were not always sidestepping tricky issues. *Belford's* argued fairly consistently that 'a writer of fiction must establish the artistic claim before his preaching can be tolerated';[74] the principle that a novel's moral structure should be implicit within its narrative structure was upheld as well by the Reverend J.A. Bray, reviewer of many popular novels in *The Canadian Spectator*.[75] The more important *Canadian Monthly* likewise observed, 'We may doubt the aesthetic propriety of fiction being laden with social moralities.'[76]

The latter periodical established a sort of double standard in its reception of fiction. It was happy to accept entertaining novels by Wilkie Collins (five of whose works were serialized in *The Canadian Monthly* and its successor) and other popular writers, so long as they eschewed the 'coarseness' of Fielding and Smollett and conformed to the code of Podsnappian respectability by not presenting 'an atmosphere redolent of conjugal infidelity and secret poisoning.'[77] But it also insisted that true literary merit was only to be found in fiction that reached the standard of George Eliot. Hence a clear distinction between the acceptable popular novel and the admirable literary novel underlies much of the *Monthly's* commentary, such as its review of George Meredith's *Beauchamp's Career*.[78]

The third option for those troubled by unpleasantly realistic literature was to avoid it entirely by calling for fiction that was simply entertaining. This position appeared as early as 1854 in the 'Editor's Shanty' column of *The Anglo-American Magazine*[79] and increased in attractiveness as the century progressed, especially to those who found Zola abhorrent. In *The Week*, after the departure of Sara Jeannette Duncan in 1888, the literary columns were dominated by writers convinced that 'the primary object of the novel is to amuse.'[80] In their campaign for fiction that was healthy, wholesome, and 'eminently respectable'[81] these commentators implicitly constructed a history of the English novel that looked back to the time of Sir Walter Scott as a lost Golden Age of romantic fiction. Among the most vocal was Graeme Mercer Adam, who mourned that 'The good old romantic and imaginative novel of our grandmothers' time seems a creation wholly of the past.'[82] In 1894 *The Week* welcomed a reprint of *The Cloister and the Hearth* with distinct relief: 'How truly refreshing is this good, old-fashioned romance in contrast with present day realism and psychological analysis: a happy substitute indeed.'[83] Most applauded were heroes and novels 'of the old school,' the latter headed by Walter Scott and including all who specialized in the creation of 'fresh wholesome romance, free from soul-harrowing incidents.'[84]

The Week's retreat from serious social fiction at the end of the nineteenth century illustrates how thoroughly prevailing cultural opinion in Canada had performed a neat reversal, from distrusting imaginative writing and demanding that fiction justify itself by relating didactically to the real world, to distrusting the subversiveness of realistic literature and demanding that fiction revert to simple entertainment. Whatever its form, throughout the century prose fiction was held to be of less literary value than poetry or history, but novels might be acceptable if they combined instruction with entertainment, presented a moral and wholesome vision of society, and reinforced conventional norms of sexual and religious behaviour. Not surprisingly, Canadian novelists were expected to conform to this standard. For Canadian writers, however, the conservative taste of their community accounted for only part of the problem of establishing the Canadian novel. One of the basic challenges to nineteenth-century Canadian writers was the land itself, and the concomitant difficulty of transferring to barely civilized territory the highly sophisticated literary traditions surrounding the European novel. The next chapter reconstructs the process by which the valorization of Canada as a location for fiction intersected with the establishment of the Canadian novel as a legitimate literary venture.

3 Problems of Place

When Robert Kroetsch remarked, 'In a sense, we haven't got an identity until somebody tells our story. The fiction makes us real,'[1] upon which E.D. Blodgett later elaborated 'for us the place, the space of the Canadian literatures, is only real because it has been turned to fiction,'[2] they gave post-modernist expression to a problem that has preoccupied Canadian writers since pre-modern times. The need for a literature which speaks to Canadians about Canadian experience in a Canadian environment was as current a topic in the 1860s as the 1960s, from the time of Thomas D'Arcy McGee's observation that 'The books that are made elsewhere, even in England, are not always the best fitted for us.'[3] Post-Confederation cultural nationalists were acutely aware of the power of creative literature to valorize a place and shape the vision of its perceivers. More than one Canadian reader of William Dean Howells' *Their Wedding Journey* and *A Chance Acquaintance*, for example, intuited the books' effects on their own sensibilities. Claimed George Stewart, 'Quebec, before we read Howells, never appeared so intoxicatingly beautiful and interesting as it did after we read his story of a few days' stay in it.'[4]

The motives underpinning the position that English Canada required an indigenous literature could be political or moral or both; taken for granted was the notion that one of the primary purposes of a national literature was the fostering of patriotism.[5] Hence basic to Canadian cultural nationalism then as now was resistance to the influence of the United States. In the sphere of fiction, nationalism was often allied with abhorrence of American-produced 'yellow-covered literature.' The Montreal *Family Herald*'s promotion of local writing which 'aims at the cultivation of taste, the diffusion of information, and the encouragement of innocent amusement' was motivated by a repudiation of 'sensation romances' and by the realization that among current popular publications 'Not one is of domestic production; not one is "racy of the soil" on which we live, or in any particular adapted to the development of qualities which, as Canadians, we desire to cultivate.'[6]

What resulted was a dilemma specific to nineteenth-century English Canada. On the one hand, nationalists of all stripes yearned for a distinctive Canadian literature both to forge a unique social and political identity and to validate Canada as a political, psychological, and geographical place. On the other, Canadian authors were confronted with the problem of creating the highly refined, lengthy Victorian prose narrative, whether realistic novel or imaginative romance, out of unpromising local raw materials.

The first literary artifacts arising from the European encounter with the New World were the accounts of the explorers, in verbal parallel to the maps that were the first visual records. These were soon followed by the documentation of travel and settlement: visitors' narratives, pioneers' letters home, and settlers' guides – word sketches often accompanied by pictorial sketches and similar in intention to the topographical drawings produced by British officers and their wives. But to proceed from the documentation of actual personal events to the distillation of a broader cultural experience into shaped story required an artistic quantum leap that was often complicated by the nature of the genre within which authors chose to work.

Before Canadian writers could begin to develop a national prose literature they had to convince themselves and their readers that Canada provided suitable settings for the requisite characters and events of popular fiction. During the period preceding the First World War several different stages of the process may be discerned. After Confederation, in the 1870s and 1880s, national confidence inspired many writers and commentators simply to assert that their country contained exciting subjects and colourful backgrounds for fiction. During the pre-Confederation period, however, the contents of periodicals and novels present a genuine struggle to discover material in an immature country suitable for the mature forms of short and extensive fictional narrative. In the last decade of the century this problem acquired a new dimension as more and more Canadian writers broke into the international market for popular fiction. Most turn-of-the-century Canadian-born novelists who became literary expatriates either forsook their Canadian origins to write novels indistinguishable from the mass of popular British and American fiction, or constructed an image of Canada that catered to the international taste for exotic colour.

During a century when a European-educated eye judged that 'The physiography of North America, though it has its regional diversities, is characteristically as simple as the European continent is varied,'[7] it is hardly surprising that the difficulty of developing a local literature in a land which lacked most of the qualities presumed necessary for literary activity preoccupied and baffled many early Canadian authors. The questions of articulation and silence raised by Dennis Lee in the 1970s reach back to the first writers desiring to create literature in an alien, colonized space. As those who originally outlined the problem did so with eloquence and in publications not currently accessible, it is worth our while to let them speak for themselves.

Immigrants attempting to write about a region without 'infinite associations of time, place and circumstance' learned that their difficulties began at the most fundamental level of nomenclature. In 1831 Andrew Shiels described his distress at discovering that the prosaic terminology of Nova Scotians undermined the romantic alignment between geographical features and descriptive language to which he had been accustomed in Scotland:

[I]nstead of the 'mountain high' and 'hills of green,' – the beautiful vale, breathing with imagery, including mouldering abbey, delapidated tower, ruin'd camp of Dane and Roman, fields of battle where the warriors fought and fell, princely palaces, classic rivers and sylvan brooks (each bearing its own specific designation and its legend besides) of my 'pleasant Teviot-dale' let the traveller in Nova-Scotia ask what is the name of yonder dwelling? the answer is almost universally Mr. Such or such-a-ones' farm, and that contains all the variations of its History; or enquire the name of the dull half forgotten, or perhaps unknown stream, in any quarter of the province, and ten to one but it is either *Nine mile* or *Salmon river*.[8]

The entire problem received considerable expansion in an important article titled 'The Literature of a New Country' published in *The Monthly Review* (Toronto) in 1841. Its anonymous author summarized the disorientation of prospective poets and novelists who found themselves in a place that challenged all their received assumptions regarding the foundations of literature:

The very nature and character of the land itself, its past history, its former inhabitants, all conspire against its literary success. Almost every one of the European or Eastern nations, that has furnished a proportion to the general array of authors, has contained within itself the ordinary materials for the formation of a national literature. Tradition, legend, tale, and song, have sent down from the floating shadows of the past, rich and exhaustless stores of mingled fact and fiction, from which the successive writers of ages could draw, as from a vast historic reservoir ... The inhabitant of this Continent has little, if any, early recollections to be entwined with the local characteristics of the land he inhabits; he has to cast his eyes beyond an ocean, should he ask for legends or memories of the past to awaken the inspiration of the present.

Moreover, the issue of language raised a fundamental irony of literary colonialism: when the new country tried to create its own culture its magnificent literary heritage reversed from an asset to a liability, depriving English-speaking North Americans of the opportunity to develop their own literature in their own language:

The language in which [the British American] speaks and thinks, is but a borrowed medium, a language in which have excelled the greatest masters that have ever ennobled an earthly tongue, and who must, in the rich excess of their brightness, outdazzle and outshine the highest efforts of a nation of imitators. Hence the [British] American writer cannot but feel, that how far soever he may outstrip all rivals that strive with him on his own shore, a hopeless contest still awaits him with the almost invincible giant of English literature, who requires from his transatlantic children unreserved homage and fealty, in return for his extending to them the rich boon of his glorious language ... In small communities, distinct in habit and peculiar in language, an author of moderate ability may rise to distinction, and be known to the world as the first poet, novelist, or historian *of his country*, though in the general assembly of literary talent, his place might be far from foremost. An American, however, cannot share this advantage. From the snows of Labrador to the Andes, he may have no equal; but till he performs the Herculean task of mounting higher than the starry names in the literary galaxy of England, the world at large will only accord him his fitting rank among the authors who spoke or sang in the language of Shakespeare and Milton.

This, then, was the formidable task facing early Canadian authors: to enter the tradition 'of Shakespeare and Milton' while stranded in a place bereft of even a basic 'store of materials from which to mould a pleasant tale or sparkling romance.'9

Charles Heavysege's only venture into fiction can be read as a rather ingenious attempt to resolve this problem. A recent immigrant awed by the great tradition of English literature, Heavysege overcompensated for his dislocation in Canada by modelling his novel on the greatest writer of all. He composed *The Advocate* (1865) in pseudo-Shakespearean rhetoric and, as in a play, located most of the action in the dialogue. The book is crammed with Shakespearean epigraphs and allusions: the evil Montreal advocate resembles Iago and Richard III, his son is a Canadian Caliban, his illegitimate daughter participates in a Romeo and Juliet style balcony scene, and she and her lover re-enact the marriage in Friar Lawrence's cell when they plan to be married secretly in the church of St Laurent. The derivative style that earned Heavysege some recognition as a poet proved less appropriate to the domain of fiction, which requires a credible alliance of language and setting not sustained by recounting contemporary Canadian events in pseudo-heroic bombast.[10] Heavysege's engagement with the problems outlined in *The Monthly Review* elucidates the dilemma facing the writer living in a place where 'Oberon and Titania held no sway.'[11]

As the century progressed, the discomfort of inhabiting a country without a mythology diminished but did not disappear. Just before Confederation a contributor to *The British American Magazine* anticipated by eight decades Earle Birney's line 'It's only by our lack of ghosts we're haunted' in his regret that

Canada has no historical past distant enough to lift its events into the clear region of the imagination, where all that is trite and common-place in the actual falls away, and the grand, heroic, poetical lineaments alone remain; – no worshipped heroes whose memory may bind the hearts of the people together, or give the poet's lyre a truly national tone; – no sacred fables, myths or traditions like those which, in the morning of the world, steeped some favoured spots of earth in an atmosphere of romance and poetry that will cling to them forever.[12]

Counter to the stream of thought that Canada was inadequate as a cradle for literature ran the opinion that what the country lacked was not suitable material but writers interested in identifying and developing its literary resources. Drawing their critical stance from popular English Romanticism rather than popular classicism, they shared Susanna Moodie's dismay at the obtuseness of native Canadians towards their country's artistic possibilities: 'Has Canada no poet to describe the glories of his parent land – no painter that can delineate her matchless scenery of land and wave? Are her children dumb and blind, that they leave to strangers the task of singing her praise?'[13]

Thus Andrew Learmont Spedon, a Lower Canadian farmer, teacher and writer, claimed that interesting material would be found by those who took the trouble to search. 'Though [Canada] cannot boast of a thousand dilapidated towers, around which the hero-spirits of a hundred ages still linger,' he argued, 'yet, there are spots, sacred to the world's history, that stand as the deathless memorials of departed glory and illustrious valour.'[14] Several pieces in his *Tales of the Canadian Forest* (1861) document just such local incidents of 'departed glory and illustrious valour' yet Spedon felt unsupported in his efforts to enhance Canada's literary identity. In his introduction to his subsequent collection he voiced his frustration at Canadians' literary indifference to their land:

Unlike many of the older countries, Canada has but few literary pioneers and sons of song. Yet what a noble field there is for the native sons of genius to gather therefrom the forest laurels of a past age, to adorn the literature of their country, and to give it that mystical enchantment which antiquity alone is capable of giving. Oh! for a shade of Scott, Cooper or Irving to call up the Indian from his tomb, – the hero from the battle-field, – the mariner from the deep; to breathe upon their dry bones, – to embody them in nobler forms, and to give to them a life and an immortality unknown before! O, ye Canadians! why will ye slumber in literary indolence and allow your noble rivers to roll on, year after year, '*unlettered and unsung*'?[15]

This same theme in a less melodramatic key was sounded by the next generation as well, usually coloured by the optimism typical of seers into Canada's literary future for the entire century following Confederation.[16] A sense of urgency was added when George Stewart warned that if Canadian writers did not act quickly to take possession of their literary potential their 'rich preserves' would be broached by enterprising American 'poachers.'[17] Likewise troubled by the invasion of 'foreign pens,' Graeme Mercer Adam enumerated all the Americans by whose efforts 'many of the localities in Quebec and the Maritime Provinces, with their rich histories and fascinating legends, are fast passing into literature'; his list included Parkman, Longfellow, Howells, Charles Dudley Warner, Charles Hallock, Thoreau, Stedman, and Whittier.[18]

However, not all Canadian writers sensitive to romantic literary associations lamented their absence. To Catharine Parr Traill, who approached the New World from a perspective akin to eighteenth-century rationalism, Canada's lack of folklore was a distinct advantage. Her published view that 'As to ghosts or spirits they appear totally banished from Canada. This is too matter-of-fact [a] country for such supernaturals to visit,'[19] was elaborated in her unpublished journals in several passages emphatically approving of a land free from mythology. In response to strange noises during an August night she observed:

Formerly imagination would have fancied these nocturnal sounds into the voices of yelling demons and all manner of evil spirits exulting sporting amid the war of the elements - Happily in this new country fancy has little food to exist upon – the toil of every day labour is before us – the hard but simple process of subduing the giants of the forest to provide the necessities of life leaves little leisure for indulging in superstitious vanities ... The Canadian settlers' children will probably never listen to any of the wild tales of ghosts and witches and robbers and fairies and seer – that formed at once the blight and terror of their parents' childhood.[20]

Her sister likewise approved of the 'utter disbelief in supernatural appearances which is common to most native-born Canadians,' but for different reasons. For Susanna Moodie the presence of ghosts indicated consciousness of sin. She read Canada's dearth of supernatural associations as a sign of the greater innocence of a land undefiled by civilization:

The unpeopled wastes of Canada must present the same aspect to the new settler that the world did to our first parents after their expulsion from the Garden of Eden; all the sin which could defile the spot, or haunt it with the association of departed evil, is concentrated in their own persons. Bad spirits cannot be supposed to linger near a place where crime has never been committed. The belief in ghosts, so prevalent in old countries, must first have had its foundation in the consciousness of guilt.[21]

In the virgin territory of the New World, freedom from ghosts may have signalled freedom from traditional sin and guilt, but it also represented detachment from the literary associations and cultural resonances conducive to imaginative literature. That the novel suffered more than any other literary form from the absence of a solid foundation of acknowledged social and historical experience is demonstrated by Moodie's own writing. Like her pre-Confederation contemporaries in other parts of the country that was to become Canada,[22] Moodie achieved her greatest literary success in the essay, the sketch, and the journal. In *Roughing It in the Bush* (1852) and *Life in the Clearings versus the Bush* (1853) she resorted primarily to non-fiction (with frequent recourse to fictional convention) to transform raw experience into enduring literary artifacts which related directly to her Canadian life. Her serialized fiction, however, published in *The Literary Garland* in the 1840s, was composed with one eye on potential markets in England and the United States. Astute at recycling her writings, Moodie took no risks by attempting to transplant to Canadian soil the complex plots and stereotyped characters required by the sentimental novel. The closest she ever came to producing a novel about Canada was *Flora Lyndsay*[23] (1854), based on the Moodies' own departure from England and terminating with the arrival of the Lyndsays in the New World. Even here Moodie found that the form of the popular novel demanded more complicated material than could be furnished by the commonplace experience of emigration. She added character and plot first by interpolating a series of sketches into Flora's preparations and embarkation, then by inserting wholesale a 100-page story that Flora writes to pass the time while their ship is becalmed off Newfoundland. This novelette, 'Noah Cotton,'[24] includes enough murder, illegitimacy, theft, and romance to compensate for Flora's more mundane activities, thus bridging the gap between the conventions of popular fiction and the material offered by the New World.[25]

One could argue that solutions to Moodie's problem had already been presented by Thomas Chandler Haliburton and Major John Richardson, who demonstrated in the 1830s and 1840s that it was not impossible to write full-length works of fiction using Canadian materials. Not only did their books fail to stimulate local literary activity, but the writers themselves left the country – Haliburton to fame and power in Britain, Richardson to poverty and obscurity in New York.[26]

That early and mid-century writers experienced considerable difficulty in adapting their literary assumptions to Canadian settings is demonstrated by two recurring narrative patterns. The first, in which the story begins and ends in Canada with the bulk of the action occurring elsewhere, was particulary favoured by writers of the 1840s. A number of *Garland* tales are narrated retrospectively, centring on a character for whom Canada serves merely as a point of termination. These individuals either die here leaving behind manuscripts describing their pre-Canadian adventures, or else verbally relate their exploits in the Old World which resulted in their residence in the New.[27]

More enduring was the inverse of the above, in which Canada serves as a place of trial and adventure but deserving characters are ultimately permitted to return to their estates in Europe. Frances Brooke's *The History of Emily Montague* (1769), English Canada's only eighteenth-century novel, may be regarded as a prototype; the pattern quickly reappeared in the first two novels published in the Canadas, Julia Catherine Beckwith Hart's *St Ursula's Convent* (1824)[28] and James Russell's

Matilda; or, The Indian's Captive (1833).[29] For the next sixty years it consistently structured stories and novels scattered across the country and its periodicals,[30] diminishing somewhat in the 1880s when the growing interest in local colour more frequently allowed fictional Canadians to live happily ever after in the New World's green fields and forests (but seldom its cities). Yet at the end of the century it still refused to vanish; for example, Agnes Maule Machar's *The Heir of Fairmount Grange* (1895) and R.L. Richardson's *Colin of the Ninth Concession* (1903) both conclude when heroic orphans displaced in the New World are eventually restored to their rightful positions in the Old.

A particularly late instance of this pattern's persistence into the twentieth century can be found in Marshall Saunders' last novel. Her most successful book, *Beautiful Joe* (1895), illustrates the general problem of national setting in that Saunders had to transform Canada's most famous canine hero into an American dog in order to qualify for the book prize that made them both famous. However, it is *Esther de Warren* (1927), her last and most autobiographical novel, which is in some ways her most dislocated work. The young Nova Scotian heroine, sent abroad (like Saunders herself) to finish her education, looks back lovingly to her Canadian home. But nothing happens there; the excitement of the plot extends from Scotland to Boston and involves secret identities, surprising benefactors, Zionism, separated twins, and picturesque manors where elegant nobles can offer gracious entertainments. Esther's discovery that her beloved Nova Scotian parents are just a foster family and that she herself was born in Boston and is heir to an estate in Scotland serves as a paradigm for the fate of the popular novel in a land which so frequently failed to provide it with an authentic home.[31]

It was primarily in the literary periodicals of the nineteenth century that the struggle to establish Canada's validity as a location for fiction took place. In pre-Confederation journals, interest in Canada ranged from *The Literary Garland*'s deliberate efforts to foster in Canada the kind of genteel literary culture its contributors and readers had enjoyed in England and Boston to *The British Colonial Magazine*'s complete indifference to its Canadian origin. Edited by William H. Smith of Toronto in 1852 and 1853, the latter consisted almost exclusively of items reprinted from popular British periodicals like *Chambers's*, *Gentleman's*, and *Fraser's* magazines, and acknowledged its nationality only in rare notices of utilitarian Canadian publications, almanacs in particular. As Smith was also author of *Smith's Canadian Gazetteer* (1846) and *Canada: Past, Present and Future* ... (1851), it is likely that the nature of his magazine was dictated less by disinterest in things Canadian than by economic expediency.

The Literary Garland, on the other hand, sustained one of the longest lifespans among pre-Confederation periodicals on the strength of Canadian interest in Canadian writing. In tone 'Anglo-Bostonian rather than Anglo-Canadian' in Carl Klinck's apt phrase,[32] it attempted to establish for Canadian letters a norm of pious middle-class gentility. While the majority of its contributions came from Canadian residents and were directed towards Canadian readers, its fiction was primarily non-Canadian in content. Especially popular were Oriental tales, Old World pastoral idylls, European medieval romances, Irish and Scottish dialect anecdotes, and English silver fork stories. When they turned to Canada, *Garland* writers sought Canadian equivalents for the conventions they favoured, although not all aspects of Old World society proved equally transplantable. Susanna Moodie and Catharine Parr Traill learned in real life that Irish peasants had relocated in the Canadian backwoods, thus making their peculiarities available to the New World littérateur, but many pieces of nineteenth-century Canadian fiction are to be admired more for the ingenuity of their authors' importation of literary conventions than for their faithfulness to the Canadian scene.

Some tales seem unconscious of their artifice, such as those whose Indians who resemble Marie Antoinette's courtly shepherds and shepherdesses, one of whose heroine's daily activity is to 'work the moccasins and ornaments of bark, and cultivate my little garden.'[33] More self-conscious is an 1840 story that represents a deliberate search for a Canadian equivalent to the watering-place romance and opens with its author's justification of her decision to write about the Caledonia Springs in eastern Upper Canada:

The watering places of Europe, and even in the States, have long enjoyed an enviable supremacy in romantic adventure. These places of gregarious resort have been from time immemorial celebrated in story, as the scene of many a love-lorn tale and ditty ...

There are as bright eyes and as susceptible hearts in Canada as in any portion of the globe, and it is self-evident to all logicians, that the same causes will produce the same effects all the world over; Caledonia has therefore had its share of adventures, and it only waits a faithful narrator to give the interesting details to the public.[34]

Not just in love stories but also in tales with descriptive titles like 'The Ruins: A Canadian Legend,' 'Canadian Legends. 1. The Ruined Cottage,' 'A Legend of the Lake,' and 'The Old Manuscript: A Mémoire of the Past,'[35] *Garland* writers devised local counterparts to the romantic narrative of the remote European past, thereby colouring the Canadian landscape with tinges of legendary tradition.

Not surprisingly, Canada was recognized as a valid location for short stories, tales, and sketches before it became a suitable setting for longer fiction. The work of Rosanna Leprohon, one of the *Garland*'s major contributors, nicely illustrates the process. Before she could write about the present and past social life of her own country in 'The Manor House of De Villerai' (1859), *Antoinette De Mirecourt* (1864), *Armand Durand* (1868), and 'Clive Weston's Wedding Anniversary' (1872), Leprohon served an apprenticeship as an author of high-life stories set in England – a country she appears never to have visited. Her five novels serialized in the *Garland* between 1847 and 1851 owe their existence entirely to the popularity of fashionable silver fork fiction in England during the 1830s and 1840s, and nothing at all to the direct experience of their Canadian author.

Few fiction writers of Leprohon's era were able similarly to effect a transition from fantasizing about England to writing about Canada. Perhaps the most cogent illustration of the difficulty of filling the form of the novel with Canadian content appears in the periodicals founded on the wave of national enthusiasm which accompanied the Confederation era. Some editors specifically sought stories set in Canada, despite the expense. In 1864 Louisa Murray received a letter from Thomas McLean of *The British American Magazine* asking:

Could you not furnish us with a Canadian Tale? It has frequently been asked of us why not republish from one of the English periodicals, a Tale. If you have to lay the scene of your best Tales in a Foreign Land, where is the difference? I must confess that there is a good deal of force in the statement, and in addition there would be nothing to pay for Copy right.

If [Cooper] could find material among the Indians for a Series of highly interesting Tales, I see no reason why a Canadian cannot also find similar material.[36]

Not many of McLean's contemporaries seem to have solicited substantial quantities of Canadian fiction. Magazines like *The New Dominion Monthly* (1867–79), *The Canadian Illustrated News* (1869–80), *The Canadian Monthly and National Review* (1872–8) and *Belford's Monthly Magazine* (1876–8) present a broad cross-section of Canadian life in their serious articles and short fiction, but to satisfy the demand for long fiction (and to attract readers) they usually serialized novels by Wilkie Collins, James Payn, the team of Walter Besant and James Rice, and other popular British and

American writers. In the case of journals like *The Saturday Reader* (1865–7) economics rather than patriotism governed the choice of serialized fiction. The avowed purpose of the latter being 'to make money,' it assumed that the road to success was paved with 'the reproductions of the works of British authors of repute.'[37] Twenty-six years later the reliable attractiveness of popular British and American novelists accounted for *The Dominion Illustrated*'s purchase of 'the exclusive rights for Canada' of serial stories by 'leading English authors' such as Robert Buchanan, Hawley Smart, W. Clark Russell, and George Manville Fenn.[38] To its credit *The Dominion Illustrated* lived up to its name by publishing many Canadian short stories, and in 1892 it began its new series by serializing 'The Raid from Beauséjour' by Charles G.D. Roberts.

The large and lavish *Canadian Illustrated News* (1869–80) represents the trajectory of its fellow periodicals. Founded in a spirit of nationalistic enthusiasm, it commenced publication by sponsoring a contest offering prizes for the best 'ROMANCES founded on Incidents in the History of Canada.'[39] During its first years this magazine's short and serialized fiction was primarily Canadian in origin and content, but by its later volumes it had turned to non-Canadian sources and was running novels by Mary Braddon, Wilkie Collins, Rhoda Broughton, and Besant and Rice.

When *The Canadian Illustrated News* decided to pursue its search for Canadian literature in the direction of the historical romance it was simply articulating the general assumption that the way to build the Canadian novel was to follow the lead of Sir Walter Scott. Scott's influence in Canada will be discussed in detail in Chapter 5; what concerns us here is his example in almost single-handedly valorizing a previously neglected locality. In 1874 the Reverend Moses Harvey of Saint John's explained Scott's significance to a society seeking self-definition. Calling for a literary saviour for Newfoundland, Harvey asked:

Who knew or cared anything about Scotland till Walter Scott lifted the veil and revealed her, not only to her own astonished and delighted inhabitants, but also to other nations who had hitherto despised or derided 'the land of mountain and of flood.' The future will no doubt produce a Walter Scott for Newfoundland, who will gather up its traditions and superstitions, its tales of peril and heroic daring among its ice-laden seas, the oddities and humors of its fisher-folk, the tragedy and comedy of human existence as here developed, and perhaps weave them into such charming romances, poems and dramas as shall win the ear of the world.[40]

Decades later, at the opposite edge of the New World, Pauline Johnson's

Legends of Vancouver (1913) was credited with having 'done for us what Walter Scott did for the Borderers'[41] in its articulation of the literary significance of place.

The process of introducing Canadian traditions, superstitions, tales, and oddities into novels began with their recognition and validation in the literary periodicals, in short fiction and sketches which focused on single incidents and events. The first examples appear in the 1820s in tales elevated to the status of legend like John Howard Willis's 'The Fairy Harp' and 'The Faithful Heart.'[42] In the later periodicals, in addition to the familiar Canadian topics of winter social life, ice accidents, hunting adventures, getting lost in the bush, historical events, encounters with Indians, and hardships of settlement, Canadian storytellers wrote about smuggling on the St Lawrence or the Great Lakes,[43] New Brunswick pirates,[44] crime and vice in Canadian villages,[45] Ontario courtroom drama, and Toronto ghosts.[46]

For novelists who sought financial success beyond Canada, the problem of Canada's validity as a location for fiction was compounded by the nature of the international fiction market. In the latter half of the nineteenth century British and American popular taste demanded complex, sensational narratives set in places that were comfortably familiar or intriguingly exotic – Canada being seen as neither. The fiction of James De Mille, a classical scholar who employed his literary talents principally to pay off his family debts during the 1860s and 1870s, illustrates some of the difficulties involved in attempting both to write fiction in Canada and to make money from it.

While many of De Mille's highly contrived plots are indistinguishable from the mass of market fiction, in a few of his 'potboilers' (as he called them)[47] he tested his ingenuity by seasoning the usual formulas with bits of Canadiana. *The American Baron* (1872), for example, is set mostly in Italy but one of its many romantic entanglements begins when an English visitor to Canada rescues a young lady from a forest fire in the Ottawa valley; *Cord and Creese* (1869), a thriller whose plot rambles from Australia to Hong Kong to England to San Salvador, likewise includes several glimpses of Canada. But aside from his juvenile BOWC (Brethren of the White Cross) series, De Mille wrote only two novels whose primary action occurs in his native land.

The first, *The Lady of the Ice* (1870), is De Mille's most accomplished piece of fiction after *A Strange Manuscript Found in a Copper Cylinder* (1888). The plot centres on an indigenous Canadian catastrophe which (with a little assistance from Harriet Beecher Stowe) became a convention in nineteenth-century Canadian fiction: the rescue of a character (usually female) trapped on the ice when a river (preferably the St Lawrence) breaks up in the spring.[48] In this instance the rescued is a mysterious young woman and her saviour a flippant young officer stationed at Quebec whose first-person narrative consistently exposes his fatuousness and conceit. This book's erudite literary humour, self-revealing narrator, and clearly delineated characters and events distinguish it from De Mille's other adult Canadian novel, a trivial historical romance titled *The Lily and the Cross* (1875).

Presumably the writing of his BOWC series of boys' adventures stories was motivated in part by De Mille's desire to demonstrate that his native region did contain valid literary material even if not of the sort to appeal to the general adult readership of his American publishers. Although bibliographical information on De Mille is sparse, his Maritime juvenile fiction appears to have remained in print long after his potboilers disappeared from publishers' lists. First issued from 1869 through the early 1870s, each of these books enjoyed at least three or four editions and in 1902 they were still listed by the Boston firm of Lee & Shepard in their American [sic] Boys' series.

In these novels, De Mille drew on his Saint John childhood and his own Grand Pré school days. He lavished much attention on the physical beauty of the Fundy area, proclaiming its superiority to even the most celebrated landscapes of Europe.[49] His Maritime material also includes detailed references to the great Miramichi fire of 1825, the Magdalen and Sable islands, the Tracadie leper colony, rumours of Captain Kidd's buried treasure, and, of course, the Acadians. While these books are not as overtly didactic as those in the same author's Young Dodge Club series, much historical and geographical information is carefully incorporated into their narratives.

De Mille's faithfulness to his setting contrasts markedly with the contempt for Canadian geography manifested by J.E. Collins in one of the more atrocious novels of the last century, *Annette the Métis Spy* (1887). In few other countries would it have been possible to issue so blatant a statement of indifference to the land: 'I have ... arranged the geography of the [Northwest] Territories to suit my own conveniences. I speak of places that no one will be able to find upon maps of the present or of the future. Wherever I want a valley or a swamp, I put the same; and I have taken the same liberty with respect to hills or waterfalls. The birds, and in some instances the plants and flowers of the prairies, I have also made to order.'[50] Such blithe fabrication of natural elements, possible only in a place utterly bereft of a sense of its own identity, can be read as a sign of eastern Canadian indifference to the west. Destined to be subsumed by the developing trend towards regional realism, Collins' attitude remains significant as the position rejected by writers like De Mille who sought a sense of authenticity in setting, if not always in characterization and plot.

Yet the new conventions De Mille was initiating in his Maritime fiction carried with them a new set of restrictions. Free of the preposterous intrigues and characters of his potboilers – in the creation of which De Mille took tongue-in-cheek delight – the BOWC books foster an image of Canada as a location appropriate for uncomplicated fiction suitable for children and Mrs Grundy.[51] This view became particularly dominant at the turn of the century when the most popular Canadian novels promoted a simplistic setting for a sanitized version of Canadian experience, such as the pastoral Ontario of Joanna Wood's *Judith Moore* (1898). The best-sellers of Ralph Connor, whose West is always governed by goodness, and L.M. Montgomery, whose Prince Edward Island basks in sunlight and blossoms, solved the problem of place by creating a land which corresponded more accurately to the map than to the experiences of its ordinary inhabitants. These writers' American success suggests that outside of Canada their work was received 'not as a potentially autonomous tradition, but as regional or "local colour" extensions of the literature of the United States.'[52] This interest in Canadian local colour produced two particular subgenres that will be discussed in later chapters, the tale of quaint French-Canadian life and the regional idyll. But for many writers, the problem of Canada's suitability as a location – both for fiction and for living – remained unresolvable. As Susie Frances Harrison tried to explain the situation to W.D. Howells:

'Canada is the grave of a good deal of talent ... and we (speaking of Canadian authors) have sometimes difficulty in impressing ourselves on foreign publishers, the only publishers worth anything to us. A great deal of good work is done in Canada which does not find its way into other countries. And there may be work which is a little good for Canada, and yet, not quite good enough for English or American markets. Then, if we are to excel in local colour, we must remain in Canada in order to observe it, live it, so to speak, and so – you see,' I ended weakly.[53]

Such inconclusiveness poignantly illustrates the situation of writers living directly within the 'Where is here?' riddle identified by Northrop Frye as a central paradox of the Canadian sensibility.[54]

In the 1890s and early 1900s authors trying to survive by their writing had to decide whether to stay national (and poor) or go international and leave Canada behind.[55] Many of the internationalists who literally became expatriates clustered around *The Idler* in London, which was edited by Robert Barr from 1892 to 1895 and published work by Barr, Gilbert Parker, Grant Allen, and Sara Jeannette Duncan. Of this group, it was Duncan who was her country's greatest loss. Because one of her major concerns as a novelist was the relation between perception and action, her own experiences in Britain and India provided richer material than Canada could supply. As she stated in an 1895 interview, 'there is such abundance of material in Anglo-Indian life – it is full of such picturesque incident, such tragic chance.'[56] But before she left Canada for good in 1891, the year of her marriage to Charles Everard Cotes, Duncan had left an indelible impression on the Canadian literary scene. An avowed moderate realist in the footsteps of Howells and James, she had vigorously assaulted the impenetrable conservatism of the Canadian public. In the 1880s her articles in *The Week*, the Toronto *Globe*, and the Montreal *Daily Star* consistently badgered Canadian readers to relinquish their taste for popular romance and to enjoy the innovations occurring in novels which would stretch the narrow vision of a colonial backwater.

4 Approaches to Realism

Articulate advocates of literary realism were rare in Victorian Canada, possibly rarer than anywhere else in the English-speaking world. In England 'an undercurrent of romantic criticism ... provoked a majority rationale' from 'thoughtful realists ... who wished to argue the case for fiction as a fully serious art form.'[1] In Canada the inverse held true – the majority opinion belonged to the proponents of romance, the subject of Chapter 5. They outnumbered and outlasted the realists whose major spokesperson, Sara Jeannette Duncan, formulated the most serious defence of moderate literary realism to be found in pre-modern Canada. Before Duncan made a brief, concerted effort to broaden the cultural horizons of her fellow Canadians during the mid-1880s, Susanna Moodie had proven the most radical mid-century Canadian commentator when she argued that social realism was permissible in fiction if directed to moral ends. Approaching the same topic from a different direction, Thomas Chandler Haliburton used his famous character Sam Slick to advocate fictional writing that was 'true to nature.' This phrase did not refer to the detail of the social anatomist but to the satirist's deployment of exaggeration and caricature to present his analysis of and solutions to current economic and political problems. Its meaning is elucidated by Slick himself in *Nature and Human Nature* (1855), the last of his books, when he is asked whether he had actually said and done everything recorded in his earlier narratives: 'I wouldn't just like to swear to every word of it, but most of it is true, though some things are embellished a little, and some are fancy sketches. But they are all true to nature ... I have tried to stick to life as close as I could, and there is nothin' like natur, it goes home to the heart of us all.'[2] Describing his literary mission as 'Holding Up the Mirror,' Slick argues that the significance of individual details arises from their support of the truth that 'natur is the same always.' Hence he praises the work of Smollett and Fielding because their books are 'true to life' and 'a picture of the times, and instructin' as well as amusin'.'[3]

In Haliburton's own practice, instruction preceded amusement. While Sara Jeannette Duncan was primarily interested in fiction as an art, Haliburton's motive was to exploit its popularity to advance specific causes. His own explanation of the genesis of Sam Slick is that after completing *An Historical and Statistical Account of Nova Scotia* (1829),

It occurred to me that it would be advisable to resort to a more popular style, and under the garb of amusement, to call attention to our noble harbors, our great mineral wealth, our healthy climate, our abundant fisheries, and our natural resources and advantages ... I was also anxious to stimulate my countrymen to exertion ... to awaken ambition and substitute it for that stimulus which is furnished in other but poorer countries than ours by necessity. For this purpose I called in the aid of the Clockmaker.[4]

Didacticism being Haliburton's primary motive and satire his genre, he did not write within the tradition of the novel – which would have required the creation of a complete fictional world – but instead created one outstanding character to perform as his persona. Distant readers responded to the humour and vitality of the fiction and adored the idiosyncratic Slick for his 'welcome unconventionality.'[5] Nova Scotians paid more attention to the underlying reality, with mixed reactions.

The Novascotian lauded Haliburton for establishing the literary validity of Nova Scotia, finding that *The Clockmaker*'s being 'so generally admired by the experienced judges of England, stamps it with the quality of sterling merit.'[6] For several decades literary equality with the mother country seemed a distinct possibility: 'If England has its *Dickens* – and Ireland her *Lever* – Nova Scotia has her *Haliburton* whose literary fame is nothing dimmed by a comparison with his most popular contemporaries.'[7] However, Haliburton's local reputation was coloured by responses both political and personal. The Liberal *Novascotian* (where the first Sam Slick books were initially serialized) stopped publishing *The Attaché* because it found Haliburton's book 'not conspicuously conducive to good morals, religious freedom of conscience, or political liberality.'[8] Also offended was the pseudonymous Julian of the *Acadian Recorder*, whose misreading of Haliburton's irony led to the accusation that the latter intended to 'libel the *Plebian* population of the Province.'[9] V.L.O.

Chittick's survey of reactions to Sam Slick indicates that *The Clockmaker* received greater acclaim abroad than at home.[10] Haliburton's local audience paid closer attention to his political views than to his literary accomplishments, with the result that 'his influence *on Canada* is political rather than literary, whereas his reputation and influence *in the world* is literary rather than political.'[11]

Of all Haliburton's books it is *The Old Judge* (1849), his sole work of fiction not narrated by Sam Slick, which best exhibits a breadth of vision characteristic of the mid-Victorian novel. In *The Old Judge* Haliburton redirected his penchant for literary realism, attempting 'to delineate Life in a Colony'[12] by assembling a collection of Nova Scotian tales and legends which, in the view of one modern critic, reveal 'an unsuspected facet of romantic feeling and talents of a high order for serious fiction.'[13] The original form of the book presents an anatomy of local life, history, and society, using several narrators to describe and satirize elements as diverse as the governor's ball and rural manners. Its structure of interspersed stories, essays, descriptive sketches, and commentary achieves an air of objectivity, despite the dominance of Haliburton's Toryism, by balancing the quiet irony of educated commentators like Barclay and Judge Sandford against the uninhibited exuberance of the common people. Not a novel, *The Old Judge* nonetheless indicates that Haliburton was capable of a degree of subtlety and restraint not present in the Sam Slick books and suggests that had he cared to do so, he might have applied his sense of literary realism to the creation of fuller works of fiction in line with the critical principles later articulated by Sara Jeannette Duncan.

A writer who is seldom discussed alongside Duncan but who shared some of her views on fiction is James De Mille. A generation older and several provinces distant from her milieu, he too understood that it was easier to disparage the stereotypes of romance than to avoid them. While both these Canadian novelists wrote comic fiction about North Americans visiting Europe, what concerns us here is De Mille's parody of romantic literary conventions.

There is no evidence that De Mille wrote criticism apart from his textbook, *Elements of Rhetoric* (1878), in which he maintains the impersonal approach expected of academic writing. Published in New York, the book takes nearly all its examples from classical and British writers. But De Mille may have tipped his hand by judging 'the very best fiction' (by Eliot, Dickens, Thackeray, and Scott) superior to 'the very best history' and by slipping in his own parodies of Tennyson and Browning.[14] More specifically, his popular romances can be read as covert criticism of prevailing literary taste. Archibald MacMechan's view that their Shan-dyean wit bespeaks 'a gentleman and a scholar possessing something like genius'[15] is only a moderate overstatement.

In the best of the novels he referred to as his potboilers De Mille maintained a humorous distance from his preposterous plots and predictable characters, hinting that his playful efforts to 'out-Braddon Miss Braddon'[16] were burlesques of the standard components of popular fiction intentionally exaggerated to underline their absurdity. Among De Mille's favourite self-reflexive strategies for calling attention to the artificiality of his narrative was the rearrangement of typography. Crucial utterances which would normally be printed as part of the text are turned into chapter headings[17] and chapters of some comic novels consist solely of titles.[18] Several novels – The Lady of the Ice (1870), An Open Question (1872), The American Baron (1872), and A Castle in Spain (1883) – openly proclaim their parodic structure, a feature they share with the book for which De Mille is best known today, A Strange Manuscript Found in a Copper Cylinder.

Published posthumously in 1888 but composed much earlier,[19] this book contains ironic commentary on both the kind of sensational adventure fiction that De Mille himself wrote and the pretentious literary critics who belittled it, thereby allowing the author the delicious experience of having his cake and eating it too. In the manuscript in the bottle picked up by Featherstone's yacht, De Mille presents an intriguing account of the discovery of an unknown country at the South Pole, the carelessness of the narration being perhaps the most convincing argument for its authenticity. It is significantly Otto Melick, the fatuous London littérateur, who suggests that the manuscript had been set afloat by 'some fellow who wanted to get up a sensation novel and introduce it to the world with a great flourish of trumpets.' Convinced that what is being read is a 'transparent hoax,'[20] Melick remains oblivious to the manuscript's deeper significance as a commentary on his own culture and retreats to the pat phraseology of the hack reviewer.[21] By attributing to this obtuse fictional man of letters the kinds of comments he was used to receiving on his own work, De Mille took a barbed parting shot at his critics. He demonstrated that his own hackwork was created in full awareness of its triviality, that he was capable of burlesquing both his potboilers and his critics, and that his decision not to produce sophisticated, philosophical, realistic fiction was not due to lack of ability.[22]

The era of De Mille's success was that of Sara Jeannette Duncan's childhood, when the dominant notion in Canada was that fiction was not expected to represent real life. Patronizing approval marked the Montreal *Family Herald*'s acknowledgment of the gap between art and experience when it commended one book whose characters 'earn the reward of all true lovers in story books and are happily married at the end'[23] and another as 'a story of the right sort' because 'All the troubles [are] at the one end of it, all the happiness at the other.' Such tales may not be true to life but they are true to tradition: 'And if some ill-natured critic should suggest that such extraordinary co-incidences never happen in real life, at least all there is of amiable critics will be delighted to find a storybook left in which the interest is wound up on the good old primitive principle, if not in the words, "So they were married, and had a large family, and lived happily ever afterwards".'[24]

Such fiction is best described as romance. In *The Progress of Romance* (1785), the first lengthy discussion of prose fiction written in England, Clara Reeve defined 'romance' and 'novel' in terms which were to remain generally applicable to the Canadian literary scene throughout the following century.

The Romance is an heroic fable, which treats of fabulous persons and things. – The Novel is a picture of real life and manners, and of the times in which it was written. The Romance in lofty and elevated language, describes what never happened nor is likely to happen. – The Novel gives a familiar relation of such things, as pass every day before our eyes, such as may happen to our friend or to ourselves; and the perfection of it, is to represent every scene, in so easy and natural a manner, and to make them appear so probable, as to deceive us into a persuasion (at least while we are reading) that all is real, until we are affected by the joys or distresses, of the persons in the story, as if they were our own.[25]

While Victorian Canada modified the realm of romance from the impossible to the improbable and from the bygone age of fable to its own more recent past (or even present), it maintained Reeve's distinction between two opposing approaches to fictional representation. Believing that 'The effort to be realistic, and to depict actual life with an unsparing hand, is in truth an unpleasantly painful one, and leads the modern novelist into many an extravagance and libel on the race,'[26] most nineteenth-century Canadians voiced a distinct preference for romantic fiction in which the author removes characters and circumstances from the arena of common experience by heightening their distinguishing characteristics so that heroes are more perfect, villains more evil, and events more coincidental, tragic, or blissful than in real life. The ease with which they interchanged the terms 'romance' and 'novel,' as indicated by their comments cited in the preceding and following chapters, suggests the tenacity of their assumption that fiction could only be romantic. In 1892 Archibald Lampman tried to dismiss the 'quarrel between realism and romanticism' as 'about as empty a one as that over the iota in the Nicene Creed.' His proposition that from Walter Scott to Henry James 'every writer of real gift is a realist'[27] fell on deaf ears. A brief overview of the Canadian response to Howells and James in the last two decades of the century illuminates the context in which Duncan was trying to promote these two Americans as appropriate models for Canadian writers.

No Canadian supporter of the literary methods of James and Howells appears to have accepted their work absolutely uncritically. E.W. Thomson, for example, writing to Ethelwyn Wetherald in 1895, remarked, 'I don't yield to anyone in appreciation of Howells and James' and then expressed his doubt that 'their theory of novel writing is broad enough, or that their novels truly express life,' judging them 'the mufflers of passion and great emotion.'[28] Earlier praise, before the romance/realism debate warmed up, was heartier. In 1878 George Stewart devoted one of his *Evenings in the Library* to Howells' first two books, *Their Wedding Journey* and *A Chance Acquaintance*, and applauded their style, characterization, depiction of Quebec, and elegant marriage of fiction and history.[29] The same year, *Rose-Belford's* found in *The Lady of the Aroostook* 'men and women [who] may be met with every day in the streets of cities and in the byways and lanes of villages' and also 'the beautiful type of perfect womanhood.'[30] On the whole the two American realists received little attention in Canada until 1885, when they began to be frequently reviewed and discussed in *The Week*.

While the reception of Howells and James in *The Week* runs the full scale from adulation to abhorrence, the dominant tone is certainly commendatory. Many of *The Week*'s reviewers responded first of all to the sheer ability of these two novelists to write well whatever their subject. And as revealed in reviews of James' *Partial Portraits* (1888) and Howells' *Criticism and Fiction* (1891), Canadians were grateful to find the primary American realists denouncing the 'revolting and indecent' work of Zola and de Maupassant and upholding the 'decorum' of a refined social order in which 'people now call a spade an agricultural implement.'[31] *The Week* sufficiently admired Howells' essay 'The Allowable in Fiction' to print it twice in six months.[32]

On the whole James raised more Canadian hackles than did Howells.

The Reverberator was described as 'slight and unpleasant' and 'almost vulgar'[33] and 'A New England Winter' was treated rather gingerly because 'in it Mr James handles some hitherto sacred subjects without gloves.'[34] *The Tragic Muse* and *Embarrassments* were both found to be all style and no substance – the reviewer of the latter challenged his audience to 'extract sunbeams from this cucumber.'[35] On the other hand, *The Week* was enraptured with *The Princess Casamassima* ('a delightful book'),[36] the four stories in *The Author of Beltraffoi* ('about as charming a bevy of novelettes as the publishing market has offered for some time'),[37] and *The Bostonians* ('some of Mr James's very best work').[38]

Reviews of Howells were almost uniformly appreciative.[39] In 1887, when Sara Jeannette Duncan was in charge of the 'Our Library Table' column and presumably wielded some editorial influence, *The Week* reprinted from the New York *Critic* a substantial interview with Howells containing a precise elucidation of his literary philosophy. This was prefaced by an editorial paragraph introducing 'the head of the American realistic school' to 'conservative Canada.'[40] But conservative Canada was not easily won, as Louisa Murray demonstrated when she accused Howells of advocating a 'communistic' literature which 'though immaculate from a moral point of view, must inevitably degrade the taste, lower the standard of art, and prove fatal to all elevation of mind and noble ambition ... Worlds away as Mr Howells' representation of life is from M. Zola's theory of realistic art, or Count Tolstoi's tragic stories of oppression and cruelty, it appears to me as thoroughly pessimistic in its tendency.'[41]

The Week did not allow this opinion to rest unchallenged. Yet it is significant that the rebuttal came not from a Canadian (Duncan was by this time on the other side of the globe) but from a Scot who admired Howells as 'the American Thackeray.'[42] The tendency of Canadians to retreat from realism at the turn of the century may account for the guarded tone of Susan Frances Harrison's 1897 *Massey's Magazine* interview with 'the most distinguished of American novelists' which does, however, credit Howells with sincerity and with having 'certainly put before us, as no one else has, the American daily life, the American citizen, the American train of thought – even the American woman.'[43]

While Sara Jeannette Duncan never ceased to admire Howells and James as 'gentlemen both engaged in developing a school of fiction most closely and subtly related to the conditions and progress of our time'[44] she maintained some independence in her views. Her Washington *Post* review of *The Bostonians*, for example, expressed admiration for James' 'art' but found his depiction of the women's suffrage movement 'the work of a man with a very bitter prejudice and very narrow vision.' (Not that she was a supporter; she added, 'A fair picture of the movement could hardly fail to deprecate it, but this is a caricature.')[45] And her gift for flippancy gained the upper hand in a July newspaper column when, as a cure for midsummer heat prostration, she recommended '"Concentrated Essence of Realism," none genuine without the signature of the patentee, one W.D. Howells, formerly of Boston, now of New York, also the endorsation of a Russian gentleman named Tolstoi, and a Frenchman *nommée* de Balzac,' the remedy consisting of minutely observing all the contents and activities of one's own backyard.[46]

Duncan's occasional liberties and disagreements with the masters of American realism merely enhanced her frequent iterations of their principles. She did her best to cultivate their personal acquaintance, from her 1886 interview with Howells' boots[47] to her request for Henry James' opinion of *His Honour and a Lady* (1896).[48] Throughout her brief career as a Canadian literary journalist she referred to the work of James and Howells whenever she applauded the way in which 'Fiction seems determined to broaden its scope in all directions.'[49] And she usually gave short shrift to writing shaped by 'the old fashioned method in fiction by which the heroine was brought safely and comfortably out of her woes and the reader was left in the agreeable certainty that only the unnecessary people had died, the evil disposed fallen into their own pit, and the truly deserving married and lived happily ever afterward.' Duncan endorsed the advancements being made in progressive literary circles, where 'modern tendencies in fiction' were fast gaining hold: 'The idea seems to be gaining ground that life should be represented as it is and not as we should like it to be, regardless of probabilities. And in life as it is the traditions of the novelist are very often reversed. There is always consolation for the disconsolate, though, on the top shelves of the circulating libraries and in the old numbers of *The Young Ladies' Journal* and similar publications.'[50]

Herself eminently a New Woman (albeit not a suffragette), Duncan acclaimed the modern heroine as one of the major achievements of the new realism:

The woman of to-day is no longer an exceptional being surrounded by exceptional circumstances. She bears a translatable relation to the world; and the novelists who translate it correctly have ceased to mark it by unduly exalting one woman by virtue of her sex to a position of interest in their books which dwarfs all other characters ... The woman of today understands herself, and is understood in her present and possible worth. The novel of today is a reflection of our present social state. The women who enter into its composition are but intelligent agents in this reflection, and show themselves as they are, not as a false ideal would have them.[51]

Nonetheless she applied clear boundaries to acceptable subjects for literature, conceding that 'The modern school of fiction, if it is fairly subject to reproach, may bear the blame of dealing too exclusively in the corporealities of human life, to the utter and scornful neglect of its idealities.'[52] Duncan's sense of propriety emerged again in her 1887 defence of female hack novelists. Bad novels were produced by men just as often as by women, she declared, and women, at least, 'have no part in contributing the depraved element of fiction which drags the average down. The work of women in fiction does not increase the statistics of crime. In being denied such contact with the world as might serve to make their books stronger and more realistic they are also deprived of the temptation of making them the dangerous social force that cheap sensational literature represents.'[53]

In a *Globe* column ostensibly describing the literary tastes of women in general, Duncan defined the qualified realism she favoured: 'The ordinary detail of humdrum life and circumstance, pen-painted by an artist with sympathies keen enough to detect the mysterious throbbing of the life that is inner and under, fascinates us like our own photographs. As a rule we dislike strong situation, and sanguinary scenes are the exception in recent novels of the better class. Coarseness we cannot tolerate, even with that saving sauce in the eyes of men – humour.'[54]

Her own preferences thus clearly articulated, Duncan understood that the major achievement of the realistic school was not to change the novel so much as to expand it: 'The novel of to-day may be written to show the culminative action of a passion, to work out an ethical problem of everyday occurrence, to give body and form to a sensation of the finest or of the coarsest kind, for almost any reason which can be shown to have a connection with the course of human life, and development of human character ... Fiction has become a law unto itself, and its field has broadened with the assumption.'[55] The flexibility implied by this acknowledgment of the breadth of the genre was borne out by her glowing, almost sentimental appreciation of *A Christmas Carol*,[56] her report of Tennyson's admiration of Kirby's *The Golden Dog* with minimal irony,[57] and her occasional scepticism regarding proponents of realism who autocratically 'announce to their scribbling emulators the only proper and acceptable form of the modern novel, announce it imperiously, and note departures from it with wrath.' When she reviewed *An Algonquin Maiden* (1887), co-authored by Graeme Mercer Adam and Ethelwyn Wetherald, Duncan sardonically admitted that old-fashioned romance retained an appeal against which all the logic and rhetoric of the literary realists were powerless:

Gentlemen of the realistic school, one is disposed to consider you very right in so far as you go, but to believe you mistaken in your idea that you go the whole distance and can persuade the whole novel-reading fraternity to take the same path through the burdocks and the briars. Failing this, you evidently believe that you can put to the edge of the sword every wretched romanticist who presumes to admire the exotic of the idea, and to publish his admiration. This is also a mistake, for both of the authors of 'An Algonquin Maiden' are alive, and, I believe, in reasonable health; and 'An Algonquin Maiden' is a romance, a romance of the most uncompromising description, a romance that might have been written if the realistic school had never been heard of.

In this review Duncan simultaneously recognized the persistence of the romantic temperament and wittily castigated the improbabilities imposed by the romantic mode. But she also admitted that romance, when well-written, could render ridiculous conventions almost palatable. Her assessment of the conclusion of *An Algonquin Maiden* begins as censure but modulates to ironic praise:

True to the traditions of romance, the authors arrange a perfectly satisfactory termination of affairs for everybody concerned. Odd numbers being incompatible with unalloyed bliss, Miss Wetherald drowns the unfortunate Algonquin maiden, in the chapter before the last, which she styles poetically 'The Passing of Wanda' – drowns her in a passage of such sympathetic grace that one becomes more than reconciled to the sad necessity of the act, and convinced that the love-smitten Algonquin maiden herself could ask no happier fate.[58]

Duncan's ability to adjust her criticism to her audience is evident in her discussion of the same book in her 'Woman's World' column in the *Globe*. Aware that she was now writing for a broader audience (and that Ethelwyn Wetherald was a popular contributor to the *Globe* under the pseudonym 'Bel Thistlethwaite'), she donned the hat of literary nationalism and enthusiastically recommended *An Algonquin Maiden* as an 'unaccustomed literary sensation ... in a land where literary sensations are about as frequent as earthquakes.'[59]

Such unabashed romance as *The Algonquin Maiden* allows little room for the kind of realism that Duncan described as 'the everlasting glorification of the commonplace.'[60] Yet she did not find romance and realism necessarily incompatible, as she reveals in her discussion of Frances Brooke's *The History of Emily Montague* (1769). Although this book was written 'in the palmy days of heroes and heroines' Duncan discovered in the first Canadian novel a valuable 'picture of contemporary British ways of thinking and writing, as well as a sprightly and presumably truthful account of our own social beginnings.'[61] And she perceived that the variability now possible in fiction was due to its democratic nature. 'The art of fiction,' she wrote, 'having for its shifting and variable basis, humanity, is bound to present itself in more diverse forms than any other – constantly to find new ones, constantly to recur to old ones.'[62] The persistence of the old forms of romance arose from the motivation of ordinary readers, which Duncan recognized to be their desire to project themselves into a world which satisfied their fantasies and reinforced their prejudices: 'The average novel reader likes above all a book in which his imagination will permit him to feel at home, a book in which the people talk as he would like to have talked, and act as he would like to have acted, and a book which makes any number of sacrifices of the probabilities in order to arrive at an orthodox and comfortable conclusion.'[63]

Taking her cue from Howells' *A Chance Acquaintance* (1873), a book she knew well,[64] Sara Jeannette Duncan put her own critical principles into practice when she played with her reader's anticipation of an 'orthodox and comfortable conclusion' in two of her lighter novels, *An American Girl in London* (1891) and its sequel, *A Voyage of Consolation* (1898). Both recount the European adventures of Mamie Wick, a bright young lady from Chicago (literary cousin to Daisy Miller as well as Kitty Ellison) whose ingenuous spirit exposes the limitations and prejudices of her British and American acquaintances. In her first narrative Mamie is courted by Mr Mafferton, a proper young Englishman whose attentions augur a wedding-bells conclusion. As *The Week*'s reviewer remarked, 'we feel we shall not be surprised if the usual fate which pursues pretty American girls overtakes our heroine. That it does not is perhaps the cleverest thing in the book.'[65]

Having deflated her readers' expectations in her first book, Mamie opens her second by declaring that both her behaviour and her apparently frank autobiographical report had been conditioned by the conventions of romantic fiction:

I once had such a good time in England that I printed my experiences, and at the very end of the volume it seemed necessary to admit that I was engaged to Mr Arthur Greenleaf Page, of Yale College, Connecticut. I remember thinking that this was indiscreet at the time, but I felt compelled to bow to the requirements of fiction. I was my own heroine, and I had to be disposed of. There seemed to be no alternative. I did not wish to marry Mr Mafferton, even for literary purposes ... So I committed that indiscretion. In order that the world might be assured that my heroine married and lived happily ever afterwards, I took it prematurely into my confidence regarding my intention. The thing that occurred, as naturally and inevitably as the rain if you leave your umbrella at home, was that within a fortnight after my return to Chicago my engagement to Mr Page terminated ...[66]

In *A Voyage of Consolation* Duncan again parodies popular literary convention. The marriage ending that Mamie rejects at the beginning of the book is affirmed with a vengeance at its conclusion. After a series of coincidental encounters across continental Europe, Mamie and all the unattached characters (including Mr Mafferton) terminate their adventures with three, possibly four marriages, Mamie becoming Mrs Arthur Greenleaf Page after all. Duncan, like James De Mille before her, understood that one way to come to terms with the conventions of the popular novel was to treat them ironically. Rather than seek new narrative modes, Duncan in these two books moulded currently popular structures to her own purpose, much to the delight of her readers. As *The Dominion Illustrated* observed in 1890, 'Those who deny women humour must go to Miss Duncan's pages to be cured of their heresy.'[67]

Yet even her comic novels signal her engagement with problems of literary form. As in her more serious fiction, she here moved away from the novel of plot towards the more Jamesian novel of character and idea which defines and reveals character by focusing on an individual's perception of the world around her and narrating through her particular viewpoint. Mamie Wick evokes more interest for her piquant comments on British society than for her amorous involvements. And Elfrida Bell, heroine of *A Daughter of Today* (1894), speaks for Duncan herself when she says that 'for a novel one wants a leading idea – the plot, of course, is of no particular consequence. Rather I should say plots have merged into leading ideas.'[68] The 'leading idea' of Duncan's serious fiction – set in India, Canada, or Britain – is to explore how modes and limitations of perception and imagination shape people's lives. Hence her concern is not narrative for the sake of recounting adventure, but the effect of events on the formation of vision. As she says of Lorne Murchison's trip to England in *The Imperialist* (1904), 'What he absorbed and took back with him is, after all, what we have to do with; his actual adventures are of no importance.'[69] Duncan's own novels tend to weaken when she constructs plots composed of 'actual adventures'; this is especially true of some of her later books like *Set in Authority* (1906), *His Royal Happiness* (1914), and *Title Clear* (1922). In her best writing she almost abandons plot, delineating characters whose pathos, comedy, and potential tragedy arise from their own short-sightedness. Her narrower characters generally reveal their limitations in contrast to the more astute perceptiveness of characters of superior and frequently ironic vision (a structure she may have assimilated from Jane Austen), one of the best examples being Mrs Farnham of 'A Mother in India.'

At the lowest end of Duncan's scale of vision sit individuals like the Brownes of *The Simple Adventures of a Memsahib* (1893), who transfer their middle-class Englishness to Anglo-India with only minute effects on their own sensibilities. More interesting and disturbing are those who not only fail to sense their limitations, but try to change the world around them by putting into practice the principles underlying their distorted vision. In Canada, idealistic Lorne Murchison of *The Imperialist* bungles his ideal of transforming Canada's political relationship with the mother country because he completely loses touch with the everyday life represented by Elgin's market square. In *The Burnt Offering* (1909), set in India, British social democrat Vulcan Miles ruins his own parliamentary career and nearly incites grave political trouble when he acts according to his European perspective without perceiving its inappropriateness in the alien East. As with Murchison, Miles' interpretation of the political situation in which he finds himself is coloured by his romantic self-image, arising in his case from his identification with

the earlier emergence of the Socialist idea, before it had learned the necessity of compromise or the value of business methods ... Vulcan's long-contemplated journey had ... brought him to the heart of a political romance where a knight was clearly needed, a mailed fist, with a pipe in it, and no nonsense about it, to take the part of the inarticulate millions. He came to it out of a world of prosaic engagements, mean streets, and wet umbrellas, and he brought a capacity for sentiment which was like the thirst of a lifetime.[70]

Through characters like Lorne Murchison and Vulcan Miles, Duncan (like Scott in *Waverley* and Flaubert in *Madame Bovary*) exposed the inability of the romantic temperament to cope with the complexities of real social and political experience, and in her literary structures she frequently rejected the novel of plot in favour of the novel of idea. But her efforts to push Canadian fiction in the direction that she identified as the mainstream of serious literary artistry were powerless against the renewed tide of romance that swept the English-speaking world in the last decade of the nineteenth century. The few turn-of-the-century Canadian writers who attempted to pursue Duncan were ignored by readers and periodicals in favour of the slick romances of popular authors like Gilbert Parker and Robert Barr, the latter crowned by *The Canadian Magazine* as 'the Prince of Canada's storytellers.'[71] Although these two novelists evinced some potential capacity for serious social fiction, Barr in *The Mutable Many* (1896) and Parker in *The Translation of a Savage* (1893), these were not the books that won the adulation of their Canadian readers and consequently represent roads not taken in their later careers. Instead, these writers sought fame and fortune by participating in the popular revival of romantic fiction of the 1890s. The trend can be seen in *The Week* itself, which swerved from its earlier support of Howellsian realism to favour literature that 'lifts us above the low level of daily surroundings and events, into a purer air, a more radiant sunshine, a loftier aspiration and achievement than the daily experience can ever bring.'[72]

The late Victorian reawakening of a supposedly dormant taste for unrealistic literature can be seen in part as a low-brow reaction against the decadence of the Beardsley circle and the disturbing productions of the realists and naturalists. British critics have offered several explanations, from the peculiar taste of the critic Andrew Lang, who wielded his power in favour of tales of adventure,[73] to the popular successes of Hall Caine and Marie Corelli in the late 1880s.[74] Other identified key figures include Richard Blackmore and Robert Louis Stevenson, the latter, according to Ernest A. Baker, being responsible for giving romantic fiction new respectability in serious literary circles.[75] Conscious that they were departing from the norm of mid-Victorian seriousness that had dominated fiction in the 1860s and 1870s, romantic novelists like Stevenson, Ouida, and Hall Caine published lively defences of the imaginative adventure novel.[76]

This turn-of-the-century surge of interest in romantic fiction appeared to signify changes in the accepted form and function of the novel, after the mid-Victorian realism of Trollope and Eliot and away from the late Victorian naturalism of Hardy and Moore. But it was less a change than a re-affirmation, this time with the blessing of some respected critics, of the persistence of popular literary forms. Beneath the broad appeal of the realists there had always flowed a stream of popular romance. It was established in an historical current by imitators of Walter Scott like G.P.R. James, Harrison Ainsworth, Bulwer Lytton, and Charles Reade, and pursued in a domestic and social course by Rhoda Broughton, Mary Braddon, and Ouida. The apparent swell in romantic fiction that occurred in the 1830s and 1840s and again in the 1880s and 1890s did not indicate changes in the taste of the general reading public so much as temporary closures of the gap between sophisticated literary artistry and popular literary entertainment.

By choosing romance as their fictional mode, most nineteenth-century Canadian novelists deliberately removed themselves from the frontiers of serious literary advancement and placed themselves directly within the mainstream of popular literature: the obvious route to local fame, possible fortune, and international recognition. In a colonial society that equated literary merit with popular success and the broadest acceptability, the highest praise was reserved for those whose work presented the least challenge to conventional mores. Conversely, writers caring to examine the profounder issues of the day had to couch these problems in terms acceptable to their community and frequently had to resort to relocation – of their settings or of themselves. What Canadians wanted in their own literature was not realism but the lamp of 'Reality' – suitably escorted by Ideality, Purity, and Chivalry – that Goldwin Smith found in Walter Scott.

5 The Long Shadow of Sir Walter Scott

The significance of Sir Walter Scott to the literary environment of Victorian Canada is suggested by two events which neatly bracket the nineteenth century. In 1814 Five Nations Chief John Norton selected *The Lady of the Lake* 'together with the Scriptures' to translate into Mohawk; seventy-five years later *The Lay of the Last Minstrel* was named a prescribed text for junior matriculation in the province of Ontario.[1] Important as Scott's poetry was to nineteenth-century Canada, in the realm of fiction he left an even greater impression upon the development of Canadian literature. Influenced by a combination of literary and extra-literary factors relating to the country's colonial position and cultural history, the role he was given in shaping the horizon of expectation of the Canadian literary community is crucial to our understanding of the way fiction was written and read in nineteenth-century Canada. What is important is not what Scott himself said or wrote but the figure Canadians made of him. Unlike Australia and the United States, Canada produced no highly visible detractor of Scott – no Marcus Clarke, Joseph Furphy, or Mark Twain to challenge Scott's eminence in a distant corner of the English-speaking world.[2]

Before 1860, during the colonial period, Scott was esteemed for having made fiction respectable and directly or indirectly received the homage of scores of imitators who filled the pages of Canadian literary periodicals with historical romances set in Europe. During the nationalistic Confederation era, from the 1860s to the 1880s, his prominence grew as commentators and writers striving to develop a national literature almost unanimously chose Scott as their model. In the last decades before the First World War, when Scott's reputation sagged in the larger world, English Canada's cultural leaders continued to venerate the Wizard of the

North, making him the yardstick by which modern writers were measured and found severely wanting if their work betrayed the influence of realists and naturalists like Thomas Hardy and Emile Zola. While Scott was received rather more cautiously in French Canada where some commentators expressed discomfort with his 'préjugés antipapistes,' he was still widely read.[3]

Despite the efforts of a few brave souls (most notably Sara Jeannette Duncan and occasionally Duncan Campbell Scott) to broaden the horizons of the Canadian literary establishment, at the turn of the century the Scott standard remained firmly in place, as evidenced by the literary views of George Moore Fairchild, a wealthy businessman and man of letters.[4] Commenting on William Kirby's place in Canadian literature, Fairchild opined that 'When Gilbert Parker is forgotten Wm Kirby will be remembered as the Walter Scott of Canada' because 'His "Chien D'Or" is the greatest of all our Canadian romances.' In the first decade of the twentieth century this middle-aged representative Canadian assumed that the appropriate direction for Canadian fiction was national romance modelled on the example of Sir Walter Scott:

I could wish that Kirby had done more on the lines he so auspiciously commenced. The material was, and is, profuse for the writer of Canadian romance.

Now that Parker has abandoned the field I wonder who will be the man to arise and do the big work? ... Alas! I am only a scribbler and can but skirt the edges of the work that some *genius* will yet do ... [T]he real heart of the thing, the big romance, with its greater setting, as done in the work by Kirby, has yet to come, and it will come in the by and bye when the right man comes, and the needing world has sickened of the nauseus [sic] stuff that now prevails.[5]

A survey of Canadian literary opinion throughout the nineteenth century reveals that Fairchild's reverence for Scott accorded with a long-enduring national attitude that valued Scott for his use of history, the nationalistic affect of his fiction, his lively characters, his 'realism,' and his unimpeachable morality. The recipient of Fairchild's letter, Sir James LeMoine, was himself one of Scott's major Canadian advocates, having authored a lengthy study in French which enjoyed at least three separate printings (1862, 1872–3, 1885),[6] and having published in English many popular volumes of French-Canadian historical and folkloric material for which he was frequently compared with Scott.[7]

With few exceptions each of the short-lived Canadian literary periodicals in existence during Scott's lifetime paid him significant attention. In

1823 the first issue of *The Canadian Magazine and Literary Repository* (Montreal) published a lengthy original anonymous article which praised the effect of Scott's writing in raising the national consciousness of his fellow countrymen by appealing to their emotions and their sense of ancestry.[8] Through the following two years Scott remained in the public eye with a three-part review of *Quentin Durward* and another of *St Ronan's Well*, an extract from *Redgauntlet*, and an article tracing scenes from *Old Mortality*.[9] As well, the editor selected from the *Aberdeen Chronicle* a piece 'On Novel Reading' which thoroughly condemned the practice – with the exception of 'the novels by the author of Waverley.'[10] During the same decade, *The Acadian Magazine* (Halifax) reviewed Scott's *Life of Napoleon Bonaparte*, reprinted his description of the Duke of York, and commented on the public identification of the author of the Waverley novels.[11] After Scott's death *The Canadian Literary Magazine* (York) took considerable pride in presenting the first portrait of Scott 'ever engraved in Upper Canada – engraved too on Canadian Stone, and from thence, by means of a Canadian press, transferred to a Canadian paper.'[12] Dissent to this chorus of adulation appears to have been confined soley to the Scottish-born Presbyterian clergyman, the Reverend Thomas McCulloch of Pictou, whose attempt to counter Scott's presentation of the Covenanters in *Old Mortality* with his own 'Auld Eppie's Tales' is preserved in an unpublished manuscript in the Nova Scotia Archives.[13]

Through the middle years of the century Canadians upheld Scott – the man as much as the writer[14] – as the pure standard from which later authorship had deviated. Typical of commentary in Montreal's *Literary Garland* was the 1848 critic who feared that 'there is far too much idle, affected sentimentality, both in the literary productions of our own country and in those which we obtain from abroad' and recommended fiction that followed the example of Johnson's *Rasselas* or Scott, for 'we think no higher or holier principles have been inculcated in the world, than those of Walter Scott.'[15] Matching views appeared in Toronto's *Anglo-American Magazine*, which bestowed its highest accolade on Alexandre Dumas' *Emmanuel Philibert*: 'Sir Walter Scott could not have done more justice to the theme.'[16]

As the century progressed so did Scott's reputation. His high standing in post-Confederation Canada may be understood as the literary counterpart to what one historian has called the 'defensive position' to which the country's influential social groups (identified as 'Businessmen, labour, professional groups, churches, and middle-class women') retreated in response to 'the threat to social chaos' which menaced the late nineteenth-century desire for stability.[17] Disorder on the literary front was being instigated by the schools of realism and naturalism, and the prescribed remedy was invariably Sir Walter Scott. The frequency with which metaphors of health occur in this context, 'wholesome' becoming a superlative adjective, suggests that Victorian Canada did indeed regard literary realism as an infection of the social organism. In 1870 *The New Dominion Monthly* (Montreal) printed an article in which Harriet Beecher Stowe answered the question 'What shall the Girls Read?' with one word - '*Ivanhoe.*'[18] The following year in *Stewart's Literary Quarterly* (Saint John) Andrew Archer praised Scott's novels for 'their natural air and healthy tone.'[19] Ten years later Goldwin Smith invoked the standard of 'the high-minded Scott'[20] to condemn Disraeli's *Endymion*. And in *The Canadian Magazine* and *The Week*, the two leading Toronto periodicals of the last decades of the century, the exalted name of Scott appeared whenever commentators encountered literature transgressing their standards of good taste. Conan Doyle was hailed as 'the modern Sir Walter Scott' and Edmund Gosse was advised to 'give no heed to the new school which philosophizes instead of narrating, and to go and sit at the feet of Walter Scott who will teach him the good and the right way.'[21] If Canadians of the last century had not been given Sir Walter Scott they would have had to invent him, as indeed they did.

What precisely were the qualities that Victorian Canada projected onto Scott and then sought to find reflected in its own reading and writing? The answer begins with the literary ramifications of the cultural nationalism which was described in the opening chapters of this book.

The decade of Confederation saw the publication of the first of Francis Parkman's books on the history of New France and the first of James LeMoine's series of *Maple Leaves*; thus content for national historical fiction became available coincidentally with the rise of political nationalism. By calling for a Walter Scott for Canada, the country's cultural leaders acknowledged and sought to exploit the political power of popular fiction, a power recently exemplified by the role of *Uncle Tom's Cabin* in assisting the abolitionist movement in the United States. The threat of cultural and political absorption by the United States further consolidated the appeal of Scott, a representative of the nation from which approximately one-quarter of English-speaking Canadians claimed descent, to those desiring to strengthen Canada's emotional ties to the British Empire.

An examination of the literary aspects of Scott's Canadian popularity must acknowledge the obvious similarities between Scotland and New

France as sources of literary material. Both nations, having suffered defeat at the hands of the English, had ceased to present a political threat. English-Canadian writers were quick to find in French Canada a New World counterpart to the folklore, history, and local colour of Scott's fiction, which they could develop with a mixture of condescension and nostalgia, as will be seen in Chapter 8. Deeper insight into the way Scott could be used to reinforce the prevailing values of Victorian Canada has been conveniently and appropriately provided by Goldwin Smith, the eminent cultural and political critic whose economic liberalism was balanced by his literary conservatism.[22]

In 1871, shortly after his arrival in Canada, Smith contributed to the Toronto celebration of the Scott centenary an address titled 'The Lamps of Fiction.'[23] Adapting his title from Ruskin's *Seven Lamps of Architecture*, Smith enunciated seven principles to guide the novelist who wished – and ought – to pursue the tradition of Walter Scott, whose 'heart, brave, pure and true, is a law unto itself.' Although a newcomer to Canada at this time, Smith was sufficiently in tune with the country's literary sensibility to crystallize the attitudes which had dominated the writing and reception of fiction in Canada for the previous fifty years and would persist for close to another half century.

Smith's seven lamps were Reality, Ideality, Impartiality, Impersonality, Purity, Humanity, and Chivalry – a list that blends features of Scott's writing with qualities of his personality. Analysis of these abstractions discloses the structure of conservative beliefs which bound the geographically disconnected regions of Victorian Canada into a coherent cultural community.

Of the seven, Purity and Impersonality most obviously define themselves. By Impersonality Smith meant that novelists should refrain from debasing their work 'by obtruding their personal vanities, favouritisms, fanaticisms, and antipathies.' According to Smith, Scott's 'high and gallant nature' could never 'use art as a cover for striking a foul blow.' Purity Smith defined simply as sexual morality. He commended Scott for having rescued the English novel from 'the impurity, half-redeemed, of Fielding, the unredeemed impurity of Smollett, the lecherous leer of Sterne, the coarseness even of Defoe.' Unlike French writers, who have made 'the divine art of Fiction "procuress to the Lords of Hell",' Scott demonstrated 'the manly purity of one who had seen the world, mingled with men of the world, known evil as well as good; but who, being a true gentleman, abhorred filth, and teaches us to abhor it too.'

Smith's privileging of Reality as the first lamp kindled by Scott echoed the literary views of his British contemporaries enamoured of Scott's innovations in realism.[24] Scott's success in the 'perilous' genre of the historical romance where according to Smith 'the fiction is apt to spoil the fact, and the fact the fiction,' was directly attributable to his practice of substantiating his characters and plots with regional dialects, frequent footnotes, and historical details. These all contributing to the Reality that Goldwin Smith defined as 'a faithful study of human nature,' distinctly echoing Scott's own pronouncements in the first chapter of *Waverley*: 'The human nature which he paints, he had seen in all its phases, gentle and simple, in burgher and shepherd, Highlander, Lowlander, Borderer and Isleman; he had come into close contact with it; he had opened it to himself by the talisman of his joyous and winning presence: he had studied it thoroughly with a clear eye and an all-embracing heart. And when his scenes are laid in the past, he has honestly studied the history.'

The significance of Scott's type of realism in valorizing the novel as a literary genre in colonial Canada can be seen in the frequency with which early critics drew a clear distinction between unacceptable sentimental romance and acceptable Scott-inspired fiction.[25] Up to about 1860 Canadian writers and reviewers generally remembered that Scott's great contribution to the English novel had been to make romance believable[26] and commended his addition of 'realism' (meaning credibility) to the earlier traditions of romance. For example, in 1832 *The Halifax Monthly Magazine* applauded James Fenimore Cooper as 'the American Scott' for presenting 'Romance and Realism married together! – the most rare, as well as the most exciting and piquant of all literary unions.'[27]

By the era of Confederation, Canadian literature was in the hands of a generation who had been raised on Scott and who therefore assumed that one of the requirements of the romantic novel was sufficient substantiating detail to assure the reader of the narrative's plausibility. The simple requirement that fiction be marginally credible had entered Canadian criticism from the beginning, in the reviews of Julia Catherine Beckwith Hart's *St Ursula's Convent*, the first novel by a native Canadian. But by the 1860s the influence of Scott's romances had permeated Canadian cultural consciousness to the point where Canadians defined the novel as prose romance and, like their American counterparts, employed the terms 'novel' and 'romance' interchangeably.[28] This lack of formal or thematic distinction underscores their expectation that all prose fiction conform to the pattern of Scott-inspired romance.

Some dissent was not uncommon, however. Two mid-century periodicals, *The Anglo-American Magazine* and *Stewart's Literary Quarterly*, occasionally argued in favour of fiction that was not only believable but probable. Unlike Sara Jeannette Duncan, they preferred realism less from their interest in the literary vanguard than from their retroversion to eighteenth-century rationalism. In *The Anglo-American*'s 'Editor's Shanty' column, realism was frequently weighed against Defoe. *Uncle Tom's Cabin*, for example, received high praise because Stowe's 'style is at once correct and familiar, and the narrative possesses all that truthful matter-of-fact like air, which was the leading characteristic of old Daniel DeFoe. Indeed, it is difficult for the reader to persuade himself that he is perusing a fiction, and not a *bona fide* relation of events that really occurred.'[29] In later columns Thackeray was favourably compared with Addison and Fielding as an illustrator of society, and now forgotten novels were lauded if they were found to resemble the work of William Godwin and Jane Austen.[30]

In 1870–1 *Stewart's* supported a similar outlook when it published Professor Lyall's articles on the history of English literature. In an era of encroaching gentility, when Fielding's 'coarseness' aroused considerable discomfort,[31] Lyall presented a rational appreciation of eighteenth-century fiction, praising *Tom Jones* for its 'closeness to nature' and for 'the naturalness of the plot – the ease and simplicity with which incident after incident arises out of the narrative and the perfect *vraisemblance* therefore of the whole production.'[32] Not surprisingly, editor George Stewart identified himself as an early admirer of Howells. In *Evenings in the Library* (1878) Stewart observed of *A Chance Acquaintance* that 'the total absence of plot and its concomitants shows how skillful an artist Howells is. He has no heroes or heroines, his characters are individuals who seem to exist in real life.'[33]

On the whole, the consistency of *The Anglo-American Magazine* and *Stewart's* preference for literary realism was exceptional. Discussions of realism in other periodicals often opened with statements in favour of 'truth to nature' which were then qualified by the essential romanticism of the writer's outlook. Typical was Miss Foster's lengthy 1843 review of Frederika Bremer's *The Neighbours*, which declared the book so realistic that 'Fiction indeed seems an inappropriate name for what bears upon almost every page the stamp of truth and nature.' Yet the next sentence, containing the phrase 'romance of real life,' reveals that Foster valued not Bremer's verisimilitude but her ability to add romantic qualities to daily experience.[34] Hence Bremer was found to have fulfilled the dictum pronounced by *Belford's* more than thirty years later that 'To surround familiar scenes, domestic incidents, and everyday pursuits with the halo of romance is the task which the average novelist of the period sets before him.'[35]

The glow cast by the lamp of Reality thus merges with that effusing from the lamp of Ideality. Victorian Canadians wanted their recreational reading unmarred by the grittier realities of sexuality, marital discord, labour unrest, social injustice, unrepentant criminals, and common depravity. While they often asked for real life they desired an illusion: life as it should be, not life as it was. When Goldwin Smith named Reality as the first of the seven lamps of fiction kindled by Scott he did not intend to separate it from the four remaining lamps which illuminate the realm of literary romance: Ideality, Impartiality, Humanity, and Chivalry.

Smith separated into four categories qualities which Victorian Canadians usually combined under the single heading of idealism. This idealism comprised two distinct but related components revealed in two rather different connotations of the word, one current through most of the century, the other belonging primarily to its last two decades. The earlier meaning - and the one used by Smith – refers to 'ideal' in the sense of 'universal' and derives from the aesthetic theory that the appeal of art lies in its ability to tap the shared universals of human experience. Goldwin Smith's description of this quality (as he found it in Scott) opens with a prescient rejection of the photography metaphor which would be associated with the realism of Howells in the next decade:

The artist is not a photographer, but a painter. He must depict not persons but humanity, otherwise he forfeits the artist's name, and the power of doing the artist's work in our hearts ... Of course, this power of idealization is the great gift of genius. It is that which distinguishes Homer, Shakespeare and Walter Scott from ordinary men. But there is also a moral effect in rising above the easy work of mere description to the height of art ... Scott's characters are never monsters or caricatures. They are full of nature, but it is universal nature. Therefore they have their place in the universal heart, and will keep that place forever.

To the above definition of Ideality Smith added Impartiality, meaning objectivity. To portray universal humanity the novelist must follow the sublime examples of Shakespeare and Scott, presenting each character detachedly with sympathy and justice. The result is a depiction of the moral structure governing human affairs, for the genuine literary artist 'never fails to bring out the true issues of virtue, or of vice, because he searched the depths of the human heart.'[36]

The duty of the novelist to represent moral law in action, using Scott and Shakespeare as his paradigms, was upheld with increasing vigour in Canada in the last decades of the nineteenth century. In reaction against the picture of human nature drawn by Social Darwinists and naturalistic novelists, the term 'idealism' now received a new connotation, signifying a concern with only the more noble aspects of social behaviour and including a vision of human perfectibility fulfilling the tenets of conventional Christianity. Louisa Murray illustrated this position in 1889 when she claimed that France was perverted by 'a literature in which the worst vices, diseases and deformities of debased humanity are employed in the services of a degraded art, of which M. Emile Zola is the great high priest.' As examples of true artistry she cited Eliot, Dickens, and Scott (the latter receiving more column space than the other two combined) as 'great spirits and fine artists' whose writings 'strongly impress us with the truth that beauty and virtue are more real and permanent parts of nature and life than vice and ugliness, and for this reason they will always have the finest uses for humanity, being good for hope, for healing, and for the strengthening and ennobling of men and women.'[37]

George Eliot presented a particularly interesting problem to critics waving the Scott standard.[38] In the 1870s she was frequently commended as a writer who upheld idealism in both senses of the word. Thus in a review repeating Smith's metaphoric comparison of photography and painting, *The Canadian Monthly* found *Far from the Madding Crowd* deficient because Hardy's portrayal of Gabriel Oak lacked Eliot's idealism:

[H]e is a noble fellow, who should have been spared the humiliation of being made a servant to such a man as Troy. Many readers will feel too that he loses some dignity in becoming a mere patient drudge, even though it be of the heroine. The total absence of the ideal element is indeed the main defect of the book as a work of art. This is a mistake that George Eliot never makes. No matter how realistic a novel of hers may be, she always retains enough of the ideal element to prevent it degenerating into a mere photograph, instead of a painting.[39]

Although the *Monthly* employed Eliot as a literary yardstick, it was not perfectly satisfied with her idealism, using the word in its second sense. At times it suspected her of pessimism and in its review of *Middlemarch* feared that her rejection of conventional Christianity left her with a 'cheerless creed' in which darkness, struggle, and a melancholy undertone nearly overwhelmed 'the stretching forth of longing arms to welcoming the dawning of the coming day.'[40] Similar discomfort with Eliot was expressed in *Belford's* judgment that *Daniel Deronda* was 'the greatest of all works of fiction' yet 'chilling and startling in its calm, cold philosophy of will, and consequence, and apparent human government.'[41] Eliot was therefore not a suitable model for Canadian authors – especially women – as Maud Pettit demonstrates in *Beth Woodburn* (1897). Beth's sense of identification with Eliot is chastized by her future husband, who regards her writing as 'too gloomy' and Eliot as dangerous for not being 'a consecrated woman.' Beth eventually sees the light, burns her manuscript, and becomes a famous evangelical novelist.[42]

Eliot's challenge to the acceptable limits of conventional Christianity deeply troubled Victorian Canada. One of the most fundamental assumptions shared by the nineteenth-century Canadian cultural community was that fiction must uphold standard Christian belief and that 'Idealism' ultimately referred to Christian principles. The primacy of religion in the country's literary and cultural affairs is abundantly evident in its periodicals, as in *The Canadian Monthly*'s position that 'In attempting to take a general view of contemporary literature, we naturally give precedence to work bearing on the subject of religion.'[43] That the religious controversies which raged during the nineteenth century served largely to consolidate Canada's religious conservatism was reflected in its response to fiction. In 1876 *The Canadian Monthly* extravagantly praised Mrs Charlesworth's *Oliver of the Mill* as a novel without 'speculation or reference to speculation' which shows 'the relation to human needs, cravings and aspirations, of those great central truths which Christianity has most fully brought to light.'[44] The effect of fiction imbued with Christian optimism, as *Stewart's* remarked of Mrs Ross's *The Wreck of the White Bear* (1870), is that 'One feels better pleased with mankind and the world and all that in it is, when the perusal of this work is complete.'[45] In this frame of mind *The Canadian Magazine* welcomed Marie Corelli's *The Mighty Atom* as 'a mighty protest against a purely scientific world, a world without faith, without the comfort of a Personal and Omniscent God.'[46]

In *The Week*, literary idealism was equated with the advancement of human dignity and spiritual values. *Marius the Epicurean* was commended for being 'pregnant with noble thoughts' while George Gissing's *In the Year of the Jubilee* was denounced for its cast of 'mostly half educated people, frivolous, mean and sordid, without a single high or elevated idea among them.'[47] Agnes Maule Machar attacked Grant Allen (a fellow native of Kingston related to her by marriage) as a Darwinist and Spencerian whose novels advocated a philosophy 'that, while it illuminates certain fields of knowledge, does not recognize its own limitations, and overlooks the deepest facts of human consciousness, with the inevitable penalty of falling short of the profoundest truth, and of robbing our human life of its true spiritual glory; and ignoring those strongest forces which have inspired humanity to its noblest victories in the past as they alone can do in the future.'[48] The same outlook was supported by *The Canadian Magazine* when it published a defence of idealism in fiction by author Stuart Livingston (who had himself contributed to the genre with a curious allegorical tale, *The History of Professor Paul* [1889]): 'Now, the idealist with all the enthusiasm of optimism, scrutinizes the events of life with an eye of faith and, believing that the good is not always borne down by the evil, he tries to raise and strengthen his fellows by bringing into their lives the glory of this hope. To do this he does not rest with depicting life as it is but strives to create it as it should be.'[49]

What Victorian Canada defined as idealism Goldwin Smith discussed as his last two lamps of fiction, Humanity and Chivalry. Humanity meant the rejection of Zolaesque coarseness and of sensationalism. Walter Scott 'knew that a novelist had no right even to introduce the terrible except for the purpose of exhibiting human heroism, developing character, awakening emotions which when awakened dignify and save from harm.' And Chivalry meant maintaining 'the ideal of a gentleman' by which the writer would never 'lower the standard of character or the aim of life.'

Throughout the nineteenth century, then, most Canadian writers and commentators shared the assumption that the appropriate model for Canadian fiction was the romantic novel derived from Scott and distinguished by the admirable qualities they found in his work. They could thus follow one of the main currents of popular British fiction while fostering an individual Canadian identity. Canadian fiction was expected to be informative, harmless, morally elevating, nationalistic, idealistic, and to contain entertaining and believable characters and events. Canadian life was to be presented in a favourable light and history was a favourite subject. Above all, Canadian writers were to eschew dime novel sensationalism. Despite the efforts of Sara Jeannette Duncan to instil a taste for the decorous social realism of Howells and James, the quest for a Canadian Scott would continue to preoccupy the mainstream of local literary commentary.

As a result there occurred occasional conflict between a reviewer's literary nationalism and his distaste for certain aspects of a particular Canadian writer's work. *The Literary Garland* suffered the dilemma of wanting to promote John Richardson as a Canadian writer for patriotic reasons while disapproving of his sensationalism. In 1839 its editor campaigned vigorously for the republication of *Wacousta* while qualifying his praise because 'we look upon the interest of the tale as too painfully intense, the reader being irresistibly borne on with the author, without a moment's breathing time in which the mind is relieved from its anxiety respecting the fate of the characters of the drama.' The appearance of *The Canadian Brothers* (1840) again elicited regret that 'to our judgment the gallant Major indulges somewhat too freely in the mysterious.'[50]

Misrepresentation of the ideals of Canadian life and lack of optimism were the most reprehensible violations of the Scott standard that Canadian authors could commit. That pessimism of any sort would not be tolerated was announced as early as 1827 when the editor of *The Acadian Magazine* simply refused to accept the unhappy ending of a tale submitted to him, and in his public letter to the author rewrote the story to suit his own conception of fictional convention.[51] The opening editorial address of *The Provincial* announced that 'cheerfulness' would be one of its qualities (just as *Saturday Night* was later to promise 'To be good-natured'),[52] and it anticipated the principles Goldwin Smith would find in Scott when it condemned William McKinnon's *St George; or The Canadian League* (1852) for 'violating the honour of humanity.'[53] More agreeable to prevailing taste was Frances Brooke's *The History of Emily Montague* (1769) where 'everything concerning Canada bears ... a *couleur de rose* tint.'[54]

Lack of such 'couleur de rose' idealism in Mrs Huddleston's *Bluebell* (1875) incensed *The Canadian Monthly*. This novel recounts the flirtations and social frivolities of British officers and Canadian girls in Toronto, Bluebell turning out to be a Canadian Becky Sharp whose first concern is always her own success. Becky Sharp may have been admissible in England (and Thackeray was widely admired in Canada), but *The Monthly* was appalled to find her transferred to Canadian soil:

[W]e feel sure that all those who look upon the purity of our domestic life, and the fair fame of our countrywomen, as objects to be conserved and held sacred from the dishonour of being lightly spoken of, will join us in deprecating the picture of society represented in 'Bluebell,' as typical of Canadian households; and in resenting so gross an offence against good taste, good feeling, and hospitality, as the authoress has in the work before us been guilty of ... [T]he book is so eminently offensive that ... [w]e should have to go back to the period of Smollett to find its match. The style is slip-shod and objectionable; and the tone vulgar and mischievous. But it is as a study of so-called Canadian society that we most object to it. We should blush for our countrywomen were the novel accepted as evidence of their manners or their bearing.[55]

The attitude that commended Mrs Dobbin's *Thos.* (1878) for its 'hopefulness and courage'[56] still flourished some forty years later when the Vancouver *Westminster Review* praised L.M. Montgomery's *Anne's House of Dreams* for being 'clean and wholesome' and 'idealizing common people and glorifying the ordinary life.'[57] One of the most vocal late upholders of the Scott tradition was the enduring *Canadian Magazine* (1893–1939), which early announced its preference for 'light and wholesome' nationalistic literature and in 1894 was continuing the search for the Canadian Walter Scott.[58] Through its first decades it praised books dwelling on 'the sunny side and the foibles of human nature' and frequently rose to the 'defence of idealism against realism [with which] wholesome story writers will concur.'[59] On the eve of the twentieth century, its editor was pleased to report the following incident:

Six men of education and culture were taking dinner in a private room in a city restaurant. The conversation turned on to the current novel and its value. Finally, some one suggested that each person write the names of his five favourite English authors on a slip of paper and hand it to one of the men for examination. The Bible and Shakespeare were barred. When the result was summed up the vote stood as follows: Scott, 4 votes; Carlyle, Dickens and Kipling, 3 each; Macaulay, Parkman, Thackeray and Ruskin, 2 each; Eliot, Pope, Leckie, Stevenson, Browning, Tennyson, Goldsmith and Arnold one each.[60]

To the above, Robert Barr retorted that the Canadian Walter Scott would probably starve because Canada was 'about the poorest book market in the world outside of Senegambia,' but he still assented to the assumption that Canada 'should produce the great historical novelist; the Sir Walter Scott of the New World.'[61]

If Scott-inspired romance was to be the preferred form for Canadian fiction, what should be its contents? History, obviously, and that is the focus of two subsequent chapters. But the first problem was how to adapt an Old World form to New World experience and shape disparate elements into coherent plots that bore some relation both to the inherited conventions of the novel and the raw new terrain to which it had been transplanted.

6 The Challenge of Form

Julia Catherine Beckwith Hart's *St Ursula's Convent, or The Nun of Canada* (1824), acclaimed as 'the first native novel that ever appeared in Canada,'[1] provides an appropriate starting point for discussion of the way several early Canadian writers met the challenge of novelistic form. A naive text composed when the author was only seventeen, this book conveniently epitomizes some of the problems tackled by Canadian creators of prose fiction throughout the nineteenth century. In her mission to awaken British North America from its 'long night of ignorance and inaction' to 'a dawn of literary illumination'[2] Hart produced a narrative which, according to *The Canadian Magazine and Literary Repository*, better deserved the title 'The Quintessence of Novels and Romances.' Viewing the novel as primarily a construct of plot, Hart self-consciously filled her two small volumes with as many conventions as she could muster from the vocabulary of popular romance. The latter journal was quick to discern the resulting overcompensation:

We cannot attempt an account of the story of the convent of St Ursula. There are so many plots and underplots in this tale that it would require an explanation equal in size to the work itself, to convey an accurate account of them. The incidents come so thick upon us; nay, they are thrown in duplicates, for we find *two* children exchanged, *two* storms at sea, *two* deceiving old (I beg the ladies pardon) young nurses; a lady who, thinking she has lost all her family, retires to a convent, emerges again from its gloom, and returns to her husband and children; some scenes of high life in England, badly described it is true; a vicious old friar's deathbed confession of his intrigues; the narrow escape of a young lady from a marriage with her own brother; and finally, the whole is wound up with three or four marriages, we forget which.[3]

The breathless pace of Hart's narrative allows little opportunity to develop character or setting. Her main characters, all from upper-class French or British families, spend a limited if complicated time in Canada straightening out their true identities and finally retire to the luxury of Old World estates. Quebec provides a tinge of indigenous romance with its contented *habitants* and a conniving Jesuit. For Hart as for most subsequent Canadian writers, the novel was a European literary artifact. The way to write a Canadian novel was to find or invent Canadian equivalents for European romantic conventions – in Hart's case Quebec's Catholicism could furnish a convent and a treacherous priest – or to import European characters and situations and simply impose them on the Canadian landscape.

Romantic novelists like Hart, for whom story overrides social pertinence, directly challenge the assumption of modernist criticism that realism is the preferred mode for fiction and romance merely an aberration or debasement. In *The Secular Scripture*, Northrop Frye deconstructs the romance/realism paradigm to argue instead that the baseline of fictional narrative is drawn by the formulas of romance and that the novel is not a new norm but 'a realistic displacement of romance.'[4] Given the stability of romance in terms of its enduring formulaic structures as well as its continuing broad appeal, it is hardly surprising that writers who were themselves displaced on the outskirts of English-language literary culture should implicitly align themselves with the mainstream of popular romantic convention. Yet they also wanted to accommodate the New World to the narrative formulas of the Old and not to antagonize the growing prestige of realism – in other words, to perform the almost impossible trick of meeting the overlapping and frequently conflicting demands for realism, nationalism, and romance. The work of John Richardson, English Canada's first self-proclaimed national novelist, aptly illustrates the problem.

A more professional and prolific writer than Hart and also more conscious of the conventions and demands of fictional forms, Richardson presented his work in relation to that of James Fenimore Cooper, whose audience he strove to capture. Richardson frequently reiterated his admiration for 'the first among American authors'[5] and in *Hardscrabble* (1851) he claimed to have modelled Mr Heywood's background on that of Cooper's Leatherstocking.[6] In his introduction to the Americanized 1851 edition of *Wacousta* Richardson classed himself with Cooper and boasted that he had scooped 'that first of vigorous American Novelists'[7] by grabbing the tale of the Pontiac conspiracy for himself. The extent to which Cooper's writing coloured Richardson's perception of North America is intimated by the latter's account of a visit to the Alleganies, where

there was a wild and romantic character about the scenery that forcibly impressed the imagination. The various descriptions of the pine, the cypress, and the hemlock, wore, amid the snows that fringed their boughs as with trellis work, an appearance of loneliness and sternness, leading one to expect, at every moment, the appearance of some savage beast of prey ... Never were the characters in Cooper's 'Leather Stocking' and the 'Pathfinder' more vividly brought before my recollection.[8]

Popularly hailed as the American Walter Scott, Cooper included among his accomplishments the identification and development of indigenous North American material suitable for literary romance. In his prefaces he evolved a coherent theory of romance as the appropriate mode for American fiction[9] and in his novels he created the romance of the American frontier. Unlike Cooper, however, Richardson did not utterly commit himself to the genre of romance; rather, he may be viewed as the first major exemplar of the dilemma of the nineteenth-century Canadian novelist: attempting to mediate between the early American engagement with romance and the waxing British practice of realism, he compromised with an uneasy hybrid. While Richardson's plot devices, characters, and language all contribute to the romantic flavour of his work, he frequently interjected authorial assertions that his fiction was 'founded on fact.' Although this cliché was easily tossed off by nineteenth-century authors of all nationalities, frequently without sincerity and often with deliberate irony, Richardson appears to have penned it in earnest.

Richardson's juggling of romance and factuality began with *Ecarté* (1829), which is set in Europe but manifests many of the formal characteristics of his later, Canadian fiction. Echoing Scott's disclaimer of romance in the opening chapter of *Waverley*, Richardson commences his first novel with a similar declaration: 'Our hero, though kind hearted and generous, was not a hero of romance.'[10] This repudiation, in Frye's words, marks 'the absorption of realistic displacement into romance itself,'[11] a signal of the ascendancy of romance which is often misread as its surrender to realism.

Richardson's convincing sketches of gambling dens, Paris slums, and French prisons persuaded his British reviewers, favourable and unfavourable alike,[12] that the book documented iniquities of real life. At the same time, these moments of verisimilitude are framed by an elaborate plot which ranges from Kentucky to India and includes duels, jealous lovers, libertine aristocrats, and misused maidens. In *Ecarté* Richardson established the structural pattern that was to shape his Canadian fiction: to fit the material he knew to his conception of the romantic novel he strung sections of detailed realistic description along a narrative thread knitted from the ritualized plots and stereotyped characters of popular romance.

The uneasiness of Richardson's combination of real life and romantic convention appears quite strikingly in his language, particularly his juxtaposition of colloquial speech with the loftiest romantic oratory. In *Ecarté* the vernacular dialogue of the gambling scenes contrasts sharply with the formal, heavily adjectival rhetoric of the lovers and heroic characters, who produce improbable utterances like 'The quick motion of my horse against a pure and refreshing air, perfumed by the various odiferous plants and flowers which grew in wild luxuriance around, enlivened my spirits, and gave energy to my feelings.'[13] While liveliness and energy may be the subjects of this sentence, these qualities are subverted by the weight of its polysyllabic diction and complex syntax. In *Wau-Nan-Gee*, one of Richardson's last novels, Captain Headly speaks ordinary English while his wife expresses herself only in the formalized inverted sentences and rhetorical constructions of romance. Their conversations can be rather incongruous as, for example, when Mrs Headley informs her husband that within the camp of the Pottowatomies there lurks an untrustworthy Indian. Headley, the plain-speaking soldier, asks, 'What purpose, what motive can he have?' His wife replies, 'The purpose and motive those which often make the gentle tigers, the timid daring, the irresolute confirmed of will – Love.' Headley then demands, 'Love! What love? whose love? and what has that to do with the fidelity of the Pottowatomies?' To which Mrs Headley eloquently responds, 'The love of Wau-Nan-Gee, the once gentle and modest son of Winnebeg, who, scarce three months since, could not gaze into a white woman's eyes without melting softness beaming from his own, and the rich, ripe peach-blush crimsoning his dark cheek.'[14]

These different rhetorical styles derive in part from their author's desire to match voice to social rank and narrative role, the commoners speaking plainly and the heroes and heroines in purple prose. As well, they arise from a basic conflict between Richardson's own historical and experiential knowledge and his sense of the formality of fiction. In spite of his desire to achieve fame as a novelist, Richardson (like many other

Canadian writers of his century) showed more talent for autobiography and chronicle than for fictitious plots and characters, and much of his most vigorous and convincing writing appears in his descriptive non-fiction. In documentary works like *The War of 1812* (1842), *Eight Years in Canada* (1847), and 'The Story of a Trip to Walpole Island and Port Sarnia' (1849),[15] he expressed his concern for historical fidelity. Upon his return to Amherstburg he accidentally discovered his own brother's grave, an anecdote he recounts 'chiefly with a view to show how truly it has been related that the romance of real life is often more stirring than that of fiction.'[16]

When Richardson turned to fiction he frequently wrote out of his own experience, presenting scenes, battles, incidents, and large historical occasions at which he or people he knew had been present and whose depiction was therefore in his view 'founded on fact.' In *Hardscrabble*, he made fidelity to history the excuse for comic relief at a moment of high tension, declaring, 'Nothing can, we conceive, be in worst taste in a fictitious narrative, than the wanton introduction of the ludicrous upon the solemn, but when in an historical tale these extremes do occur fidelity forbids the suppression of the one, lest it should mar the effect of the other.'[17] His introduction to *The Canadian Brothers* stresses his respect for history, for 'although works of fiction are not usually dedicated to the Sovereign, an exception was made in favour of the following tale, which is now for the first time submitted to the public, and which, from its historical character, was deemed of sufficient importance not to be confused with mere works of fiction.'[18]

Richardson's last books, the fruits of desperation and poverty, were written directly for the American sensation market after he had relinquished his goal of achieving recognition as a Canadian novelist. It was in his two most overtly Canadian novels, *Wacousta* and *The Canadian Brothers*, that he continued the quest timidly initiated by Hart: to do for Canada what Scott had done for Scotland and Cooper for America by valorizing his country as a location for fiction and founding a national literary identity. As Richardson frequently reminded the Canadian public, during his time he was indeed 'the first and only writer of historical fiction the country has yet produced.'[19]

Whatever the circumstances of its composition, the introduction to the 1851 edition of *Wacousta* contributes significantly to our understanding of Richardson's conception of the novel. Here Richardson presents the historical background to the Pontiac conspiracy in distinctly personal terms, describing the experiences of his maternal grandparents. For

Richardson, historical importance arose from the intersection of personal history with national history; *Wacousta* was initially inspired by his grandmother, who 'used to enchain my young interest by detailing various facts connected with the siege she so well remembered, and infused into me a longing to grow up to manhood that I might write a book about it.' In Richardson's view his grandmother's tales were indeed 'facts,' for he considered history itself to be objective and verifiable. Hence his concern in this introduction with justifying 'Two objections [which] have been urged against Wacousta as a consistent tale – the one involving an improbability, the other a geographical error.' The improbability is Wacousta's ability to escape from the fort by climbing the flagpole with Clara in his arms; the geographical error concerns the narrowness of the St Clair River.

Richardson's anxiety about these two relatively minor components of a romance composed almost entirely of improbabilities may strike the modern reader as incongruous. Although his plot takes great liberties with the logic of real life, Richardson felt that only his tampering with geography required the excuse of 'the license usually accorded to a writer of fiction, in order to give greater effect.' In this regard he was implementing a consistent if limited theory of fiction. When he declared that 'The story is founded solely on the artifice of Ponteac to possess himself of those last two British forts. All else is imaginary,'[20] he posited a clear distinction between history and imagination. Only alterations connected with the historical reality of 'the artifice of Ponteac' required justification; for the rest, licence was simply assumed to be the author's right.

Within the text of *Wacousta* Richardson adds to this initial distinction between historical reality and imagination a further distinction between emotional reality and imagination. After Wacousta has captured Clara and Madeline de Haldimar and Sir Everard Valletort, he discovers that Ellen Halloway, whom he had abducted, has been the wife of two Reginald Mortons – himself and his nephew. Richardson plots this coincidence, which forms part of the 'imaginary' action, without authorial comment. But as soon as attention turns to the love affair of Clara and Sir Everard, the author insists, 'ours is a tale of sad reality ... Within the bounds of probability have we, therefore, confined ourselves'(440). True to the tradition of the novel of sensibility, improbability of plot is perfectly acceptable so long as conventional probabilities of the heart are properly respected.

The narrative structure of *Wacousta* reflects some of the problems its author encountered in transplanting an Old World literary form to 'a ground hitherto untouched by the wand of the modern novelist'(3). The book opens in the besieged garrison of Detroit where the sudden appearance of a mysterious stranger has intensified existing tensions between the English and the Indians. At first the plot appears to grow from a uniquely North American situation, the historical event of Pontiac's resistance to the British. But the ultimate identification of the visitor (haunting the stockade like the ghost of Hamlet's father) as Reginald Morton, alias Wacousta, demonstrates that local history forms only the skeleton of Richardson's novel which he fleshes out with a romantic narrative motivated entirely by rivalries transplanted from Europe. Tracing the historical roots of the plot of Wacousta reveals the line of literary descent that Richardson followed when he decided to transform history into fiction.

The immediate present is the autumn of 1763. The historical past quickly intrudes when Frank Halloway, on trial for treason, refers to 1759 when he had saved Frederick De Haldimar's life on the Plains of Abraham. While serving with Wolfe, Frederick had been attacked by a gigantic French officer, actually Wacousta in disguise. The connections between Wacousta and De Haldimar which produce the dramatic abductions and confrontations of the present plot extend northeastward from Detroit through Quebec to Britain and back in time to the Jacobite rebellions of the 1740s, when both men were English officers stationed in Scotland. For his 'imaginary' material Richardson looked not just to England by making both Reginald Mortons Cornishmen, but to Scotland, where the Jacobite troubles mustered the ill-fated trio of Morton, De Haldimar, and Clara Beverley. Behind Clara lies even more Scottish history: her misanthropic father, 'of English name, but Scottish connections' (462), had retreated to his Highland wilderness Eden after losing his fortune and his wife due to his participation in the Rebellion of 1715. Richardson's recourse to Scotland for the primary impetus of a novel about the Pontiac conspiracy demonstrates that in 1832 even a native-born Canadian found it impossible to divorce the romantic novel from its connection with Sir Walter Scott.[21]

Although Richardson turned to Scott's territory for the historical background of Wacousta, his actual method of adapting Old World conventions to North America drew more heavily on the conventions of revenge tragedy and gothic and sentimental fiction[22] than on the historical novel as developed by Scott. Scott's characters are usually motivated by their political and class allegiances at particular eras of historical crisis. In Wacousta and The Canadian Brothers, however, Richardson's plots of curses and revenge risk losing sight of the historical issues at hand. While historical events provide a factual anchor as well as local colour and sensational effects, the politically based moral claims of the conflicting parties soon evaporate. This is especially evident in *The Canadian Brothers*, which does commence like a true historical novel. The scene is Amherstburg at the beginning of the War of 1812. The Indians under Tecumseh are gathering to join the British; within the British camp smoulder rivalries between British-born and Canadian-born soldiers. Americans, reliable as well as treacherous, dwell on both sides of the border. Some British deserters have joined the Americans and the British have just captured an American ship. All in all, Richardson assembles a rich array of potential conflicts arising directly out of national, political, and cultural circumstances, yet the war soon ceases to be the focus of attention. The novel transmutes instead into a revenge thriller as Matilda Montgomery, granddaughter of Ellen Halloway, tries to implement the curse laid by her grandmother upon the descendants of Colonel De Haldimar.

The Canadian Brothers continues the transformation of history into gothic romance initiated in *Wacousta*. Wacousta joined Pontiac's war party not out of sympathy with the cause of the Indians but to avenge himself on De Haldimar. As a pseudo-Indian he outdoes the natives in savagery, indicating how closely Richardson intuited the critique of colonialism later articulated as Conrad's *Heart of Darkness*. What Richardson actually achieves in *Wacousta* is less an historical novel about the Pontiac conspiracy than a tragic clash between good and evil in the chaotic New World wilderness, where the ostensible villain later earns our sympathy while his apparently upright opponent is revealed to have a less than virtuous past.

To achieve this archetypal impact Richardson draws on the popular traditions of the literature of emotion: gothic terror and sentimental sympathy. Both Charles De Haldimar and his sister Clara appear to have wandered into the North American forest directly out of a European novel of sensibility. Charles, very much a Man of Feeling, speaks in 'accents of almost feminine sweetness' (25) and has a ready tear for all touching occasions. Throughout *Wacousta* 'the young, the generous, the feeling Charles de Haldimar' (37) enacts the stereotype of the eighteenth-century sentimental hero, from his fainting fit and tears when it appears that his brother has been killed to his own murder by Wacousta, who captures his victim because the latter is too 'overcome by his emotion' (504) to flee. In accordance with the practice of sentimental fiction, the narrative relentlessly analyses the finer emotions of Charles, his close friend Valletort, and his sister Clara. Even more sensitive and delicate than her brother, Clara faints as frequently and conveniently as her namesake, Samuel Richardson's Clarissa. As the innocent virgin pursued by the malevolent Wacousta – whose feelings also received detailed scrutiny when he is transmuted to a rather sympathetic Byronic hero redressing his wrongs – Clara links Richardson's use of the sentimental literary tradition with his adaptation of European gothicism.

Unlike the majority of nineteenth-century English-Canadian writers interested in gothic effects, Richardson did not avail himself of the Roman Catholicism, crumbling châteaux, and demonic folklore of Quebec. Instead he inverted some of the conventions of European gothicism to accommodate the devices of prophecy and portent, mysterious coincidences, concealed identities, and virtue in distress to North America. He transformed the locale of confinement, rape, and horror from the convent or castle to the labyrinthine wilderness so that for his displaced Europeans 'The forest, in a word, formed, as it were, the gloomy and impenetrable walls of the prison-house' (286). Instead of safety occurring in escape from man-made edifices into the outer social or natural world, the only refuge from the terrors of Richardson's wilderness lies within the garrison. Richardson reverses the claustrophobia which animates most European gothicism to a fear of unknown, uncivilized space. Within the 'dark, dense forest' (286) Indians, the 'cunning and midnight enemy' (19) replace mad monks and dissolute aristocrats as the personification of danger and persecution.[23] In the New World, moreover, virtue is less assured of victory than it was in the Old. Wacousta successfully and brutally destroys Clara and Charles De Haldimar, the two characters most redolent of the Old World cult of sensibility, precisely because their fragility unfits them for the New, just as the genre they represent is unsuited to the American continent and is itself deconstructed in Wacousta.

Richardson's gothic inclination generated a third stylistic feature of his work. In addition to lofty romantic rhetoric and straightforward documentation, he frequently indulged a penchant for gory and pornographic sensationalism. Far removed from the gentility of Scott, Richardson's lurid touches recall the style of 'Monk' Lewis. From the scene in Ecarté when De Forsac tries to rape Adeline to the sensuous description of a bullet being removed from Mrs Headley's 'magnificent' arm in Wau-Nan-Gee, Richardson maintained a lusty interest in depicting violence and both natural and unnatural sexuality that climaxed in The Monk Knight of Saint John. In Wacousta details of blood and mutilation abound, most strikingly in the description of mad Ellen Halloway which unites fascination with 'reeking corpses' with a lascivious eye for the female form in an act of subtextual necrophilia:

Her long fair hair was wild and streaming – her feet, and legs, and arms were naked – and one solitary and scanty garment displayed rather than concealed the symmetry of her delicate person. She flew to the fatal bridge, threw herself on the body of her bleeding husband, and imprinting her warm kisses on his bloody lips, for a moment or two presented the image of one whose reason has fled forever. Suddenly she started from the earth; her face, her hands, and her garments so saturated with the blood of her husband that a feeling of horror crept through the veins of all who beheld her. (153).

The 1851 version of *Wacousta*, edited in the interest of gentility as well as brevity and American national sentiment, modifies much of the blasphemy and overt sexuality of the original. Also cut are the words which conclude the above scene, when Wacousta carries Ellen off pressing 'his lips to hers, yet red and moist with blood spots from the wounds of her husband' (154). One result of the demolition of the novel so carefully documented by Douglas Cronk[24] was to remove from *Wacousta* many of its links with the conventions of eighteenth-century sensibility and lurid gothicism. By gentrifying the original into a text closer to the wholesome Victorian romance of high adventure conforming to Smith's Lamps of Fiction, the American editors responsible for its corruption may have also inadvertently rendered Richardson more palatable to his Canadian readers.

John Richardson's formula for Canadian fiction was to base his novels upon actual historical events, thereby satisfying the need for Reality, and then graft on various elements from European literary traditions. For many writers the mere matter of length proved a complicating factor in the quest for appropriate forms for Canadian fiction. Stories in nineteenth-century periodicals show that a serious pitfall awaiting unskilled authors was the tendency of their plots to escape authorial control. Serialization often complicated the problem, as in the case of John George Bourinot's 'Marguerite, a Tale of Forest Life in the New Dominion,' which ran in *The New Dominion Monthly* for the first six months of 1870. Well versed in Canadian history and an experienced writer of non-fiction, Bourinot set out to dramatize the conflicts between the English, the French, and the Indians in Nova Scotia in 1757, his debt to Scott suggested by his selections from Scott's poetry as chapter headings. The story commences promisingly with a restrained narrative style which is then overtaken by the melodramatic intrigue. There ensues a web of chases involving a kidnapped girl who eventually returns to her family, her brother who pursues an Acadian spy who is also an Indian chief, and an English officer who is captured and recaptured by hostile Indians and rescued and re-rescued by a mysterious Indian maiden until he finally marries Marguerite, the nominal heroine of the piece. Not surprisingly, 'Marguerite' appears to have been Bourinot's only extended prose fiction; in his short stories,[25] which occasionally suggest the influence of Wilkie Collins, he confined himself to tighter plots and was able to draw on his knowledge of French Canada with greater aplomb.

The problems illustrated by Bourinot's infrequent ventures into fiction represent the general fate of nineteenth-century Canadian writers who attempted the big romance of high adventure. When they aimed for full-length narratives constructed from exotic Canadian material, their enthusiasm often overwhelmed their ability as they overcompensated for their colonial insecurity by cramming their pages with an astonishing array of romantic conventions. But when they restricted themselves to shorter fictional forms, frequently the mystery tale modelled on Poe, they concentrated instead on credibility, making a Canadian town or rural setting the scene of a single unified action. Stories such as 'A Night of Terror in the Backwoods of Canada' (1872),[26] 'The Secret Passage; a Tale of Ottawa City' (1882),[27] 'A Ghostly Warning (1878),'[28] 'My Grandfather's Ghost Story' (1878),[29] and John Charles Dent's 'The Gerrard Street Mystery' and 'The Haunted House on Duchess Street' (1888)[30] proved that Canada could hold its own as a location for effective tales of terror, crime, suspense, and encounters with the unknown.

That it would become possible to harmonize real life and literary romance in a full-length narrative is evidenced by William McLennan's *Spanish John* (1898). This book expands upon a memoir composed by Colonel John McDonell some time before his death at Cornwall in 1810 and published in *The Canadian Magazine and Literary Repository* in 1825. McLennan closely follows McDonell's description of his youthful adventures in the Spanish Catholic army striving to reinstate the deposed Stuarts. He maintains the straightforward voice of the original and bolsters its unstructured narrative by adding subplots involving characters who figure only occasionally in McDonell's text. Even when McLennan adds a didactic incident by having his hero play the good Samaritan the moral implications remain unobtrusive. The result is a restrained and occasionally compelling transformation of an early Canadian document into a fictional romance which was later commended by Pelham Edgar for its 'literary merit' although never inducted into the national canon.[31]

The comic side of the prevailing taste for romantic fiction, later immortalized in Leacock's *Nonsense Novels* (1911), proved irresistible to a few of his predecessors. The parodies of James De Mille discussed in Chapter 4 were preceded by Abraham Holmes' *Belinda; or, The Rivals* (1843), which will be considered in Chapter 9. Stella Mackay's 1867 satire, 'The Vow. A Tale of Love – Blood – Thunder – And Happiness,'[32] may be the most concise send-up of romantic convention published in Victorian Canada. Later in the century two hilarious burlesques of popular literature by Walter Blackburn Harte, temporarily domiciled in Montreal, entertained readers of *The Dominion Illustrated*. 'Noblesse Oblige: A British Society Novel, By a Crowned Head. Abridged and Mutilated by W. Blackburn Harte' demolished high-life fantasy and 'Something in the Wild West' performed the same operation on the romance of the American West.[33] Robert Barr was also not averse to exploiting the comic side of the work from which he made his living. *In the Midst of Alarms* (1894), one of Barr's two specifically Canadian novels, is less a literary parody than a lighthearted love story which refuses to take history seriously. A brash Yankee reporter seeking rest and solitude in the Canadian backwoods unexpectedly finds himself embroiled in the Fenian troubles of 1866. Far from being heroic, the battle of Ridgeway is so minor that 'the result of the struggle was similar in effect to an American railway accident of the first class.'[34] The effectiveness of Barr's comedy arises largely from his deflation of the high romantic tone usually associated with fiction relating to Canadian history.

With effort one can trace in Canada a minor vein of literary satire burlesquing the prevailing forms of romantic fiction. But during the last century most writers of historical romance took their history far more seriously than did Barr, their romance more seriously than did De Mille, and worked more directly within the tradition of Sir Walter Scott than did Richardson. In their efforts to provide Canada with a suitable local literature they earnestly tried to kindly all seven of Goldwin Smith's Lamps of Fiction, promoting the historical romance as the genre which would develop a national identity by popularizing and mythologizing Canada's neglected history.

7 The Past Tense of English Canada

It is not the literal past that rules us, save, possibly, in a biological sense. It is images of the past. These are often as highly structured and selective as myths ... A society requires antecedents. Where these are not naturally at hand, where a community is new or reassembled after a long interval of dispersal or subjection, a necessary past tense to the grammar of being is created by intellectual and emotional fiat.[1]

The creation of appropriate antecedents and the valorization of the social mythology underpinning Victorian Canada's conservatism[2] were primary motives in its literary élite's approval of indigenous fiction for mass consumption. At the top of the list was the historical romance, whose proliferation indicates that publishers and authors expected a large audience for fiction celebrating 'the heroic times of Canada.'[3] Such times were to be found in the general pioneer past and in particular events such as the War of 1812, which was always interpreted as the vindication of monarchism and British values, and the 1837 uprising, whose repression was usually celebrated as the assertion of law and order.

Before examining some of the 'images of the past' promoted by English Canada in its fiction, we must consider the significance of history itself in the literary consciousness of a new country where the anti-fiction bias of many critics led to lively debate about the role of history in imaginative writing. For John Richardson, as we have seen, the inclusion of historical material in a fictional narrative validated imaginative literature, marrying national chronicle with family tradition and personal experience. Throughout the nineteenth century most Canadian writers and critics shared Richardson's reverence for history based on the assumption that history was objective, factual, one of the classical pursuits, and therefore unquestionably superior to 'mere works of fiction.'[4] Diverse evaluations of historical fiction ensued. Some writers, like Richardson, asserted that the inclusion of historical material increased the moral and didactic value of a novel; others trembled lest fiction be confused with history and historical truth suffer distortion.

For pre-Confederation literary analysts the issue was both significant and complex. The position of *The Literary Garland* was to 'highly approve of what are generally designated Historical Novels' with the proviso that 'Many people, however, especially the young and inexperienced, in reading such works, are apt to attach too much credit to the statements they contain – to mistake for historical accuracy a plausible and circumstantial train of events and occurrences distorted and exaggerated, and not unfrequently invented to suit the purpose of the story teller. This is an error to be carefully guarded against.' Yet the *Garland* also acknowledged that in its ability to communicate character and social texture, fiction can be truer than history:

let anyone read as carefully as he may, the best written life of Oliver Cromwell, even his Life and Times by Carlyle for instance, and then read Sir Walter Scott's Historical Novel of Woodstock, and he will close the book with a much more perfect knowledge of the real character of that extraordinary and peculiarly talented man than he had before, although no single circumstance in the fictitious tale should be found to correspond with the statements in the authentic history.[5]

It was therefore consistent for this periodical to decide that the historical basis of Richardson's *The Canadian Brothers* rendered the book so 'useful' that the word bore repeating several times in its review.[6]

Contributors to the *Garland* represented several schools of thought. While the Reverend Henry Giles supported the editorial position,[7] others believed that 'There is much more real poetry in science than in fiction' and deplored the misrepresentation of the Middle Ages in novels which 'romance history.'[8] According to W.P.C., all the delights of fiction can be found in history itself, whose characters are 'the more interesting since we are confident of their reality,' for 'After all, History is the highest and noblest species of literature!'[9]

Post-Confederation Canada continued the discussion. *The New Dominion Monthly* waved the banner of Sir Walter Scott when it published an article by Harriet Beecher Stowe advising girls to read history during their summer holidays. Her own works an apt illustration of the social power of literature, Stowe promoted well-written fiction as a valid educational medium and recommended *Ivanhoe* as 'a study in style and as a study in history.' Scott would educate the taste as well as the mind: 'If you like it, relish it, feel its beauties, you will find that you have gained more than a knowledge of history – you will have *formed a taste for first-class writing.*'[10] Readers of such literature would have to remain alert, however; as *The Canadian Monthly* warned, 'It is so much more pleasant to float through pages of picturesque narrative, sweetened with mellifluous sentiment, than to inquire whether the narrative is true.'[11]

In Canada, distortion of historical truth was discovered in abundance in Disraeli's *Endymion.* Severely censured by Goldwin Smith for violating the standards of Walter Scott,[12] Disraeli was also reprimanded by *Rose-Belford's* for violating the sanctity of history:

Do not doubtful facts and erroneous statements already creep in among the records of our national progress with sufficient ease, and must we needs deliberately add to the confusion and difficulty by foisting them in by wholesale? ... When the present generation has passed away, what opportunity for error, for misconception, and misappreciation, will be found in the pages of the Earl of Beaconsfield's historical novels![13]

Admonitions of this sort were not intended to discourage Canadians from writing historical fiction but to encourage them to write the right kind. Throughout the nineteenth century and especially after Confederation, many Canadian writers were engaged in discovering and preserving Canadian history in formal historiography and the historical romance. To claim a distinct national identity, they believed, their country had to know and cherish its past.[14] The popularity of historical fiction in Europe fortified Canadians' interest in indigenous material and reinforced their view that the development of a recognizable literary tradition was inseparable from the establishment of a distinctive historical identity. Thus in one of its many discussions of the possibility of a Canadian literature *The Canadian Magazine* listed history as the primary distinguishing feature: 'It influences our lives, our thoughts and our institutions, and, consequently, it influences the literature produced in this country; and just so far as it does this, we have a literature which, by reason of its special character, must be designated Canadian.'[15] No critic questioned the importance of history and most presumed a direct correspondence between a country's awareness of its past and and the quality of its imaginative literature, yet different opinions emerged regarding the specific situation of Canada.

Least optimistic were those who asserted that the paucity of good

Canadian literature resulted directly from the country's relative newness, the historical apathy of its population, and the blandness of its political history. Assuming that only the resonances of antiquity could inspire great imaginative writing, they recommended that Canada relinquish its quest for its own Shakespeare, Milton, or Scott for several thousand years. Canadians' apparent lack of interest in their own past exacerbated the situation. In the experience of an 1841 observer, to the average Canadian 'History is a pursuit naturally foreign to his habit of thinking.' Canada's necessary absorption in 'the matter of fact, sober, plodding routine of Colonial existence,' its lack of history and lack of interest in history meant that 'years, long years must elapse, before a Colony, situated like Canada, can cause her voice to be heard in the literary world.'[16]

After Confederation some writers still described the relation between history and literature in European terms, and like occasional poet John E. Logan argued that there would arise 'a distinctive Canadian literature' only

when all the unknown and undreamt changes and influences of centuries have wrought their impress on the people; when revolutions have marked eras in our history, and history, itself grown old, is phosphorescent with the halo of romance ... That we will have a literature long before such things happen I do not question; but he is doomed to awake unsatisfied who dreams of a *distinctive* literature from the hands of a genius, who, at a single bound, has leaped from chaos to cosmos across the evolution of ages.[17]

Scanning the past from the perspective of 1912, Pelham Edgar offered as one reason why 'No [writer] ... has yet synthesized for us the meaning of our Canadian life, nor revealed us to ourselves' the inappropriateness of English-Canadian history: 'We are what we are as a people by virtue of the struggle for responsible government, but what poet could read a tune into such refractory material?'[18]

Exponents of the latter view were outnumbered by those who asserted that Canada did indeed possess a distinctive history sufficiently colourful to inspire a national literature, and filled the pages of the country's literary periodicals with exhortations to Canadians to study and write about their past. The movement to recover Canadian history began in earnest in the 1830s and expanded considerably with the surge of nationalism that accompanied Confederation. One of the most prominent journals in this regard was *The Canadian Monthly and National Review*, whose frequent pieces on Canadian history were, according to J.G.

Bourinot, 'of especial value, in the way of attracting attention to the stores of interesting lore which lies around us in old Canadian archives.'[19] In conjunction there appeared in *The Monthly* a number of corrective statements rejecting the European outlook that denied Canada a valid history because the country had been settled for only a few centuries. Their authors declared that to appreciate the Canadian situation it was necessary to redefine European standards of antiquity and approach the time scheme of the New World on its own terms. As Daniel Wilson explained, 'The olden times of our Ontario capital must be measured by the scale of the New World to which it belongs; and the young Dominion in which it occupies so prominent a place; but youthful as it is, its beginnings already pertain to elder generations; and it has a history of its own not without interest to others besides its modern denizens.' Wilson demonstrated Toronto's status by comparing its origins with those of Thebes, Rome, and London;[20] likewise M.J. Griffin equated the ancestors of Victorian Canada with the heroes of classical antiquity:

surely it is not too much to claim that the Canadian reader shall have a kindly and deep interest in the men who began the history of our country. It is a history to which we look back as the Greeks looked back to the Homeric heroes, or the Roman to the dim figures which fill the epoch of his country's foundation, and which will ever be the prologue to the recital of the most splendid developments to which these colonies may in the future attain.[21]

The quest for Canadian history suitably 'rich in association and stirring in story'[22] permeated the literary consciousness of Victorian Canada. Many stories in pre-Confederation periodicals attempted to add historical associations to the apparently timeless wilderness, combing the local landscape for resemblances to the Old World where 'Every valley, every mountain, every ruin, has its tale of legendary lore.'[23] Typical of this fiction was 'The Gibbet Tree' (1844), written to show that 'this country, although unknown to fame, can produce its romantic incidents also, which, if happy in a historian, would be devoured by the reader with as much avidity as the marvellous tales and legends of older and more favored lands.'[24] In another tale, 'Leaves from the Life Romance of Merne Dillamer,' author H.T. Devon acted more insistently to add 'the charms of association' to Upper Canadian soil in a love story set thirty years previously and involving a descendant of 'one of those intrepid United Empire Loyalists.' This author's Tory loyalism, reverence for history, and desire to enrich Canadians with a sense of their past all culminate in his final paragraphs when the narrator switches his focus from the past to the present, speaking in his own voice to establish a concrete connection between past events and a specific Canadian locality.[25] The West was subject to the same desire to endow the country with a sense of legend based on history. 'A Tale of the Red River' (1855), set a vague 'number of years' ago, recounts how the Red River received its name from the blood of massacred settlers (the etymology given by *The Canadian Encyclopaedia* is rather more subdued), and concludes that 'a halo of glory must ever surround the names of those pioneers of civilization in the far Northwest, as bright as that which encircles the heroes of Balaclava or Inkermann.'[26]

That Confederation would stimulate new activity in the realm of historiography and historical romance was quickly recognized by George Stewart. 'There is a mine of historic and romantic literature to be worked by the student of this or a later day,' he declared in 1867, 'and we trust that when the flag of the Dominion shall wave proudly over all the confederated states, from the Atlantic to the Pacific, we shall endeavour to preserve from oblivion many a faded annal of the past, or weave into romantic fiction ... scraps of legendary lore.'[27] The key words in this statement are 'historic' and 'romantic' in parallel syntax. The kind of history which excited post-Confederation Canada was a construct of incidents and characters meriting the adjectives 'romantic' and 'heroic' and therefore able to furnish material for novels modelled on the works of Sir Walter Scott and faithful to Goldwin Smith's 'Lamps of Fiction.' Because of its emotive power the import of this view was political as well as literary and reinforced the nationalism of the Canada First movement. W.A. Foster's 1871 address, *Canada First; or, Our New Nationality*, opened with a paean to the romance of Canada's past:

what a land of adventure and romance has this been! We may have no native ballad for the nursery, or home-born epic for the study; no tourney feats to rhapsodise over, or mock heroics to emblazon on our escutcheon; we may have no prismatic fables to illumine and adorn the preface of our existence, or curious myths to obscure and soften the sharp outline of our early history; yet woven into the tapestry of our past, are whole volumes of touching poetry and great tomes of glowing prose that rival fiction in eagerness of incident, and in marvellous climax put fable to the blush. We need not ransack foreign romance for valorous deeds, nor are we compelled to go abroad for sad tales of privation and suffering. The most chivalrous we can match; the most tried we can parallel.

In concluding that 'there are few heroes in our Pantheon. Where every

man does his duty, heroes are not wanted and not missed,'[28] Foster was
not denying interest in national heroes so much as suggesting that the
foundation of the new nation lay in the work of its often anonymous
pioneers whose heroism resided in the day-to-day labours of colonization.
Sharing the sentiment that 'the noblest chapters in the history of Canada
are buried in the graves of the early pioneers throughout this land,' the
major periodicals of his era published many accounts of early Canadian
life in the form of journalistic sketches or personal memoirs.[29] In the
realm of fiction, however, the autocratic sceptre of romance allowed scant
opportunity for accounts of ordinary life to enter the mainstream of
Canadian writing.

One author who tried to alter his country's literary tastes, newspaper-
man Robert Sellar, met with continual disappointment in his quest for an
audience for his simple, moving stories of early pioneer life based on
interviews with the first settlers in the area of Huntingdon, Quebec. His
first book, *Gleaner Tales* (1886), was virtually ignored by the community
for which it was written and he was forced to print his later stories himself
after rejection by other publishers.[30] Sellar's colloquial eloquence, political honesty (the Loyalism of the displaced Highlanders of *Morven* is
presented as a matter of accident rather than patriotism), and unromantic
narratives of pioneer hardship distinguish his fiction from that of the
romantic writers who achieved greater contemporary success.

Like Sellar, Coll McLean Sinclair wrote fiction to illustrate that 'history
was made and is being made from day to day and week to week along the
back lanes and concessions of our own and every other country.' His only
book, *The Dear Old Farm* (1897), stresses the unsung heroism of Ontario's
first settlers with only a few lapses into melodrama. But most writers
interested in recovering Canadian history and establishing Canadian
literature through the medium of the historical novel subscribed to the
'great men' approach rejected by Sinclair[31] and turned instead to men and
women whom history had endowed with distinction or to eras of great
historical crisis appropriately 'rich in association and stirring in story,' to
return to the phrase coined by *The Canadian Monthly*.

Among the most prominent supporters of Canadian efforts in the
fields of historical research and romance were three founding members
of the Royal Society of Canada. James MacPherson LeMoine, John
George Bourinot, and John Talon-Lesperance all published copiously on
Canadian historical subjects in monographs and the major post-
Confederation periodicals.[32] In his later years Bourinot valued historiography above fiction and encouraged the writing of historical romance in

concession to popular taste. But in the 1870s, when he penned a few stories himself, Bourinot joined LeMoine and Lesperance in believing that far from corrupting history, the historical romance performed the dual role of educating the Canadian public and developing a distinctive Canadian literature. These cultural leaders, later joined by W.D. Lighthall, performed their mission of directing the development of Canadian fiction by continually reminding their readers that 'The early times of Canada abound with incidents of the most dramatic interest – inexhaustible stores of materials for the novelist.'[33] And as to be expected, the ghost of Walter Scott flits through their catalogues of potential Canadian material like LeMoine's still unfulfilled prediction that 'D'Iberville, M'lle de Verchères, Latour, Dollard des Ormeaux, Lambert Close, will yet, we opine, receive from the magic wand of a Canadian Walter Scott a halo of glory as bright as that which, in the eyes of Scotia's sons, surrounds a Flora McIvor, a Jeannie Deans, a Claverhouse, or a Rob Roy.'[34]

LeMoine's essays on the history and traditions of early Canada and Quebec, collected in his six volumes of *Maple Leaves* (1863–1906) and other works, did indeed inspire several creative writers, most notably William Kirby. *The Canadian Monthly*'s review of LeMoine's *Past and Present* (1876) gratefully acknowledged the 'deep obligation' under which 'Mr LeMoine's energy and industry have laid his own Province and the Dominion at large.'[35] Bourinot gave LeMoine's research a romantic cast when he remarked that 'To him the natural beauty of the St Lawrence and its historic and legendary lore are as familiar as were the picturesque scenery and the history of Scotland to Sir Walter Scott.'[36] Scott's name appeared again in the Royal Society's obituary of LeMoine: 'Ce que furent Sir Walter Besant pour Londres, Frédéric Mistral pour le Provence, Sir Walter Scott pour l'Ecosse, Sir James LeMoine l'a été pour la ville et la région du Québec.'[37]

Like LeMoine, Bourinot determined to resurrect the forgotten heroes and heroines of early Canada. While he approached the topic with less fervour, setting Canada within the larger spectrum of world history, his object was the thoroughly nationalistic goal of calling attention to 'Canadian Materials for History, Poetry and Romance' as he titled an 1871 essay. Canada would take centuries, Bourinot felt, to acquire the historical resonances of the Old World, but it still possessed its own 'record of heroic endeavour and suffering, of the struggle between antagonistic principles and systems, of human passion, frailty, and virtue' that comprise the true 'essence of history, romance, and poetry.' The period richest in 'prolific materials for the novelist' terminated with the War of 1812, which marked the end of the country's romantic history and the beginning of its preoccupation with utilitarian progress. 'Since that time,' he declared, 'our history has been wanting in the elements of dramatic interest; it has had no episodes of stirring import, except the fruitless rebellion from 1836–37 which after all was little more than a faction fight in some Irish county. Our history for the past half century has been the record of material progress ...'[38] Bourinot compiled a generous list of historical materials suitable for romantic fiction, but like other literary nationalists he found it easy to make such recommendations and difficult to persuade others to pursue them. Twenty-two years later, in one of his last assessments of his country's cultural standing, he was disappointed that no Canadian had yet achieved international recognition in 'the novel or romance' and that the country still lacked a national literature which successfully gave 'form and vitality to the abundant materials that exist in the Dominion ... for the true story-teller.'[39]

In contrast to LeMoine and Bourinot, John Talon-Lesperance contributed to the encouragement of Canadian historical romance more conspicuously as a novelist and journalist than as an historian or cultural critic. As editor of the weekly *Canadian Illustrated News* from 1873 to 1880 and founding editor of the *Dominion Illustrated Weekly* in 1888, Lesperance favoured romantic tales based on Canadian history. For the first number of the new periodical he wrote a story combining Canadian history with one of the most popular forms of magazine fiction, the summer love story. For all its good intentions, 'A Missisquoi Holiday' is more successful as an illustration of the difficulty of blending ancient history with contemporary amours than as a piece of entertainment. In unexpert hands such fiction can become clumsily didactic, as shown by Lesperance's interruption of a sunset scene on Lake Champlain with a catalogue of dates:

It was now sunset, and we had the glorious view which Sharpe had promised me. The great lake – scene of so much history, in two hundred years – the incursions of the Iroquois to Quebec; the expedition of de Tracy into the Mohawk Valley; the ascent of Montcalm in 1758; the descent of the British in 1760; the triumph and flight of the Continentals in 1776–77; the disastrous march of Burgoyne, which culminated at Saratoga in 1780; the naval encounters of 1812–15; and the lesser incidents of the Canadian rebellion of 1837–38, the great lake seemed to reflect in sanguine glory all these deeds of victory and defeat as the sun poured his departing fires upon its bosom, tempered by streaks of storm clouds. We sat in rapt wonder for over ten minutes ...[40]

His earnest concern with publicizing Canadian history through the medium of fiction, central to his best-known work, *The Bastonnais* (1877), enhanced Lesperance's reputation in Canadian literary circles. *Canadiana* complimented his editorial direction of the *Dominion Illustrated*, particularly in the department of historical fiction,[41] and upon his death W.D. Lighthall eulogized him for having shown 'more than any man how much interest can be awakened in the romance of the regions around us, and there is little doubt that he educated not a few permanently in that culture of the heart which alone makes the gentleman and gentlewoman.'[42]

The terms of Lighthall's praise for Lesperance return us to the glow cast by the Lamps of Fiction. Following Scott's example and sharing Smith's code of literary chivalry, English-Canadian novelists (including Lighthall himself) turned to various phases of Canadian history. Resolved to create a national literature, they tailored Canadian material to the pattern of historical romance. Canadian content, not Canadian form, was their object; as one theorist stated in 1881, an

atmosphere of nationalism, indeed ... should more penetratively pervade all our literature than it does. If that literature is ever to fire the heart of the nation, and to create a distinguishing type of national character, it must cease to be imitative, and find the materials of its art and occupation at home. It may borrow the literary forms of the authorcraft of the Old World, but its themes must be those of the New.[43]

The attraction of the majority of historically inclined English-Canadian novelists to French Canada is the topic of the next chapter of this book; less visible was the inclination of a smaller group – mostly from Upper Canada – to fictionalize the past of their own English-speaking communities. Surprisingly few wrote directly about the Loyalists although there was apparently an audience for the subject.[44] In this area, one of the more widely publicized books was Graeme Mercer Adam and Ethelwyn Wetherald's jointly authored *An Algonquin Maiden* (1887), a deliberate attempt to establish the historical romance as the proper mode for Canadian fiction. In her discussion of this book in *The Week*, Sara Jeannette Duncan quickly derided its authors' intention to counter the realistic direction of the modern novel:

'An Algonquin Maiden' is a romance, a romance of the most uncompromising description, a romance that might have been written if the realistic school had never been heard of. One need go no further than the title to discover it a romance; 'maidens' are unknown to the literary methods of a later date. They have become extinct, and are less euphonically replaced ... More than this, the title boldly states, as well as implies, the character of the book. 'A Romance' its authors have had the temerity to subtitle it, 'of the Early Days of Upper Canada.' This must be regarded as nothing less than a challenge to the modern idea of the form of latter-day fiction.[45]

From the first paragraph, which invokes 'the romantic halo which the mist of years loves to weave about the heads of departed pioneers,'[46] the vision remains consistent. In 1832 William Dunlop (who was to lend his name to the hero of this book) observed of Canada that 'I can conceive no possibility of its becoming for centuries a fitting stage for the heroes or heroines of the fashionable novels of Mr Bulwer or the young D'Israeli.'[47] Such details of social history did not trouble Adam and Wetherald, however. Relying on chronological distance to lend enchantment to the past, they present 'flat Ontario'[48] with a local cultural fantasy that reinforces the Tory mythology of social class while soft-pedalling contentious religious and political issues. By populating Upper Canada with European families whose nobility is represented in their bloodlines and their homes, the authors engage the reader with a caste of characters who enact the creation of a Canadian upper class based not simply on heredity but also on the principle of noblesse oblige. As the plot unfolds, blending of Canada's linguistic heritages is permissible – so long as English remains dominant – but mixing of classes, races, and religious groups is strictly controlled.

Hélène deBerczy, one of the three maidens whose heartthrobs shape the plot, descends from a Huguenot family now living thirty miles from York in a community settled by 'French officers of the noblesse order' (14) who received land grants from the Crown after escaping the French Revolution. The English counterpart to this romantically French (and conveniently Protestant) royalist element is the Macleod family, headed by emphatically Tory Commodore Ralph Macleod. A 'grand specimen of the sturdy British seamen, who contributed by their prowess to make England mistress of the seas,' Macleod retired to Canada where he built 'a palatial residence' (26) on the shore of Lake Simcoe. His Toryism and political activities on the Legislative Council link him with the Family Compact and he bitterly opposes the reformist work of young Allan Dunlop, friend of his son Edward and eventually husband of his daughter Rose.

Dunlop adds another social dimension to this romantic structure. An upstart Reformer of humble status yet incarnating 'all that became a patriot and a high-minded gentleman' (29), he at first seems too lowly ever to attain the maiden he loves. But Dunlop proves a hero in disguise. '[T]hough born and bred on a farm,' he 'had in him the springs of a higher and finer life. He was a man of delicate instincts, refined feelings, and great native sensibility, inherited from his mother' (91), an English gentlewoman who had eloped with her riding master. Dunlop's high maternal ancestry and even higher soul eventually earn him his bride as both he and Ralph Macleod learn to take 'a more dispassionate view of the questions which disturbed the country and which had ranged them politically on opposite sides' (237). Into this classic romance plot, in which the obscure hero realizes his true identity and noble love triumphs over political and parental obstacles, the authors insert a subplot centring on the Algonquin maiden.

Although Wanda scarcely touches the primary action, the fact that this post-Wordsworthian child of nature gives the book its title indicates the prominence of romance in the minds of its authors.[49] Described as 'a beauty. Half-wild, of course, but with a sort of barbaric splendour about her that dazzles and bewilders one' (58), Wanda epitomizes the innocence and eroticism of the female noble savage in a series of clichés remarkable only for their candour. Her creators place her in a paradisal natural world, to her far superior to the comforts of European civilization. Rose Macleod and Wanda are friends, but Wanda's

admiration of Rose was tinged with pity. Poor garden flower, confined for life to the dull walks and prim parterres of a fixed enclosure, when she might roam the wild paths of the forest; condemned to sleep in a close room, on stifling feathers, and bathe in an elongated tub, when she might feel the elasticity of hemlock boughs beneath her, inhale the perfumed breath of myriad trees, and plunge at sunrise into the gleaming waters of the lake. It was indeed a pitiable life (49).

Then a serpent invades Wanda's Edenic wilderness in the form of Rose's philandering brother. Haunted by the 'intense recollection of a tawny woman, beautiful and warm-blooded' (98), Edward spurns Hélène DeBerczy. Eventually Wanda discredits herself with white society, in whose eyes she behaves 'precisely like an overgrown child of five years who has "never had any bringing up"' (193). Yet for a long time Edward continues to vacillate between the two women – one representing the refinement of Europe, the other the passion of the wilderness – until he finally returns to Hélène and his proper social niche. The once innocent Wanda, now deeply in love with Edward, is too much a victim of civilization to return to her idyllic forest and decorously withdraws from the scene by drowning herself, having 'committed the god-like sin of loving too much' (233).

In the close literary circles of post-Confederation Toronto, Sara Jeannette Duncan learned enough about the process of this book's composition to attribute the stylistic embellishments to Wetherald, noting 'In any love story there are plenty of opportunities for the divine afflatus to precipitate itself, as it were, into prose, and Miss Wetherald has improved every opportunity.'[50] More to Duncan's taste were the chapters based on Canada's political history: 'The historical and political parts of the volume, which form by no means too much ballast for Miss Wetherald's areial writing, we owe entirely to Mr Adam; and it will probably be wished in many quarters that we had been given more chapters like that upon "Politics at the Capital," even at the expense of a few of the sort of that upon "A Kiss and its Consequences".'[51]

Like most Canadian historical fictions *An Algonquin Maiden* embraces a purpose that is political as well as literary. In addition to advocating romance as the appropriate mode for Canadian fiction and attempting to instil a sense of patriotism, this novel illustrates the conflicts leading up to the 1837 rebellion and the achievement of Responsible Government so as to prescribe a code of political chivalry. Allan Dunlop represents the ideal temperate political reformer: 'He was one of the few in the Legislature who, while they recognized that the old system of government was becoming less and less suited to the genius and wants of the young Canadian community, at the same time wished to usher in the new *régime* with the moderation and tact which mark the work of the thoughtful politician and the aims of the true statesman' (29). While siding with the reformers, Dunlop eschews republicanism, for he is 'too loyal a man to rank with the "heated enthusiasts" who were threatening to overturn the Constitution and make a republic out of the colony' (168). To maintain political peace he learns to adopt 'a point of view which was eminently statesmanlike and discreet' and he therefore refrains from 'pressing many reforms which time, he knew, would quietly and with less acrimony bring about' (237).

Such impeccable diplomacy cannot fail to win over Colonel Macleod, the crusty old Tory whose 'kindly, sympathetic heart' respects 'those whose aims were high and whose motives were good' (237). Compromise without republicanism (and implicitly a rejection of American values) is the overriding message of the political portion of the book. In Duncan's analysis, Adam's tactful efforts to paint both sides in their best colours arose from his being 'aware that the foibles of both the early pioneers of Reform and the upholders of the Family Compact have descended almost intact unto the second and third generations, and doubtless desirous, above all things, to avoid fanning the flames of Provincial party strife.' But of his apparent refusal to take sides she also remarked: 'While congratulating Mr Adam upon the diplomacy with which he has compassed a somewhat difficult situation, one cannot help observing in the necessity for it another and an unsuspected difficulty which besets Canadian authorship.'[52]

Tact and diplomacy meant less to other authors of historical fiction about English Canada, many of whom were motivated by political partisanship. In the 1850s there appeared several stories about the 1837 uprising which expressly sided with the government. William Charles McKinnon, for example, claimed in his preface to *Saint George: or, The Canadian League* (1852) that 'the author has not allied himself to any party or taken the view of any particular faction with regard to the insurrection,'[53] yet he depicted all Mackenzie's associates as consummate villains. 'A Backwoodsman' states his political allegiance even more clearly with rebels who attempt the 'act of sacrilege' of kissing the heroine and converse 'in language too debased for these pages.'[54]

During the same period, Catharine Parr Traill also portrayed the rebels in unsavoury terms. Susanna Moodie later expressed some sympathy with Mackenzie's cause, most notably in the essay titled 'Canada: A Contrast' appended to the 1871 edition of *Roughing It in the Bush*. But her sister's earlier juvenile story, 'The Volunteer's Bride' (1854), gives voice only to the government view, using the occasion to teach patriotism to young readers. Duty overcomes love when the bridegroom troops off with the government forces minutes after the marriage ceremony. Traill underscores the virtues of 'our brave Canadian volunteers' and their selfless wives when the tale ends with the suppression of the rebellion and the final cutting of the wedding cake with 'three cheers – one for the bride, one for the bridegroom, and the third for the colony and its brave volunteers.'[55]

Later writers treated the rebellion more dispassionately. In a rambling potpourri of literary styles, plots, and characters serialized in *The Maritime Monthly* in 1874 under the title 'Josiah Garth' Dr Daniel Clark expressed sympathy with Mackenzie. And in 'Rosalba; or, Faithful to two Lovers,' the second prize winner in *The Canadian Illustrated News*'s historical romance competition, John Talon-Lesperance [pseud. Arthur Faverel] even discounted the political significance of the uprising. His Canadian narrator explains to an American that

The rebellion ... marks an era in our history. It is an event to date from. To men of my generation it is a starting point, but that is because it is the era of our Union. Outside of this fact, I can trace no direct influence it has had on the Canadian people. The rebellion was crushed before it became a revolution, and it is only revolutions, you know, that can materially alter a national character, one way or the other. Hence the Canadian people, barring always their steady advance with the wave of universal progress, have remained ever since the rebellion pretty much what they were before it.

For Lesperance the rebellion acquires literary importance because 'there are numerous episodes connected with that event – scraps of legendary and ballad literature of our village firesides, most of them still unwritten'[56] which fulfil the conventions of romance. Hence in 'Rosalba' greater emphasis is placed on the narrative complications produced by the rebellion than on its political significance.

Nationalists wishing to avoid the troubling civil turbulence of 1837–8 sometimes turned to the opportunities for patriotic rhetoric afforded by the War of 1812. Agnes Maule Machar's *For King and Country*, serialized in *The Canadian Monthly* before its publication in book form, supported that periodical's Canada First point of view.[57] The story combines the romance of love with that of history as lowly Ernest Heathcote proves worthy of his upper-class Upper Canadian sweetheart by fighting bravely with General Brock. The situation is complicated by Ernest's American birth; that an American can support the Canadian cause authenticates British morality and justice. Heathcote devotes himself to Canada because he feels that

a reckless, unscrupulous invasion of a peaceful country, brought about by base men for selfish ends, must be resisted by every honest man. To take up arms in such a cause was to fight not only for King and Country, but for peace and good order, – for the sacred rights of man, – for home and the dear helpless ones around the hearth-stone; and against murder, rapine, crime, – all the countless villainies that must attend the success of reckless marauders.[58]

A similar position is taken by the hero of W.H. Withrow's *Neville Trueman, or The Pioneer Preacher* (1880), a young American-born Methodist who finds himself in Canada in 1812 when hostilities break out. Trueman stays with the Canadians, believing 'this invasion of a peaceful territory by an armed host is a wanton outrage, and cannot have the smile of Heaven.'[59] Also designed to uphold British virtues against American self-interest was Robert Sellar's *Hemlock, A Tale of the War of 1812* (1890). But by far the most polished Canadian novel about this conflict is William

Wilfred Campbell's *A Beautiful Rebel* (1909), in which the 'unofficial poet laureate of Canadian imperialism'[60] turned the conventions of romance into a statement of imperialist sentiment.

Campbell had earlier proclaimed his penchant for allegorical fiction when he selected *The Scarlet Letter* and *Silas Marner* as the two greatest novels written in English.[61] In *A Beautiful Rebel* the announced purpose of the story is both national and imperial: to recreate 'in romantic form the early vicissitudes of fortune in the life of my native province,' to demonstrate that 'no portion of our continent contains more fascinating and tragic material for the novelist, than does the triangular peninsula bounded by the Great Lakes, the Ottawa River, and the Upper St Lawrence,' and above all to situate Canada within the Empire: 'To the British over-sea, but in the Empire I present these pages, in the hope that they will realize that the true strength of Empire depends not on trade or commerce, not on force or political diplomacy; but on the common loyalty of her children at home and abroad to the highest instincts and traditions of a great people.'[62] Brock is therefore distinguished as 'a brave soldier of the Empire' (5) and the battle of Queenston Heights as the occasion when 'the first great victory in the battle for the preservation of Canada to the British Crown was won' (264).

To relate the War of 1812 to British readers, Campbell created a story whose central conflict occurs not between Canadians and Americans but between two families of British descent who carry to the New World the historic friction between the Roundheads and the Cavaliers. The Bradfords, republicans 'by reason of their heredity of blood from their regicide ancestor' (62–3), plot with the Americans against the British aristocrats living in Upper Canada. Their main target is Colonel Monmouth, whose garden, 'like a bit of the Old World,' represents the transplanting of his class. Outside his fence is 'the rough squalor and coarseness of a primitive backwoods yard' while within exists 'a condition showing infinite care, toil and ideality, a refinement of garden hedge and orchard-wall, which suggested England' (125). By removing the conflict to Canada, Campbell is able to provide a Royalist resolution to the English Civil War, a feat that will hardly surprise readers familiar with the Tory bias of Canadian historical romance. This outcome is accomplished symbolically through the titular heroine, Lydia Bradford, who 'instinctively, loved and worshipped beauty and refinement' (222) despite her republican origins. Converted through love, she marries Monmouth's heir and together they settle down in Upper Canada, talking of compromise but perpetuating the wealth and values of Old World gentry.

Like Adam and Wetherald, Campbell required the sanction of Old World aristocracy and its historical associations to render English-Canadian life suitable for literary romance, thereby giving his society 'a past tense to the grammar of being' (to return to George Steiner's phrase) more congruent with the literary genre being employed than with the community being represented. Their fictional heroes and heroines are born in Canada but mostly to families who have transplanted upper-class European life wholesale to the New World and established grand estates in the wilds of Upper Canada – a pattern that would later culminate in Mazo de la Roche's stupendously popular Jalna books. This kind of creative nostalgia for a form of high life which did not exist in contemporary Canada and could be found in its past only with some difficulty appears also in Casca's 1863 discussion of *The History of Emily Montague*,[63] in the initial chapters of Margaret A. Brown's *My Lady of the Snows* (1908), and in Agatha Armour's *Lady Rosamond's Secret* (1878). The latter, set in Fredericton during the administration of Lord Howard Douglas in the late 1820s, describes the period as 'Fredericton's glorious days – days of sport; days of chivalry; days of splendour and high life' when 'proud knighthood was the ruling passion in the breasts of the sterner sex, when true heroic bravery was the quality which won the maiden fair,' an age now lost to 'Progress and Reform.'[64]

Agnes Laut's *Lords of the North* (1900) illustrates that the impulse to medievalize could be directed westward as well. Dick Harrison regrets the failure of nineteenth-century Canadian writers to successfully adapt the prose romance to the opening of the Northwest, citing Laut as a particular disappointment because her 'careful research' is presented in 'a romance of tangled intrigue, reminiscent of Walter Scott's lighter works.'[65] Yet Laut's insistence on taking her direction from Scott was thoroughly consistent with the outlook of her audience, who relished her character-ization of the rival trading Companies as feudal robber barons, her pseudo-medieval diction, and her advocacy of chivalry in an unruly land.[66]

The straining of social history for romantic effect in the novels of Campbell and Adam and Wetherald shows how little English Canada could offer its romantic novelists in the way of dramatic social, cultural, and political history. Their efforts to provide their society with romantic fictional antecedents concurred with J.G. Bourinot's view that the history of Canada, 'under the English *régime*, labours under the disadvantage of want of unity ... being for the most part a record of comparatively insignificant political controversy.' While Bourinot called for dedicated historians to 'lift [English-] Canadian history out of the slough of dulness into which so many have succeeded in throwing it'[67] few novelists rose to the challenge. Instead English-Canadian writers turned to the regions within their national borders which most readily provided exciting history, romantic folklore, and a European social order, and adopted as their own the past of the French Canadians, in Acadia and Quebec.

8 The Old World of America

In a certain sense Quebec is the Old World of America. Its claims to distinction depend not upon any untrustworthy hopes of future greatness; they rest with a confidence of assurance upon an unforgettable and richly dowered past. Patriotism may be cherished by the ordinary Canadian as a fit and proper sentiment, but for it to thrill his imagination and touch his heart it is necessary that he should dwell in Lower Canada.[1]

Thus Ethelwyn Wetherald expressed the significance of Quebec's vibrant history and apparently secure culture to post-Confederation Canada's continual quest for identity. In the pages of pre-Confederation periodicals we can see how Victorian Canada's literary love affair with New France arose from the union of a taste for romance with a desire for cultural distinction. Over the course of the nineteenth century, fascination with the otherness of French Canada muted into a sense of identification with Québécois and Acadian culture, folklore, and history which helped enrich English Canada's own relatively barren national image. In the 1860s, as the colonies approached nationhood, French Canada's literary and imaginative importance increased correspondingly so that by the turn of the century English-Canadian writers were looking to French Canada not only for the stuff of historical romance, but also for quaint contemporary material in tune with the international taste and American magazine market for local colour and folk realism.

English-Canadian writers drew upon the 'unforgettable and richly dowered past' of Quebec and Acadia with the genial approval of influential cultural figures like John George Bourinot, J.M. LeMoine, W.D. Lighthall, and the editors and reviewers of literary periodicals, who all shared the assumption that English-Canadian literature should be romantic and French Canada could provide that romance. Before the appearance of Francis Parkman's major studies that would valorize and popularize the past of New France, *The British American Magazine* pronounced the first volume of LeMoine's *Maple Leaves* a 'godsend' for filling the void felt by the English-speaking inhabitants of a country without a mythology: 'We have, within the limits of British America, no such strongholds of romance, as Quebec, and its surroundings. Nowhere else are such tragedies native to the scene, as the stories of Château Bigot, the *Chien D'or*, and the "Iron Cage".'[2]

By playing up Quebec's colourful history and idealizing both early and contemporary French-Canadian life, Victorian Canada sought to fulfil its yearning for national romance. Trapped in a relatively prosaic society preoccupied with material progress, writers projected onto French Canada their own society's desire for cultural distinctiveness from Great Britain on the one hand and the United States on the other. Goldwin Smith's pronouncements that Canada had no reason to exist as a separate entity spurred English Canada's interest in Quebec, its manifestations ranging from the antiquarian activities of LeMoine to the wish fulfilment voiced by Blanche Macdonell, author of several stories and novels set in Quebec, when she excused the lack of early literary activity in New France by explaining that 'These people lived poetry and romance' although they 'had no time to write it.'[3] To such writers the vision of Old Quebec as a unified, self-contained world, founded on an heroic past and composed of individuals representing distinct class and social types secure in their language, religion, history, and traditions, fulfilled a purpose that was simultaneously political and literary and eminently suited to the genre of fiction modelled on Sir Walter Scott.

Early nineteenth-century tales of French Canada bear evidence of less interest in its documented history than in settings, characters, and folklore associated with its antiquity and foreignness. The imaginative role played by Lower Canada as a setting for gothicism and mystery – a role that would be significantly developed at the end of the century in the stories of Susie Frances Harrison and D.C. Scott and later in Margaret Atwood's *Surfacing* – hearkens back to the 1820s, with John Howard Willis' stories 'The Fairy Harp' and 'Midsummer Eve. A Tale of the Ottawa.'[4] Religion constituted another facet of Lower Canada's literary appeal by offering some English-Canadian writers an opportunity to import the anti-Catholicism characteristic of much European gothic fiction. In 1824, when Julia Beckwith Hart included in *St Ursula's Convent* a Jesuit priest who conspires to confine a lady in a Quebec convent, the first Canadian novel initiated a pattern that was to recur occasionally but consistently until about 1875. In a well-documented study of Mrs Ellen Ross, author of *Violet Keith* (1868), Jeffrey L. Wollock discusses the role of Montreal in nineteenth-century anti-Catholic literature and lists a number of sensational publications which appeared in the United States, primarily in the 1830s. The most infamous and frequently reprinted were *Lorette: The History of Louise, Daughter of a Canadian Nun* (1833), the *Awful Disclosures, by Maria Monk, of the Hotel Dieu Nunnery of Montreal* (1836), and *Further Disclosures* (1837), all wholly or partially written by George Bourne, an English-born Presbyterian minister who spent some time in Quebec.[5] These scurrilous productions, along with incidents in Canadian fiction such as the seduction of the heroine of John Richardson's *Westbrook* (1851) by a lascivious priest attached to the Montreal convent of Notre Dame, the 'damp cell episode' of *Violet Keith*, and the enforced nunhood of the heroine of 'Adrienne Cachelle,' a story serialized in *The New Dominion Monthly* in 1871, illustrate how Quebec's Catholicism provided North American writers with indigenous equivalents to the dark convents and monasteries of Italy and Spain, favourite settings for the horrors of European gothic romance.

Contributors to *The Literary Garland*, however, cared more for the courtly elegance and high adventure they could ascribe to New France than for fabricating nefarious religious practices. Their polished tales of heroic devotion and sacrifice, set in the early days of Quebec and Acadia, are usually placed within a verifiable historical context but concern affairs of love and honour peripheral to the main historical action. Writers like Eliza Lanesford Cushing and her sister Harriet Vining Cheney, who produced stories with historically suggestive titles such as 'Jacques Cartier and the Little Indian Girl,' and 'The Old Manuscript; A Mémoire of the Past,' viewed their literary creations as something quite distinct from history. Mrs Cushing explained that her role was not to write history but to embellish it by expanding upon the 'numerous affecting incidents, that developed the character of individuals, and which lent ... a tinge of romantic interest, that sheds a mellow lustre over the dry and scanty detail of the historian.'[6]

In the mid-1860s, when LeMoine and Parkman brought out the first volumes of their expansive works relating to French-Canadian history, English-speaking Canadians awoke en masse to the fact that their past – or at least that of Quebec – was anything but 'dry and scanty.' In 1863 LeMoine gathered his scattered magazine articles into the first volume of *Maple Leaves*, subtitled 'a Budget of Legendary, Historical, Critical and

Sporting Intelligence.' This collection of assorted facts, anecdotes, and observations, 'many written offhand from self-memory of persons or events, and others with more research into the records of the past, or reminiscences of the living,'[7] presented social, cultural, folkloric, and historical aspects of Quebec that immediately captured the attention of English Canada. When Parkman published *Pioneers of France in the New World* in 1865, his dramatic style of historical narrative further encouraged English Canada to adopt and romanticize the history of New France. Indeed Parkman almost single-handedly determined the direction of Canadian historiography and historical fiction for the last three decades of the nineteenth century.[8] *The Dominion Annual Register* for 1880–1 spoke for that era as a whole when it commented, 'The chief interest in Canadian history, it is almost trite now to say, has hitherto centered in the French *régime*, the heroic incidents of which Mr Francis Parkman has anticipated Canadian writers in depicting, though his charming narratives ... reconcile us to the thought that the period has found its first and best historian in an American.'[9] Parkman's organized research and LeMoine's more random but equally engaging tidbits together inspired a literary interest in historical and contemporary French Canada that was to thrive into the twentieth century. Foremost among its consequences was the writing of William Kirby's *The Golden Dog* (1877), revered in late Victorian Canada as 'our finest novel'[10] and never out of print.[11]

The Golden Dog was inspired by LeMoine and approved by Parkman. In a letter to LeMoine written after his book had finally appeared in print Kirby described its conception:

In 1865 I think – I was in attendance at Parliament in Quebec ... when your excellent 'Maple Leaves' came into my hands. I read it with great interest, and sitting with Sulte one day in the window of the St Louis Hotel, I read portions of it to him, remarking that here was the finest subject for a romance that I knew of. We talked much of Château Bigot and the Chien d'Or. I wanted Sulte, as a clever French Canadian, to write the story, and finally half in jest, half in earnest, threatened him, that if he would not write the story of the Chien d'Or I would! That was the beginning of it.[12]

Kirby, his friends, and his reviewers concurred regarding the didactic, nationalistic, and literary value of *The Golden Dog*. The Toronto *Mail*'s approval of its historical content was amplified when *The Canadian Monthly* endorsed Kirby's version of the last decades of French rule in New France, finding the novel informative, entertaining, and supportive of its own political bias:

This admirable historical fiction deserves the warmest commendation, not merely for its lucid and flowing style, and the artistic construction of its plot, but especially for the light it throws on the institutions of the old French *régime* and the real causes of the collapse of Bourbon power in the Dominion ... [T]he natural fruit of a vicious system began to appear the moment France neglected her colony and bad men assumed the reins of power.

It accepted Kirby's excuse that he 'had to perpetrate an anachronism or two to make the ends of it tie together'[13] since 'the slight liberties taken with received accounts not only do not mar the story but were absolutely necessary to ensure the unities of time and action and give completeness to the plot.' Indeed the *Monthly* felt that 'As compared with Scott, [Kirby] is accuracy itself.' Kirby's contribution to the development of a national literature overrode any minor quibbles, and the *Monthly* concluded that 'as a whole, the work deserves to be attentively read by all who relish an interesting book, but more especially by those who love Canada and her traditions, and desire to foster and encourage native literature.'[14] The French press also responded warmly. *La Revue Canadienne* was impressed by Kirby's historical research and in *L'Opinion Publique* Kirby's friend Benjamin Sulte enthused, 'Saluons un Anglais qui a étudié l'histoire de la Nouvelle-France. Saluons l'un des meilleurs romans canadiens qui aient été écrits en langue anglaise.'[15]

Although he consulted LeMoine regarding historical details, Kirby remained fully aware that he was not writing history. As he later explained, 'Historical inaccuracies may be discovered in the history of the Chien d'or but this book is not a history – but a romance – and must be judged by the higher laws of poetic and dramatic fiction than by the dry rule & figures work of history.' Moreover, 'the MS was read by the late Francis Parkman at the request of the Lovells – and by him strongly recommended for publication. His imprimatur has always been a pleasing recollection.'[16] Kirby regarded history as the common property of the literary world and he leaped to LeMoine's defence when the latter was accused of plagiarism in his *Chronicles of the St Lawrence* (1878):

[P]lagiarism indeed! as if historical facts, legends & traditions were not the stuff, the raw material out of which every writer who is worth reading does not exercise his genius in forming them into works of art and things of beauty – if he can! We take things that are brute matter, common property, like unappointed land, and by our work give them value, beauty, life, and they become a right & an inheritance. As well dispute Shakespear a title to his plays, because they are a new fusion of old stories refined & recast in his immortal mind![17]

It was Kirby's recasting of Canadian history that won the praise of Benjamin Sulte, his personal friend and later his associate in the Royal Society. Sulte valued *The Golden Dog* precisely because it was not history and therefore would reach and educate a much larger audience:

Mr Parkman, que les lecteurs anglais admirent avec raison, n'a pourtant rien fait que de coucher dans la langue qu'il parle des pages bien connues de l'histoire du Canada, mais connues des Canadiens-français seulement. En exploitant la même mine, vous aurez comme lui la vogue et le charme de la nouveauté. De plus, la partie de vos récits qui ressort de l'imagination pur et simple contribuera à populariser le *Chien d'or*, – ceci n'arrivera pas pour Mr Parkman, car du moment que l'on traite l'histoire pour l'histoire, on ne se fait connaître que d'une classe de la société.

As an historical novelist Kirby joined distinguished company. Although Lorne Pierce was later to fault him for having 'studied the novel as developed by Scott and Dumas père and applied the rules of these craftsmen with little originality,'[18] Kirby's resemblance to these writers was a major strength in the eyes of his contemporaries: 'L'avantage du roman sur les autres genres est très visible. Quant à la renomme littéraire qui en déroule, je pense qu'on peut être content de se nommer Walter Scott, Fenimore Cooper, ou Alexandre Dumas. Dans notre pays, cette place est à prendre, et laissez-moi vous dire que vous semblez le comprendre parfaitement.'[19]

While *The Golden Dog* may not have fulfilled its lofty mission of bridging the two solitudes[20] it certainly did succeed in crystallizing English Canada's formulation of the myth of Quebec. In his now famous conclusion to the first edition of the *Literary History of Canada*, Northrop Frye places English Canada's literary fascination with French Canada in the pastoral tradition:

At the heart of all social mythology lies what may be called, because it is usually called, a pastoral myth, the vision of a social ideal. The pastoral in its most common form is associated with childhood, or with some earlier social condition – pioneer life, the small town, the *habitant* rooted to his land – that can be identified with childhood. The nostalgia for a world of peace and protection, with a spontaneous response to the nature around it, with a leisure and composure not to be found today, is particularly strong in Canada.

In Victorian Canada this nostalgia frequently took the form of 'the evocation of an earlier period of history which is made romantic by having a more uninhibited expression of passion or virtue or courage attached to it. This of course links the pastoral myth with the vision of vanished grandeur that comes into the novels about the *ancien régime*.'[21] The eager participation in this myth on the part of *The Golden Dog*'s contemporary readers prompted their celebration of its 'realism.' LeMoine's praise for Kirby's characters was echoed by *The Canadian Monthly*'s observation that 'The sketches of manners and institutions under the old *régime* are exceedingly well wrought in.'[22] Benjamin Sulte in *L'Opinion Publique* and Pamphile Le May in his introduction to his translation of *The Golden Dog* indicated that the book also satisfied French Canada's desire for a romantic vision of its past.[23]

Although Kirby conceived of his novel as tragedy, the book is pastoral in Frye's sense in its depiction of a once ideal social order whose noble principles and personages are gradually blighted by the serpents of corruption and self-interest. Structuring the story of the Philiberts, the Repentignys, Bigot, Angélique des Meloises, and La Corriveau is the archetypal confrontation of good and evil, figured forth in human terms. On Kirby's romantic stage absolute good (Amélie de Repentigny and Bourgeois Philibert) and absolute wickedness (La Corriveau) clearly declare themselves. Through the gradual corruption of Bigot and Angélique, who infect the wavering and destroy the virtuous, New France yields to the ascendancy of evil with all the inevitability of preordained action contained in 'received traditions.'[24] Apparently casual references to Eden and Adam and Eve uttered by various characters and the omniscient narrator (1, 48–9, 79, 161, 280–1, 476) reinforce the book's mythic structure as a New World version of the first fall and demonstrate the vulnerability of the virgin continent to the decadence of European civilization.

In his concluding paragraph Kirby summarizes the moral and imaginative relationship between his fictional romance based on history and the real world in which similar actions transpire. He gives his tale a fable quality: 'It ends in all sadness, as most true tales of this world do! There is in it neither poetic nor human justice. Fain would we have had it otherwise, for the heart longs for happiness as the eye for light! But truth is stronger as well as stranger than fiction ...' (678) This assertion that the book illustrates the absence of justice in a fallen world so disturbed *The Canadian Monthly*'s reviewer that the latter carried the story beyond the conclusion of the novel to reassure readers of the historical fate of 'Bigot and his vile crew ... for it is eminently satisfactory to one's sense of justice.'[25] But Kirby himself was more concerned with the imaginative connection between old Quebec and the present than with demonstrating the reliability of Providence. The sentence that begins 'But truth is stronger as well as stranger than fiction ... ' continues 'and while the tablet of the *Chien d'Or* overlooks the Rue Buade; while the lamp of Repentigny burns in the ancient chapel of the Ursulines; while the ruins of Beaumanoir cover the dust of Caroline de St Castin; and Amélie sleeps her long sleep by the side of Héloise de Lotbinière, this writer has neither courage nor power to deviate from the received traditions in relating the story of the Golden Dog' (678). Repetition of the word 'while' emphasizes both the temporal and the physical continuity of relics and 'received traditions' from the past which shape the present, signalling how Kirby and his compatriots looked to old Quebec for the desired 'vision of vanished grandeur' (Frye's phrase) lacking in the social mythology of English Canada.

Kirby's Tory social vision projects onto New France an irretrievable, idyllic feudal past. His description of May-Day celebrations on the estate of Lady de Tilly, one of the last representatives of an idealized aristocracy, is interrupted by the authorial reflection that 'The revels of May in New France, the king and queen of St Philip, the rejoicings of a frank, loyal peasantry – illiterate in books but not unlearned in the art of life – have wholly disappeared before the levelling spirit of the nineteenth century' (284). While the depravity of Bigot's administration which is responsible for the loss of this paradise aroused Kirby's moral indignation, its luxury and debauchery also excited his sensual imagination. The elaborate descriptions of the furnishings of Caroline de St Castin's secret apartment, where 'Nothing that luxury could desire, or art furnish, had been spared' (67), of Angélique's boudoir as a 'nest of luxury and elegance' (155), and of Bigot's revelries which 'defied the very order of nature by [their] audacious disregard of all decency of time, place and circumstance' (51) suggest the perverse attraction of Gallic decadence to the upright Upper Canadian Tory mind.

In addition to presenting pre-Conquest Quebec as the scene of startling contrasts of order and disorder, Kirby exploited the gothic associations of New France. The combined attraction to manifest evil and repulsion from it that constitute the 'gothic shudder' inspired him to include the legendary poisoner, La Corriveau, in his tale. Parallel to the way Bigot's administration infects the New World with the depravity of the Old, La Corriveau preserves horrible secrets inherited from Renaissance France and Italy, her murder of Caroline de St Castin transporting to Quebec the archetypal gothic pursuit of an innocent maiden. The agent of 'wickedness, fell and artful' (479), La Corriveau performs on a functional level by expediting Kirby's plot. On a structural level she unifies several of the legends popularized by LeMoine and on an imaginative level she personifies unregenerate evil. Some of the best writing in *The Golden Dog* occurs in Kirby's account of the history and activities of La Corriveau, and Kirby's own obvious fascination with the darker traditions of French Canada helped consolidate English Canada's sense that Quebec's folk culture was largely gothic.[26] At the same time, Kirby drew on less sinister aspects of the romantic tradition. He approached folklore sentimentally when he adapted LeMoine's account of 'The Grave of Cadieux'[27] to provide Amélie de Repentigny with a song 'of wonderful pathos and beauty' (271) and he turned to the pastoral (in the common sense of the word) in his portrait of the *habitants*.

Kirby's depiction of a happy, humble peasantry reinforced the view of French Canada introduced in the first native English-Canadian novel. In *St Ursula's Convent*, Hart's characters describe the *habitants* as an 'honest, peaceful contented people' whose filial obedience to their Seigneur recalls 'the golden ages.'[28] Kirby's development of this image emphasizes the innocence and simplicity which allow the rustics to endure and prosper, untouched by the decadence of the governing classes despite their cognizance of Bigot's debauchery. In their devotion to God and King, their perpetuation of a folk culture indigenous to their class, their lack of material ambition, and their willingness to remain in their inherited social station, Kirby's *habitants* incarnate an idealized pastoral purity.[29] By intertwining documented history with popular legend, idealizing a stratified social order, and presenting contrasting extremes of chivalry and luxury, debauchery, and religious devotion, *The Golden Dog* in all its massiveness provided a solid foundation to support the flimsier constructions of Kirby's fellow romancers who were drawn to Lower Canada's local and historical colour.

The novel most frequently paired with Kirby's as evidence of English Canada's growing literary accomplishment was John Talon-Lesperance's *The Bastonnais*, published the same year as *The Golden Dog* and greeted as 'an interesting historical tale in which the facts of history are handled with scrupulous reverence.'[30] Indeed, the scrupulousness of Lesperance's reverence for history somewhat oppresses his 'Tale of the American Invasion of Canada in 1775–76' as the historian wrestles with the romancer to present detailed references to 'the researches we have made.'[31] More germane is his recourse to certain stereotypes of plot and character which recur frequently in nineteenth-century Canadian fiction.

The story concerns the entanglements of two French-Canadian women with two English-speaking men, one American, the other originally from Britain. Roderick Hardinge, born in Scotland but raised in Murray Bay (La Malbaie), incarnates all the virtues of Canada's multiple heritages. In addition to being perfectly bilingual, he 'was tall, robust, athletic and active. He was very fond of field sports. He had made many a tramp on snow-shoes with the *coureurs de bois* far into the heart of the wilderness. He had often wandered for months with some of the young Hurons of Lorette in quest of the deer and the bison. He was a magnificent horseman' (85).

The American counterpart to this sterling specimen of Canadian manhood is Cary Singleton, an equally valiant, honourable, bilingual officer descended from 'a good stock, Maryland on the side of his father, Virginia on that of his mother' (137). Together these paragons vie for the affections of two *belles Québécoises*: Pauline Belmont, 'the true type of the loveable woman' (88) and exotic Zulma Sarpy, educated in France, 'fair as a filament of summer gorse, and statuesque in all her poses' (96). The complicated amours of this quartet represent conflicting political and cultural allegiances, the ultimate marriages of Roderick and Zulma, and Pauline and Cary allegorizing the union of English and French, and Canadian and American interests in North America. In the book's final paragraph the narrator encounters a young woman who turns out to be the granddaughter of the two couples; when 'at last, the blood of all the lovers had mingled together in one' (359) the resolution of sexual strife signals the assurance of continental peace.

The separation of lovers by political discord is of course a classic component of both comedy and tragedy. In Canadian fiction like *The Bastonnais* this convention frequently acquires symbolic overtones, especially when a French-Canadian maiden is wooed and won by an English-Canadian suitor. Love triumphs and resolves national disputes when the Québécoise heroine of 'Rosalba; or, Faithful to Two Lovers' eventually marries her English-Canadian sweetheart after the trauma of the 1837 rebellion. However, not just any Anglophone will do, as Rosanna Leprohon's Antoinette De Mirecourt discovers. In her 1864 sentimental novel set in post-Conquest Quebec, Leprohon allows her heroine to make the mistake of marrying the wrong Englishman, the violent, fortune-hunting Audley Sternfield, before settling down with the romantic wanderer, Captain Evelyn. Although Antoinette's father would prefer her to remain within her culture and espouse her childhood sweetheart, Louis Beauchesne, Leprohon simultaneously disposes of both that option and the odious Sternfield by having Beauchesne shoot his rival. Unlike most subsequent English-Canadian fiction set in historic Quebec, *Antoinette De Mirecourt* (whose source is Garneau rather than Parkman) makes little use of colourful adventure and picturesque customs. Instead, Leprohon manipulates the social and moral complications presented by the sudden influx of British officers into Montreal society just after the Seven Years' War to convey a message of emotional honesty and filial obedience.

The ease with which Leprohon marries Antoinette, daughter of a defeated nation, to one of her conquerors may have been in reply to Philippe Aubert de Gaspé, whose enormously popular *Les anciens canadiens* (1862) she would certainly have read. In his novel about the conquest of Quebec, de Gaspé develops a refined romance between Blanche D'Haberville, daughter of a seigneurial Quebec family, and Archibald Cameron of Lochiel, a Jacobite exile who has found refuge in Quebec. At the outbreak of the Seven Years' War, Cameron reverts to his origins by joining a Highland regiment and he is eventually ordered to burn down the Manoir D'Haberville. After the war he makes his peace with his old friends and proposes to Blanche. Although she makes no secret of her love for 'Arché,' Blanche refuses marriage, declaring

Il est naturel, il est même à souhaiter que les races française et anglo-saxonne, ayant maintenant une même patrie, vivant sous les mêmes lois, après des haines, après des luttes seculaires, se rapprochent par des alliances intimes; mais il serait indigne de moi d'en donner l'exemple après tant de désastres; on croirait, comme je l'ai dit à Arché, que le fier Breton, après avoir vaincu et ruiné le père, a acheté avec son or la pauvre fille canadienne, trop heureuse de se donner à ce prix. Oh! jamais! jamais![32]

Blanche will allow her brother to marry 'une Anglaise' but for her to espouse her conqueror would amount to utter capitulation. De Gaspé's acceptance of marriage between a French-Canadian man and an English-Canadian woman and rejection of the converse justifies our reading the frequency of marriages between *belles Québécoises* and valiant English men in nineteenth-century English-Canadian fiction as a signal of English Canada's political supremacy. Such a union predicates the absorption of the female partner into the dominant culture of the male, the sexual submission of the individual symbolizing the political submission of the group. If *La Revue Canadienne*'s comments on *Antoinette De Mirecourt* are representative, French-Canadian critics were very sensitive to the implications of fictional intermarriage. Joseph-Edouard Lefebvre de Bellefeuille (nephew of Leprohon's husband) praised Leprohon's book extravagantly but took exception to its ending:

Si je devais trouver un défaut dans le livre de Mme Leprohon, ce serait peut-être d'avoir fait marier successivement son héroïne, sa belle *Antoinette*, avec deux officiers anglais ... Je pense bien que l'auteur n'a pas voulu le proposer en cela comme un modèle à nos jeunes Canadiennes, mais la peinture d'un bonheur fictif peut quelquefois vivement séduire un jeune coeur nourri d'idéal loin de la trompeuse réalité ... Il est vrai que le Col. *Evelyn*, le second mari d'*Antoinette*, était catholique; c'est quelque chose, mais ce n'est pas tout ce que je désire voir dans l'époux d'une de mes jeunes compatriotes: il n'était pas Canadien.[33]

In the polished historical fiction of Charles G.D. Roberts, however, love between two representatives of opposing political forces is less reflective of national allegory than of the predictable plot formulas of turn-of-the-century romance. While central Canadians interested in French Canada followed Parkman and turned to historic Quebec, Maritimers pursued the direction taken by Longfellow (who had himself been inspired by Haliburton)[34] and looked to Acadia. Victorian Canada's irksome debt to this pair of Americans was a subject of frequent commentary such as *The Canadian Monthly*'s quip that 'Mr Parkman is our best chronicler, and Mr Longfellow, in his Evangeline, our national poet.'[35] Early in his career Roberts paid homage to Longfellow whose 'handling of the Acadian story has simply glorified the theme for later singers.'[36] This view was shared by most Canadians with the crusty exception of Goldwin Smith, who protested that 'The false and calumnious version of [the expulsion of the Acadians] has been made popular by the barley-sugar composition which is styled the poetry of Longfellow. Perhaps the moralists will some day give us, for the benefit of history, their opinion as to the proper limits of lying in verse.'[37] Smith notwithstanding, *The Canadian Magazine* was sufficiently convinced of the 'sacredness' of the name 'Evangeline' to confer on its possessor the status of a 'national heroine'[38] and thoroughly supported the way the romance of Acadia captured the attention of Maritimers interested in exploring their local counterpart to the romance of Quebec.

When Roberts published his Acadian novels in the 1890s and 1900s he was working within an area already charted by several predecessors. Long before Kirby incorporated into *The Golden Dog* legendary material concerning the daughter of Baron de Saint-Castin and his Abenaki wife, two Nova Scotians had produced fictional accounts of the prolific Baron's half-Indian progeny. Douglas Huyghue's *Argimou* (1847), published the same year as *Evangeline*, elegizes the decline of the once-noble 'aborigines of America' while describing the loves and trials of Argimou, Grand Sachem of the Micmac nation, and his 'fawn-like' Waswetchcul, Saint-Castin's daughter.[39] Centring his tale on the English conquest of Fort Beauséjour in 1755, Huyghue used the occasion to lament the white man's destruction of the Indian. In *St Castine: A Legend of Cape Breton* (1850), William Charles McKinnon also contrasted 'the degenerate Micmac of to-day' with their forefathers, 'Haughty as the knights of old, and easily affronted.'[40]

Unlike much of the historical fiction about Quebec, English-language fiction about Acadia demonstrates little direct interest in reconstructing the past through references to documented history.[41] Instead, Maritimers drew upon the French-Canadian side of their heritage as a convenient source of local colour and sentimentality. In Clotilda Jennings' *The White Rose in Acadia* (1855), the expulsion provides a tragic ending to a romance foredoomed by its conflicts of nationality and religion. Likewise, Roberts' historical tales exploit the sentimental associations surrounding the expulsion of the Acadians with little exploration of the event's historical complexity.

Written primarily after Roberts left Canada for New York and published by American firms, his Acadian romances specifically cater to an international taste for light, swashbuckling romance, meeting the American market for French-Canadian historical fiction first established by Mary Hartwell Catherwood in the late 1880s. Roberts' contribution to the international image of Canadian literature was recognized by a New York reviewer of *The Prisoner of Mademoiselle* (1904), a deft tale of love and pursuit, who appreciated the book's particularly Canadian quality: 'It possesses a peculiar attraction which we recognize in almost all works of fiction which come to us from Canada; an atmosphere of refinement and a certain loftiness characterise their romance ... It has gleams of humour in its high romance, and is told with a certain elegance characteristic of its origin.'[42]

To suit the conventions of high romance Roberts populated the land of Evangeline with humble peasants, a balance of bloodthirsty Indians under the leadership of the vicious Black Abbé and noble savages who assist the heroes, a demented prophet who wanders through several volumes chanting 'Woe, woe to Acadie the fair,' and various couples for whom historical discord provides barriers to be overcome by love. Faithful to the aim of his genre to comfort its audience, Roberts gave a happier ending to Longfellow's melodrama by having the exiles of *A Sister to Evangeline* (1898) take over their ship and remain in New France, eventually integrating into a submissive post-Conquest Quebec. His ploy of making Abbé Le Loutre the villainous instigator of Acadian resistance allowed him to ameliorate the image of the British and also generate sympathy for the Acadians; a similar desire to make amends for errors of history motivates the hero of Marshall Saunders' *Rose à Charlitte* (1898), a romance set among contemporary Acadians.

The historical novels of Charles G.D. Roberts and Gilbert Parker illustrate how English Canada's treatment of New France shifted, from the earnest interest in its culture and history manifested in the serious historical fiction of the late 1870s to the more superficial use of French Canada's picturesqueness typical of the stories composed for the popular periodicals of the 1890s. One way to avoid the polarization of the increasingly bitter debate about realism and naturalism in fiction was to withdraw into a less troubling pre-industrial past where political friction could be resolved on the battlefield, social status was determined by birth, and sexual tension could be sublimated into the drama of courtship. 'In a historical romance,' noted one journalist with evident relief, 'there is no room for that psychological treatment which, for good or ill, asserts itself so prominently in the novel-writing of the day.'[43]

Like Roberts, Parker viewed history as dull fabric to be embroidered by the romancer. Modern critics agree that Parker's costume romances exhibit none of the determined faithfulness to the past, appreciation of historical forces, or complex patterns of motivation which distinguish *The Golden Dog*.[44] Yet most contemporary reviewers praised 'the pre-Raphaelite fidelity with which Mr Parker's vivid and picturesque scenes are painted.'[45] *Massey's Magazine* pronounced *The Seats of the Mighty* a work of 'considerable' historical value[46] and *The Canadian Magazine* declared its author 'Canada's greatest novelist' because he was seen to maintain the qualities Goldwin Smith had valued in Walter Scott: 'His works ... are wholesome and fruitful, bright and interesting, polished and refined. His historical romances compare with the best work of this class in the English language. He is progressive and stable. He is never flippant and always instructive.'[47]

Particularly intrinsic to the development of Canadian literature and literary attitudes are Parker's stories of contemporary French-Canadian life. The late nineteenth-century interest in local colour that inspired American and British writers like Bret Harte and Rudyard Kipling to fictionalize the manners and dialects of far corners of their domains sent

Parker to the Northwest and Quebec. Parker claimed that his tales, first published in popular British and American periodicals before being collected in *Pierre and His People* (1892), opened up the Canadian North in fiction. To unify his melodramatic stories of the Hudson's Bay region – with which he had scant personal acquaintance – Parker concocted Pretty Pierre, an elegant French-speaking Métis gambler 'begat in an hour between a fighting and a mass' who was, Parker always insisted, 'true to life – to his race, to his environment, to the conditions of pioneer life through which he moved.'[48]

Sensing that the charismatic Parker (who had trained as an elocutionist) possessed the knack of playing to his audience, Bliss Carman astutely predicted in 1894 that Parker was 'one of the half dozen English novelists to whom the opening of the twentieth century is likely to belong.'[49] Three of his books – *The Seats of the Mighty* (1896), *The Right of Way* (1901), and *The Weavers* (1907) – became best and 'better' sellers in the United States[50] and most of his Canadian readers, thrilled at the international success of a native son, pronounced themselves 'thankful to Sir Gilbert for idealizing Canada.'[51] Well into the modern era Parker's eulogizers enjoyed the way his books upheld the principles of Smith's Lamps of Fiction. In 1927 Lorne Pierce demonstrated that Canadian criticism remained firmly entrenched in the nineteenth century when he declared 'There are many elevated moral passages in his work, as well as a fine use of Scriptures. Mr. Parker is also free from morbidity, sombre psychology and sex; he is wholesome and yet virile.'[52]

But Parker did not receive quite the unanimous acclaim enjoyed by William Kirby and Sir Walter Scott. One of the most vehement denunciations of his superficiality appeared in the Toronto *Evening Star,* which accused him of callously exploiting his country:

Gilbert Parker ... is a poseur from first to last. He is romantic and idealistic, and has the faults of his qualities. Able to write limpid prose, he prefers to strain after those meretricious blank verse effects which spoil true style. He is popular because he had the commercial shrewdness to give the reading public the only part of the British Empire that had not been exploited. When Pierre and His People was published, Haggard had worked Africa and Kipling India, and the other habitable portions of the globe had likewise their manipulators. Parker served up Canada and the Canadian Northwest, giving the latter region a local colour that existed largely in his own imagination. At any rate, invidious people say that Parker's Northwest is as much like the real thing as a peacock is like a Moor hen, and as for the preposterous Pierre, with his everlasting cigaret and his graceful insouciance – such a half-breed as that could hardly escape the Lieutenant Governorship of the Territories.[53]

Parker carried his self-conscious romanticism from the North to Quebec in *The Pomp of the Lavilettes* (1896), *The Lane that Had no Turning* (1900), *The Right of Way* (1901), and *The Money Master* (1915). In the prefaces to the Imperial Edition of his Collected Works he claimed that these books were realistic studies of French-Canadian life. The perspective of his English-Canadian readers who praised their 'atmosphere of the old French-Canadian life so truthfully depicted that its very naturalness is the highest tribute to the author's ability'[54] had been shaped by authoritative commentaries like those reviewed in the March 1899 issue of *The Canadian Magazine*,[55] which reinforced the stereotype of the simple, contented *habitant*.

Melodrama, condescension, and distance from his subject impeded Parker's efforts to create a Quebec counterpart to Thomas Hardy's Wessex. Although *The Money Master*, for example, overtly recalls *The Mayor of Casterbridge*, Parker's decision to populate Quebec with gothic eccentrics and romantic stereotypes suggests that his inspiration came more directly from popular convention than from first-hand acquaintance with the society being represented.

In several interviews Parker expounded the literary principles responsible for his staggering success in his day and his equally astonishing current neglect. He explicitly rejected the kind of realism advocated by Sara Jeannette Duncan:

I appreciate the talent of the writer who takes a slab of life, who anatomizes it as a skilled surgeon would a body, who brings out its details even though they may be hideous, but there is no urge in me for such dissection.

I have the romantic tendency ... I make my characters a little better, a little more adventurous, a little more superlative in all their qualities than they would be possibly in real life.[56]

Hence he found Quebec the only part of Canada with any 'glamor' in a country that was otherwise 'serenely unpicturesque.' Claiming that he needed 'the clash of race' and 'great elements of contrast' to provide dramatic material, he struck a pose of false humility to explain why these could be found in the North and Quebec:

You have, at the present day in Canada, human life, and that is immensely interesting, and to bring it out of unpicturesque surroundings and give it eminence requires not only great art, but great humanity; therefore, we who are not great, have a hard task because we have no adventitious aids to fame ... That is why I went where there were contrasts – to Hudson's Bay which still provided great elements of contrast ... It is also provided in Quebec, by reason of the clash of race – English and French.[57]

Parker was the most conspicuous of the many Canadian writers who contributed local colour tales of French Canada to major American periodicals before collecting them in book form. Like the late nineteenth-century painters who 'created an image of Quebec widespread through Canada, an image of quaint folk customs and superstitions, of a country people who were likeable yet slightly backward and out of touch with reality and current life,' they 'sought for the picturesque and quaint elements in Quebec life as their subject matter.'[58] Most of their books, such as E.W. Thomson's *Old Man Savarin Stories* (1895), William McLennan's *In Old France and New* (1899), H.C. Walsh's *Bonhomme* (1899), and G.M. Fairchild's *A Ridiculous Courting and Other Stories of French Canada* (1900), will strike the modern reader as being as condescending, melodramatic, and sentimental as Parker's work. Yet the tendency of their turn-of-the-century English-Canadian audience to read these stories as realistic and sympathetic portrayals of Quebec went almost unchallenged,[59] while at the same time they ignored Francis W. Grey's *The Curé of St Philippe* (1899), the one Canadian fiction of that era to apply the methods of the British social realists to Quebec village life. Throughout 1896, for example, *The Canadian Magazine* followed the progress of Clifford Smith's *A Lover in Homespun and Other Stories of French Canada*, commending 'these glimpses of French-Canadian life' for being 'photographic in their fidelity' and happily reporting in August that this was the best-selling Canadian book of the month.[60] So prominent was the genre that several members of the next generation chose it for their first venture into print. Both Florence Randal Livesay and Mazo de la Roche published French-Canadian stories before going on to the work for which they became better known; intriguing is the latter's later amnesia regarding her reason for the choice.[61] The popularity of *habitant* stories into the 1920s elicited W.A. Deacon's complaint of 'weariness with the veneration with which the habitant has been treated in Canadian literature for the past ten years.'[62]

Archibald Lampman, from whom criticism of some astuteness might be expected, particularly lauded the work of his friend E.W. Thomson. The qualities for which he commended Thomson are less applicable to the actual volume of *Old Man Savarin Stories* than to Lampman's conception of a truly Canadian literature. Out of his desire for authenticity he praised the book for having been 'written not by a foreign littérateur who has scoured this country on the hunt for new sensations, but by a Canadian who has lived in the places the very scent of whose pines and the pure breath of whose atmosphere he brings before us, and worked with the people whose simple humanity and genuine talk lend humour and life to his pages.' In the language of Thomson's stories, some written in the *habitant* dialect soon to be popularized by W.H. Drummond, Lampman thought he detected a genuine Canadian voice which is 'often extraordinarily simple, but it is the kindly offspring of genuine conception, and direct spontaneous feeling, and ... often something particularly apt to a Canadian ear.'[63]

Thomson's skilfully written stories are good specimens of magazine fiction. Two other writers did add a special dimension to English Canada's literary treatment of French Canada by transforming the local colour tale from an entertaining account of a quaint culture to an intense imaginative experience. The Quebec fiction of Susie Frances Harrison and Duncan Campbell Scott follows an approach to Lower Canada first adumbrated in *The Golden Dog*.

Victorian Canadians enjoyed *The Golden Dog* because like their Queen they 'liked a novel.'[64] In this book Kirby's handling of time suggests that in writing about French Canada he was tackling a problem more subtle than the recounting of historical facts and legends. When dealing with historical characters Kirby occasionally leaps out of the present time of his novel to forecast future events. From his opening chapter to his final paragraph, projections into the future underscore the relation of each historical moment to previous and future historical time. Simultaneously, he constructs a superhistorical perspective when he refers to areas and events beyond the range of verifiable history. Geological prehistory enters Peter Kalm's scientific speculations (412–16) and suggests the brevity of the love between Pierre Philibert and Amélie de Repentigny when the lovers are seated on 'a boulder which had dropped millions of years before out of an iceberg as it sailed slowly over the glacial ocean which then covered the place of New France' (299–300). To these scientific references to time beyond human knowledge Kirby adds the dimension of mythic time with frequent allusions to the Bible and to classical mythology. By making New France the confluence of time and timelessness he effectively elevated Lower Canada from a geographical place to an imaginative space, 'a symbolic landscape, at once familiar and foreign.'[65] It was as an imaginative space that Quebec appealed to Harrison and Scott.

In her poetry and her fiction Harrison creates a Quebec removed from English Canada in both space and time: not a Lower Canada composed only of conventional cheerful peasants and gothic fireside tales, but also a place where her protagonists – usually English-speaking outsiders – encounter their own lower depths. Several of the pieces in *Crowded Out! and Other Sketches* (1886) strikingly illustrate an imaginative relationship between English Canada and Quebec in which the Lower Province serves as a looking-glass for the Upper, where fears and desires can be clothed and confronted in tangible, outer forms. The narrator of the title story is a young English-Canadian musician/writer failing to achieve recognition in London. As he descends into madness and death he calls the name of his beloved Hortense, a high-born Québécoise. Hortense Angélique de Repentigny de St Hilaire[66] is not only a disdainful mistress whose image haunts her lover; she is also under the domination of a lecherous old priest who 'has brought her up like a nun, crushed the life out of her ... my God! that night while I watched them studying and bending over those cursed works on the Martyrs and the Saints and the Mission houses – I saw him – him – that old priest – take her in his arms and caress her, drink her breath, feast on her eyes, her hair, her delicate skin ...'[67]

This experience with perverted religion and sexuality destroys the young man, who dies murmuring, 'Descendez à l'ombre, / Ma jolie blonde.' The same lines from a Quebec ballad, 'so weird, so solemn, so earnest, yet so pathetic, so sweet, so melodious,'[68] form the title of a story in which they again signal death for the English outsider, this time from smallpox contracted from a French Canadian. Other English-speaking visitors discover Quebec to be the locale of gothicism, romance, and inversion in 'The Story of Delle Josephine Boulanger' when a reserved old maid turns out to be a harmless maniac, and 'The Story of Etienne Chezy D'Alencourt' when an English immigrant learns that the man he had thought the epitome of the *habitant* is actually of noble descent.

Harrison's two novels, *The Forest of Bourg-Marie* (1898) and *Ringfield* (1912), expand upon this literary approach to Quebec. Joshua Ringfield, the protagonist of the second book, is an Ontario Methodist preacher whose traumatic experiences in the isolated village of St Ignace ultimately inspire his retreat from English Protestantism to the secure arms of the Roman Catholic Church. An ambitious, practical man, Ringfield first arrives in the village at the request of the Americanized Poussette, an entrepreneur hoping to bring progress and enlightenment to his native parish. But his design backfires when Ringfield's repressed passions break through his cool, Protestant exterior and he falls hopelessly in love with Pauline Clairville, an actress descended from the region's seigneurial family. Pauline's fatal decadence is aptly symbolized by the white peacock wandering about the decaying family manor which she shares with her demented brother. Ringfield suffers terrible conflicts between emotion and intellect when his infatuation with Pauline forces him to acknowledge much that his Methodism abhors – aristocracy, the stage, hints of illegitimacy, sexuality – in short, the region of suppressed passion and irrationality. In his inevitable nervous breakdown he succumbs to the overwhelming psychic underworld that Anglophone writers can project onto Quebec. When Pauline finally marries his rival, Ringfield cannot return to Ontario. The invitation of the Roman Catholic Church, the backbone of French Canada, proves irresistible, and the former Methodist retires forever to 'The cloister, the cross, the strange, hooded, cloaked men ... the rich symbolism of even the simplest service ... that beckoning world of monks and monastic quiet.'[69]

In *The Forest of Bourg-Marie* the role of the Anglophone outsider is not given to a character within the novel but conferred upon the English-speaking reader. Harrison introduces English Canada to the alien wilderness of Quebec in her dramatic opening paragraphs:

Bordering the mighty river of the Yamachiche there are three notable forests, dark, uncleared, untrodden, and unfrequented by man, lofty as Atlas, lonely as Lethe, sombre as Hades. In their Plutonian shades stalk spectral shapes of trapper and voyageur, Algonquin and Iroquois, Breton and Highlander, Saxon and Celt ...

The forest of Bourg-Marie is the darkest, the deepest, the most impenetrable, the most forbidding of the three. The stars of spring that light up other woods seem here rarely to pierce through the cold, hard ground to the sun: the sun itself seldom penetrates the thick branches of fir and pine and hemlock ... Fitting soil for fable and legend, for the tale of the Dead Man's Tree, for the livelier story of ill-fated Rose Latulippe, for countless minor myths that the old women and the old men, even the young men and maidens, have at their fingers' ends ...[70]

Harrison's alliance of classical references and Quebec folklore creates a foreboding backdrop for the dramatization of mythic conflicts between past and present, tradition and materialism, and, ultimately, good and evil. Old Mikel Caron, forest ranger for Yamachiche, makes himself fully at home in the primeval wilderness. Descended from the noble family that originally possessed the land, he still owns the ruined manoir where he has constructed a secret room furnished with an elaborately set dining table. This chamber symbolizes his dream of restoring past glory through his grandson, Magloire, whom he had envisaged as a great French-Canadian leader. But Magloire has completely betrayed his identity by Americanizing himself to the extent of Anglicizing his name. Now a gambler, he regards his home and family only as potential sources of funds. In disgust Mikel chooses for his heir Nicholas Laurière, a *habitant* and 'the worthiest, most virtuous, most respectable young man in the parish.'[71]

Like the English-speaking outsiders who appear as characters within Harrison's other works, the reader of *The Forest of Bourg-Marie* is drawn into a gothic landscape to witness the triumph of darkness when Nicholas is destroyed by Magloire and the manoir itself is devastated by a windstorm. Magloire escapes unpunished to prosper in the United States. The book concludes on an elegaic note similar to the ending of *The Golden Dog*: all that finally remains is Mikel's strength to endure.

Stylistically judged 'a distinct revelation of power and mastery of material,'[72] *The Forest of Bourg-Marie* demonstrates the effectiveness of controlled romance. So powerful was its hold on one fellow author that he blurted into one breathless sentence:

'The Forest of Bourg Marie' is a notable work of genius, a book superb in its character drawing, noble in diction, thrilling in incident, and so strongly constructed that it dispenses with conventional love-making, without losing an atom of its interest, a feat which has not been accomplished, to my knowledge, since Robinson Crusoe, and I doubt if there is a novelist living, however famous, who would have had the courage to put forth a romance without a heroine in it.[73]

Powerful writing of a different sort distinguishes Duncan Campbell Scott's stories of the village of Viger, the 'restrained intensity'[74] of his fine literary skill combining with his conception of Quebec as an imaginative space in a sequence of tales which transcend the conventions of the genre. *In the Village of Viger* (1896) is sharpened by the tension between Viger's identity as a 'pleasant' retreat from 'The complex joys and ills of life' in the words of Scott's epigrah, and the threat of the expanding city which is described on the next page.[75] This balancing of dualities – idyll and threat, illusion and reality – permeates the village as Scott establishes a world in which boundaries between fact and fantasy blur and blend until reality ceases to be verifiable, and magic and mystery are not only possible but occasionally the norm. Individual transformations of myth into reality are confirmed on a communal level when the entire village shares the belief that a mysterious blind peddler may be 'the old Devil himself.' Building on the gothicism more possible in Quebec than the Ottawa where he spent most of his life, Scott did not rest with the conventions at the level of entertainment but engaged with them in a process of psychological exploration.[76]

The reviewer for *Massey's Magazine* appreciated the contribution of Scott's style to his effectiveness and commended his 'brief exactness' – 'every word is made to count ... There is so much suggested in it, so much left to the imagination.'[77] Scott's innovation was to reject the dialect humour, melodrama, and sentimentality typical of local colour fiction and to depict the unpredictable life of the imagination in a pared down style utterly removed from the emotive language of his contemporaries. His stories thus mark a high point in Victorian Canada's literary love affair with Quebec – and also illustrate that for Canadian writers of this era the short story was frequently a more hospitable genre than the novel.

Scott's ability to mediate the fine line between realism and romance was not shared by most of his contemporaries. When they turned from the exotic subject of French Canada to the everyday life of their own communities they retained their taste for didacticism and romance. The stuff of realistic fiction – pioneer life, religious doubt, labour issues, social and sexual complications, unwed mothers – attracted many authors, who invariably turned these subjects into occasions to preach, or to confirm 'the romance of real life.'

9 Soulager le Bourgeois

'[T]he empire of the novel,' wrote R.H. Hutton in 1869, 'is really based on the desire of a self-conscious race to look at itself in the glass, and to see itself, as it were, under analysis, – to study itself either clothed, as with [Anthony] Trollope; or nude, as with Thackeray; or under the anatomist's knife, as with the author of *Romola*.'[1] Intrinsic to the nineteenth-century social novel is an appreciation of the complex connections between individual human beings and the labyrinthine social and economic structures within which they function and attempt to make sense of their lives. Fictional characters develop through their struggles to heed or resist social expectations and restrictions; plots recount the consequences visited by the social order upon its darlings and its reprobates. Canadian fiction from this period reflects a country that was struggling to conceive of itself as a place, had little notion of its identity as a society, and shrank from the intimate self-examination practised by Trollope, Thackeray, and Eliot. Far from challenging accepted values, Canadian critics and novelists perceived literature as a medium for reinforcing prevailing norms; 'épater les bourgeois' was never their intention[2] but rather 'soulager' – to comfort and disburden – the middle class.

As illustrated earlier, the problem of realism begins at the basic level of valorizing Canada as a setting for literature. In the fiction published in periodicals as well as that influenced by travel writing it is certainly possible to trace a continuing strain of faithful geographical description, but the realism usually peters out beyond this point. Topographical accuracy is sometimes not even extended to descriptions of climate, thereby omitting the effects of weather conditions on social relations (for example, although Montgomery's diaries record the chill of a Prince

Edward Island winter, that season seldom appears in *Anne of Green Gables*) and very seldom is it matched by accounts of normal life within that landscape.

The few writers who essayed the path towards social realism met with meagre encouragement from a community eager to escape 'the miasma of modern novels.'[3] Around the turn of the century the interest of authors like Robert Sellar, Albert Carman, C.M. Sinclair, Francis W. Grey, and the Lizars sisters in creating fiction out of the materials of folk history and small town daily life was ignored by a readership smitten with Gilbert Parker. Hence in concession to popular taste these writers usually blended genres, their plots suddenly blossoming into unexpected events such as the multiple deaths and coincidences of the second half of the Lizars' *Committed to His Charge* (1900) and the sensational New York material (including a near marriage to a half-sister) which Sinclair added to the later portion of *The Dear Old Farm* (1897). Much of the now forgotten Canadian fiction from this era shares a common pattern of commencing with realistic descriptions of setting and social interaction which then dissolve into the plot conventions of popular romance. Composed just after the period under consideration in this book, the early novels of Robert Stead present an apt illustration of the problem.

Now canonized as a realist principally because of *Grain* (1926), Stead first wrestled with the relation of setting and plot in *The Bail Jumper* (1914) and *The Homesteaders* (1916), in which initial faithfulness to the prairie setting and stark local living conditions gradually succumbs to the intricacies of intrigue. Considerably younger than the authors listed above, Stead was to become 'the only writer to span the development of prairie fiction from the popular genre of romances of pioneering to realistic novels scrutinizing the values of prairie society.'[4] Many of his predecessors simply gave up. Whereas Robert Sellar resorted to printing his work himself, Kathleen Lizars later returned to the better received genre of local history and Grey, Carman, and Sinclair wrote no subsequent fiction about Canada.[5]

Even Sara Jeannette Duncan was to discover that Canada posed particular problems for the social realist. A novel of Canadian life especially intended to appeal to Canadian readers, *The Imperialist* exhibits a narrative division between its political content and its love story similar to the gap Duncan had criticized in *An Algonquin Maiden*, although Duncan handles the problem with considerably more dexterity than did Adam and Wetherald. In *The Curé of St Philippe* (1899), Francis W. Grey pursued a different course by creating a one-sided anatomy that dissects the political machinations of 1894–7 in a Quebec parish in such fine detail as to exclude the uninitiated reader.[6] Presenting electioneering as a masculine domain, he populated his novel with fleshless male characters representing positions rather than persons. Consequently lacking are the dimensions of physicality and domesticity, and the dense texture of daily social interaction in a mixed society where Irish Catholics and Scottish Presbyterians have settled in a traditional French-Canadian community – in other words, the hum of distinctive characters of all ages and sexes going about their usual business in their home environment that contextualizes the political side of *The Imperialist*.

This chapter will later focus on two specific topics selected as touchstones of social realism. Labour strife and illicit sexual activity timidly entered Canadian fiction in the 1890s, more than half a century after they had become familiar subjects in international writing. The first social interests of Canadian writers, however, were uncontroversial. Early Canadian fiction dealing overtly with local daily life tends to conform to one of two distinct categories: the didactic prescription of social conduct, and the fictive pioneer guide. It is at this very elementary level of fictionalizing, of shaping raw experience with the tools of received narrative structure, that the significance of the common mid-century phrase 'the romance of real life' becomes evident.

An 1839 entry from the journal of Anne Langton illustrates the perspective of the immigrant viewing her experience in the New World through eyes educated in the Old:

We have had a thunderstorm today. My mother amused herself during the storm with repeating poetry, a thing I have not done for a very long time. The old world is the world of romance and poetry. I daresay our lakes, waterfalls, rapids, canoes, forests, Indian encampments, sound very well to you dwellers in the suburbs of a manufacturing town; nevertheless I assure you there cannot well be a more unpoetical and anti-romantic existence than ours.[7]

In the 1830s, the second decade of serious efforts to produce Canadian fiction, to valorize 'unpoetical and anti-romantic' Canadian life as literary material it was necessary to call attention to its 'romance.' Rearranging the prevailing criteria for fiction which deemed fictional romance acceptable only if it contained a discernible element of Reality, many stories of Canadian life which were presented as versions of actual experience qualified as literary artifacts by their participation in the conventions of romance. A typical example is John Howard Willis's story, 'Lionel

Hammond.' Claimed to be 'founded on one of those occurrences which sometimes jut out from the commonplace incidents of life,' this sentimental tale is offered as an illustration of 'the romance of reality.'[8] The following decade saw several applications of the phrase 'the romance of real life,'[9] one of the more extensive appearing in Miss Foster's review of Frederika Bremer's *The Neighbours*. Foster found this European novel of domestic life distinguished by 'deep beauty,' 'poetic inspiration,' and 'a high tone of moral feeling.' Her view that 'the romance of real life far exceeds in wildness, aye, and in improbability, the imaginings of the most fantastic brain'[10] exemplifies the attitude of those Victorian Canadians who did indeed want to read and write fiction about moral and social aspects of daily life, but could not conceive of the novel as other than romantic.

When this outlook was directed specifically towards Canadian writing it resulted in statements like J.W. Longley's call for 'the delineator of Canadian life' to 'picture the quiet scenes of industry, the simple incidents of ordinary life, the joys, sorrows, hopes, disappointments, successes and failures which are incident to men in the common routine of life,' not because these are intrinsically interesting, but because 'There is more tragedy in the life of the poorest wood-cutter than ever the most brilliant novelist has conceived and written.'[11] The notion that participation in the grander genres of tragedy and romance would elevate common Canadian experience surfaces again in Coll McLean Sinclair's conclusion of his defence of literary democracy – 'nothing can be commonplace or unimportant, which directly concerns the every day life of the common people' – with the validation of romance: 'no life has more of the element of romance in it than that of the ordinary dweller in rural Canada.'[12]

Ordinary life in rural Canada frequently found successful literary expression in the forms of the emigrant's handbook and the settler's autobiography, Catherine Parr Traill's *The Backwoods of Canada* (1836) and *The Female Emigrant's Guide* (1854), and Susanna Moodie's *Roughing It in the Bush* (1852) having been canonized as representative classics. The impulse to transpose experience into fiction, imported by the first immigrants along with their axes and crockery, resulted in the indigenous genre of the fictionalized survival guide, an ambitious hybrid of practical information and high adventure. Probably the earliest example is the third volume of John Galt's *Bogle Corbet* (1831), which enlivens instructions for the demanding labour of clearing the land and establishing a community with a thin plot reworking familiar conventions of identities lost and found. The author's original intention of 'publishing, for the

benefit of Emigrants, a Statistical Account of Upper Canada'[13] resonates
through his text and its appendix, the narrative taking its direction from
the author's didactic intention which, like Moodie's, is to advise prospective emigrants. Justification for this particular blend of fact and fiction
appears in the preface to *Sketches of Canadian Life, Lay and Ecclesiastical*
(1849) by the Reverend William Stewart Darling, who chose to cast his
'portraiture of Canadian life' in 'the form of a narrative, because a book
written in that style appeared to the author not only less irksome to write,
and more easy to read, but also because he thought, that to trace the
fortunes of an imaginary individual would afford an opportunity of
describing more correctly the numerous minute details of a settler's
experience than a work of higher pretensions and more important
character.'[14]

The appeal of fiction to younger readers jusifies Catharine Parr Traill's
presentation of practical information in fictional form in several works
published in the 1850s. Natural history is the focus of *Lady Mary and Her
Nurse; or, A Peep into the Canadian Forest* (1856)[15] and wilderness survival
the subject of the once popular *Canadian Crusoes: A Tale of the Rice Lake
Plains* (1852).[16] Set in the romantic post-Conquest past, this story of lost
children (which also incorporates a brief captivity narrative) owes its sense
of realism to its copious factual details as three adolescents – a pair of
half-Scottish, half-French siblings and their French-Canadian cousin –
aided by a Mohawk girl whom they rescue, create their own little domestic
paradise when they wander into the primeval forest near Rice Lake.
Relying on their knowledge and their wits, these well-trained young
pioneers enjoy a two-year retreat from the world of their parents,
interrupted only by hostile Indians whose efforts to capture the children
are ultimately foiled. A combination of rational behaviour and divine
beneficence triumphs over adversity, demonstrating that with faith, will,
and judgment the wilderness can easily be tamed. The plot is fleshed out
with encyclopedic nature lore, instructions on conduct, and Christian
proselytizing as the white children convert their Indian friend, the
religious ethos of the book more redolent of its author's own Protestantism than of the Catholicism attributed to the young heroes in accordance
with their ethnicity. Once baptized Indiana becomes an acceptable spouse
for one of her white playmates. After the children are found, the
narrative stage expands to national dimensions as the tale is eventually
rounded off with a double marriage blending the country's British,
French, and Indian heritages, the latter two being subsumed into the
dominant white, English-speaking order.

Adult readers were the presumed audience for the first novel of the Canadian West, Alexander Begg's *Dot-It-Down* (1871), which is better known for its caricature of poet Charles Mair than for its investment of pioneer life with romantic intrigue. Begg's main concerns were to delineate Northwest life, defend the Hudson's Bay Company, and demonstrate that the West was suitable for settlement. To prove that the region's promise was literary as well as agricultural he chose to document it in the sophisticated form of the romantic novel. The narrative's supplementary 'Emigrant's Guide to Manitoba' suggests its author's awareness that his description of emigrant experience had become so mired in romantic conventions (including a deathbed marriage) that he required an appendix to clarify his intentions.

The fictionalized pioneer guide may be seen as a colonial variant of one of the more familiar forms of mainstream popular writing, the fictionalized conduct manual. Most pre-Confederation Canadian writers who drew their material from everyday life saw the connection between their fiction and the real world not as literary verisimilitude but as moral edification. Thomas McCulloch's pair of cautionary tales published in Scotland as *Colonial Gleanings: William, and Melville* (1826) was intended for 'the information of those parents and children in Britain, who found their hopes of happiness upon the acquisition of wealth in foreign lands.' The two young Scotsmen forfeit their dreams of prosperity in the New World: William because he yields to materialism, Sabbath-breaking, and dissipation; Melville because he remains 'a complete stranger to the Christian system.'[17]

A similar strain of didacticism colours the real life stories published in *The Literary Garland*, which unswervingly uphold conventional standards of religious and social behaviour, preaching temperance, industry, and godliness. Few *Garland* writers descended to the mundanity of 'The First Cow: A Story of the Back-Woods,'[18] a tale unusual for the concreteness of its depiction of immigrant life though typical in its message that hard work and occasional sacrifice will lead to prosperity. Accounts of success were balanced by those highlighting 'the vanity of wealth';[19] after Confederation, periodicals continued to publish stories using local characters in local settings to teach Canadians not to gamble, flirt, or try to rise above their proper station in life. One need read no further than their titles to predict the tenor of pieces like 'A Mistake in Life. A Canadian Story Founded on Facts,'[20] 'Loss and Gain; or, The Bensons,'[21] 'The Story of a Flirt,'[22] or 'Marian's Miseries.'[23]

Not surprisingly, foreign settings dominate much of the prescriptive social fiction written in Canada (although often published elsewhere) and directed to Canadian readers as well as to the larger English-speaking world. Illustrative of the situation of the mid-century Canadian novelist are the careers of Susanna Moodie and Rosanna Leprohon, two authors with rich local experience who looked instead to the sophisticated social life of England for literary conventions to illustrate their familiar themes of filial obedience, faithfulness, generosity, honesty, and the supremacy of virtue. As discussed earlier, Moodie's now-forgotten fiction imaginatively enacts a return to England no longer possible in her own life. More directly concerned with Canadian society is the fiction of Rosanna Leprohon, who began her career with five exposés of the frivolity and hypocrisy of fashionable society, serialized in *The Literary Garland* between 1846 and 1851.[24]

In these stories, all set in England, Leprohon refined the themes she was to employ in her best-known Canadian novel, *Antoinette De Mirecourt; or, Secret Marrying and Secret Sorrowing* (1864). Four centre on a young woman whose difficulties arise from the inadequacy of her education or the irresponsibility of her parents or guardians. All are cast in a high romantic mould with appropriately intricate love complications recounted in elegant language. Leprohon's skilful handling of typical *Garland* materials was noticed by Moodie, who praised the 'power and vigor' of her writing and predicted she would become 'the pride and ornament of a great and rising country.'[25] The intervention of marriage and a dozen children reduced Leprohon's subsequent output of fiction to several stories in *The Canadian Illustrated News* and three novels of manners, her focus now her own society. In the first two she transferred her youthful interest in high life from England to Quebec, describing the effects of the Seven Years' War on the upper classes of New France. John Talon-Lesperance considered her best work to be her first Canadian novel, *The Manor House of De Villerai*, serialized in the Montreal *Family Herald* (1859–60) and published in translation as *Le Manoir de Villerai* (1861) but not issued in book form in English until 1986.[26]

Class conflict provides one of the major tensions of the plot when a young nobleman, engaged since childhood to a fellow aristocrat, falls in love with the village beauty. With careful historical fidelity the novel follows the characters through the traumatic period of the Conquest, smallpox and the hazards of war eventually conspiring to allow the lovers to marry. Leprohon removed the union of the prince and the peasant from the real life world of Quebec when she sent the happy couple back to Europe after the fall of New France. Refusing to extend the tragedy of the historical situation to her characters, she transformed a study of virtue in distress to a romance of virtue rewarded similar to the way she would later permit Antoinette to survive and thrive despite her marital misadventures.

Antoinette De Mirecourt, unsubtly subtitled 'Secret Marrying and Secret Sorrowing,' is a moral survival guide for young women being wooed to transgress the will of their parents. In the setting of post-Conquest Quebec, Leprohon details the fall and redemption of a heroine too vital to accept the Clarissa role her community tries to thrust upon her: 'Despite the opinions of friends and acquaintances, who had obligingly decided that Antoinette should at once enter a convent, or retire to Valmont, there to live and die in the strictest seclusion, she was publicly united a year after to Colonel Evelyn. It is hard to say whether surprise or indignation predominated ...'[27]

Having ironically suppressed the voice of convention, Leprohon went on to extend the range of her writing in two stories analyzing contemporary domestic life and marital discord. *Armand Durand; or, A Promise Fulfilled* (1868) signalled a new direction as Leprohon turned from the aristocracy of the past to the society of her own time. She describes the careers of two half-brothers, one remaining on the family farm, the other becoming a lawyer and progressing up the social scale to eventually earn the hand of a descendant from the old nobility. Armand's first marriage, however, is a loveless union to a beautiful, frivolous shrew who drives him to drink and conveniently dies repentant, freeing him to espouse the 'good angel' who teaches him abstinence and forgiveness and will support his imminent brilliant political career. Detailed descriptions of the daily life and manners of rural and urban Quebec sufficiently relieve Leprohon's moralizing to earn her the distinction of being both the best and the most overlooked English-Canadian fiction writer of her generation. On the whole, her work fared much better in translation; *Armand Durand*, for example, appeared three times as a serial and twice as a book in French, compared with only once in each form in English.[28] In her last significant fiction, the story 'Clive Weston's Wedding Anniversary' (1872), Leprohon retreated from her new social realism to the more familiar realm of high life, this time set in Anglo Montreal. Here too she altered standard romantic convention by beginning rather than ending with a wedding and by analysing some of the tensions of marital life, albeit her solution is wifely submission to duty and abandonment of pride.[29]

Although religion figures quite explicitly in Leprohon's work as in all the domestic fiction of Victorian Canada, there was as well a steady stream of specifically evangelical writing. Long before Charles W. Gordon's brand of muscular Christianity made godliness a best-selling quality at the turn of the century, Canadian readers were presented with localized Sunday school fictions offering easy solutions to complex problems.[30] The deliberate inversion of the usual order of title and subtitle in Mary E. Herbert's *Woman as She Should Be: or, Agnes Wiltshire* (1861) signals that in such writing the message overrides the medium, subordinating characterization to moral imperative.[31]

One of the most prominent tillers of this field was Agnes Maule Machar, Kingston woman of letters who was initiated into fiction by twice winning first prize in a competition sponsored by a Toronto publisher 'for the book best suited to the needs of the Sunday School Library.'[32] The resulting novels, *Katie Johnstone's Cross: A Canadian Tale* (1870) and *Lucy Raymond; or, The Children's Watchword* (1871) describe the religious lives of Ontario adolescents while preaching good works, self-control, the subduing of pride, and the primacy of religious values. Machar's early fiction is typical of its time and place in that its most pressing social problems are poverty and alcoholism and its solution is the Social Gospel of individual religious conversion combined with good deeds among the poor.[33] In 'Lost and Won: A Canadian Romance' (serialized in *The Canadian Monthly* in 1875 and never issued as a book) she spells out her view that life in the Canadian countryside is intrinsically Arcadian, economic and emotional misery resulting from the intrusion of tavern-keepers and sharp, town-educated lawyers.

In this romantic distinction between rural virtue and urban vice may be found one thread of the thin fabric of social realism woven by nineteenth-century Canadian fiction writers. The social and economic complexity of the contemporary city, so dominant a feature of international fiction of the last century, is virtually absent from Canadian writing before the First World War; when a Canadian author did choose to describe middle- or working-class urban life the setting was usually deflected to Britain or the United States. One analyst of late nineteenth-century English-Canadian novels suggests that Canadian writers did not perceive urban slums as a Canadian problem because 'Their concern is the reflected concern of Britons and Americans, gleaned from British and American press reports and contemporary literature.'[34] Certainly the few mid-century novels to give Canadian cities more than a passing glance take their cue from the master of the Victorian urban novel, Charles Dickens. The detailed description of Toronto poverty and unemployment in *Canadian Homes; or, The Mystery Solved* (1858), written by Londoner Ebenezer Clemo shortly after his arrival in Canada, owes its style to Dickens and its content to its publisher, John Lovell, who had commissioned the book as a tract to promote protection for Canadian industry. If, as advertised, 30,000 copies were indeed published and sold (along with another 20,000 in French), this rare and now-forgotten novel was one of the major Canadian best-sellers of the century.[35] Dickensian echoes also permeate *My Own Story. A Canadian Christmas Tale* (1869) by the pseudonymous 'Grodenk,'[36] who must have composed his address to the reader with his tongue firmly planted in his cheek. Claiming that his story is 'one of Canadian every day life. It contains nothing sensational – nothing exciting – but is true to the letter,'[37] he presents a plot which carries Dickens' penchant for coincidence to new heights of improbability. And while the primary setting is indeed Ontario, the street scenes reminiscent of *Oliver Twist* are placed in Boston.

For whatever accident of social history, Maritime writers seem to have been more willing than other Canadians to admit the iniquity of their cities. In a story from the 1820s Thomas McCulloch warned of Halifax that 'Its allurements to vice are fearful'[38] and in the year of Confederation a Saint John story-teller acknowledged that 'within the precincts of the city there was misery – poverty, sickness, want and hardship – perhaps not so much as usually falls to the share of every large city; but yet a great deal ...'[39] Marshall Saunders conducts her reader into Halifax tenements in *The House of Armour* (1897) with the aim of promoting improved housing, childcare, and playgrounds for the poor. In most fiction of Victorian Canada poverty is chronicled chiefly to promote benevolence; hence rather surprising for its honest presentation of social values is Mary E. Herbert's *Belinda Dalton; or, Scenes in the Life of a Halifax Belle* (1859), which describes the economic vulnerability of a single woman lacking male protection and refuses to solve the heroine's problem by providing her with a husband.

The extent to which romanticism imbued the late Victorian English-Canadian cultural establishment can be seen in its fostering of the regional idyll, a mode whose features are outlined in Francis Sherman's appreciative review of Charles G.D. Roberts' *Earth's Enigmas*. Sherman begins by praising the current vogue of local colour fiction for making 'some hitherto commonplace locality or people alive and full of interest for us,' citing Thomas Hardy, Kipling, and J.M. Barrie as British examples and George Washington Cable, Hamlin Garland, and Gilbert Parker as North Americans. Roberts he applauds for the authenticity of his settings: 'We feel, reading here, that it would be but an hour's journey to get to the scene of any one of these tales.' Sherman then transposes this realized sense of place onto its denizens, congratulating Roberts for having chosen the 'plain, truthful narration' of his 'stories of live, healthy men and women; stories echoing with the sound of our saw-mills and our tides, and redolent of our marshes and newly-cut lumber' over 'that morbid class of fiction which is now such a favorite of the reading public.'[40]

The qualities that Sherman admired in Roberts became the regional idyll's identifying characteristics: a blending of the appearance of realism (primarily in details of place) with the outlook of romance, giving Smith's Lamps of Fiction a local, contemporary setting which could scarcely offend the conservative taste of the genteel popular reader. This genre earned international sanction when Ralph Connor and L.M. Montgomery joined Gilbert Parker at the head of the American best-seller lists around the turn of the twentieth century, confirming that Canadians from coast to coast preferred to conceive of their country as the Garden that Dick Harrison finds the dominant myth in prairie fiction of this era.[41] The prevailing qualities of this pastoral vision accord with the insistent idealism of the English-Canadian literary community: the natural world is perceived as manageable and regenerative; emphasis is laid on the promise of future success rather than on the trials of the present; an ultimately beneficent order plots the course of human affairs.

The virtual absence of the contemporary city and its problems from pre-modern Canadian fiction is symptomatic of the selectivity of writers concerned with social issues. The safer the topic the more frequent its appearance; Canadian adulation of Stowe suggests that emancipation would have been a major cause in Canadian literature had slavery been a Canadian problem. In the last century's abundance of temperance tales the prevailing attitude towards reform, as expressed in fiction, was to cure economic hardship and family abuse by locking the taverns and opening the churches. Poverty was perceived as an individual problem inevitably ascribed to laziness, alcoholism, or the wickedness of a particular individual, and therefore to be relieved by personal conversion. Sharp businessmen are not uncommon; the successors of Sam Slick appear in the guise of land speculators and self-interested lawyers and usually receive their appropriate come-uppance. But the more painful questions that would be raised by analysing a socio-economic structure which permitted gouging landlords, exploitive factory owners, and prostitution rarely appear in the literature of a country trying to present itself in congruence with the ideals it found in Sir Walter Scott. *The Canadian*

Magazine's plaint that 'The romance of the Canadian North-West is fast passing into history – for there is little romance where the threshing-machines, the railroad, the steamboat and the town-constable are to be found'[42] implies that both the problems and the appurtenances of modern progress held meagre literary appeal.

A few realistic glimpses into the working lives of ordinary people appear sporadically in turn-of-the-century periodicals. For *Saturday Night*'s 1890 summer supplement, editor Edmund Sheppard wrote a story remarkable for its unidealized portrayal of economic strife in an unpicturesque rural community.[43] Two *Canadian Magazine* stories from 1897 stand out, one for its unsentimental acknowledgment of the precarious economic position of the small self-employed shopkeeper, the other for its depiction of the toil of the mill worker.[44] However, direct consideration of the plight of the factory worker and unionism is limited to a scattering of ephemeral novels. The heroine of Lottie McAlister's *Clipped Wings* (1899) spends one week drudging in a city shirt-waist factory, concludes that she cannot live on her earnings, and then drops this cause for more individualized good works in her home town. M.A. Foran's 'The Other Side' (1872), the most radical nineteenth-century novel discovered by Frank Watt in his quest for Canada's elusive literature of protest, resorts to a complex web of romantic plot devices to describe the triumph of unionism and the defeat of bloodthirsty capitalists. Although published in *The Ontario Workman* the narrative is set in Chicago; the same geographical deflection occured twenty years later in Agnes Maule Machar's *Roland Graeme, Knight: A Novel of Our Time*.

While Machar's hero is Canadian, the place where he founds a workers' newspaper and joins the Knights of Labour is the fictional mill town of Minton in the United States. In accordance with her Social Gospelism, Machar shows her hero's quest for religious understanding to be as important as his attempt to improve the lot of the workers. When the latter threaten to strike against their boss's attempt to increase wages and cut hours, Graeme acts as peacemaker, resolving the issue by appealing to the better nature of both parties. Machar's decision to set her labour novel in the United States may appear evasive and her resolution just the simplistic doctrine of 'noblesse oblige' as Frank Watt puts it,[45] yet her recognition of workers' needs as a pressing issue is almost unique among novelists of Victorian Canada and appears to have been shared only by fellow Social Gospeller Albert Carman, author of *The Preparation of Ryerson Embury* (1900).[46]

The setting of Carman's novel is Ithica, Canada, a fictional college and mill town where the divinity student of the title, unable to resolve his religious doubts, becomes involved instead in the strike of the local foundry workers. Their desperate situation resulting from wage cuts receives sustained attention, and only with difficulty does Embury eventually persuade them to return to work and carry on their struggle through the ballot box. Free of the cumbersome subplots of Machar's book, this surprisingly well-written novel combines a critical analysis of small-town Ontario society and its established religious institutions with a commitment to social progress.

The few nineteenth-century Canadian novelists willing to rock the boat of social complacency by addressing problems of labour unrest were matched in scarcity by those daring to give serious attention to sexual impropriety in contemporary life. The notion of a Canadian Emma Bovary, Anna Karenina, Hetty Sorrel, or Tess Durbeyfield was unthinkable in a culture that supported *Saturday Night*'s position that 'The journey of life is naturally over many rough places, and those are not friends of society who add to the ruggedness of the road or increase the disquiet and turmoil ...'[47] Or as *The Canadian Magazine* succinctly opined,[48] 'Our dirty linen should be washed in private, not in public.' While the latter was willing to publish one contributer's opinion that a writer may attempt to 'eradicate evil by the exposure of oppressive and dishonest social conditions,'[49] its editorial commentary consistently preferred 'fiction which deals with real people, that is, people such as we find every day in real life, and deals with them not realistically, but in a healthy way.'[50] Hence it concurred with American disapproval of Stephen Crane's Bowery tales, *George's Mother* and *Maggie*,[51] and would have been appalled by a comparable Canadian girl of the streets – or by Abraham Holmes' Belinda.

Published in 1843, *Belinda; or, The Rivals. A Tale of Real Life* is now known from recent attention drawn to the sole surviving copy found in the Detroit Public Library.[52] Holmes' modern advocates view this novel of seduction in Canada West as 'a competent spoof of the sentimental seduction tale'[53] which inverts convention by presenting a lively Canadian coquette who assumes various genteel and religious guises to seduce a series of vulnerable men. Similar to the way James De Mille was later to use the form of the adventure novel to ridicule the extravagances of romantic fiction, Holmes manipulates the form of the sentimental novel to unmask the hypocrisy which frequently underlies moralistic tales of seduction and betrayal. Carl Klinck argues that 'Coquetry becomes in Holmes' hands a literary mode, governing the general plan and every paragraph of the book, just as Belinda, within the scheme, governs her suitors.'[54]

While there is clear authorial disapproval of Belinda's perversion of love and religion, Holmes seldom relaxes his tone of witty ambiguity. Even when he kills off his heroine after she presents her husband with a fine son just six weeks past her marriage, he creates a deathbed scene refreshing in its irreverence. Belinda's momentary contrition quickly dissolves into assurance, and after a life of dissimulation she dies with 'a confident expectation of being welcomed to the realms of bliss immediately upon her dissolution.' Forgiven by her family, the promiscuous frontier belle receives tribute 'as if some patriot hero, the pillar and support of his community, had fallen.' Although Holmes' language remains unimpeachable, he writes about sexuality with an air of coy frankness that leaves no doubt regarding the activities of an energetic young woman who is 'as intimate as Antony and Cleopatra' with her various lovers. Speculation that the book was intended to be read as a roman à clef is supported internally by the author's announced intention *to give every dog his due* to tell what certain characters actually were'[55] and by the fact that there was once a list identifying the characters pasted into the only copy to escape destruction.

Like the Winnipeg matron in Zero's *One Mistake* (1886) who announces 'We don't use "leg" in Canada,'[56] Canadian literary commentators supported the illusion of their country's pristine sexual demeanour. As demonstrated by the anonymously authored *Sir Peter Pettysham* (1882), 'a satirical story of Canadian life marked by considerable ability,'[57] politics, religion, and business were fair targets so long as the sanctity of domestic life remained intact. Hence one novel that reached the shelves of few Canadian readers was Mary Leslie's *The Cromaboo Mail Carrier* (1878), possibly the only nineteenth-century Canadian fiction to explicitly employ the word 'rape.'

Mary Anne Sadlier had earlier used fiction to warn single young female emigrants of 'the numerous dangers to which their virtue is exposed';[58] Leslie describes a village where 'there is an illegitimate child in every house – in some two, in others three, in one six – and the people think it no sin.' Reputedly the citizens of Erin, Ontario, were so incensed by Leslie's presentation of 'the most blackguard village in Canada'[59] that the book was banned. At its centre is a detailed account of the impregnation of a fifteen-year-old by a philandering visitor. Mary Smith is neither martyred nor punished; she makes the best of her lot by marrying a widower and enduring the normal hardships of rural family life.

Although her son's delinquent father later returns and is reconciled with his child, Leslie refuses to clean up the scene by eventually wedding the victim to her seducer.

Later decades saw several better-known efforts to break with Canada's romantic tradition which relegated sexual irregularity to the *ancien régime* and permitted no more than discreet hints at sexual transgressions in contemporary Canadian life. Thomas Stinson Jarvis, Joanna Wood, Grant Allen, and Charles G.D. Roberts offered rather different treatments of illegitimate pregnancy in their novels, the most shocking being Allen's *The Woman Who Did* (1895), published the same year as *Jude the Obscure*. Although Allen had severed all connection with the land of his birth long before he began to write fiction, the Canadian press followed him as a successful native son. Allen's complaint that 'The education of an English novelist consists entirely in learning to subordinate all his own ideas and tastes and opinions to the wishes and beliefs of the inexorable British matron' suggests how uncomfortable he would have been had he remained in Canada – and his description of the way he was forced to alter the conclusion to his first novel to meet the hypothetical British matron's preference for happy endings should serve as a precaution to any critic tempted to infer an author's personal views from the fates of his characters.[60] Allen's sympathetic presentation of Herminia Barton, a British 'free woman' who intends to carry on the protest of George Eliot and Mary Godwin by avoiding the hypocrisy of conventional marriage, thoroughly offended his Canadian readers (as well as many in England). The Ottawa *Citizen* denounced *The Woman Who Did* as an 'abortive production of an unhealthy brain ... free-love being frankly advocated'[61] while *The Canadian Magazine*, claiming that 'There is little doubt that Grant Allen has injured himself in Canada by his outré writings,' was relieved to be able to 'safely' recommend a later novel.[62]

The other three authors located their errant women in Canada, in novels which share the problem of how to shape an unacceptable social situation into an acceptable narrative form. The result is three books which acknowledge the problem of premarital pregnancy and then resort to extraordinary devices to arrive at a printable resolution. Most deliberately sensational is Jarvis's *Geoffrey Hampstead* (1890), a story of the disruption effected on moral Toronto society by a thoroughly amoral intruder. To account for Hampstead's villainy Jarvis gives him a Tartar father, thereby suggesting that no purebred Britisher could be so attractive and irrational a seducer, embezzler, daredevil, and suicide. Hampstead's victim is nouveau riche Nina Linton, whose father wants her to marry a 'dook' and whose mother spends her time and money on charities for fallen women while her beautiful daughter quietly goes her own way, falls under Hampstead's spell, and melodramatically dies in a shipwreck, pregnant and unmarried. Myron Holder of Joanna Wood's *The Untempered Wind* (1894) also dies at the end of her story, just after finally marrying the father of her child. This intense novel of a young woman who is 'a mother, but not a wife' contains a sharp critique of social attitudes in Jamestown, a 'cruel, sordid, babbling little village'[63] that cannot forgive Myron's refusal to name her lover. While the book's major strength is its social analyis, its specific setting is blurred. A careful reading suggests that Jamestown is Wood's home of Queenston, yet the book was published in the United States and heralded by *Current Opinion* as 'the strongest and best American novel of the year.'[64] Despite Wood's care to tidy up her heroine's life with a deathbed marriage after putting her through the punishing grief of losing her child, Canadians were less than eager to claim *The Untempered Wind* as the Canadian *Tess of the D'Urbervilles* or *Scarlet Letter*.[65]

Charles G.D. Roberts' *The Heart That Knows* (1906) likewise concludes tidily. As a study in social realism the book effectively portrays the various attitudes expressed by a small New Brunswick community towards a young woman who bears a child out of wedlock. Very much a Canadian Tess in her confrontation with social convention, Luella Warden finds her difficulties compounded by a jealous rival and a forged letter which by comparison reduce the accidental loss of Tess's crucial letter to Angel to a rather minor liberty on Hardy's part. Roberts' refusal to subscribe to Hardy's tragic vision leads to even greater improbabilities since his congenial resolution depends upon the romantic convention that unknown parents and children may intuitively recognize one other. The discrepancy between the novel's acutely realized setting and its melodramatic plot has led to its current minor position in the Roberts canon, where it is admired as a regional idyll and ignored as a serious literary venture.[66] Fiction, clearly, was not the arena in which to argue for social change in Canada. In Victorian England, as George Watt has demonstrated, fictional fallen women made an important contribution to reform movements. The Canadian counterpart to his study of *The Fallen Woman in the Nineteenth-Century English Novel* would be a slim volume indeed.[67]

If prematurely passionate but ultimately faithful lovers are rare in early Canadian fiction, prostitutes are almost non-existent. Acknowledgment of their presence was usually accompanied by the same kind of geographical deflection that characterized literary depictions of labour strife.

Stinson Jarvis (in *She Lived in New York* [1894]) and Joanna Wood (in *A Martyr to Love* [1897]) went on to write sensational fictions describing the careers of high-life courtesans, both books being set and published in New York. When Marshall Saunders gave a brief example of how poverty could lead to prostitution, she sent her Halifax victim to the streets of Montreal.[68] In *The Measure of a Man* (1911) Norman Duncan includes in his frontier logging town a 'shameless red house' run by unscrupulous saloon-keepers, but the emphasis is on eliminating alcoholism and the setting is Minnesota.[69] Canadian writers who did admit that their nation contained a few women of ill repute usually gave them short shrift. For example, in *If Any Man Sin* (1915) H.A. Cody concedes that a northern gold rush will attract 'bad women who flock into every camp such as this. They drink, gamble, and – lead men astray'[70] but he refrains from individualizing them or involving any in his plot.

To a small number of socially oriented writers the New Woman[71] was a more attractive figure than the fallen woman. Lottie McAlister (in *Clipped Wings* [1899]) and Amelia Fytche (in *Kerchiefs to Hunt Souls* [1895]) used the form of the novel to argue for women's rights, both writers carefully conventionalizing their requests for social change. Hence after working publicly as a nurse and speaking out for emancipation McAlister's 'Saint Agnes' retires into marriage and domesticity, her husband now the one who writes articles on women's suffrage. For Fytche's New Woman, Canada is unsuitable as a testing ground for women's liberation. In Europe, Dorothea Pembroke must define her principles in relation to current trends in art and literature. Weary of 'indecorous nudity' in painting, she concludes that 'realism in art' is the 'outcome of an effete civilization' and is pleased to inform a Frenchman that Canadians 'have no realistic writers like Zola; our literature is far purer than yours. That which is called emancipated ... is written with a purpose and an object; that purpose is to counteract this very depravity of the age that we are now discussing.'[72] As documents of their era, these two fictions with a purpose capture the blend of indignation, moralism, and innocence that characterized this stage of the women's suffrage movement in Canada.

Thus it was up to Sara Jeannette Duncan to create the most memorable New Women in early Canadian fiction – not by expounding a particular thesis but by creating literary projections of her own lively, adventuresome personality, her flippant dedication of her first novel to Mrs Grundy signalling her willingness to question convention. This defiance was always to remain cautious; it was hardly extended to sexual matters and in her Canadian fiction remained confined to asserting a woman's right to travel freely and pursue a career, and to maintaining her own characteristically ironic perspective on social platitudes. Of her heroines, the most popular seems to have been the thinly disguised but Americanized persona who narrates *A Social Departure* (1890), believed to have been her greatest seller.[73] This witty travel narrative avoids serious social analysis. The reader who accepts its premise that two young women may travel around the world unchaperoned will encounter few subsequent challenges to the liberal middle-class Anglo-Saxon point of view.

In *The Imperialist*'s Advena Murchison, 'bookish and unconventional'[74] and apparently doomed to spinsterhood in a small Ontario town, Duncan modestly raises the issue of women's social place. Her subdued treatment of the subject in her most deliberately Canadian novel contrasts markedly with the challenge to conventional London society posed by Illinois-born Elfrida Bell of *A Daughter of Today* (1893). Determined to make her own way in the world, Elfrida suffers a tragedy shaped largely by her impulsiveness, which Duncan presents as a typically American trait. For Advena, on the other hand, she contrives a thoroughly conventional resolution by matching her heroine with a husband who is her equal in both intellect and social ineptness – a happy ending more likely to ingratiate her with her Canadian readers[75] through the familiar medium of the regional novel.

Unlike Adeline Teskey's Mapleton, L.M. Montgomery's Avonlea, R.L. Richardson's Ontario 'Scotch Settlement,' Connor's Glengarry, and most of the other small Canadian communities sentimentalized in fiction in the first decades of the twentieth century, Duncan's Elgin is portrayed with as much irony as nostalgia. Her perspective sharpened by her experience of Anglo India, Duncan strikes a delicate balance between affection for the security of small-town life and criticism of its limitations. As a social anatomist she describes Elgin in its shirtsleeves but refrains from further disrobing the body politic, wielding a gentle scalpel (if we return to R.H. Hutton's metaphors) in her dissection of its social practices. Her introduction of sexual and political misdemeanours serves only to reinforce the town's essential innocence: the 'ambiguous' Miss Belton is an American predator whose exploitation of young Ormiston's chivalry is duly exposed, and the murky electioneering which unseats Lorne occurs beyond the borders of the town itself, conveniently scapegoated to the Indian reservation.

Life in Elgin is no idyll for those with 'horizons' and intellectual ambition. Advena chafes against the restrictions of a town where 'the arts conspired to be absent' (91) and 'No one could dream with impunity ...

except in bed'(63); for 'a difference is the one thing a small community, accustomed comfortably to scan its own intelligible averages, will not tolerate' (62). At the same time, what Duncan emphasizes is not the fixedness of small-town Ontario life but its fluidity – the process of 'the making of a nation' (67). Taking Elgin as representative of 'the biography of Fox County and, in little, the history of the whole Province' (117), she presents the evolution of a shifting social order, beginning with a glimpse of the Murchisons' early insecure days before settling them in middle-class comfort. We can, I think, correctly infer that her sensitivity to the nuances of distinction between the shoemaker's and the greengrocer's aprons reflects her own first-hand knowledge of the rigid class and caste systems of England and India. In Elgin such differences are only 'little prejudices' subject to modification by 'a certain bright freedom' (68) embodied in the 'melting-pot' process of the Collegiate Institute: 'you went in as your simple opportunities had made you; how you shaped coming out depended upon what was hidden in the core of you.' Above all, 'You could not in any case be the same as your father before you; education in a new country is too powerful a stimulant for that' (121) even though the primary goal of the population is material success. The pulpit and the press – shown in cheerful collusion at the Murchison teatable – are the unacknowledged legislators of this self-confident community whose narrowness defies the possibility of grand romance or tragedy.

The greatest permissible divergence from social norms appears in the Murchison family who contain a 'strain of temperament' (62) that subliminally threatens to develop into eccentricity or genius. Idiosyncratic in their humour, irregularity, and decision to live in a rambling old house designed according to 'large ideas' (34), the otherwise unimpeachable parents produce two remarkable children whose political and amatory involvements carry romantic idealism as far as it can travel within the town's prosaic limits. Because Elgin's commonplace standards can admit neither tragic nor saccharine resolutions to the experiences of its citizens, Duncan carefully balances the conclusions to the parallel adventures of Lorne and Advena, Advena's happy marriage countered by the rejection of Lorne's imperialism. In each case normality triumphs as the couple who belong together are relieved of the idealism that kept them apart, and the political visionary is betrayed by a community which refuses to subordinate prosperity to ideology.[76]

It is not surprising that Canada's most articulate advocate of realism in fiction should also prove its most accomplished practitioner. Duncan's version of reality is, of course, carefully laundered, a celebration of Elgin's strengths as much as an inventory of its limitations. Elgin is untroubled by labour unrest, significant poverty, or serious sexual scandal. What the novel best represents is a marriage of form and content almost unique in Canadian fiction until the modern era. The gentle irony of its narrative voice matches its dissection of small town values and manners, and the plot and characters complement each other with minimal external intervention.

10 Conclusion

Establishing the novel in pre-modern Canada was not an easy venture. Believing that 'A nation without a native literature is like a body without a soul,'[1] the country's cultural leaders fostered the development of a literature that would fulfil their idealized national aspirations. In the realm of fiction, the resulting discourse of gentility masked the society it represented, to the degree that modernist critics have found it simpler to fault early Canadian fiction than to attempt to understand it and have shown little inclination to investigate its composition and milieu.[2] In 1912, the year he became head of the English Department at Victoria College (Toronto), Pelham Edgar published an essay titled 'A Fresh View of Canadian Literature.' Assessing the scene at the very end of the period we have been examining, Edgar concluded that 'the gravest charge our literature has to bear' is that 'No one ... has yet synthesized for us the meaning of our Canadian life, nor revealed us to ourselves. Mere scattered hints and faint suggestions we find, but no convincing picture.'[3] His failure to notice Sara Jeannette Duncan, who was not inducted into the canon of significant Canadian writers until the late 1970s, suggests why his native culture had produced little fiction of interest to a scholar nurtured in the great tradition of European literature. So distinctly was its horizon of expectation shaped by the taste for national romance that even the foremost spokesperson and practitioner of realism could elude the attention of a major critic.

Gerda Lerner's view that 'Idealization is very frequently a defensive ideology and an expression of tension within society'[4] is amply borne out in this book's analysis of the structure of attitudes that shaped the literary culture of English Canada during the nineteenth century and persisted well into the twentieth. The attachment of the early twentieth-century

Canadian literary establishment to its Victorian roots was clearly articulated by two of its major power brokers. In 1922, William Arthur Deacon wrote to B.K. Sandwell, 'The deep-seated liking of the natural Canadian for the romantic in fiction, I admit, and commend, believing that while this depressing English realism is natural to an Englishman, and therefore right and wholesome for him, that it is not the next step on the evolutionary path for the Canadian.'[5] This attitude was shared by Lorne Pierce, ardent nationalist and member of the Royal Society from the age of thirty-six. As chief editor at Ryerson Press from 1922 to 1960 he played a crucial role in the formation of modern Canadian literature that has yet to be fully assessed; his 1927 *Outline of Canadian Literature* proclaimed his allegiance to the principles of the past. Admitting that the weaknesses of Canadian writers include 'diffuse style, shadowy characters, and ephemeral thinking' as well as the tendency to 'offer a moral epigram as a substitute' for penetrating characterization, he went on to commend precisely those features of Canadian writing that resisted realistic social and psychological analysis. What he liked in Canadian literature was its 'simplicity and sincerity,' 'optimism,' 'courage,' 'pioneering spirit,' 'power and rugged dignity,' independence, and decorum. It is possible that his statement that 'With all our simplicity we rarely become so naive as to ask improper and embarrassing questions, and those who do so are promptly labelled erotic and so done to death forever' was offered in amends for his decision to bring out Grove's naturalistic *Settlers of the Marsh* (1925); in any case, it is surprising to find Grove's publisher approving of the way Canadian realism 'lacks the stern philosophy and morbid psychology of the Continent, and on the whole is more optimistic and wholesome.'[6] After the First World War, Goldwin Smith's Seven Lamps still so burned brightly that works of fiction marked by social and sexual realism, such as Jessie Sime's *Sister Woman* (1919) and *Our Little Life* (1921) and Madge Macbeth's *Shackles* (1926), were summarily excluded from the canon created by the country's conservative, androcentric literary gatekeepers.

The problem of how to deal with the mass of Canadian fiction written by the glow of these lamps has troubled more recent literary and cultural historians. Underlying Desmond Pacey's 1945 generalization that 'Our novelists of the past, with a few honourable exceptions, have been cautious souls, afraid to incur the wrath of the public, and producing either sugar-coated tracts or novels of escape'[7] is the modernist assumption that the place of the serious fiction writer is at the vanguard of social and artistic progress, and that in faithfulness to their art early Canadian writers should have repudiated their community's taste for harmless, edifying entertainment. As the preceding chapters have shown, incurring the wrath of the public was the last thing most nineteenth-century Canadian writers had in mind. Far from challenging their society, these writers shared and stabilized its values. They regarded their proper place as the mainstream, not the forefront (or underground) of artistic and social thought. Hence the primary significance of their work is to be found in its reflection of prevailing cultural attitudes. 'It cannot be emphasized too urgently that any age in the past can be understood only when we analyze it so far as possible in its own terms,' observed D.W. Robertson, jr.[8] When examined within its own context, early Canadian fiction illustrates the social role of fiction and the relation between cultural attitudes and literary performance in a community struggling towards self-definition. Against the constant threat of American cultural domination, Victorian Canada's continual reaffirmation that its national literature should be patriotic and ameliorative, based on the models of Shakespeare and Scott, reflected the conviction of a colonial society that in cultural affairs, nationhood would be achieved only by transplanting the most admirable traditions of the Old World to the New.

Abbreviations

Titles of periodicals and several volumes which are frequently cited are abbreviated as follows:

Acadian	*The Acadian Magazine* Halifax 1826–8
AAM	*The Anglo-American Magazine* Toronto 1852–5
BAM	*The British American Magazine* Toronto 1863–4
BMM	*Belford's Monthly Magazine* Toronto 1876–8
CIN	*The Canadian Illustrated News* Montreal 1869–83
CJ	*The Canadian Journal* Toronto 1852–88
CL	*Canadian Literature* Vancouver 1959–
CM	*The Canadian Magazine* Toronto 1893–1939
CMLR	*The Canadian Magazine and Literary Repository* Montreal 1823–5
CMNR	*The Canadian Monthly and National Review* Toronto 1872–8
CNN	*Canadian Novelists and the Novel*, ed. Douglas Daymond and Leslie Monkman. Ottawa: Borealis 1981
CN&Q	*Canadian Notes and Queries* Kingston 1968–
CRLHJ	*The Canadian Review and Literary and Historical Journal* Montreal 1824–6
DAR	*The Dominion Annual Register and Review* Ottawa, Montreal, Toronto 1878–86
DI	*The Dominion Illustrated* Montreal 1888–95
ECW	*Essays on Canadian Writing* Toronto 1974–
HMM	*The Halifax Monthly Magazine* Halifax 1830–3
JCanS	*Journal of Canadian Studies* Peterborough 1966–
JCF	*Journal of Canadian Fiction* Montreal 1972–
LG	*The Literary Garland* Montreal 1838–51

LHC   *The Literary History of Canada: Canadian Literature in English*, ed.
            Carl F. Klinck. 2nd ed. 3 vols. Toronto: University of Toronto
            Press 1977
MM   *The Maritime Monthly* Halifax, St John, Montreal 1873–5
NDM   *The New Dominion Monthly* Montreal 1867–79
PBSC   *Papers of the Bibliographical Society of Canada* Toronto, 1962–
Provincial *The Provincial; or, Halifax Monthly Magazine* Halifax 1852–3
RBCM   *Rose-Belford's Canadian Monthly and National Review* Toronto
            1878–82
SCL   *Studies in Canadian Literature* Fredericton 1976–
SECL   *The Search for English-Canadian Literature*, ed. Carl Ballstadt.
            Toronto: University of Toronto Press 1975
SN   *Saturday Night* Toronto 1887–
Stewart's   *Stewart's Literary Quarterly* St John 1867–72
TCL   *Towards a Canadian Literature*, ed. Douglas Daymond and Leslie
            Monkman. vol. 1 Ottawa: Tecumseh 1984

Notes

PREFACE AND ACKNOWLEDGMENTS

1 John Metcalf, 'The Curate's Egg,' *ECW* 30 (1984–5) 36
2 D.W. Robertson, jr, 'Some Observations on Method in Literary Studies,' *New Literary History* 1 (1969) 3–31
3 Leslie Fiedler, *What Was Literature?: Class Culture and Mass Society* (New York: Simon and Schuster 1982) 143, 58
4 Along with *The University Magazine* (1907–20) these periodicals have been indexed, rendering their contents accessible to the modern researcher. See D.M.R. Bentley and MaryLynn Wickens, *A Checklist of Literary Materials in 'The Week'* (Ottawa: Golden Dog Press 1978); Mary Markham Brown, *An Index to 'The Literary Garland'* (Toronto: Bibliographical Society of Canada 1962); Marilyn Flitton, *An Index to 'The Canadian Monthly and National Review' and to 'Rose-Belford's Canadian Monthly and National Review'* (Toronto: Bibliographical Society of Canada 1976). The *University Magazine* is indexed from 1910 to 1920: Kim Jones, 'A Content guide and Index to *The University Magazine* vols. IX–XIX, 1910–1920,' MA, Queen's 1954. The indexing project being carried out by Professor Thomas Vincent at the Royal Military College of Canada (Kingston) will greatly improve the resources available for this kind of research. Completed are indexes to *The Acadian Magazine* (1826–8), *The Amaranth* (181–2), *The Canadian Magazine and Literary Repository* (1823–5), *The Nova-Scotia Magazine* (1789–92), and *The Provincial* (1841–3).
5 Paul Rutherford, *A Victorian Authority: The Daily Press in Late Nineteenth-Century Canada* (Toronto: University of Toronto Press 1982) 39, 46, 70, 128. This approach follows also the example of Nina Baym, whose impressively thorough study of the mid-century view of fiction in the United

States draws only on the leading literary periodicals of the era. See her *Novels, Readers and Reviewers: Responses to Fiction in Antebellum America* (Ithaca: Cornell University Press 1984). Mary Lu MacDonald's detailed content analysis of newspapers published in the Canadas from 1830 to 1850 shows that newspapers were far more likely to publish local poetry than local fiction. See her 'Literature and Society in the Canadas, 1830–1850,' diss., Carleton 1984, 99.

6 Sara Jeannette Duncan, 'Saunterings,' *The Week* 3 (30 Sept. 1886) 708; *TCL* 115

7 Garvin's letters to W.D. Lighthall concerning the Masterworks, dated from 27 Dec. 1922 to 20 Mar. 1923, are preserved in the Lighthall Papers, NAC, MG 29 D93 vol. 2. Later announcements for the series, found in the Garvin Papers at Queen's University, show that the list of titles underwent continuous revision. The number of volumes was cut from 25 to 15 and many of the literary items were dropped in favour of explorers' narratives by Pierre Radisson, Alexander Henry, and Alexander Mackenzie. In the end, only two or three books were actually published, including Mair's *Tecumseh, etc.* (1926) and Mackenzie's *Voyages ...* (1927). For a detailed account of a parallel series of critical texts see Margery Fee, 'Lorne Pierce, Ryerson Press, and The Makers of Canadian Literature Series,' *PBSC* 24 (1985) 51–69.

8 See Morris Dickstein, 'Popular Fiction and Critical Values: The Novel as a Challenge to Literary History,' in Sacvan Bercovitch, ed., *Reconstructing American Literary History* (Harvard University Press 1986) 35–7.

9 Q.D. Leavis, *Fiction and the Reading Public* (1932); Amy Cruse, *The Victorians and Their Reading* (1936); Margaret Dalziel, *Popular Fiction 100 Years Ago* (1957); Richard Altick, *The English Common Reader* (1957)

10 E.D. Blodgett, 'After Pierre Berton What?: In Search of a Canadian Literature,' *ECW* 30 (1984–5) 63

11 The term is from Hans Jauss, *Towards an Aesthetic of Reception*, trans. Timothy Bahti (Minneapolis: University of Minnesota Press 1982) 24–8.

CHAPTER ONE: READERS AND WRITERS

1 Thomas D'Arcy McGee, 'The Mental Outfit of the New Dominion' [Nov. 1867], rpt *TCL* 85

2 George Parker, *The Beginnings of the Book Trade in Canada* (Toronto: University of Toronto Press 1985) 18–22

3 Harvey Graf claims that Canada West contained fewer adult illiterates than the British Isles or the (white) United States, and in Elgin county, 'a settled and stable agrarian area,' the rate of adult literacy reached an astonishing

97.8%. The rate for Canada as whole, of 80.2%, was lowered by 64.2% figure for Canada East; in Canada West, the rate was 92.8%. Harvey Graf, 'Literacy and Social Structure in Elgin County, Canada West: 1861,' *Histoire sociale/Social History* 11 (1973) 45

4 Paul Rutherford, *A Victorian Authority: The Daily Press in Late Nineteenth-Century Canada* (Toronto: University of Toronto Press 1982) 26–7, 30. He describes the problem with census vagaries as follows:

> The 1861 census of the two Canadas noted only the inability to read among male and female adults, likely overestimating the number of people who had any competence. The Nova Scotia census was far better, since it surveyed the ability to read and write among children and young teens as well as everyone over 15. New Brunswick did not bother to probe the illiteracy of its population, thus saving its masters the shock experienced by school teachers and politicians in the sister colony. The census of 1871 was a wider and apparently more accurate survey of all adults by place and sex. In 1881 the census takers did not publish information on literacy at all. In 1891 they provided an extensive breakdown of the statistics on the ability to read and write by age cohort, invaluable to demonstrate the advance of literacy over the decades. Most irritating, the census bureau in 1901 lumped all of its figures together in a silly attempt to discover the literacy of people aged five and over. Since people did not normally acquire competence in reading and writing until after a few years of schooling, around age ten, the findings contained an unknown number of children who had lacked the opportunity to become literate (26).

5 McGee, *TCL* 83–4

6 James Douglas, jr, 'The Intellectual Progress of Canada During the Last Fifty Years, and the Present State of Its Literature, *CMNR* 7 (1875) 466–7; *TCL* 101–2

7 Eric C. Bow, 'The Public Library Movement in Nineteenth-Century Ontario,' *Ontario Library Review* 66 (1982) 2

8 E.A. Hardy, 'One Hundred Years of Public Service: The Dundas Public Library, 1841–1941,' *Ontario Library Review* 26 (1942) 5

9 Bow, 'The Public Library Movement' 5

10 National Council of Women, *Women of Canada* (1900) 175. These figures are offered as a general indication of library services, and differ slightly from those of James Bain, jr, 'The Public Libraries of Canada,' in J. Castell Hopkins, *Canada: An Encyclopaedia of the Country* (Toronto: Linscott 1899) vol. 5, 207–11. As with the computation of literacy rates there is some inconsistency in the definition and enumeration of libraries. Yvan Lamonde

has noted the existence of 171 'collective libraries' in Montreal between 1659 and 1900, and John Wiseman counts 9,186 libraries in Ontario in 1914; this total includes 4,802 belonging to public and private schools and 4,000 attached to Sunday schools. See Yvan Lamonde, 'Social Origins of the Public Library in Montreal,' *Canadian Library Journal* 38 (1981) 363–70, and John A. Wiseman, 'Phoenix in Flight: Ontario Mechanics' Institutes, 1880–1920,' *Canadian Library Journal* 38 (1981) 401–5.

11 David Hayne, 'A Survey: Quebec Library History,' *Canadian Library Journal* 38 (1981) 359. Hayne's source is Fernande Turcotte, 'Les Bibliothèques paroissiales: bibliographie analytique de la littérature française parue sur le sujet dans la province du Québec,' BLS thesis, Laval 1952.

12 Hayne, 'A Survey,' 357. His source in Yvan Lamonde, *Les Bibliothèques de collectivités à Montréal (17e–19e siècle): sources et problèmes* (Montréal: Bibliothèque nationale de Québec 1979).

13 *The Family Herald*, 4 Apr. 1860, 168

14 'A Lover of Literature,' *The Pearl*, 28 Dec. 1838, 414

15 Susanna Moodie, Introduction to *Mark Hurdlestone, the Gold Worshipper*, 1853; rpt in *Life in the Clearings*, ed. Robert L. McDougall (Toronto: Macmillan 1976) 292

16 MacDonald, diss. 134–7

17 Randolph Lee, 'Literary Societies and Culture,' *Westminster Review* 134 (1890) 311. His comment continued: 'and we may here express a doubt whether a loss has not been sustained in the disappearance, to a very large extent, of the more substantial basis which belonged to these associated pioneers of self-improvement.' As further evidence that the word 'literary' connoted prestige, note the name of the Canadian Literary Institute, which was actually a Baptist college founded in 1857 that later merged with Woodstock College. See D.K. Clarke, 'Woodstock College, Early Days,' *McMaster University Monthly* (Oct. 1906) 3–11

18 Ginette Bernatchez, 'La Société Littéraire et Historique de Québec (The Literary and Historical Society of Quebec), 1824–1890,' *Revue d'Histoire de l'Amérique française* 35 (1981) 188

19 'A Lover of Literature,' *The Pearl*, 28 Dec. 1838, 414

20 Minutes of the Burrard Literary Club, Vancouver City Archives, Add. Mss 257

21 Mrs G.M. Armstrong, *The First Eighty Years of the Women's Literary Club of St Catharines, 1892–1972*. Available from Brock University Library

22 Papers of the Calgary Women's Literary Club (1906–82) are held by the Glenbow-Alberta Institute Archives. Some other serious reading clubs whose records have survived are the Griswold Reading Club (1900–21) and

the Searchlight Book Club (1910–73), both of whose records are at the Public Archives of Manitoba, and the Canadian Literature Club of Toronto (1914–73), whose papers are in the Baldwin Room, Metro Toronto Reference Library.

23 *Women in Canada* 396–8. Known western literary clubs, many founded later than 1900, include the Medicine Hat Women's Literary Club (founded 1923) and the Fortnightly Club in Macleod, Alberta (active 1929–30), as well as those listed above.

24 MacDonald, diss. 39

25 Parker, *Beginnings of the Book Trade in Canada* 187

26 Allan Smith, 'The Imported Image: American Publications and American Ideas in the Evolution of the English-Canadian Mind, 1820–1900,' diss. Toronto 1971, 53–87. See also his essay, 'American Publications in Nineteenth-Century Canada,' *PBSC* 9 (1970) 15–29.

27 Mary Vipond, 'Best Sellers in English Canada, 1899–1918: An Overview,' *JCF* 24 (1979) 108

28 Stephen Beckow, 'A Majestic Study of Orderly Progress: English Canadian Novelists on Canadian Society, 1896–1900,' MA Carleton 1969. L.M. Grayson and J. Paul Grayson, 'The Canadian Literary Elite: A Socio-Historical Perspective,' *Canadian Journal of Sociology* 3 (1978) 291–308. J. Paul Grayson and L.M. Grayson, 'Canadian Literary and Other Elites: The Historical and Institutional Bases of Shared Realities,' *Canadian Review of Sociology and Anthropology* 17 (1980) 338–56. However, it should be noted that Grayson and Grayson base their research on the writers included in Guy Sylvestre, Brandon Conron, and Carl F. Klinck, *Canadian Writers / Ecrivains canadiens: A Biographical Dictionary* (Toronto: Ryerson 1970), which is particularly weak on secondary women writers.

29 MacDonald, diss. 155–6

30 See Gordon R. Elliott, 'The Games Bibliographers Play,' *PBSC* 10 (1971) 10–11.

31 E.H. Dewart, *Selections from Canadian Poets*, 1864; rpt ed. Douglas Lochhead (Toronto: University of Toronto Press 1973) ix

32 Mary Lu MacDonald, 'Some Notes on the Montreal Literary Scene in the Mid-1820's,' *Canadian Poetry* (1979) 29–40

33 P.B. Waite, 'John Sparrow Thompson,' *Dictionary of Canadian Biography*, IX, 785–7. See also Gwendolyn Davies, 'A Literary Study of Selected Periodicals from Maritime Canada,' diss., York 1979.

34 Mrs Cheney and Mrs Cushing edited *The Snow Drop* (1847–53); Mrs Cushing also edited *The Literary Garland* during its last year (1850–1); Eleanor Lay took over *The Maple Leaf* (1852–4) after the death of her husband in 1853;

Mary Jane Katzmann edited *The Provincial; or, Halifax Monthly Magazine* (1852–3); Susanna Moodie co-edited *The Victoria Magazine* (1847–8) with her husband.

35 Daniel Wilson to J.W. Dawson, 12 Jan. 1882, Dawson Papers, McGill University Archives

36 George Stewart, jr, 'Literature in Canada,' *Canadian Leaves*, ed. G.M. Fairchild (New York: Nelson 1887) 138

37 *CM*, 8 (1897) 463–6. Present were Hon. Thomas Ballantyne, ex-Speaker of the Ontario Legislative Assembly, Barlow Cumberland, MA, John A. Cooper, editor of *The Canadian Magazine*, Bourinot, Stewart, W.H. Drummond, Hon. G.W. Allan, Principal Parkin, President Loudon of the University of Toronto, Professor Mavor, Mr E.B. Walker of the Bank of Commerce, Alexander Muir (author of 'The Maple Leaf'), O.A. Howland, MPP, Lieut.-Col. G.T. Denison, E.E. Sheppard (editor of *Saturday Night*), J.S. Willison (editor of *The Globe*), W.J. Douglas (*Mail and Empire*), Alexander Fraser, Toronto, and Frank Rossire, New York. Regrets were sent by Hon. J.C. Patterson, Lieutenant-Governor of Manitoba, the Governor General, members of the Dominion and Ontario cabinets, Lieut.-Governor Mackintosh, Hon. R.R. Dobell, Sir James M. LeMoine, Charles G.D. Roberts, D.C. Scott, Archibald Lampman, F.G. Scott, Professor Clark, Hon. J.W. Longley (Attorney-General of Nova Scotia), John Reade, Louis Fréchette, Chancellor Boyd, Martin J. Griffin, Dr G. Dawson, Speaker J.D. Edgar, Hugh Graham, and Archbishop O'Brien, President of the Royal Society.

38 For an analysis of some features of this optimism see S.M. Beckow, 'From the Watch-Towers of Patriotism: Theories of Literary Growth in English Canada, 1864–1914,' *JCS* 9 (1974) 3–15.

39 *HMM*, Monthly Advertiser (July 1831). See also the opening address by the editor of *The Literary Garland*, John Gibson, 'To Our Readers,' *LG* 1 (1839) 3

40 For example, John George Bourinot, in *Stewart's* 3 (1869) 124, and again in *The Intellectual Development of the Canadian People* (Toronto: Hunter Rose 1881) 125–6

41 William Kirby to George Stewart, jr, 30 January 1883, Harvard University Library, BMS Can 3

42 *CM* 8 (1897) 364

43 Mrs Holiwell, 'The Love of Reading,' *BAM* 2 (1864) 271

44 Dewart, x; *TCL* 51

45 John Richardson, petition to Baron Sydenham. nd, arrd. 20 July 1841. NAC, Governor General's Office, Civil Secretary's Correspondence, RG 7 G 20. A year later Richardson did manage to obtain a grant of 250 pounds to

continue his history of the War of 1812. See David Beasley, *The Canadian Don Quixote: The Life and Works of Major John Richardson, Canada's First Novelist* (Erin: Porcupine's Quill 1977) 125–35 for details of his various petitions.

46 John Richardson, *Eight Years in Canada* (Montreal: Cunningham 1847) 92

47 John Richardson, *Wacousta; or, The Prophecy; A Tale of the Canadas* (1832; rpt Ottawa: Carleton University Press 1987) 587

48 James Douglas, jr, 'The Intellectual Progress of Canada,' 476

49 *CIN* 15 (24 Feb. 1877) 114

50 'Saunterings,' *The Week* 4 (20 Jan. 1887) 120

51 *CM* 14 (1899), 3; Richardson to W.H. Merritt, 17 Dec. 1839, in Beasley, 117

52 Parker, *Beginnings of the Book Trade in Canada*, 106–7

53 Ibid. 191, 174–5

54 Graeme Mercer Adam, 'The Copyright Law,' *Canada Bookseller* ns 1 (1872) 17

55 Elizabeth Brady, 'A Bibliographical Essay on William Kirby's *The Golden Dog*,' *PBSC* 15 (1976) 24–48; Parker, *Beginnings of the Book Trade in Canada*, 190–2

56 'American Influence on Canadian Thought,' *The Week* 4 (7 July 1887) 518; *TCL* 120; *SECL* 41

57 See Douglas Lochhead, 'John Ross Robertson, Uncommon Publisher for the Common Readers: His First years as a Toronto Book Publisher,' *JCS* 11 (1976) 19–26; and 'J. Ross Robertson -Publisher: Aspects of the Book Trade in Nineteenth-Century Toronto,' in *Book Selling and Book Buying: Aspects of the Nineteenth-Century British and North American Book Trade* (Chicago: American Library Association 1978) 73–86.

58 G. Mercer Adam, 'Garth Grafton's Triumph,' *The Globe* 28 June 1890, 5

59 Goldwin Smith, *Canada and the Canadian Question* (1891; rpt Toronto: University of Toronto Press 1971) 212

60 Goldwin Smith, 'What Is the Matter with Canadian Literature?' *The Week* 11 (31 Aug. 1894) 950; *TCL* 124–5; *SECL* 86–8.

61 Goldwin Smith, *Bystander* 1 (Jan. 1880) 55

62 'Saunterings,' *The Week* 3 (30 Sept. 1886) 708; *TCL* 116; *SECL* 35

63 J.G. Bourinot, 'Views on Canadian Literature,' *The Week* 11 (16 Mar. 1894) 368

64 Graeme Mercer Adam, 'Canadian Literature,' *The Week* 8 (4 July 1890) 486

65 Evelyn Durand, 'A Further Word on Canadian Literature,' *Canada Educational Monthly* (Apr. 1897); rpt in *Elise Le Beau ...* ed. Laura Durand (Toronto: University of Toronto Press 1921) xxiii

66 For a concise summary of the whole problem, see W. Blackburn Harte, 'Intellectual Life and Literature in Canada,' *New England Magazine* (Oct. 1889) 377–80.

CHAPTER TWO: THE RECEPTION OF THE NOVEL

1 Frederick Sinnett, 'The Fiction Fields of Australia' (1856) in John Barnes, ed., *The Writer in Australia: A Collection of Literary Documents, 1856–1964* (Melbourne: Oxford University Press 1969) 8

2 John Lambert, *Travels through Canada* I 325. Cited by Parker, *The Beginnings of the Book Trade in Canada* (Toronto: University of Toronto Press 1985) 20

3 McGee, 'The Mental Outfit of the New Dominion,' *TCL* 80; Nora Robins, 'The Montreal Mechanics' Institute: 1828–1870,' *Canadian Library Journal* 38 (1981) 378; Jim Blanchard, 'Anatomy of Failure: Ontario Mechanics' Institutes, 1835–1895,' *Canadian Library Journal* 38 (1981) 397. *The Canadian Bibliographer*, summarizing the 1888 report of Dr S.P. May to the Ontario Ministry of Education, stated that fiction accounted for 54% of the circulation of Mechanics' Institutes and 70% of that of free libraries (rpt *PBSC* 6 [1967]).

4 Yves Dostaler, *Les infortunes du roman dans le Québec du XIXe siècle* (Montreal: Hurtubise HMH 1977) 63; Jean-Paul Tardivel, 'Avant-Propos,' *Pour la Patrie* (1895), in Guido Rousseau, ed., *Préfaces des romans québécoises du XIXe siècle* (Montreal/Sherbrooke: Editions Cosmos 1970) 87

5 Nina Baym, *Novels, Readers, and Reviewers: Responses to Fiction in Antebellum America* (Ithaca and London: Cornell University Press 1984)

6 John Tinnon Taylor, *Early Opposition to the English Novel: The Popular Reaction from 1760 to 1830* (New York: King's Crown Press 1943). The thorny problem of discussing Canadian attitudes on issues influenced by factors outside the immediate Canadian context affects all areas of Canadian intellectual history. I favour the resolution offered by a scholar of religious history and cited in an article on medical history:

> No doubt the stock of Canadian ideas is replenished every generation from European and American sources; and doubtless it should be an important function of the Canadian intellectual historian to perform the sort of operation that will trace Canadian ideas to their ultimate external source. But his major task, surely, is to analyse the manner in which externally derived ideas have been adapted to a variety of local and regional environments, in such a way that a body of assumptions uniquely Canadian has been built up; and to trace the changing content of such assumptions.

S.F. Wise, 'Sermon Literature and Canadian Intellectual History,' in M. Cross and G. Kealy, eds, *Readings in Canadian Society History, Vol. 2: Pre-*

Industrial Canada, 1760–1849 (Toronto: McClelland & Stewart 1982) 80; cited by Wendy Mitchinson, 'Hysteria and Insanity in Women: A Nineteenth-Century Canadian Perspective,' *JCS* 21, no. 3 (1986) 101

7 Susanna Moodie, *Life in the Clearings versus the Bush* (1853; rpt ed. R.L. McDougall, Toronto: Macmillan 1959) xxxiii

8 'On the Influence of Literature,' *CRLHJ* 1 (July 1824) 67

9 Mary Jane Katzmann, rev. of *St George; or The Canadian League* by William Charles McKinnon, *Provincial* 1 (Apr. 1852) 148

10 Matthew Arnold, 'Count Leo Tolstoi,' *Essays in Criticism: Second Series*, ed. S.R. Littlewood (London: Macmillan 1939) 150

11 Charles Mair, 'Views on Canadian Literature,' *The Week* 11 (9 Mar. 1894) 344

12 Archibald MacMechan, *Headwaters of Canadian Literature* (Toronto: McClelland & Stewart 1924) 14

13 'New Publications. *St Ursula's Convent; or, The Nun of Canada*,' *CRLHJ* 1 (July 1824) 49–53. Samuel Hull Wilcocke's withering review in *The Scribbler* (8 July 1824, 225–34) opens with a denunciation of the book's genre and recommends it to 'juvenile readers who delight in pages full of tittle-tattle.'

14 Rev. of *Paul Clifford*, by Edward Bulwer-Lytton, *HMM* 1 (1830) 81–2

15 I. [James Irving], 'Cursory Thoughts and Literary Reminiscences,' *Acadian Magazine* 1 (1827) 259–61. For an account of the misadventures resulting from Irving's literary tastes see Gwendolyn Davies, 'James Irving: Literature and Libel in Early Nova Scotia,' *ECW* 29 (1984) 48–65.

16 Later published in book form under several different titles: *Lady Mary and Her Nurse* (London: Hall 1856); *Stories of the Canadian Forest* (Boston: Crosby & Nichols 1861); *Afar in the Forest* (London: Nelson 1869)

17 *Maple Leaf* 2 (Jan. 1853) inside back cover

18 Catharine Parr Traill, *The Backwoods of Canada* (London: Knight 1836) 9

19 For example, her footnote to 'The Baron. A Tale of the Nineteenth Century – not of Fiction' (*LG* n.s. 4 [1846] 184): 'Romantic as this story may appear, it is strictly true; to the honor of human nature, I can say, the Baron is no creature of the imagination. This episode in my life is no fiction.'

20 Catharine Parr Traill, *Narratives of Nature* (London: Edward Lacey, nd) v

21 Henry Youle Hind, 'Introduction,' *CJ* 1 (1852) 3

22 Goldwin Smith, *Bystander* 1 (1880) 55

23 J.L. Stewart, 'George Eliot,' *BMM* 3 (1878) 675

24 J.G. Bourinot, *Our Intellectual Strength and Weakness* (1893), rpt ed. Clara Thomas (Toronto: University of Toronto Press 1973) 30

25 J.P., 'Novels and Novel Readers,' *LG* n.s. 8 (1850) 212

26 Henry Giles, 'Fiction,' *LG* n.s. 8 (1850) 264

27 'Our Table,' *LG* n.s. 8 (1850) 238

28 'Our Table,' *LG* 1 (1839) 144
29 See Carter Troop, 'On the Horrible in Fiction,' *The Week* 6 (8 Feb. 1889) 15.
30 Angus M'Kinnon, 'Reading,' *NDM* 1 (1868) 284
31 'The Effects of Literary Cultivation on Morals,' *Canadian Literary Magazine* 1 (1833), 38. See also Henry Giles, 'Fiction,' *LG* n.s. 8 (1850) 267
32 George Stewart, 'Introductory,' *Stewart's* 1 (1867) 1; *TCL* 90. Similarly, M.W.C., 'The Use of Books,' *The Harp* 4 (1879) 495; 'Publisher's Department,' *NDM* Mar. 1876, 237; John A. Cooper, 'A Boy's Reading,' *CM* 6 (1896) 282–5; *CM* 8 (1897) 547–8. Edmund Sheppard, editor of *Saturday Night*, took a more sanguine view: 'I doubt if a boy with any head on him can be spoiled by reading the average dime novel. It is the sort of thing that cures itself ...' *SN* 14 July 1888, 1.
33 'Answers to Correspondents,' *Family Herald* 1 (1860) 128
34 Northrop Frye, *The Secular Scripture: A Study of the Structure of Romance* (Cambridge, MA: Harvard University Press 1976) 25–6
35 'Book Reviews,' *CMNR* 4 (1873) 357–9. Daniel Fowler identifies himself as the author in his autobiographical manuscript published in Frances K. Smith, *Daniel Fowler of Amherst Island* (Kingston: Agnes Etherington Art Centre 1979) 162.
36 J.G. Bourinot, 'Notes in My Library,' *The Week* 12 (5 Apr. 1895) 445
37 J.P., 'Novels and Novel Readers,' *LG* n.s. 8 (1850) 209
38 'The Purser's Cabin,' *AAM* 5 (1854) 334. The character reappears in MacGeorge's *Tales, Sketches and Lyrics* (Toronto: Armour 1858) in 'Count or Counterfeit. A Tale of Lake Ontario.'
39 Rosanna Leprohon, *Antoinette De Mirecourt; or, Secret Marrying and Secret Sorrowing* (Montreal: Lovell 1864) 126
40 'Editor's Shanty,' *AAM* 5 (1854) 609
41 J.P., 'Novels and Novel Readers,' *LG* n.s. 8 (1850) 211
42 'The Editor's Address to the Public,' *Canadian Literary Magazine* 1 (1833) 2; Senex, 'Modern Literature,' *Acadian* 1 (1827) 436
43 'Editor's Shanty,' *AAM* 1 (1852) 173; also 2 (1853) 206
44 I. Allan Jack, 'Harriet Beacher Stowe on Lady Byron's Life,' *Stewart's* 3 (1869) 279
45 'Canadian Books,' *Saturday Reader* 1 (30 Dec. 1865) 261
46 *CMNR* 1 (1872) 152
47 'Current Literature,' *BMM* 1 (1877) 708
48 'Saunterings,' *The Week* 3 (7 Oct. 1886) 723
49 'Our Table,' *LG* n.s. 5 (1847) 435
50 Miss Foster (T.D.F.), 'Jane Eyre – An Autobiography,' *LG* n.s. 6 (1848) 335–8; Susanna Moodie, 'A Word for the Novel Writers,' *LG* n.s. 9 (1851) 348–51; *CNN* 44–50

51 Goldwin Smith, *Bystander* 1 (1880) 390
52 'Our Library Table,' *The Week* 8 (17 Apr. 1891) 319. Zola did not generate the same kind of response in *The Canadian Magazine* where he was usually ignored. A translation of *Le Ventre de Paris* was noted simply as a detailed but rather dull book: *CM* 6 (1896) 488
53 McGee, *TCL* 80
54 G.M. Adam, 'Recent Fiction in Britain,' *CM* 4 (1895) 218
55 'Bric A Brac,' Montreal *Daily Star*, 5 Dec. 1887, 2. The experience of living in India may have broadened her literary perspective, for in an 1896 review of Conrad she commended him for possessing 'not inconsiderably the power of Zola and of Hardy ... of transmuting the unspeakable things of life, with the effect that they are not only bearable upon the printed paged, but serve undeniable ends of art.' *Indian Daily News*, 12 Oct. 1896; rpt in T.E. Tausky, ed., *Sara Jeannette Duncan, Selected Journalism* (Ottawa: Tecumseh Press 1978) 120
56 D.C. Scott, 'At the Mermaid Inn,' 10 June 1893; rpt in Barrie Davies, ed., *At the Mermaid Inn* (Toronto: University of Toronto Press 1979) 329
57 Bernard Smith, *Forces in American Criticism* (New York: Harcourt Brace 1939) 37
58 A.R. [Andrew Robertson], 'Retrospective Reviews,' *LG* 2 (1840) 307
59 'New Publications,' *CRLHJ* 1 (1824) 49
60 'The Bravo: A Venetian Story,' *HMM* 32 (1832) 410
61 'Our Table,' *LG* n.s. 8 (1850) 289
62 Michèle Lacombe, 'Colonialism and Nationalism in English- and French-Canadian Literary Journals from Montreal, 1846–1879,' diss. York 1984, 213–14, 252–3
63 For example, *Provincial*, 2 (1853) 196–7, 316–17
64 Moodie, *LG* n.s. 9 (1851) 348–51; *CNN* 44–50
65 'Our Table,' *LG* 1 (1839) 192
66 'Our Table,' *LG* n.s. 3 (1845) 190. Mary Jane Katzmann praised *Nicholas Nickleby* and *Oliver Twist* for 'the bold manly spirit that dared to strike a blow for poor and wronged children' but she very much disliked *Martin Chuzzlewit*, *Dombey and Son*, and *David Copperfield* for their 'broad vulgarisms' and 'revolting scenes' ('A Gossip About Literature,' *Provincial* 2 [1853] 321–30). Dickens was admired by Richardson (Beasley, *The Canadian Don Quixote* 133) and upon his death received a lengthy, thoroughly laudatory tribute from the Reverend Moses Harvey (*Stewart's* 5 [1872] 134–9).
67 'Our Table,' *LG* n.s. 3 (1845) 336
68 'George Sand,' *LG* n.s. 7 (1849) 63. Sand was not universally condemned in Canada, however. A generation later she was named 'the author who,

next to George Eliot, has done most to redeem the modern novel from decaying along with the modern drama,' *CMNR* 12 (1877) 664

69 Charles Pelham Mulvaney, 'Some French Novels of the Eighteenth Century,' *BMM* 3 (1878) 385

70 'Our Library Table,' *The Week* 3 (1 July 1886) 500

71 'Our Library Table,' *The Week* 3 (22 Apr. 1886) 338

72 *The Week* 7 (20 June 1890) 461

73 'Recent Fiction,' *The Week* 12 (3 Aug. 1895) 951

74 'Current Literature,' *BMM* 2 (1877) 856

75 'Current Literature,' *Canadian Spectator* 1 (26 Jan. 1878) 36

76 'Book Reviews,' *CMNR* 12 (1877) 100

77 'Book Reviews,' *CMNR* 13 (1878) 224; 10 (1876) 87

78 'Book Reviews,' *CMNR* 9 (1876) 341

79 'Editor's Shanty,' *AAM* 6 (1855) 103; 5 (1854) 511

80 C. Davis English, 'The Immoral in Fiction,' *The Week* 2 (8 Oct. 1885) 709; Carter Troop, 'On the Horrible in Fiction,' *The Week* 6 (8 Feb. 1889) 152–3

81 Roderick Random, 'Letters to Living Authors – Mr Robert Louis Stevenson,' *The Week* 6 (15 July 1889) 487

82 G. Mercer Adam, 'Some Books of the Past Year,' *The Week* 2 (15 Jan. 1885) 103

83 'Library Table,' *The Week* 11 (2 Feb. 1894) 232

84 E.G., 'Recent Fiction,' *The Week* 13 (1 May 1896) 550

CHAPTER THREE: PROBLEMS OF PLACE

1 Robert Kroetsch, 'A Conversation with Margaret Laurence,' in *creation*, ed. Robert Kroetsch (Toronto: new press 1970) 63

2 E.D. Blodgett, 'After Pierre Berton What?: In Search of a Canadian Literature,' *ECW* 30 (1984–5) 62

3 McGee, 'The Mental Outfit of the New Dominion'; *TCL* 85

4 George Stewart, *Evenings in the Library. Bits of Gossip About Books and those who Write them* (St John: Morrow 1878) 201

5 See, for example, *CM* 2 (1894) 199.

6 'Prospectus of the Family Herald,' *Family Herald*, 16 Nov. 1859, 2

7 G. Mercer Adam, 'Outline History of Canadian Literature,' in William H. Withrow, *An Abridged History of Canada* (Toronto: Briggs 1887) 180

8 Andrew Shiels, *The Witch of the Westcot* (Halifax: Joseph Howe 1831) preface

9 'The Literature of a New Country,' *The Monthly Review* 1 (Jan. 1841) 59–61. A modern discussion of the problem which scarcely mentions Canada

appears in David T. Haberly, 'The Search for a National Language: A Problem in the Comparative History of Postcolonial Literatures,' *Comparative Literature Studies* 11 (1974) 85–97.

10 Hence Desmond Pacey christened *The Advocate* 'the worst of the many bad novels produced in Canada.' *Creative Writing in Canada* new ed. (Toronto: McGraw-Hill Ryerson 1967) 25

11 *Monthly Review* 61

12 'Canadian Poetry and Poets,' *BAM* 1 (1863) 416–17

13 Susanna Moodie, Introduction to *Mark Hurdlestone* 292

14 Andrew Learmont Spedon, *Tales of the Canadian Forest* (Montreal: Lovell 1861) 203

15 Andrew Learmont Spedon, *Canadian Summer Evening Tales* (Montreal: Lovell 1866) 5

16 For example, Hector W. Charlesworth, 'The Canadian Girl: An Appreciative Medley,' *CM* 1 (1893) 186

17 George Stewart, jr, 'Canada in Fiction,' *The Week* 4 (6 Oct. 1887) 720

18 Adam, 'Outline History of Canadian Literature' 182

19 Catharine Parr Traill, *The Backwoods of Canada* (London: Knight 1836) 153–4

20 Catharine Parr Traill, Journal, 16 Aug. 1837, NAC, Traill Family Papers, vol. 2. A similar comment appears 29 Jan. 1838.

21 Susanna Moodie, *Roughing It in the Bush* (London: Bentley 1852) vol. 2, 13–14

22 See George L. Parker, 'Literary Journalism before Confederation,' *CL* No. 68–9 (1976) 97

23 *Flora Lyndsay; or, Passages in an Eventful Life* (London: Bentley 1854). First serialized as 'Trifles from the Burthen of a Life,' *LG* n.s. 9 (Mar.–July 1851)

24 First serialized *LG* n.s. 9 (Sept.–Dec. 1851)

25 In 1856 Moodie gave her publisher, Richard Bentley, a different reason for no longer writing about Canada: 'It is difficult to write a work of fiction, placing the scene in Canada, without rousing up the whole country against me. Whatever locality I chose, the people would insist, that my characters were *really* natives of the place. That I had a malicious motive ... Will they ever forgive me for writing *Roughing It*? ... If I write about this country again, it shall never be published till my head is under the sod.' *Letters of a Lifetime*, ed. Carl Ballstadt, Elizabeth Hopkins, and Michael Peterman (Toronto: University of Toronto Press 1985) 169–70

26 That theirs was an era of little interest in Canadian subjects for any artistic venture is suggested by the 1834 exhibition of the Society of Artists and Amateurs of Toronto in which only 28 of 196 items bore any evidence of their Canadian context. See G. MacInnes, *A Short History of Canadian Art* (Toronto: Macmillan 1939) 38.

27 Examples are John Gibson, 'The Hermit of Saint Maurice,' *LG* 1 (1838) 5–15;
Diana Bayley, 'The Elopement,' *LG* n.s. 1 (Jan.–Feb. 1843); M.W., 'The Gibbet
Tree,' *LG* n.s. 2 (1844) 69–78; C., 'The Old Man's Tale,' *LG* n.s. 3 (1845)
41–5; Clarence Ormond, 'Canadian Legends. 1. The Ruined Cottage,' *LG*
n.s. 4 (1846) 177–9; Hamilton Aylmer, 'Alciphron Leicester,' *Victoria Magazine* 1 (Jan.–Mar. 1848); anon., 'The Hermit of Niagara,' *Amaranth* 2 (1842)
178–83. A later instance occurs in Mrs Sadlier's *Elinor Preston* (1861).

28 This is not the case with her 'American' novel, *Tonnewonte, or, The Adopted Son
of America* (1825), in which the hero chooses the space and freedom of the
United States over caste and property in France.

29 Awareness of this little book is itself an instructive fable for historians
of Canadian literature. Published in Three Rivers and set largely in
Canada, it remained unknown to Canadians until it was reprinted in 1977
in the Garland Library of Narratives of North American Captivities and
drawn to the attention of Canadians by Mary Lu MacDonald (*CL* No. 91, 1981
181–3). In contrast to the first English-language Canadian novels, the
first French-Canadian novel, Aubert de Gaspé's *L'Influence d'un livre* (1837),
imports none of its characters, settings, or resolutions explicitly from the
Old World.

30 Representative examples include Mrs Cushing, 'A Canadian Legend,' *LG* 1
(1839) 167–80; Douglas Huyghue, *Argimou* (1847); Andrew Learmont
Spedon, 'Marriage in Middle Life' in his *Tales of the Canadian Forest* (1861);
Mrs J.V. Noel, 'The Secret of Stanley Hall,' *Saturday Reader*, 3 Feb.–10
Mar. 1866; Mrs Ross, *Violet Keith* (1868); J.G. Bourinot, 'Marguerite: a Tale
of Forest Life in the New Dominion,' *NDM*, Jan.–June 1870; Annie Louisa
Walker Coghill, *A Canadian Heroine* (1873), Mrs Huddlestone, *Bluebell*
(1875); Agatha Armour, *Lady Rosamond's Secret* (1878).

31 For a discussion of the pattern in early prairie fiction see Dick Harrison,
Unnamed Country: The Struggle for a Canadian Prairie Fiction (Edmonton:
University of Alberta Press 1977) 58–9.

32 Carl F. Klinck, 'Literary Activity in Canada East and Canada West (1841–
1880),' *LHC*, vol. 1, 160

33 Mrs MacLachlan (E.M.M.), 'The Pride of Lorette: A Tale Founded on Fact,'
LG 2 (1840) 337–51

34 A., 'The Heiress: An Adventure at the Springs,' *LG* 2 (1840) 161–4

35 T., 'The Ruins. A Canadian Legend,' *LG* n.s. 2 (1844) 467–8; Clarence
Ormond, 'Canadian Legends. 1. The Ruined Cottage,' *LG* n.s. 4 (1846)
177–9; Mrs Cheney, 'A Legend of the Lake,' *LG* n.s. 9 (1851) 74–9; Mrs
Cheney, 'The Old Manuscript; a Mémoire of the Past,' *LG* n.s. 9 (Apr.–Sept.
1851)

36 Thomas McLean to Louisa Murray, 7 Jan. 1864. Louisa Murray papers

(copied from originals in the possession of Louisa King), York University Archives.

37 'Our Undertaking,' *Saturday Reader* 1 (1865) 1

38 'To Our Readers,' *DI* 6 (1891) 2

39 'Prospectus,' *CIN* 1869

40 Rev. M. Harvey, 'A Trio of Forgotten Worthies,' *MM* 4 (1874) 408–9

41 Robert Allison Hood, *The Chivalry of Keith Leicester. A Romance of British Columbia* (New York: Doran 1918) 197

42 John Howard Willis ('H.'), 'The Fairy Harp,' *CRLHJ* 1 (1824) [343–8]; 'The Faithful Heart,' *CMLR* 4 (1825) 416–18

43 Ned Caldwell, 'Sam Horton's Last Trip,' *LG* n.s. 1 (1843) 522–4; James McCarroll, 'The Adventures of a Night,' *AAM* 6 (1854) 553–60

44 anon., 'Dark Harbour. A Tale of Grand Manan,' *Amaranth* 1 (1841) 122–6

45 'Sketches of Village Life,' *LG* 3 (Jan.–May 1841); Harry Bloomfield, 'Richard Craighton,' *LG* n.s. 5 (Jan.–June 1847)

46 C.W. Cooper, 'Jessie's Lawsuit,' *CMNR* 2 (1872) 25–36; John Charles Dent, 'The Gerrard Street Mystery,' *BMM* 1 (1877) 761–81

47 See A.J. Crockett, 'Concerning James De Mille,' *More Studies in Nova Scotian History*, ed. George Patterson (Halifax: Imperial Publishing 1941) 124–5.

48 Ice accidents also appear in Philippe Aubert de Gaspé, *Les Anciens Canadiens* (1863); J.A.H., 'The Story of Jenny Stuart,' *NDM* 2 (Sept. 1868) 335–9; John Talon-Lesperance (pseud. 'Arthur Faverel') 'Rosalba, or: Faithful to Two Lovers,' *CIN* 1 (19 Mar.–16 Apr. 1870); Susan Frances Harrison, *Ringfield* (1912).

49 James De Mille, *The Boys of Grand Pré School* (Boston: Lee & Shepard 1871) 66

50 J.E. Collins, *Annette the Métis Spy* (Toronto: Rose-Belford 1886) 142. It is particularly intriguing to see such utter disdain for geographical reality expressed by the author of two historical books, *Life and Times of Sir John A. Macdonald* (1883) and *Canada under the Administration of Lord Lorne* (1884).

51 For a detailed analysis of the image of Canada presented to English juvenile readers, see R.G. Moyles, 'A "Boys' Own" View of Canada,' *Canadian Children's Literature* 34 (1984) 41–56.

52 James Doyle, 'Canadian Poetry and American Magazines, 1885–1905,' *Canadian Poetry* 5 (1979) 75

53 S. Frances Harrison ('Seranus'), 'William Dean Howells: An Interview,' *Massey's Magazine* 3 (1897) 334

54 Northrop Frye, 'Conclusion,' *LHC*, vol. 2, 338

55 For example, *CM* 2 (1894) 199–200:

Some time ago, in an American paper, there appeared, from the pen of a well-known critic and writer, a list and eulogistic notice of Canadian writers and writings. Of the men on that list two have found their home in England, and the remainder, with two exceptions, in the United States. Men must live, and will ever go where they find a market for their wares, but it is contended here that if there were the lively interest among Canadians in Canadian subjects which the latter deserve, these writers would not have had to go so far afield for an audience.

56 G.B. Burgin, 'A Chat with Sara Jeannette Duncan,' *Idler* 8 (1895) 117

CHAPTER FOUR: APPROACHES TO REALISM

1 Edwin M. Eigner and George J. Worth, 'Introductory Essay,' *Victorian Criticism of the Novel* (Cambridge University Press 1985) 2–3

2 Thomas Chandler Haliburton, *Nature and Human Nature* (1855; rpt London: Hurst & Blackett 1859) 83

3 Ibid. 245

4 *The Novascotian*, 13 June 1839. Quoted by V.L.O. Chittick, *Thomas Chandler Haliburton: A Study in Provincial Toryism* (New York: Columbia University Press 1924) 179

5 V.L.O. Chittick, *Thomas Chandler Haliburton* 206

6 *The Novascotian*, 27 Sept. 1838. Chittick, ibid. 233

7 *The NovaScotian*, 24 July 1843. Chittick, ibid. 477

8 *The Novascotian*, 4 Sept. 1843. Chittick, ibid. 479

9 *Acadian Recorder*, 10 June 1837. Chittick, ibid. 211

10 Chittick, *Thomas Chandler Haliburton* 350–7

11 J.D. Logan, *Thomas Chandler Haliburton* (Toronto: Ryerson 1923) 23

12 Thomas Chandler Haliburton, *The Old Judge; or, Life in a Colony* (London: Colburn 1849) I 5

13 Fred Cogswell, 'Haliburton,' *LHC*, vol. 1, 114

14 James De Mille, *Elements of Rhetoric* (New York: Harper 1878) 309, 417–18

15 Archibald MacMechan, *Headwaters of Canadian Literature* (Toronto: McClelland & Stewart 1924) 48

16 Rev. of *The Living Link*, *CIN* 10 (22 Aug. 1874) 118

17 For example, *The Lady of the Ice* (New York: Appleton 1870) 9

18 For example, chapters XVIII and XXVII of *The Dodge Club* (1869) and the final chapter of *The Lady of the Ice*. For a theoretical analysis see Richard Cavell, 'Bakhtin Reads De Mille: Canadian Literature, Post-modernism, and the Theory of Dialogism,' John Moss, ed., *Future Indicative. Literary Theory and Canadian Literature* (Ottawa: University of Ottawa Press 1987) 205–11.

19 M.G. Parks, 'Strange to Strangers Only,' *CL* 70 (1976) 61–78

20 James De Mille, *A Strange Manuscript Found in a Copper Cylinder*, 1888; rpt ed. M.G. Parks (Ottawa: Carleton University Press 1986) 61

21 Ibid. 228

22 For a fuller discussion of De Mille's work, see Carole Gerson, 'Three Writers of Victorian Canada' (Toronto: ECW 1981).

23 Rev. of *Seven Years and Other Tales* by Julia Kavanagh, *Family Herald*, 25 Jan. 1860, 96

24 Rev. of *The Abby of Rathmore and Other Tales*, by Mrs J.V. Noel, *Family Herald*, 4 Apr. 1860, 168

25 Clara Reeve, *The Progress of Romance* (1785; rpt New York: Garland 1970) 111

26 Graeme Mercer Adam, 'Recent Fiction in Britain,' *CM* 4 (1895) 218

27 *At the Mermaid Inn* 146

28 E.W. Thomson to Ethelwyn Wetherald, 14 May 1895, Lorne Pierce Collection, Queen's University Archives, 2001b BO34 File 16 Item 02

29 Stewart, *Evenings in the Library* 200–7

30 'Current Literature,' *RBCM* 2 (1879) 511

31 *The Week* 5 (19 July 1888) 545, 8 (17 July 1891) 531

32 *The Week* 8 (3 July 1891) 497–98, 9 (8 Jan. 1892) 93

33 *The Week* 5 (19 July 1888) 544

34 *The Week* 1 (20 Nov. 1884) 811

35 *The Week* 13 (28 Aug. 1896) 958

36 *The Week* 4 (3 Mar. 1887) 223

37 *The Week* 2 (26 Feb. 1885) 204

38 *The Week* 3 (8 Apr. 1886) 301

39 However, an 1885 reprint of *Their Wedding Journey* elicited the comment that 'It is fair to presume that Mr Howells has long since seen cause to modify some of the views expressed in this story. His estimates of English and Canadian characters are absurd and grossly unjust.' *The Week* 2 (17 Sept. 1885) 667

40 *The Week* 4 (21 July 1887) 549, 552

41 Louisa Murray, 'Democracy in Literature,' *The Week* 6 (2 Aug. 1889) 550

42 Thomas Dick, 'Howells Again,' *The Week* 6 (27 Sept. 1889) 683

43 S. Frances Harrison, *Massey's Magazine* 3 (1897), 333–6

44 'Literary Pabulum,' *The Week* 4 (24 Nov. 1887) 831

45 Washington *Post*, 4 Apr. 1886; rpt as 'The Bostonians' in *Sara Jeannette Duncan. Selected Journalism*, ed. T.E. Tausky (Ottawa: Tecumseh 1978) 103–5

46 'Bric A Brac,' *Montreal Daily Star*, 28 July 1888, 4

47 Marjory MacMurchy, 'The Bookman Gallery. Mrs Everard Cotes,' *The Bookman* 48 (1915) 39. The chief evidence of continuing personal contact

between the two writers is a letter from Duncan to Howells held by the Houghton Library and reprinted by Thomas Tausky, *JCF* 13 (1975) 148.

48 Evidence of this interchange is James' reply, dated 26 Jan. 1900, in Leon Edel, ed., *Henry James Letters* iv (Cambridge, MA: Harvard University Press 1984) 131–2

49 'Saunterings,' *The Week* 5 (2 Aug. 1888) 574

50 'Bric A Brac,' Montreal *Daily Star*, 17 Jan. 1888, 2

51 'Saunterings,' *The Week* 3 (28 Oct. 1886) 772

52 *The Week* 3 (15 July 1886) 533

53 'Bric A Brac,' Montreal *Daily Star*, 31 Dec. 1887, 4. Note the contrast with the diatribe of Graeme Mercer Adam against 'the degeneracy of the novel in the hands of the new woman' cited in Chapter 3.

54 'Other People and I,' *Globe*, 17 June 1885, 3

55 'Outworn Literary Methods,' *The Week* 4 (9 June 1887) 451; *CNN* 86–8

56 'Saunterings,' *The Week* 4 (23 Dec. 1886) 56–7

57 *The Week* 4 (3 Feb. 1887) 159

58 'Saunterings,' *The Week* 4 (13 Jan. 1887) 111–12; *CNN* 80–6

59 'Women's World,' *Globe*, 13 Jan. 1887, 6

60 'Saunterings,' *The Week* 4 (13 Jan. 1887) 111

61 'Bric A Brac,' Montreal *Daily Star*, 26 May 1888, 2

62 *The Week* 4 (13 Jan. 1887) 111

63 'Saunterings,' *The Week* 5 (2 Aug. 1888) 574

64 For a thorough discussion of Duncan's indebtedness to Howells see Thomas Tausky, 'The American Girls of William Dean Howells and Sara Jeannette Duncan,' *JCF* 13 (1975) 146–58.

65 'Our Library Table,' *The Week* 8 (3 Apr. 1891) 288

66 Sara Jeannette Duncan, *A Voyage of Consolation* (New York: Appleton 1898) 1–2

67 67 *DI* 5 (27 Sept. 1890) 214. (She also merited a portrait on p 212.)

68 Sara Jeannette Duncan, *A Daughter of Today* (New York: Appleton 1894) 258

69 Duncan, *The Imperialist* (Toronto: Copp Clark 1904) 190. See Carole Gerson, 'Duncan's Web,' *CL* 63 (1975) 73–80.

70 Sara Jeannette Duncan, *The Burnt Offering* (1909; rpt London: Methuen 1919) 117–18

71 'Books and Authors,' *CM* 13 (Sept. 1899) 487

72 *The Week* 12 (1895) 413

73 Forrest Reid, 'Minor Fiction in the Eighties,' in *The Eighteen-Eighties*, ed. Walter de la Mare (Cambridge: Cambridge University Press 1930) 107–35

74 Amy Cruse, *The Victorians and Their Reading* (Boston and New York: Houghton Mifflin 1935) 417

75 Ernest A. Baker, *History of the English Novel* (1936; rpt New York: Barnes & Noble 1963) IX 290–3, 296–338; Hugh Walpole, 'The Historical Novel in England since Sir Walter Scott,' in *Sir Walter Scott Today*, ed. H.J.C. Grierson (London: Constable 1932) 183

76 See George L. Barnett, ed., *Nineteenth-Century British Novelists on the Novel* (New York: Appleton-Century-Crofts 1971).

CHAPTER FIVE: THE LONG SHADOW OF SIR WALTER SCOTT

1 Carl F. Klinck and J.J. Talman, eds, *The Journals of Major John Norton 1816* (Toronto: Champlain Society 1970) xx; Charles E. Phillips, *The Development of Education in Canada* (Toronto: Gage 1957) 477. Thanks to Ian MacLaren for the Norton reference.

2 See Chris Worth, 'Sir Walter Scott and Nineteenth-Century Australian Fiction,' presented at the 'Scott and His Influence' conference, University of Alberta, August 1987. Elizabeth Webby's series of articles on early Australian literature published in *Southerly* document Scott's presence before 1850. See 27 (1967) 266–85; 29 (1969) 17–42; 36 (1976) 200–22, 297–317.

3 Yves Dostaler, *Les Infortunes du roman dans le Québec du XIXe siècle* (Montreal: Hurtubise 1977), 33–4. See Eva-Marie Kröller, 'Walter Scott in America, English Canada, and Québec: A Comparison,' *Canadian Review of Comparative Literature* (Winter 1980) 44–6.

4 He was a literary collector and author of several books, including *A Ridiculous Courting and Other Stories of French Canada* (Chicago: Donelly 1900).

5 Fairchild to Le Moine, 1 Jan. 1903, Lorne Pierce Collection, Queen's University, Box 41

6 Raoul Renault's *Bibliographie de Sir James-M. Le Moine* (Quebec: Leger Brousseau 1897) lists *Etude sur Walter Scott, comme poète, romancier, historien* (Montreal 1862). What is probably the same piece was serialized in *L'Opinion Publique* (5 déc. 1872–21 mai 1873); the latter was republished with a few minor modifications as 'Sir Walter Scott, Poète, Romancier, Historien,' in LeMoine's *Monographies et esquisses* (1885).

7 For example, see his obituary, *Proceedings and Transactions of the Royal Society of Canada* ser. 3, vol. 6 (1912) v–vii

8 'Sir Walter Scott,' *CMLR* 1 (1823) 19–24. The fact that its first editor, David Chisholme, was a recent emigrant from Scotland likely influenced the magazine's interest in Scott. After the appointment of a new editor, Dr A.J. Christie (also a Scot), early in 1824, Scott's presence diminished slightly. Surprisingly, Chisholme's new periodical, *The Canadian Review and Literary and Historical Journal* (5 nos, 1824–6), paid Scott scant attention.

9 *CMLR* 1 (1823) 25–32, 121–8, 249–56; 2 (1824) 97–110; 3 (1824) 49–60; 4 (1825) 336–41

10 *CMLR* (1824) 306–8

11 *Acadian* 2 (1827) 175–83; 1 (1827) 399–401; 1 (1827) 469–71

12 *Canadian Literary Magazine* 1 (1833) 41. The portrait was accompanied by a tribute from Robert Douglas Hamilton, MD (pseud. 'Guy Pollock').

13 In *The Life of Thomas McCulloch, DD*, his son, William McCulloch, dates its completion as the late 1820s (141–3).

14 See Kröller, 'Walter Scott in America, English Canada, and Québec: A Comparison' 36–7. Veneration of Scott as the incarnation of human nobility (in contrast with Byron as the exemplar of 'wretched principles' suitably manifested in a 'wretched' life) can be found in Andrew Robertson's articles on the two writers in the first two volumes of *The Literary Garland* 1 (1839) 318–20; 2 (1840) 433–43.

15 W.P.C., 'Our Literature Present and Prospective,' *LG* n.s. 6 (1848) 246. Similar views abound; see, for example, B.F.M., 'Romance,' *LG* 3 (1841) 302–4 and Rev. Henry Giles, 'Fiction,' *LG* n.s. 8 (1850) 268. The *Garland*'s editorial pages commented as well on the availability of Scott's work in Canada, in 1842 and 1843 welcoming the lavish Abbotsford Edition and the inexpensive People's Edition, both available in Montreal.

16 'Editor's Shanty,' *AAM* 5 (1854) 610

17 William E. De Villiers-Westfall, 'The Dominion of the Lord: An Introduction to the Cultural History of Protestant Ontario in the Victorian Period,' *Queen's Quarterly* 83 (1976) 63

18 Harriet Beecher Stowe, 'What Shall the Girls Read?' *NDM*, Aug. 1870, 39

19 Andrew Archer, 'Scott,' *Stewart's* 5 (1871) 145–8

20 Goldwin Smith, *Bystander* 2 (1881) 47

21 'Library Table,' *The Week* 10 (1 Sept. 1893) 952; (6 Jan. 1893) 135. Similar examples include Louisa Murray, 'Democracy in Literature,' *The Week* 6 (2 Aug. 1889), 550; Graeme Mercer Adam, 'Recent Fiction in Britain,' *CM* 4 (1895) 218–23. It was therefore quite fitting for *The Canadian Magazine* to publish British writer David Christie Murray's complaint about 'the use which the modern critic makes of Sir Walter Scott' 8 (1897) 245.

22 It may seem ironic that while Smith never ceased to venerate Scott he later became a proponent of Canadian union with the United States, anathema to those promoting the quest for the Canadian Scott to intensify Canadian nationalism. Smith's involvement in the cultural life of Canada included his association with two of the major post-Confederation periodicals, *The Canadian Monthly and National Review* (1872–8) and *The Week* (1883–96), his publication of his own *Bystander* (irreg. 1880–90), as well as his eminent position as author and historian.

23 Published in *The Canadian Journal* 13 (1871–3), 347–51; rpt in Smith's *Lectures and Essays* (Toronto: Hunter Rose 1881) and *CNN* 53–8. Due to the brevity of the article, page numbers for each quotation have been omitted. For an examination of Smith's non-literary thought, see Wayne Roberts, 'Goldwin's Myth,' *CL* 83 (1979) 50–71.

24 John Henry Raleigh, 'What Scott Meant to the Victorians,' *Victorian Studies* (1963); rpt in his *Time, Place, and Idea* (Carbondale: Southern Illinois University Press 1968) 96– 125

25 See, for example, *HMM* 1 (1830) 81–2 and Rosanna Leprohon's comments on acceptable reading material in 'Florence; or, Wit and Wisdom,' *LG* n.s. 7 (1849) 247–8.

26 As Raleigh points out, *Waverley*, like the novels of Austen, Fielding, and Cervantes before, initially had been inspired by a desire to 'laugh off the stage the currently fashionable romances in the name of realism' (101).

27 'The Bravo,' *HMM* 2 (1832) 409

28 Nina Baym, *Novels, Readers and Reviewers. Responses to Fiction in Antebellum America* (Ithaca: Cornell University Press 1984) 225–35. See, for example, Clarence Ormond, 'Leaves from the Notebook of an Idler,' *LG* n.s. 3 (1845) 475–6; 'Current Literature,' *BMM* 1 (1877) 708; Annie G. Savigny, *A Romance of Toronto (Founded on Fact). A Novel* (Toronto: Briggs 1888); J.G. Bourinot, *Our Intellectual Strength and Weakness* (1893), rpt ed. Clara Thomas (Toronto: University of Toronto Press 1973) 27; Robert Barr, 'Literature in Canada,' *CM* 14 (1899) 135.

29 'Editor's Shanty,' *AAM* 1 (1852) 174

30 Ibid. 265; 4 (1854) 326; 7 (1855) 246

31 See, for example, 'Editor's Shanty,' *AAM* 1 (1852) 560; *Family Herald*, 29 Feb. 1860, 128; Goldwin Smith, above.

32 Professor Lyall, 'From the Augustan Age to the Present Time,' *Stewart's* 4 (1871) 356

33 George Stewart, jr, *Evenings in the Library* (Toronto: Belford 1878) 203

34 Miss Foster (T.D.F.), 'The Neighbours,' *LG* n.s. 1 (1843) 309. The same book was similarly praised in *The Amaranth* 3 (1843) 286–8.

35 'Current Literature,' *BMM* 1 (1877) 708. See also *AAM* 3 (1853) 416–17.

36 Richard Lewis, 'Shakespearean Studies,' *BMM* 2 (1877) 70

37 Louisa Murray, 'Democracy in Literature,' *The Week* 6 (2 Aug. 1889) 550

38 See E.M. Kröller, 'George Eliot in Canada: *Romola* and *The Golden Dog*,' *American Review of Canadian Studies* 14 (1984) 312–13.

39 'Book Reviews,' *CMNR* 7 (1875) 99

40 'Book Reviews,' *CMNR* 3 (1873) 170, 551–2

41 'Current Literature,' *BMM* 2 (1877) 471

42 Maud Pettit, *Beth Woodburn* (Toronto: Briggs 1897) 32, 40

43 'Literary Notes,' *CMNR* 1 (1872) 94
44 'Book Reviews,' *CMNR* 10 (1876) 88
45 *Stewart's* 4 (1870) 330
46 *CM* 7 (1896) 488
47 *The Week*, 2 (30 Apr. 1885) 348; 12 (12 Apr. 1895) 471
48 Agnes Maule Machar, 'Prominent Canadians – XXXVII – Grant Allen,' *The Week* 8 (10 July 1891) 510
49 Stuart Livingston, 'Bjornstjerne Bjornson,' *CM* 1 (1893) 99
50 'Our Table,' *LG* 1 (1839) 144; 2 (1840) 139
51 'To Correspondents,' *Acadian* 1 (1827) 360
52 'Salutary,' 3 Dec. 1887, 6
53 'Our Address,' *Provincial* 1 (1852) 2, 146–8
54 Casca, 'Emily Montague; or, Quebec a Century Ago,' *British Canadian Review* 1 (1863) 87
55 'Book Reviews,' *CMNR* 8 (1875) 184
56 'Current Literature,' *Canadian Spectator* 1 (1878) 300
57 'Book Notes,' *Westminster Review* 11 (1917) 16
58 'Announcement,' *CM* 1 (1893) ii; *CM* 2 (1894) 200
59 *CM* 1 (1893) 164, 328
60 John A. Cooper, 'The Strength and Weakness of Current Books,' *CM* 13 (1899) 10; *TCL* 156–7
61 Robert Barr, 'Literature in Canada,' *CM* 14 (1899) 1–5, 130–6

CHAPTER SIX: THE CHALLENGE OF FORM

1 *CRLHJ* 1 (1824) 49
2 Julia Catherine Beckwith Hart, *St Ursula's Convent, or The Nun of Canada* (Kingston: Thomson 1824) I, v; *TCL* 15; *CNN* 23
3 *CMLR* 2 (1824) 464
4 Northrop Frye, *The Secular Scripture: A Study of the Structure of Romance* (Cambridge: Harvard University Press 1976) 38
5 John Richardson, *Eight Years in Canada* (Montreal: Cunningham 1847) 14, 95
6 John Richardson, *Hardscrabble; or The Fall of Chicago* (New York: De Witt [1851]) 66–7
7 John Richardson, *Wacousta; or, The Prophecy; A Tale of the Canadas*. 1832. Rpt ed. Douglas Cronk (Ottawa: Carleton University Press 1987) 581. All subsequent quotations will be taken from this edition, which reprints the introduction to the 1851 edition (581–8).
8 Richardson, *Eight Years in Canada* 161
9 See Arvid Shulenherger, *Cooper's Theory of Fiction* (Lawrence: University of

Kansas Press 1955); George Perkins, ed., *The Theory of the American Novel* (New York: Holt, Rinehart & Winston 1970) 17–30.

10 John Richardson, *Ecarté, or, The Salons of Paris* (London: Coburn 1829) I 13. Similar statements appear I 197, 229; II 49–50, 117. Likewise, Susanna Moodie announced that Flora Lyndsay 'was no heroine of romance, but a veritable human creature' *Flora Lyndsay* (New York: DeWitt & Davenport 1854) 67.

11 Frye, *The Secular Scripture* 40

12 *Westminster Review* 11 (Oct. 1829) 303–26

13 Richardson, *Ecarté* I 79

14 John Richardson, *Wau-Nan-Gee; or, The Massacre at Chicago* (Philadelphia: Peterson [1852]) 8–9

15 *LG* n.s. 7 (1849) 17–46

16 Richardson, *Eight Years in Canada* 91

17 Richardson, *Hardscrabble* 43

18 John Richardson, *The Canadian Brothers; or, The Prophecy Fulfilled* (Montreal: Armour & Ramsay 1840) I, x. The preface to *Wau-Nan-Gee* contains a similar assertion that 'the whole of the text approaches ... nearly to Historical fact' iii.

19 Advertisement from the Niagara *Chronicle and Advertiser*, 15 May 1838. In William Morley, *A Bibliographical Study of Major John Richardson* (Toronto: Bibliographical Society of Canada 1973) 108

20 *Wacousta* 585–7

21 I.S. MacLaren discusses *The Lady of the Lake* as one of Richardson's sources and Jay Macpherson notes some of Richardson's debts to Scott in their articles in Catherine Sheldrick Ross, ed., *Recovering Canada's First Novelist: Proceedings from the John Richardson Conference* (Erin: Porcupine's Quill 1984) esp. 49–53, 69–72.

22 Recent commentaries on this aspect of Richardson's work include the articles by McLaren and Macpherson (above) as well as L.R. Early, 'Myth and Prejudice in Kirby, Richardson and Parker,' *CL* 81 (1979), 24–36 and Sandra Djwa, 'Letters in Canada,' *University of Toronto Quarterly*, 46 (1976) 47–75. Michael Hurley discusses Byronic aspects of Wacousta in 'The Burden of Nightmare: A Study of the Fiction of John Richardson,' diss., Queen's 1984, 392–405.

23 In *Love and Death in the American Novel* (New York: Dell 1969) 149, Leslie Fiedler identifies this pattern as American.

24 The conclusions of his MA thesis appear in 'The Amercanization of *Wacousta*,' in Ross, *Recovering Canada's First Novelist* 33–48 and in his Introduction to the edition of *Wacousta* published by the Centre for Editing Early Canadian Texts (Ottawa: Carleton University Press 1987).

25 These are: 'The Mystery at Chateau des Ormeaux,' *Stewart's* 3 (1869) 242–51; 'What Happened at Beaumanoir One Christmas Eve,' *CIN* 2 (24–30 Dec. 1870); 'Stories We Heard Among the Pines,' *Stewart's* 5 (1872) 242–68; 'The Old Japanese Cabinet,' *CMNR* 12 (1877) 139–52.

26 Mrs M.E. Muchall, *CMNR* 1 (1872) 138–41

27 *RBCM* 8 (1882) 184–91

28 E.C.G., *BMM* 3 (1878) 259–65

29 W.I.D., *BMM* 3 (1878) 301–8

30 In *The Gerrard Street Mystery and Other Weird Tales* (Toronto: Rose 1888)

31 Pelham Edgar, 'English-Canadian Literature,' *Cambridge History of English Literature* XIV (1917) 400

32 *Stamp Collector's Monthly Gazette* 2 (1867) 92–3. First noticed by Carol Fullerton, 'George Stewart, Jr: Nineteenth-Century Canadian Man of Letters,' diss., Calgary 1985, 42

33 *DI* 1 (28 July 1888) 59; 1 (24 Nov.–1 Dec. 1888)

34 Robert Barr, *In the Midst of Alarms* (New York: Stokes 1894) 230

CHAPTER SEVEN: THE PAST TENSE OF ENGLISH CANADA

1 George Steiner, *In Bluebeard's Castle: Some Notes Towards a Redefinition of Culture* (New Haven: Yale University Press 1971) 3

2 For a thorough analysis of the social vision of Victorian Canada see Allan Smith, 'The Myth of the Self-Made Man in English Canada, 1850–1914,' in J. Paul Grayson, ed., *Class, State, Ideology and Change* (Toronto: Holt, Rinehart & Winston 1980) 187–205

3 'One can readily enter into the meaning of one of our late Governors, the Earl of Elgin, who, in one of his dispatches to the Home Government, in speaking of the primitive days of the colony, describes them as "the heroic times of Canada." The expression was as eloquent as it was truthful.' J.M. LeMoine, *Stewart's* 3 (1869) 85

4 John Richardson, *The Canadian Brothers* I, x

5 'Our Table,' *LG* n.s. 5 (1847) 242

6 'Our Table,' *LG* 2 (1840) 138

7 Henry Giles, 'Fiction,' *LG* n.s. 6 (1850) 265

8 J.P., 'Novels and Novel Readers,' *LG* n.s. 8 (1850) 212, 208

9 W.P.C., 'Our Literature, Present and Prospective,' *LG* n.s. 6 (1848) 246; *TCL* 40

10 Harriet Beecher Stowe, 'What Shall the Girls Read?' *NDM*, Aug. 1870, 140

11 'Book Reviews,' *CMNR* 1 (1872) 475

12 *Bystander* 2 (1881) 47–50

13 'Current Literature,' *RBCM* 6 (1881) 98. The publication of a Canadian edition by Dawson Brothers was probably instrumental in attracting Canadian reviewers. See Parker, *The Beginnings of the Book Trade in Canada* (Toronto: University of Toronto Press 1985) 186.

14 See Carl Berger, *The Writing of Canadian History* (Toronto: University of Toronto Press 1976) 2; Lorne Pierce, *Outline of Canadian Literature* (Toronto: Ryerson 1927) 237; Stephen Beckow, 'From the Watch-Towers of Patriotism: Theories of Literary Growth in English Canada, 1864–1914,' *JCanS* 9 (1974) 3–15.

15 *CM* 8 (1897) 544–5

16 'The Literature of a New Country,' *Monthly Review* 1 (1841) 59–61

17 John E. Logan ('Barry Dane'), 'National Literature,' *The Week* 1 (21 Aug. 1884) 600–1

18 Pelham Edgar, 'A Fresh View of Canadian Literature,' *University Magazine* 11 (1912) 484–5

19 J.G. Bourinot, 'Review of Literature, Science and Art,' *DAR*, 1879, 266

20 Daniel Wilson, 'Toronto of Old,' *CMNR* 4 (1874) 89. For a similar approach to Kingston see Agnes Maule Machar, 'An Old Canadian Town,' *CMNR* 4 (1874) 1.

21 M.J. Griffin, 'The Romance of the Wilderness Missions. A Chapter of Our Early History,' *CMNR* 1 (1872) 344

22 'Literary Notes,' *CMNR* 3 (1873) 176

23 J.G. Bourinot, 'Canadian Materials for History, Poetry and Romance,' *NDM* 7 (1871) 193

24 M.W., 'The Gibbet Tree,' *LG* n.s. 2 (1844) 69

25 H.T. Devon, 'Leaves from the Life Romance of Merne Dillamer,' *BAM* 2 (1863) 140–2; (1864) 416–17

26 *AAM* 7 (1855) 44, 49

27 *Stewart's* 1 (1867) 77

28 W.A. Foster, *Canada First; or, Our New Nationality; An Address* (Toronto: Adam Stevenson 1871) 5–6

29 'Book Notices,' *Canadian Methodist Magazine* 19 (1884) 381–2. Examples of this kind of writing include William Wye Smith's series of 'Illustrations of Canadian Life,' *RBCM* 8 (Feb.–May 1882); Rev. T. Webster, 'Early Scenes in Canadian Life,' *NDM* 2 (Aug.–Sept. 1868), Samuel Webster, *Reminiscences of a Canadian Pioneer for the last Fifty Years* (1882). Graeme Mercer Adam also called for the preservation of pioneer history in his 'Outline History of Canadian Literature' 188, 216.

30 Sellar's Diary, Sellar Papers, NAC MG 30 D314 vol. 1

31 Coll McLean Sinclair ('Malcolm'), *The Dear Old Farm* (St Thomas, Ontario: Journal Publishers 1897) 139

32 For a bibliography (not always accurate) of Bourinot's writings, see *Royal Society of Canada, Proceedings and Transactions* 12 (1894) 16–17. For LeMoine see Raoul Renault, *Bibliographie de Sir James M. LeMoine* (Quebec: Leger Brousseau 1897).

33 LeMoine, *Stewart's* 2 (1871) 326

34 'The Heroine of Verchères,' *Stewart's* 3 (1869) 85

35 'Book Reviews,' *CMNR* 10 (1876) 453

36 J.G. Bourinot, *The Intellectual Development of the Canadian People* (Toronto: Hunter Rose 1881) 110–11

37 *Royal Society of Canada: Proceedings and Transactions*, series 3, 6 (1912) vi

38 J.G. Bourinot, 'Canadian Materials for History, Poetry and Romance,' *NDM* 7 (1871) 193–204

39 Bourinot, *Our Intellectual Strength and Weakness* 27–9

40 John Talon-Lesperance, 'A Missisquoi Holiday,' *DI* 1 (7 July 1888) 10

41 'Current Items,' *Canadiana* 1 (1889) 159

42 W.D. Lighthall, 'John Talon-Lesperance,' *DI* 6 (21 Mar. 1891) 267

43 'Review of Science, Literature and Art,' *DAR* 1880–1, 282. The author may have been John Reade, or more likely Graeme Mercer Adam.

44 See the review of W.H. Withrow's *Barbara Heck* in *Massey's* 1 (1896) 57, and the four pages of 'Opinions of the Press' bound with the Reverend Joseph H. Hilts' *Among the Forest Trees, or, How the Bushman Family Got Their Homes* (Toronto: Briggs 1888). The scarcity of creative literature about the Loyalists in the 1830–50 period was noted by Mary Lu MacDonald, diss., 287, 316–17.

45 'Saunterings,' *The Week* 4 (13 Jan. 1887) 111–12; *CNN* 83

46 Adam and Wetherald, *An Algonquin Maiden. A Romance of the Early Days of Upper Canada* (Montreal: Lovell; Toronto: Williamson 1887) 9. All further quotations from this book are identified by page number.

47 William Dunlop, *Statistical Sketches of Upper Canada for the Use of Emigrants* (London: Murray 1832) 10

48 S.F. Harrison, *Pine, Rose & Fleur de Lis* (Toronto: Hart 1891) 7

49 The magnitude and importance of the topic of the presentation of native people in Canadian literature requires book-length treatment. See Leslie Monkman's *A Native Heritage: Images of the Indian in English-Canadian Literature* (Toronto: University of Toronto Press 1981) and Terry Goldie's forthcoming study of indigenous peoples in Commonwealth literatures.

50 'Women's World,' *Globe*, 13 Jan. 1887, 6

51 'Saunterings,' *The Week* 4 (13 Jan. 1887) 112; *CNN* 85

52 Ibid.

53 William Charles McKinnon, *St George; or, The Canadian League* (Halifax: Fuller 1852) x

54 *Two and Twenty Years Ago. A Tale of the Canadian Rebellion*. By a Backwoods-man (Toronto: Cleland's 1858) 98–9. Watters identifies 'a Backwoods-man' as William Dunlop who used this pseudonym, although the latter's 1848 death makes this attribution suspect. In 1889 Sarah Anne Curzon adapted and serialized the book under the title 'In the Thick of It,' *DI* 3–4 (12 Oct. 1889–18 Jan. 1890).

55 Catharine Parr Traill, 'The Volunteer's Bride,' *Maple Leaf* 4 (1854) 138

56 'Rosalba,' *CIN* 1 (19 March 1870) 318

57 Carl Berger, *The Sense of Power* (Toronto: University of Toronto Press 1970) 70

58 Agnes Maule Machar, 'For King and Country,' *CMNR* 5 (1874) 197

59 W.H. Withrow, *Neville Trueman, the Pioneer Preacher* (1880; rpt Toronto: Briggs 1900) 18

60 Berger, *The Writing of Canadian History* 192. The centrality of this neglected novel to the romantic Loyalist strain in Canadian writing has been recognized by Dennis Duffy in *Gardens, Covenants, Exiles: Loyalism in the Literature of Upper Canada/Ontario* (Toronto: University of Toronto Press 1982) 70–5.

61 *At The Mermaid Inn* 43

62 W.W. Campbell, *A Beautiful Rebel* (Toronto: Westminster 1909) 5–6. All further quotations will be identified by page number.

63 Casca, 'Emily Montague; or, Quebec a Century Ago,' *British Canadian Review* 1 (1863) 87

64 Agatha Armour, *Lady Rosamond's Secret. A Romance of Fredericton* (St John: Telegraph Printing and Publishing 1878) 17, 107

65 Dick Harrison, *Unnamed Country: The Struggle for a Canadian Prairie Fiction* (Edmonton: University of Alberta Press 1977), 52–3

66 See reviews, *CM* 16 (1901) 289–90; 19 (1902) 185.

67 Bourinot, *The Intellectual Development of the Canadian People* (Toronto: Hunter Rose 1881) 109

CHAPTER EIGHT: THE OLD WORLD OF AMERICA

1 A. Ethelwyn Wetherald, 'Some Canadian Literary Women – I. Seranus [S.F. Harrison],' *The Week* 5 (22 Mar. 1888) 268

2 'Reviews,' *BAM* 1 (1863) 638

3 Blanche L. Macdonell, 'The Literary Movement in Canada up to 1841,' *Canadiana* 2 (1890) 17–18

4 These first appeared in *The Canadian Review and Literary and Historical Journal* in 1824 and 1826 before being reprinted in *Scraps and Sketches of a Literary Lounger* (1831).

5 Jeffrey L. Wollock, 'Violet Keith and All that Sort of thing,' *JCF* 3 (1974) 80–8

6 *LG* 1 (1839), 167

7 Thomas Storrow Brown, 'On the "Maple Leaves" of J.M. LeMoine,' *NDM* (Jan. 1874) 61

8 See Carl Berger, *The Sense of Power* (Toronto: University of Toronto Press 1970) 94; John Robert Sorfleet, 'French Canada in Nineteenth-Century English-Canadian Fiction,' diss., New Brunswick 1975, 12–37, 330–2. As an illustration of his enduring popularity, in 1896–7 one of *Massey's Magazine*'s main features was William Clark's series, 'With Parkman Through Canada.'

9 'Review of Literature, Science and Art,' *DAR*, 1880–1, 283

10 W.D. Lighthall, 'William Kirby,' *DI* 2 (11 May 1889) 298

11 Elizabeth Brady, 'A Bibliographical Essay on William Kirby's *The Golden Dog*,' *PBSC* 15 (1976) 5. Some indication of the impact of this work upon subsequent generations of readers and writers appears in W.D. Lighthall's *The False Chevalier* (1898) which he wanted to subtitle 'the sequel to the Legend of the Golden Dog,' Marshall Saunders' *The House of Armour* (1897) which recommends as 'that *rara avis*, a Canadian novel ... The glittering romance of the Golden Dog' (185), and Pelham Edgar's 1917 assessment of English-Canadian literature in the *Cambridge History of English Literature*.

12 Kirby to LeMoine, 7 Mar. 1877, LeMoine Correspondence, Kirby Collection, Archives of Ontario. Lorne Pierce reprints it in *William Kirby: The Portrait of a Tory Loyalist* (Toronto: Ryerson 1929) 262, with slightly altered puntuation and the date 7 April 1877, which on the original letter is written in a hand other than Kirby's.

13 Ibid.

14 'Book Reviews,' *CMNR* 11 (May 1877) 564–5; Toronto *Mail* (4 Apr. 1877) 2

15 'Bibliographie,' *La Revue Canadienne* 14 (mars 1877) 227; Benjamin Sulte, 'Le Chien D'Or,' *L'Opinion Publique* 8 (3 mai 1877) 208

16 Kirby to John A. Cooper, 20 Jan. 1904, 27 Jan. 1904, NAC John Alexander Cooper Papers MG 30 D34

17 Kirby to LeMoine, 23 Jan. 1879, LeMoine Corresp., Archives of Ontario; rpt ed. Pierce, *William Kirby*, 264

18 Pierce, *William Kirby*, 259

19 Sulte to Kirby, 9 avr. 1877, Kirby Collection, Archives of Ontario

20 Sulte to Kirby, 17 mai 1877 and 7 jan. 1878; Kirby to Sulte, 18 juil. 1878

21 Northrop Frye, 'Conclusion,' *LHC*, vol. 2, 352–3

22 LeMoine to Kirby, 22 Mar. 1877, Archives of Ontario; *CMNR* 11 (1877) 565; W.D. Lighthall likewise praised Kirby's presentation of 'pictures of that

picturesque epoch which are rich in their fulness of historic detail.' *DI* 2 (11 May 1889) 298

23 Sulte, *L'Opinion Publique* 8 (3 mai 1877) 208

24 William Kirby, *The Chien D'Or. The Golden Dog. A Legend of Quebec* (New York & Montreal: Lovell, Adam, Wesson 1877) 678. All further quotations from this edition will be identified by page number. For a description of the various editions of this book, see Elizabeth Brady, 'A Bibliographical Essay on William Kirby's *The Golden Dog* 1877–1977,' *PBSC* 15 (1976), 24–48.

25 *CMNR* 11 (1877) 565

26 In *Surfacing* (1972), for example, Margaret Atwood continues this tradition.

27 J.M. LeMoine, *Maple Leaves* (Quebec: Hunter Rose 1863) 1–7

28 Julia Catherine Beckwith Hart, *St Ursula's Convent, or, The Nun of Canada* (Kingston: Hugh Thomson 1824) I, 63

29 The contrast between their innate wholesomeness and the depravity of their rulers appears even in the kinds of music preferred by the two classes: 'The popular songs of the French Canadians are simple, almost infantine in their language, and as chaste in expression as the hymns of other countries. Impure songs originate in classes who know better, and revel from choice in musical slang and indecency' (260).

30 See Graeme Mercer Adam, 'Outline History of Canadian Literature,' 212; Mabel, 'Le Chien d'Or,' *Canadiana* 2 (1890) 118; *CMNR* 11 (1877) 543.

31 John Talon-Lesperance, *The Bastonnais. Tale of the American Invasion of Canada in 1775–76* (Toronto: Belford 1877) 91. All subsequent quotations from this edition will be identified by page number.

32 Philippe Aubert de Gaspé, *Les anciens canadiens* (1862; rpt Montreal: Fides 1967) 268

33 *La Revue Canadienne* 1 (1864) 444. In Clotilda Jennings' *The White Rose in Acadia* (1855), intermarriage between an Acadian man and his English sweetheart is tragically prevented by the Expulsion.

34 V.L.O. Chittick, *Thomas Chandler Haliburton: A Study in Provincial Toryism* (New York: Columbia University Press 1924) 134

35 *CMNR* 11 (1877) 564

36 Charles G.D. Roberts, 'The Outlook for Literature. Acadia's Field for Poetry, History and Romance,' *Halifax Herald*, 1 Jan. 1886; rpt W.J. Keith ed., *Charles G.D. Roberts: Selected Poetry and Critical Prose* (Toronto: University of Toronto Press 1974) 260–4

37 *Bystander*, n.s. Feb. 1890, 170

38 *CM* 8 (1897) 192

39 Douglas Huyghue, *Argimou: A Legend of the Micmac* (Halifax: Morning Courier Office 1847) 6

40 William Charles McKinnon, *St Castine. A Legend of Cape-Breton* (Sydney: Cape Breton Herald Office 1850) 13

41 See Carrie Macmillan, 'Seaward Vision and Sense of Place: The Maritime Novel, 1880–1920,' *SCL* 11 (1986) 23–4

42 From publisher's announcement bound with Sara Jeannette Duncan's *Set in Authority* (London: Constable 1906). *The Saturday Review* commented that 'for all its slightness the book has a peculiar charm.' 24 Dec. 1904, 802

43 *BMM* 1 (1877) 579

44 See Fred Cogsell, 'The Canadian Novel from Confederation to World War I,' MA, New Brunswick 1950; John Robert Sorfleet, 'Fiction and the Fall of New France,' *JCF* 2 No. 3 (1973) 132–46.

45 W.L. Alden, 'The Book Hunter,' *The Idler* 6 (1894) 504

46 'Book Notices,' *Massey's* 2 (1896) 72

47 *CM* 7 (1896) 190. Also *The Week* 10 (1893), 687, 905–6

48 Gilbert Parker, 'Preface,' *Pierre and His People*, Imperial Edition (New York: Scribner's 1912) xii–xiii, 28

49 Bliss Carman, 'Mr Gilbert Parker,' *The Chap-Book* 1 (1894) 343

50 Frank Luther Mott, *Golden Multitudes. The Story of Best Sellers in the United States* (New York: Macmillan 1947) 324–9

51 'Sir Gilbert's Critics,' Toronto *Daily Star*, 5 Oct. 1904, 6

52 Lorne Pierce, *Outline of Canadian Literature* (Toronto: Ryerson 1927) 31

53 Toronto *Evening Star*, 2 June 1898, 5. See also T.G. Marquis, *The Week* 13 (29 May 1896) 643. For British pans of Parker, see 'Sir Gilbert's Puppets,' *Saturday Review*, 24 Sept. 1904, 402; and *The Athenaeum*, 3810 (3 Nov. 1900) 575.

54 *Prince Edward Island Magazine* 2 (1900) 298

55 These were a volume of speeches published by the Ontario Minister of Education in commemoration of the Toronto Normal School Jubilee Celebration and William Parker Greenough's *Canadian Folk-Life and Folk-Lore*.

56 Undated clipping, Parker Papers, Lorne Pierce Collection, Queen's University Archives

57 W.J. Thorold, 'Gilbert Parker, An Interview,' *Massey's* 3 (1897) 118–21

58 Russell Harper, *Painting in Canada: A History* (Toronto: University of Toronto Press, 2nd ed. 1977) 244

59 A dissenter was Errol Bouchette, 'French Canada and Canada,' *CM* 14 (1900) 313

60 *CM* 6 (1896) 486; 7 (1896) 97. In Nov. 1896 *Massey's* reported that the first edition was already out of print.

61 'For some reason I chose to write about French-Canadians, in this my first venture. Why I did this I do not know ... something in me drove me to place the scene of this story in Quebec.' Mazo de la Roche, *Ringing the Changes, An Autobiography* (Toronto: Macmillan 1957) 95. De la Roche's first stories were 'The Thief of St Loo' and 'Son of a Miser' in *Munsey's* 28 (1902) 182–7; 29 (1903) 750–7. Livesay's were 'La Bonne Sainte Anne,' *Massey's* 3 (1897) 168–70; and 'The Spire of St Ignatius,' *CM* 13 (1899) 169–71.

62 W.A. Deacon to Georges Bugnet, 6 Feb. 1930. In *Dear Bill: The Correspondence of William Arthur Deacon*, ed. John Lennox and Michèle Lacombe (Toronto: University of Toronto Press 1988) 96

63 Archibald Lampman, 'Mr Thomson's "Old Man Savarin",' *The Week* 12 (9 Aug. 1895) 880–1

64 Kirby's papers at Queen's University contain several copies of an anecdote relating that Princess Louise informed Kirby that her mother enjoyed his book because 'She likes a novel.' See Pierce, *William Kirby* 266

65 W.H. New, *Dreams of Speech and Violence: The Art of the Short Story in Canada and New Zealand* (Toronto: University of Toronto Press 1987) 181. Other writers sensed in Quebec a similar feeling of timelessness and displacement, as in Blanche Macdonell's 'The Heroism of La Petite Marie,' *RBCM* 5 (1880) 309. Dennis Duffy has remarked on the significance of New France as 'symbolic space' and as English Canada's 'mythical second self' in 'Nouvelle(s) France: An Impression,' *Queen's Quarterly* 88 (1981) 46–62

66 Her name echoes both major female characters of *The Golden Dog*, Amélie de Repentigny and Angélique des Meloises.

67 Susan Frances Harrison, *Crowded Out! and Other Sketches* (Ottawa: Evening Journal Office 1886) 9

68 Ibid. 87

69 Susan Frances Harrison, *Ringfield. A Novel* (Toronto: Musson [1912]) 304

70 Susan Frances Harrison, *The Forest of Bourg-Marie* (Toronto: Morang 1898) 1–2

71 Harrison, *Bourg-Marie* 167

72 *CM* 12 (1898) 182

73 Robert Barr, 'Literature in Canada,' *CM* 14 (1899) 135

74 E.K. Brown, *On Canadian Poetry* (1934; rpt Ottawa: Tecumseh 1973) 125

75 Duncan Campbell Scott, *In the Village of Viger* (1896; rpt Toronto: Ryerson 1945) 1

76 See Carole Gerson, 'The Piper's Forgotten Tune,' *JCF* 16 (1976) 138–53 and W.H. New, *Dreams of Speech and Violence* 45–52, 177–86

77 'Book Notices,' *Massey's* 2 (1896) 73

CHAPTER NINE: SOULAGER LE BOURGEOIS

1 *Spectator*; cited by Edwin M. Eigner and George J. Worth, eds, 'Introductory Essay,' *Victorian Criticism of the Novel* (Cambridge University Press 1985) 3.
2 Alain Robbe-Grillet, *Pour un nouveau roman* (Paris: Editions de Minuit 1963) 26
3 *Massey's* 1 (1896) 57
4 Dick Harrison, 'Robert Stead,' *Oxford Companion to Canadian Literature* (Toronto: Oxford University Press 1983) 771
5 The mere title of Carman's second novel indicates the degree to which he abandoned Canada: *The Pensionnaires. The Story of an American Girl Who Took a Voice to Europe and Found – Many Things* (Toronto: Briggs 1903)
6 *The Athenaeum* 3737, 10 June 1899, 720
7 H.H. Langton, ed., *A Gentlewoman in Upper Canada: The Journals of Anne Langton* (Toronto: Clark Irwin 1950) 114
8 John Howard Willis, *Scraps and Sketches, or, The Album of a Literary Lounger* (Montreal: Cunningham 1831) 137
9 John Richardson used it as well, in *Eight Years in Canada*, 91, and Mary Anne Sadlier in *Elinor Preston* (New York: Sadlier 1861) 186.
10 *LG* n.s. 1 (1843) 309
11 J.W. Longley, 'Canadian Literature,' *Maritime Monthly* 2 (1873) 259–60
12 Coll McLean Sinclair, *The Dear Old Farm* (St Thomas: Journal Publishers 1897) 140
13 John Galt, *Bogle Corbet; or, The Emigrants* (London: Colburn & Bentley 1831) III 303
14 William Stewart Darling, *Sketches of Canadian Life, Lay and Ecclesiastical. By a Presbyter of the Diocese of Toronto* (London: Bogue 1849) iii. A later example is the Reverend Joseph Henry Hilts, *Among the Forest Trees; or, How the Bushman Family Got Their Homes* (Toronto: Briggs 1888), subtitled 'A Book of Facts and Incidents of Pioneer Life in Upper Canada, Arranged in the Form of a Story.'
15 First serialized in the *Maple Leaf* in 1853 as 'The Governor's Daughter, or, Rambles in the Canadian Forest' and issued in later editions under various titles: *Lady Mary and Her Nurse; or, A Peep into the Canadian Forest* (London: Arthur, Hall, Virtue 1856); *Stories of the Canadian Forest; or, Lady Mary and Her Nurse* (Boston: Crosby and Nichols 1861); *Afar in the Forest; or, Pictures of Life and Scenery in the Woods of Canada. A Tale* (London: Nelson 1869); *In the Forest; or, Pictures of Life and Scenery in the Woods of Canada: A Tale* (London: Nelson 1881)
16 The book remained steadily in print in British and American editions and

impressions until its belated appearance in a Canadian edition in 1923. See Rupert Schieder's introduction and bibliographical information in the edition prepared by the Centre for Editing Early Canadian Texts (Ottawa 1986).

17 Thomas McCulloch, *Colonial Gleanings. William, and Melville* (Edinburgh: Oliphant 1826) preface, 78. 'William' appeared in *The Novascotian* in 1824.

18 *LG* n.s. 2 (1844) 376–8

19 Non, 'Memgog,' *LG* n.s. 2 (1844) 451

20 C.E.W., *NDM*, Nov.–Dec. 1874

21 Edith Auburn, *NDM*, Apr.–June 1875

22 F.T., *BMM* 2 (1877) 669–79

23 Charles Pelham Mulvaney, *RBCM* 5 (1880) 37–49

24 'The Stepmother,' *LG* n.s. 5 (Feb.–June 1847); 'Ida Beresford; or, The Child of Fashion,' *LG* n.s. 6 (Jan.–Sept 1848); 'Florence; or, Wit and Wisdom,' *LG* n.s. 7 (Feb.–Dec. 1849); 'Eva Huntingdon,' *LG* n.s. 8 (Jan.–Dec. 1850); 'Clarence Fitz-Clarence,' *LG* n.s. 9 (Jan.–May 1851)

25 'Editor's Table,' *Victoria Magazine* 1 (1848) 240

26 John Talon-Lesperance, 'The Literary Standing of the New Dominion,' *CIN* 15 (24 Feb. 1877) 118. *The Manor House of De Villerai* appeared as No. 34 of *The Journal of Canadian Fiction* (1986) with an introduction by John Sorfleet.

27 Leprohon, *Antoinette De Mirecourt; or, Secret Marrying and Secret Sorrowing* (Montreal: Lovell 1864) 279

28 *Dictionnaire des ouevres littéraires du Québec* I 40

29 For a more detailed analysis of Leprohon's writing and reputation see Carole Gerson, 'Three Writers of Victorian Canada: Rosanna Leprohon, James De Mille, Agnes Maule Machar,' in Robert Lecker, Jack David, and Ellen Quigley, eds, *Canadian Writers and Their Works. Fiction Series* I (Toronto: ECW 1983) 195–256

30 Margaret Robertson, Charles W. Gordon's maternal aunt, contributed to the genre with *Shenac's Work at Home. A Story of Canadian Life* (1868) and *The Bairns; or, Janet's Love and Service* (1870). A New Brunswick example is Mrs William T. Savage's *Miramichi* (1865); in Ontario, a well-known practioner was the Reverend William H. Withrow, editor of *The Canadian Methodist Magazine* and author of *Neville Truman, The Pioneer Preacher* (1880) and *Barbara Heck* (1895). For a discussion of several novels from the 1880–1920 period see Ken MacLean, 'Evangelical and Ecclesiastical Fiction,' *JCF* No. 21 (1977–8) 105–19.

31 In contrast to the more conventional title of her earlier novel of character, *Belinda Dalton; or, Scenes in the Life of a Halifax Belle* (1855)

32 For more information on Machar see Gerson, 'Three Writers of Victorian Canada.'

33 For Machar's connection with the Social Gospel movement see Ramsay Cook, *The Regenerators: Social Criticism in Late Victorian English Canada* (Toronto: University of Toronto Press 1985) 186–91.

34 Stephen Mark Beckow, 'A Majestic Story of Orderly Progress: English Canadian Novelists on Canadian Soceity, 1896–1900,' MA, Carleton 1969, 85

35 See Mary Jane Edwards, 'The Case of *Canadian Homes*,' CL No. 81 (1979) 147–54.

36 Identified in the *Canada Bookseller* (Toronto) as an occupant of 'a prominent position on the editorial staff of one of our leading dailies,' Mar. 1879, 9

37 'Grodenk,' *My Own Story. A Canadian Christmas Tale* (Toronto: Irving 1869) iii

38 McCulloch, *William and Melville* 10

39 W. St John, 'Christmas Eve,' *Stewart's* 1 (1867) 127–31

40 Francis Sherman, 'Roberts' New Volume,' *CM* 7 (1896) 179–80

41 Dick Harrison, *Unnamed Country: The Search for A Canadian Prairie Fiction* (Edmonton: University of Alberta Press 1977) 72–9

42 *CM* 8 (1897) 460

43 'Where Roads Meet,' *SN* (Summer 1890) 9–18

44 G.L. Drew, 'Jack,' *CM* 8 (1897) 349–53; Ella S. Atkinson (Madge Merton), 'The Bankrupt's Easter Sunday' 499–501

45 Frank W. Watt, 'Literature of Protest,' *LHC*, vol. 1, 477

46 See Cook, *The Regenerators* 192–4. *The Mutable Many* (1896), Robert Barr's labour novel set in England and written after Barr's permanent removal from Canada, appears to have received scant attention in Canada. In 1939, Irene Baird was under the impression that her *Waste Heritage* was the first labour novel written in Canada. See her letter to Hugh Eayrs, 10 July 1939, Macmillan Collection, McMaster University Archives.

47 'Salutory,' *SN*, 3 Dec. 1887, 6

48 *CM* 6 (1896) 390

49 W.A. Sherwood, 'Hall Caine,' *CM* 6 (1895) 168

50 'Books and Authors,' *CM* 7 (1896) 95

51 'Books and Authors,' *CM* 7 (1897) 579–80

52 Fred C. Hamil, 'A Pioneer Novelist of Kent County,' *Ontario History* 39 (1947) 101–13; Marilyn I. Davis, 'Anglo-Boston Bamboozled on the Canadian Thames: Holmes's *Belinda; or, The Rivals*' *JCF* 2 No. 3 (1973) 56–61. The book was reprinted by the Alcuin Society in 1973 with an introduction by Carl F. Klinck and by Anansi in 1975 with an introduction by James Polk. For information about the author see Mary Lu MacDonald, 'Abraham S. Holmes,' *CN&Q* 30 (1983) 11

53 Davis, 'Anglo-Boston Bamboozled,' 57

54 Klinck, introduction.
55 A.S.H. [Abraham S. Holmes], *Belinda; or, The Rivals* (1843; rpt Toronto: Anansi 1975) 119, 121, 97, 54–5
56 Zero, *One Mistake. A Manitoban Reminiscence* (Montreal: Canada Bank Note Company 1888) 71
57 'Review of Literature, Science and Art,' *DAR*, 1882, 275
58 *Elinor Preston* 198
59 Mary Leslie (pseud. James Thomas Jones), *The Cromaboo Mail Carrier. A Canadian Love Story* (Guelph: Hacking 1878) 3
60 Grant Allen, 'My First Book,' *Idler* 2 (1892) 162
61 'Grant Allen's Latest,' *Citizen* (Mar. 1895); clipping in Henry Morgan papers, NAC
62 *CM* 7 (1896) 584. The *Canadian Magazine*'s review of Paul Bourget's *The Land of Promise* states that 'illicit love' could appear in a novel if it also 'tells most forcibly of the shame that is entailed by wrong doing.' *CM* 6 (1896) 196
63 Joanna Wood, *The Untempered Wind* (New York: Selwin Tait 1894) 299, 6
64 *Current Opinion* 16 (1894) 298
65 *Ottawa Events* denounced it as 'an unnatural and essentially pessimistic picture of life,' preferring *Committed to His Charge* as 'essentially optimistic, and evidently drawn from life,' 15 Dec. 1900. (clipping in Lizars Papers, Regional Collection, University of Western Ontario Library)
66 See Michael J. MacDonald, 'Introduction' to the 1984 reprint of *The Heart that Knows* published by the Ralph Pickard Bell Library, Mount Allison University. The short story which preceded the novel, 'On the Tantramar Dyke' (in the 1903 edition of *Earth's Enigmas*), describes an unwed mother's confrontation with the husband of her child, their reconciliation effected when the father rescues the toddler from drowning.
67 According to Mary Lu MacDonald, '[t]here are only three "bad" women in Canadian writing of [the 1830–50] period: Holmes' Belinda, Richardson's Matilda, and Gustave's Greek wife in *Les Fiancés de 1812*. All are punished.' diss. 373
68 Marshall Saunders, *The House of Armour* (Philadelphia: Rowland 1897) 242
69 Norman Duncan, *The Measure of a Man. A Tale of the Big Woods* (New York: Revell 1911) 57
70 H.A. Cody, *If Any Man Sin* (New York: Grosset & Dunlap 1915?) 218
71 For a discussion of the subject from a different perspective, see Barbara Godard, 'A Portrait with Three Faces: The New Woman in Fiction by Canadian Women, 1880–1920,' *Literary Criterion* 19 (1984) 72–92.
72 Maria Amelia Fytche, *Kerchiefs to Hunt Souls* (1895; rpt Sackville: Ralph Pickard Bell Library 1980) 158–9
73 Thomas E. Tausky, *Sara Jeannette Duncan: Novelist of Empire* (Port Credit:

Meany 1980) 54; Marian Fowler, *Redney: A Life of Sara Jeannette Duncan* (Toronto: Anansi 1983) 186–7

74 Sara Jeannette Duncan, *The Imperialist* (Toronto: Copp Clark 1904) 62. All subsequent quotations will be from this edition.

75 Fowler, *Redney*, 250–60, 267–8

76 See Carole Gerson,'Duncan's Web,' *CL* 63 (1975) 73–80.

CONCLUSION

1 *Saturday Reader* 1 (1865) 26

2 For example, see Archibald MacMechan, *Headwaters of Canadian Literature* (1924; rpt Toronto: McClelland & Stewart 1974) 214.

3 Pelham Edgar, 'A Fresh View of Canadian Literature,' *University Magazine* 11 (1912) 484–5; *SECL* 112

4 Gerda Lerner, 'Placing Women in History: Definitions and Challenges,' *Feminist Studies* 3 no. 1/2 (1975) 7

5 *Dear Bill: The Correspondence of William Arthur Deacon*, ed. John Lennox and Michèle Lacombe (Toronto: University of Toronto Press 1988) 25

6 Lorne Pierce, *Outline of Canadian Literature* (Toronto: Ryerson 1927) 239–42

7 Desmond Pacey, 'The Canadian Novel' (1945); rpt in his *Essays in Canadian Criticism* (Toronto: Ryerson 1969) 25

8 'Some Observations on Method in Literary Studies,' *New Literary History* 1 (1969) 29

Selected Bibliography

The following list of monographs, selected to assist the newcomer to the field of nineteenth-century Canadian fiction, cites recent editions when these are fairly reliable. Most of the pre-1901 imprints are available in the microfiche set issued by the Canadian Institute for Historical Microreproduction. The notes to each chapter contain fuller details regarding other books, unpublished theses and dissertations, and articles and reviews from periodicals.

NINETEENTH-CENTURY CANADIAN FICTION AND CREATIVE NON-FICTION

Adam, Graeme Mercer, and Wetherald, Ethelwyn *An Algonquin Maiden. A Romance of the Early Days of Upper Canada* Montreal: Lovell 1887

Allen, Grant *The Woman Who Did* Boston: Roberts 1895

anon. *Sir Peter Pettysham. A Satirical Story of Canadian Life* Montreal: Railway News Co. 1882

Armour, Agatha *Lady Rosamond's Secret. A Romance of Fredericton* St John: Telegraph 1878

Backwoodsman, A. *Two and Twenty Years Ago. A Tale of the Canadian Rebellion* Toronto: Cleland's 1858

Barr, Robert *In the Midst of Alarms* New York: Stokes 1894

Barry, Kate [pseud. Vera] *Honor Edgeworth; or, Ottawa's Present Tense* Ottawa: Woodburn 1882

Begg, Alexander *'Dot-It-Down.' A Story of Life in the Northwest* Toronto: Hunter Rose 1871

Brown, Margaret A. *My Lady of the Snows* Toronto: Briggs 1908

Campbell, Wilfred *A Beautiful Rebel. A Romance of Upper Canada in Eighteen Hundred and Twelve* Toronto: Westminster 1909

Carman, Albert Richardson *The Preparation of Ryerson Embury. A Purpose* London: Unwin 1900

Clemo, Ebenezer [pseud Maple Knot] *Canadian Homes; or, The Mystery Solved. A Christmas Tale* Montreal: Lovell 1858

Collins, Joseph Edmund *Annette the Métis Spy; A Heroine of the N.W. Rebellion* Toronto: Rose 1886

Darling, William Stewart *Sketches of Canadian Life, Lay and Ecclesiastical* London: Bogue 1849

De Mille, James *The Boys of Grand Pré School* Boston: Lee & Shepard 1870

– *The Dodge Club; or, Italy in MDCCCLIX* 1869; rpt Sackville: Ralph Pickard Bell Library 1981

– *The Lady of the Ice. A Novel* New York: Appleton 1870

– *A Strange Manuscript Found in a Copper Cylinder* 1888; rpt Ottawa: Carleton University Press 1986

Dent, John Charles *The Gerrard Street Mystery and Other Weird Tales* Toronto: Rose 1888

Duncan, Sara Jeannette *An American Girl in London* London: Chatto 1891

– *The Burnt Offering* London: Methuen 1909

– *A Daughter of Today* New York: Appleton 1894

– *The Imperialist* 1904; rpt Toronto: McClelland & Stewart 1961

– *Selected Journalism* ed. T.E. Tausky Ottawa: Tecumseh 1978

– *The Simple Adventures of a Memsahib* 1893; rpt Ottawa: Tecumseh 1986

– *A Social Departure. How Orthodocia and I Went Around the World by Ourselves* New York: Appleton 1890

– *A Voyage of Consolation* London: Methuen 1898

Fytche, Maria Amelia *Kerchiefs to Hunt Souls* 1895; rpt Sackville: Ralph Pickard Bell Library 1980

Galt John *Bogle Corbet* 1831; vol. 3 rpt Toronto: McClelland & Stewart 1977

Gordon, Charles William *The Man from Glengarry. A Tale of the Ottawa* 1901; rpt Toronto: McClelland & Stewart 1965

'Grodenk' *My Own Story. A Canadian Christmas Tale* Toronto: Irving 1869

Haliburton, Thomas Chandler *The Clockmaker* 1836; rpt Ottawa: Tecumseh 1984

– *Nature and Human Nature* London: Hurst & Blackett 1855

– *The Old Judge; or, Life in a Colony* 1849; rpt Ottawa: Tecumseh 1978

Harrison, Susan Frances *Crowded Out! and Other Sketches* Ottawa: Evening Journal 1886

– *The Forest of Bourg-Marie* Toronto: Morang 1898

– *Ringfield. A Novel* Toronto: Musson 1914

Hart, Julia Catherine Beckwith *St Ursula's Convent; or The Nun of Canada. Containing Scenes from Real Life* 1824; rpt Sackville: Ralph Pickard Bell Library 1978

– *Tonnewonte, or, The Adopted Son of America. A Tale, Containing Scenes from Real Life* Waterton, N.Y.: Adams 1825

Heavysege, Charles *The Advocate. A Novel* Montreal:
  Worthington 1865
Herbert, Mary E. *Belinda Dalton; or, Scenes in the Life of a Halifax Belle* Halifax 1859
– *Woman as She Should Be; or, Agnes Wiltshire* Halifax 1861
Hilts, Rev. Joseph H. *Among the Forest Trees; or, How the Bushman Family Got Their
  Homes* Toronto: Briggs 1888
Holmes, Abraham S. *Belinda; or, The Rivals. A Tale of Real Life* 1843; rpt Toronto:
  Anansi 1975
Huddleston, Mrs George Croft *Bluebell. A Novel* Toronto: Belford 1875
Huyghue, Douglas [pseud. Eugene] *Argimou. A Legend of the Micmac* 1847; rpt
  Sackville: Ralph Pickard Bell Library 1977
Jarvis, Thomas Stinson *Geoffrey Hampstead. A Novel* New York: Appleton 1890
Jennings, Clotilda *The White Rose in Acadia* ... Halifax: Bowes 1855
Kirby, William *The Golden Dog (Le Chien d'Or). A Legend of Quebec* Montreal: Lovell
  1877
Langton, Anne *A Gentlewoman in Upper Canada: The Journals of Anne Langton*
  Toronto: Clark Irwin 1950
Laut, Agnes *Lords of the North. A Romance of the Northwest* New York: Taylor 1900
LeMoine, John MacPherson *Maple Leaves. A Budget of Legendary, Historical, Criti-
  cal and Sporting Intelligence* 7 vols. Quebec: Hunter Rose 1863–1906
Leprohon, Rosanna *Antoinette De Mirecourt; or, Secret Marrying and Secret Sorrowing*
  1864; rpt Toronto: McClelland & Stewart 1973
– *Armand Durand; or, A Promise Fulfilled* Montreal: Lovell 1868
– *The Manor House of De Villerai.* 1859–60; rpt *Journal of Canadian Fiction* No. 34
Leslie, Mary [pseud. James Thomas Jones] *The Cromaboo Mail Carrier. A Canadian
  Love Story* Guelph: Hacking 1878
Lesperance, John Talon *The Bastonnais. Tale of the American Invasion of Canada in
  1775–76* Toronto: Belford 1877
Lizars, Kathleen and Robina *Committed to His Charge. A Canadian Chronicle*
  Toronto: Morang 1900
McAlister, Lottie *Clipped Wings* Toronto: Briggs 1899
McCulloch, Thomas *Colonial Gleanings. William, and Melville* Edinburgh: Oliphant
  1826
Machar, Agnes Maule *The Heir of Fairmount Grange* London: Digby Long 1895
– *Katie Johnstone's Cross. A Canadian Tale* Toronto: Campbell 1870
– *Roland Graeme: Knight. A Novel of Our Times* Montreal: Drysdale 1892
McKinnon, William Charles *St Castine. A Legend of Cape-Breton* Sydney: Cape
  Breton Herald 1850
– *St George; or, The Canadian League. A Tale of the Outbreak in 1837* Halifax: Fuller
  1852

McLennan, William *Spanish John* New York: Harper 1898

Montgomery, L.M. *Anne of Green Gables* 1908; many reprints

Moodie, Susanna *Flora Lyndsay; or, Passages in an Eventful Life* London: Bentley 1854

– *Letters of a Lifetime* Toronto: University of Toronto Press 1985

– *Life in the Clearings versus the Bush* 1853; rpt Toronto: Macmillan 1959

– *Roughing It in the Bush* 2 vols. London: Bentley 1852 (many reprints of later editions)

Parker, Gilbert *Pierre and His People. Tales of the Far North.* London: Methuen 1892

– *The Seats of the Mighty* 1896; rpt Toronto: McClelland & Stewart 1971

– *The Translation of a Savage* New York: Appleton 1893

Petitt, Maud *Beth Woodburn* Toronto: Briggs 1897

Richardson, John *The Canadian Brothers; or, The Prophecy Fulfilled* 1840; rpt Toronto: University of Toronto Press 1976

– *Ecarté; or, The Salons of Paris* London: Colburn 1829

– *Eight Years in Canada* Montreal: Cunningham 1847

– *Hardscrabble; or The Fall of Chicago: A Tale of Indian Warfare* New York: Dewitt [1851?]

– *Wacousta; or, The Prophecy: A Tale of the Canadas* 1832; rpt Ottawa: Carleton University Press 1987

– *Wau-Nan-Gee; or, The Massacre at Chicago* Philadelphia: Peterson [1852]

Richardson, Robert Lorne *Colin of the Ninth Concession* Toronto: Morang 1903

Roberts, Charles G.D. *Earth's Enigmas. A Book of Animal and Nature Life* Boston: Lamson Wolffe 1896

– *The Heart That Knows* 1906; rpt Sackville: Ralph Pickard Bell Library 1984

– *The Prisoner of Mademoiselle. A Love Story* Boston: Page 1904

– *A Sister to Evangeline. Being the Story of Yvonne de Lamourie* Boston: Lamson Wolffe 1898

Robertson, Margaret *The Bairns; or, Janet's Love and Service. A Story from Canada* London: Hodder 1870

Ross, Ellen *Violet Keith; or, Convent Life in Canada. An Autobiography* Montreal: Lovell 1868

Russell, James *Matilda; or, The Indian's Captive* 1833; rpt New York: Garland 1978

Sadlier, Mary Anne *Elinor Preston; or, Scenes at Home and Abroad* New York: Sadlier 1861

Saunders, Marshall *Esther de Warren. The Story of a Mid-Victorian Maiden* New York: Doran 1927

– *The House of Armour* Philadelphia: Rowland 1897

– *Rose à Charlitte. An Acadian Romance* Boston: Page 1898

Savage, Mrs William T. *Miramichi* Boston: Loring 1865
Scott, Duncan Campbell *In the Village of Viger* 1896; rpt Toronto: Ryerson 1945
Sellar, Robert *Gleaner Tales* Huntingdon, Que.: Canadian Gleaner Office 1886
– *Hemlock. A Tale of the War of 1812* Montreal: Grafton 1890
– *Morven. The Highland United Empire Loyalist* Huntingdon, Que.: Gleaner 1911
Sinclair, Coll McLean [pseud. Malcolm] *The Dear Old Farm. A Canadian Story* St
  Thomas: The Journal 1897
Smith, Frank Clifford *A Lover in Homespun and Other Stories* Toronto: Briggs 1896
Spedon, Andrew Learmont *Canadian Summer Evening Tales* Montreal: Lovell
  1866
– *Tales of the Canadian Forest* Montreal: Lovell 1861
Thomson, E.W. *Old Man Savarin, and Other Stories* 1895; rpt as *Old Man Savarin
  Stories: Tales of Canada and Canadians* Toronto: University of Toronto Press
  1974
Traill, Catharine Parr *The Backwoods of Canada* 1836; rpt Toronto: Coles 1971
– *Canadian Crusoes. A Tale of the Rice Lake Plains* 1850; rpt Ottawa: Carleton
  University Press 1986
– *Lady Mary and Her Nurse; or, A Peep into the Canadian Forest* London: Hall 1856
Willis, John Howard *Scraps and Sketches, or, The Album of a Literary Lounger* Mon-
  treal: Cunningham 1831
Withrow, W.H. *Neville Trueman, The Pioneer Preacher. A Tale of the War of 1812*
  Toronto: Briggs 1880
Wood, Joanna *Judith Moore; or, Fashioning a Pipe* Toronto: Ontario Publishing
  Co. 1898
– *The Untempered Wind* New York: Tait 1894
Zero *One Mistake. A Manitoban Reminiscence* Montreal: Canada Bank Note Co.
  1888

CRITICISM AND HISTORY

Adam, G. Mercer 'Outline History of Canadian Literature' in William H. With-
  row, *An Abridged History of Canada* Toronto: Briggs 1887
Adams, John Coldwell *Seated with the Mighty: A Biography of Sir Gilbert Parker*
  Ottawa: Borealis 1979
Ballstadt, Carl, ed. *The Search for English-Canadian Literature: An Anthology of
  Critical Articles from the Nineteenth and Early Twentieth Centuries* Toronto:
  University of Toronto Press 1975
Baym, Nina *Novels, Readers and Reviewers: Responses to Fiction in Antebellum America*
  Ithaca: Cornell University Press 1984
Beasley, David *The Canadian Don Quixote: The Life and Works of Major John
  Richardson, Canada's First Novelist* Erin, Ont.: Porcupine's Quill 1977

Berger, Carl *The Sense of Power: Studies in the Ideas of Canadian Imperialism* Toronto: University of Toronto Press 1970

Bourinot, John G. *Our Intellectual Strength and Weakness* 1893; rpt Toronto: University of Toronto Press 1973

– *The Intellectual Development of the Canadian People* Toronto: Hunter Rose 1881

Chittick, V.L.O. *Thomas Chandler Haliburton: A Study in Provincial Toryism* New York: Columbia University Press 1924

Cook, Ramsay. *The Regenerators: Social Criticism in Late Victorian English Canada* Toronto: University of Toronto Press 1985

Cruse, Amy *The Victorians and Their Reading* Boston: Houghton Mifflin 1935

Davies, Barry, ed. *At The Mermaid Inn: Wilfred Campbell, Archibald Lampman, Duncan Campbell Scott in 'The Globe' 1892–3* Toronto: University of Toronto Press 1979

Daymond, Douglas and Monkman, Leslie, eds *Canadian Novelists and the Novel* Ottawa: Borealis 1981

– *Towards a Canadian Literature: Essays, Editorials & Manifestos* vol. 1 Ottawa: Tecumseh 1984

Dostaler, Yves *Les Infortunes du roman dans le Québec du XIXe siècle* Montreal: Hurtubise HMH 1977

Duffy, Dennis *Gardens, Covenants, Exiles: Loyalism in the Literature of Upper Canada/ Ontario* Toronto: University of Toronto Press 1982

Fiedler, Leslie *What Was Literature?: Class Culture and Mass Society* New York: Simon & Schuster 1982

Foster, W.A. *Canada First; or, Our New Nationality: An Address* Toronto: Adam Stevenson 1871

Frye, Northrop. *The Secular Scripture: A Study of the Structure of Romance* Cambridge, Mass.: Harvard University Press 1976

Gerson, Carole *Three Writers of Victorian Canada: Rosanna Leprohon, James De Mille, Agnes Maule Machar* Toronto: ECW 1981

Harrison, Dick *Unnamed Country: The Struggle for a Canadian Prairie Fiction* Edmonton: University of Albert Press 1977

Klinck, Carl F ed. *Literary History of Canada* 2nd ed. 3 vols. Toronto: University of Toronto Press 1977

Monkman, Leslie *A Native Heritage: Images of the Indian in English-Canadian Literature* Toronto: University of Toronto Press 1981

Morley, William *A Bibliographical Study of Major John Richardson* Toronto: Bibliographical Society of Canada 1973

Mott, Frank Luther *Golden Multitudes: The Story of Best Sellers in the United States* New York: Macmillan 1947

National Council of Women *Women in Canada* 1900

New, W.H. *Dreams of Speech and Violence: The Art of the Short Story in Canada and New Zealand* Toronto: University of Toronto Press 1987

Parker, George *The Beginnings of the Book Trade in Canada* Toronto: University of Toronto Press 1985

Parkman, Francis. *France and England in North America* 7 vols., 1865–92. rpt New York: Viking 1983

Pierce, Lorne *Outline of Canadian Literature* Toronto: Ryerson 1927

– *William Kirby: The Portrait of a Tory Loyalist* Toronto: Ryerson 1929

Ross, Catherine Sheldrick, ed. *Recovering Canada's First Novelist: Proceedings from the John Richardson Conference* Erin, Ont.: Porcupine's Quill 1984

Rutherford, Paul *A Victorian Authority: The Daily Press in Late Nineteenth-Century Canada* Toronto: University of Toronto Press 1982

Stewart, George *Evenings in the Library. Bits of Gossip about Books and those who Write them.* Toronto: Belford 1878

Tausky, Thomas E. *Sara Jeannette Duncan: Novelist of Empire* Port Credit, Ont.: Meany 1980

Tompkins, Jane *Sensational Designs: The Cultural Work of American Fiction, 1790–1860* New York: Oxford University Press 1985

Index